CHINESE PUZZLE

ALSO BY T. M. RAYMOND

Madness

Fear The Living

No Sin In The House Of Death

For Carole and Dick

CHARACTERS

Zephyr Davies
Born of wealth, he travels the world in search of adventure, finding more than he bargained for.

Wong Gou Sing (Nicknamed No Sin.)
A cocky Chinese teenager who works for an antiques dealer.

Wong Wing Hsu
Gou Sing's brutish father.

Monica Marshall
A beautiful Eurasian who won't speak.

Madame Lin
An austere and dignified woman in her early sixties. She hires Davies to investigate her niece, Monica Marshall.

Mr. Lin
Madame Lin's reserved husband - a small man who harbors a ferocious temper.

Hong Fat
The corpulent owner of a curio shop and Gou Sing's beloved employer. Poor Hong Fat is a man with many worries.

John Crockwood
A British attache and a debauched drinking buddy of Davies.'

Max
Davies' Mongolian chauffeur - an honorable man.

Mrs. Kissler
A matronly widow with a sharp tongue and horrendous taste.

Mrs. Kissler's Maid
An attractive African American saddled with an unattractive job.

Leibowitz
A thin, bespectacled, unassuming man hired by Davies to keep watch on Monica Marshall.

Horace Willows
A nasty tycoon who lords over acres of pretentious statuary at his Hillsborough, California estate. Despite being envied as a "boy wonder," he brings absolutely nothing of value to the table of humanity.

Fredricks
Willows' much maligned butler - acerbic but honorable.

Elder Brother
The head of the Chinese underworld, tiny, big eared, and dangerous – a real person known to history as Du Yuesheng.

The Interpreter
A trusted employee of Elder brother's - so well mannered and bland as to be nearly invisible.

Inspector Singletone
An English police detective. A dowdy man with a droll sense of humor.

Sergeant Smixon
A policeman who loves to abuse power.

The Hawaiian House Detective
Affable and corrupt, he works at the Moana Hotel.

The Hotel Manager
Tall, thin, humorless.

The Japanese Captain
The master of a run-down Japanese freighter – a man who's
tubby, dumpy and shady.

Surgeon Major Devor-Hyde
A world traveler, sixtyish, distinguished, very proper.

Alexander Wu
The Surgeon Major's Chinese Associate
Effete, vengeful and a loyal friend.

PREFACE

A while back I spent many hours listening to Puccini's Turandot – I loved the drama and majesty of the music, and was intrigued by the storyline, which portrayed China as an impossibly cruel and beautiful place. Was China ever really like that, I wondered, or was the kingdom dramatized in Turandot pure fantasy? I decided to research the subject, simply to satisfy my own curiosity, and the first book that I stumbled upon was "My Twenty-five Years In China," by John B. Powell. Rather than describing court life in ancient China, this memoir began in Shanghai in the early nineteen twenties. After a few pages I was hooked – what an incredible place – far more outlandish, frightening, funny, optimistic, glamorous, and tragic than anything my imagination could conjure. I decided that I had to set a story in this incredible city.

I devoured books on the subject and was lucky enough to be able to interview several people who had actually lived in Shanghai back in the twenties and the thirties. A number of their accounts, as well as the fruits of my research, were woven into my appropriately convoluted mystery. Many of the events that I invented are dramatic in the extreme, Chinese Puzzle is no cozy mystery, but what I concocted can barely compete with the reality of the place. As a rule of thumb, the more unbelievable and over the top a passage in Chinese Puzzle seems to be, the more likely that it is true. Citizens really were beheaded for inappropriate attire, pirates were a real danger on the rivers and the open sea, nearly every month a new warlord took over control of the city, the Chinese parts anyway, and social norms did dictate that only the loveliest and most expensive prostitutes be allowed to service the better neighborhoods. In the midst of all this madness, life went on with gusto. No European or American city surpassed Shanghai for its luxuries, its nightlife, its cosmopolitan glamour, or its ability to have a good time. One of the ex-patriots, whom I interviewed, recollected how, as a boy, he tagged along with his father at the golf course and was entertained, (perhaps not the proper choice of words,) by the Japanese shells that would sail overhead every afternoon at a regularly scheduled time and blow homes to smithereens in the old Chinese city that bordered the green. The Caucasians who frequented the golf course were simply amused, it was understood that the fighting was strictly between the Japanese and the Chinese and no one else would be affected – it was that kind of place.

Much of Chinese Puzzle is told from the perspective of wealthy, amateur detective Zephyr Davies. Though a progressive in his day, many of his attitudes would be currently regarded as highly politically incorrect. He refers to a fully grown individual as a "girl," or a "boy," and the term "Chinaman," is one that he uses with abandon.

In the interest of accuracy, persons and places are spelled as they would have been by an occidental in the nineteen twenties. For instance, no one travels to Beijing, because the city didn't go by that name in those days.

Additional background information, along with historical photographs, can be found at tmraymondonline.com

CHINESE PUZZLE

I. PROTECTED BY A SHOE

Wednesday, August 8, 1928 – Shanghai

A little beauty goes a long way Zephyr Davies thought as he gazed at the late afternoon sunlight streaming softly through the partially shuttered windows, causing glass bottles and ceramic jars to dance with color. The teeming sounds of the docks, magnified by the nearby water, drifted up from below, and a block away Chinese voices were arguing over the price of something. Far across the river a boatman was singing - it was the perfect time to surrender to the fanciful idea that the world was a glorious place.

As the druggist labored to fill his order, Davies was aware of a flurry of bitter smells. The source might have been the dried frogs piled in a mound, or the herbs and fish bladders beside them. The odors were an unwelcome antidote to his good cheer, returning his emotions to the dark pit they had occupied for weeks – why were lovely images and charming sounds so easily nullified by smell, the most disposable of the five senses?

Carrying the herbs, which would, hopefully, help him to sleep, Davies left the Chinese druggist's shop, going out onto a trash-strewn balcony where he was assaulted by the intense, summer heat. He made his way down a shivering wooden stairway to where Max, his stocky Mongol chauffeur, stood by the Hispano-Suiza, dutifully, holding the rear door open. The remarkable motorcar had an open body made of tulip wood, and an impossibly long, polished aluminum hood that culminated in a radiator crowned by a graceful, flying stork. The sight of it gave Davies a small, much needed jolt of pleasure.

Once they were rolling, Davies surveyed his trembling, mobile kingdom, lit a cigarette, and attempted to calm his thoughts. Things had not been going well; the past few weeks had been so brutal that we was actually considering turning tail and running home to the West.

They were skirting along the Bund, and as Davies wiped an itching dribble of perspiration from his eyebrow he thought that this part of town didn't look a bit Chinese; it was more like Wichita or Omaha. No, Shanghai was far too majestic to be a grown-up cow town. Rising arrogantly from the banks of the Whangpoo, corpulent, Western-style buildings lined the riverfront like lavishly costumed actors preparing for a curtain call.

Reaching an intersection, Max stopped as a fierce, bearded Indian Sikh policeman waved through a long flow of cross traffic. Davies was nudged out of his musings as a rickshaw drew to a stop slightly ahead of the Hispano-Suiza, its driver bent over and panting like an overworked horse. In the chair of the rickshaw was an obese man with a fat nose, a deep fencing scar on his cheek, and a straw-colored mustache - one of those unkempt mustaches that looked like a wild growth of nostril hair.

"Dummkoph!" the fat man shouted. "Rechte! Rechte!" He leaned forward and savagely struck the bare-backed coolie with his stick.

The exhausted coolie responded by collapsing into a ball on the pavement, his ribs swelling and unswelling rapidly to the sound of labored breathing. His dark, leathery skin and deeply creased face suggested that he was in his fifties - too old for his job.

Furious, the fat man lumbered out of the disabled rickshaw and employed a common but not very effective method of prodding an unsatisfactory servant back on task by kicking the coolie in the side. The Chinese man grunted feebly.

The spectacle was blocking the Hispano's path, and Davies felt his temper swell. It was blisteringly hot, his head throbbed - he was tired and groggy and he just wanted to get home. Before he knew what he was doing, he found himself out on the street. "Terrible when these chaps have minds of their own," Davies said to the fat-nosed man, while horns honked behind him, and the Sikh policeman blew his whistle and waved the Hispano-Suiza forward.

"Ja?" the scarred Bavarian answered, and, with an aggression that came easily to a man of his girth, he slammed his stick across the coolie's back. Davies could hear the sharp smack of wood hitting damp flesh. "Lazy schweinehund. Stupid China."

Davies shook his head, disapprovingly. "No, no, your technique's all wrong. Surely you've beaten a servant before, you need to go for the face – underhanded - imagine you're swinging a golf club and his nose is the ball."

Staring down at the coolie, the Bavarian nodded impatiently, then raised the stick to try out this new technique.

No," Davies said sharply, "I said underhanded. You want to knock out a couple of teeth – then they remember. Here, let me show you." Grasping his own walking stick firmly, Davies drew it back and swung it toward the cowering coolie, abruptly reversing into a savage uppercut, which struck the fat-nosed man hard in the face. The corpulent fellow stared stupidly as blood spurted from his split lip. With a sharp snap of his arm, Davies rammed the walking stick into the plump man's ample midsection.

Grunting, the German grasped his stomach and doubled over, giving Davies a strong whiff of some Teutonic hair tonic whose syrupy sweet, cloying odor seemed intrusive amongst the earthy smells of China.

Again Davies lifted the stick, more than happy to entertain a bemused crowd, which had gathered. With a flourish he brought the cane down with a whack against the back of the man's skull. Spewing out a final whimper, the Bavarian bully sprawled onto the pavement.

"Lazy student," Davies muttered. He glanced at Max who was watching the whole business with indifference; then he turned to the bewildered rickshaw driver and tossed him a handful of Mex silver dollars.

The coolie stared up at Davies like he was a crazy man. Still panting alarmingly, he snatched up the silver dollars, rose, bowed seven times, picked up the wooden arms of his rickshaw and scurried around the corner.

Davies climbed aboard the Hispano and settled into the rear seat. He heard the snicking sounds of his chauffeur's gloved hand moving levers, and they were rolling again.

Behind them, the big Sikh policeman with his turban and his Khaki tunic was walking slowly across the intersection toward the prone body of the fat man. Davies turned away from the receding scene of his crime and realized that his wrist was sore. It was inconsequential, because he somehow felt as if dry, clean air was blowing gently through the caverns and ridges of his brain; a fresh, soothing sensation on such a hot day.

* * *

Hong Fat sold the finest of curios, artifacts, and works of art. Within his unpretentious shop were countless pieces of jade, ivory, brass, silver, bronze and copper. There were vases that had adorned the palaces of China's greatest emperors, emerald studded combs that had belonged to their courtesans, and a priceless opium pipe used on languid afternoons by Emperor Tao Kuang. The display room was dark and cool, filled with the scent of newly opened sea chests, of far away places and strange perfumes. Hints of incense and sandalwood mingled with the subtler odors of rat urine and stale herbs. The shop's dusty shelves were laden with secrets. Some items were cursed - all were for sale.

Wong Gou Sing, Hong Fat's assistant, stood in the center of the room, worried that fate was ready to confirm his most bitter fear. Like many of his countrymen, he believed that only so much happiness is allotted to a man in his lifetime, and an early abundance brings a later scarcity. As a safeguard, he had prayed that tiny, reasonable misfortunes would come into his life on soft feet, but losing his job would not be a tiny misfortune - it implied that the happiness portioned to him was much smaller than he'd expected; after reaching nineteen he had used it all up.

He forced his attention back to the shop's sole customer: a short, fat, white man who had entered the shop five minutes earlier and loudly announced that he had something to sell to Hong Fat. Gou Sing didn't like the man; he didn't like his smell, or his theatrical limp, or the way he held tightly to a long box wrapped in paper - like a child who was afraid that someone would snatch his favorite toy. Maybe this first impression was unfair but, for better or worse, Gou Sing's first impression was always right.

It was a taunting prank of fate that this annoying little man held the key to Gou Sing's future. If his boss, Hong Fat, bought what the small, poorly dressed, foul-smelling white face had to sell he intended to stay in business. However, if the man was sent away it would confirm Hong Fat's recent threat to sell the shop. If this catastrophe happened, Gou Sing would be unemployed and a disgrace to his family. There would be no more money for his education and the hope of a better life. Like a fish who'd slipped out of the net, only to be discovered before he could escape to the sea, he'd be thrown, thrashing, back onto the wriggling pile that comprised the day's catch. His father would go back to beating him nearly every evening, (an activity that had stopped during the two and a half years Gou Sing had been employed by Hong Fat,) and the only future left to him would be as a wretched coolie, again toiling on the docks. Working for Hong Fat had been his only chance, he would never get another – he could not allow such a magnificent opportunity to slide away.

The white man picked up a dainty teacup with his pudgy, soiled fingers. "Me likee," he said in an unmelodious voice, which betrayed him as an American. "Wantchee price."

Gou Sing despised the recognized business tongue of China known as Pidgin English. It required each race to make small linguistic concessions to the other, rendering the grown men who spoke it into little children mouthing baby talk.

"Be careful please," he said sternly, annoyance helping him to suppress his stomach churning anxiety. "That china once belong to great Emperor Kuang Hsu."

The man whistled. "An Emperor, huh?"

"Yes. Emperor Kuang Hsu was very brave man. He want to institute great reform."

As an assistant storekeeper, Gou Sing had been required to memorize facts about China's history, a duty that he'd grown to love. History was nothing but gossip from the past, and finding gossip irresistible it had been a pleasure to learn about the treasures in the shop. Besides, his knowledge provided him with frequent opportunities to put ignorant foreigners soundly in their places. "You see," Gou Sing said, "young Emperor was to ascend throne upon death of very wicked aunt, Empress Dowager, Tsu Hsi. But in evening in nineteen-oh-eight, he sit down to a meal serve on that very beautiful china set and die, just like that. The 'old dragon,' she hate his reforms, she die the next day – gods punish her." Hoping that the American would appreciate the implication, he extracted the teacup from the man's grip and returned it to its place on a long wooden table.

Like a bad dog sneaking up on another dog's food, the American made his way to the opposite end of the table. Gou Sing followed, ready to intervene if the ill-bred customer should try and touch another sample of the valuable dinner ware. Not that Gou Sing was any less guilty - when the china set had first arrived, he'd examined the dishes for traces of the Emperor's last meal, even licking some of them. Afterwards he felt light-headed, but had finally decided that his dizziness was not caused by lingering poison, rather from the anticipation of dying on the spot.

"How much is this?" The little man had abandoned the dinnerware and was holding up a cheap, porcelain Buddha.

"A dollar," Gou Sing replied. "You should buy it, it look like you."

The man studied him through tiny, flesh-shrouded eyes. "You're pretty cocky."

"Yes."

"What have you got to be cocky about, boy?"

"I'm young, I'm handsome, I'm very clever."

"You're not very tall."

"Neither are you." Gou Sing pointed out.

The fat man chuckled. "How old are you, boy?"

"Nineteen."

"Nineteen year olds are always wicked. Are you wicked?"

"Of course," Gou Sing answered, thinking that this little man was strange as well as ugly.

Abruptly, the little man turned. Hong Fat had appeared in the office doorway; today his colorful silk clothes, even the delicate jade ring on one finger seemed gaudy against his sallow, soft skin and his humorless expression. Hong Fat gestured coarsely toward his office. "You takee little bit time talk? Plum deal for sure. You come office side?" The short, squat shopkeeper disappeared through the narrow doorway, expecting the equally small American to follow.

Finally, a good omen. "Follow me," Gou Sing said, and he led the white man toward the curio shop's back office, praying that his luck would hold for just a little longer.

* * *

Thursday, August 9, 1928

The Chinese drugs had worked. Late in the morning, Davies awakened from the most industrious sleep he'd experienced in weeks, one where he dreamed that he'd been chased through his garden by thirty irate Chinamen who wanted him to pay a chit for a meal he'd never ordered. This was followed by a more disturbing dream where a greasy, black cockroach tried to burrow through his back into the center of his heart. Now awake, he resolved to think about pleasant things, reminding himself that one or two of the tomatoes in the small garden at the side of the house should be about ripe. There was nothing more wonderful than the spicy, "straw candy" flavor of a good homegrown tomato in August. Funny that a cross-dressing fruit could bind the eastern and western hemispheres together.

Tomato plants flourishing in his garden made him feel less perched on the edge of the world, not that he didn't relish living on the edge. That was one of the delights of residence in China; after half a decade, it still it thrilled him to wake up in a strange, exotic place.

Unfortunately, the thrill had been wearing thin, of late – or more accurately life had become far *too* thrilling. Yet, the very idea of heading home to the states made him feel ill. Over the years he'd stared down bandits, warlords and gangsters – but the most frightening encounter he could imagine was back in San Francisco sitting down to face his mother. "The prodigal returns," he imagined her saying, "like a stray tom cat coming in from the rain mewing for a saucer of warm milk. Your father will be so happy to learn that after putting you through Harvard,..."

"Business School – Harvard Business School," he'd probably sputter, as if that somehow diminished the scandal he'd created when one week *before* graduating with honors, he'd packed his trunk and climbed aboard a tramp steamer bound for British Honduras. There'd be no point in explaining that with graduation came an obligation he couldn't bear - that he give his life over to a suffocating Country Club existence as he helped to run the family empire, a shamefully successful conglomeration of lumber mills, copper mines, oil wells and an ironically respectable brokerage house.

After fleeing Harvard, Davies toured the world seeking adventure and finding it. Along the way he'd learned to fight, drink to excess, and developed a knack for befriending the most questionable of questionable characters. His trust fund paid the bills, and not just monetarily. Its very existence fueled a sense of guilt that drove him to be useful and a benefit to others. Unfortunately, his insatiable curiosity frequently sabotaged his noble intentions, often leading him astray as he pursued women, exotic food and drink, occasional drugs, and exceptionally bizarre "once in a lifetime" experiences, such as participating in the Famadihana in Madagascar, where he was granted the honor of dancing with several well-dressed corpses.

Finally, he landed in China, where for the past five years he'd dabbled in gun running, not for profit, but in a naive attempt to back the one warlord who'd actually bring hope and order to a country that operated like an unruly first grade class where the teacher had dropped dead at the chalkboard.

Glancing up at the heavy, dark beams in the ceiling above his bed, he wondered if his mother would even care that he'd supported himself by channeling some of his trust fund money into Asian business ventures, a rubber plantation in French Indo-China, a new hotel and department store in Shanghai, a corporation that exported rice - and that he'd proved an exceptionally lucky financier, rewarded with successes that made it increasingly unnecessary to dip into the family till. Of course, if she'd done her homework, she could easily smack him down with the charge that anyone could make money in Shanghai. Wicked, brazen Shanghai, a fabulous place, peopled with swindlers, newly-minted millionaires, titled expatriates and their sad, restless wives, gangsters, beggars, and whores. Indeed, it was easy to make money here, and just as easy to lose a fortune. Yes, he *had* been lucky, especially as he chose investments that demanded a minimum of his time, and as the money kept rolling in, he only felt guiltier. He soothed his shamed conscience by donating liberally to local schools, hospitals and benevolent societies.

But now it seemed that everything was finally turning against him. Chiang Kai Shek, whom he had a supported as hero who could unite the country, had turned out to be a sadistic thug - sickening Chinese on Chinese violence was growing by the day, and one of his friends had recently been killed in the crossfire. In response, he'd drifted away from noble causes, instead frittering away his time searching for love - he'd found plenty of takers, but things never worked out; he still couldn't understand why. Maybe he'd expected too much, perhaps he'd expected too little, either way he'd fallen into the habit of rising each day and missing someone he'd never met. The incident with the bloated Prussian hadn't brought him any closer to finding a soul mate, but striking a blow for justice, literally, had helped him to reclaim a part of himself that he had worried was lost forever.

Sitting up in bed, and gazing out into his garden, Davies thought that, thanks to his encounter with the odious German, there was one less coolie living without hope, at least, he wanted to believe that. The money he'd tossed to the man was enough to pay his bills for the next six months. Reflecting on this, Davies felt a new sense of optimism. Wouldn't it be splendid if he could pass his new positive attitude on to his servants? Why not give them the day off? Unfortunately, when he'd tried that once before, he'd only caused them to worry that they were all about to be dismissed - rather than taking him up on his offer, they'd continued their daily labors with more fervor than normal. It didn't seem fair that the Chinese had cursed themselves with such an unyielding work ethic. Doubly unjust was how so many of his spoiled, insulated, white acquaintances looked for every possible opportunity to complain about their "lazy" Chinese servants.

A daring idea came to him. How about holding a family picnic? He could invite his servants to bring their wives and children, even their teeter tottering parents and grand parents. Why not rent out Hongkew Park for the day? His ever-petulant number one, Lo-Chien, could be counted on to object, but perhaps the time had come for Davies to lay down the law: "Come and damned well have fun or you really will be fired!"

Now inspired, Davies swung out of bed, stretched dutifully, and made his way through his exquisitely paneled bedroom. Musty-smelling, filled with shadows, the enormous chambers' wooden walls were a well-aged chocolate brown. Adorned with fanciful friezes, trimmed in red and gold gilt, the room made him feel like a feudal emperor.

Arriving in his modern bathroom, done up in crimson and black tile, and sporting one of China's rare, glass-enclosed showers, he stood before his mirror, ran a hand through his sandy hair, and gauged the stubble that had grown in the night. He had to admit that he was a good-looking fellow, and somehow his appearance improved when he was a bit of a mess.

His back itched in the area between his shoulder blades. In fact, it had been itching most of the night, and he reached to scratch. Christ, something was stuck there; it felt hard and about two inches long. It was the wrong shape for a cancerous tumor, still, visions of a grim doctor proclaiming, "two months left to live," whirled through his brain. Mildly panicked, he tried to swat the object away, but it didn't budge. Maybe he'd cut himself without realizing it, and the lump was nothing but a large scab. This idea calmed him slightly.

Unable to get a good view in the hanging mirror, he selected a hand mirror and carefully pulled off his silk pajama top. He disliked pajamas, but they were a necessity when one had so many servants hovering about. The pajama top fell to the floor and he angled the mirror for a cautious look. *Oh God.* Something dark brown and glossy was stuck to his back. The object looked like a bumpy, fat, leech - jagged around the edges with an ugly, raised spine.

His mouth dried up and his stomach took a swan dive as he remembered a bearer, hired in Burma, who'd suffered searing pain and a nearly fatal fever from the bite of a centipede. Then there were screwworms, *God.* Related to maggots, and looking like the broken tip of a screw, they'd burrow into the smallest of wounds and secrete a chemical that prevented healing. Soon the wound would putrefy and attract even more flies. He shuddered from the image; nothing scared him more than the insects of the Orient. It didn't help that he couldn't tell what the thing on his back was; he'd never seen anything like it.

On jellyish legs, he returned to his bedroom and ransacked a desk drawer in search of a letter opener. Finding one, he held the mirror in one hand, took the letter opener in the other, and prepared to pry the thing off. A sneak attack was the best option, poking at the tiny horror might warn it, causing it to dig in its fangs, or suckers, or whatever it might have - and he'd have to take care not to stab himself. *Okay,* he thought, *okay, just take it easy.*

He brought the tip of the letter opener very close to the greasy, brown, outer shell. Had it squirmed just a little? *Jesus!*

Immediately, he jammed the letter opener beneath the leading edge of the spiny shell and applied pressure.

The thing popped off with surprising ease and flew smartly across the room. He inspected his back with the mirror, expecting the worst - there was a little redness, but he didn't see any blood or puncture wounds. *Thank God.*

Taking a deep, grateful breath, he went in search of whatever had been attached to him, carrying an upraised shoe in case the small monstrosity had any fight left in it.

He found it near the foot of his bed, dying apparently, with something pale yellow protruding from the glossy brown shell. He picked at it with his letter opener, and the yellow object came out, slowly uncoiling itself. To his surprise, it wasn't the entrails of an insect, rather a rolled up piece of paper. Puzzled, he turned his attention back to the glossy brown thing that had enclosed the paper. It was made of some kind of ceramic, and had been deliberately created to resemble a ferocious, spiny-backed leech.

Cautiously, Davies smoothed out the coiled paper. It was sticky, and about the size and shape of the label on a medicine bottle. Neatly penned on it, in English, were the words, "Every breath that you take is a gift."

* * *

II. POOR TIMING

Friday, August 10, 1928

With growing excitement, Wong Gou Sing looked down the dark, narrow street, shaded by banners and flags that hung from rope nets strung overhead. An American millionaire had phoned for an appointment to view a jeweled walking stick, recently acquired from the strange, small, bad smelling man, and Gou Sing must be sure that the white face found his way to their shop. How the American had learned about the walking stick so quickly was a mystery, but soon he would enter the gates of the old Chinese city from crowded Du Ma Lu. Moments later he would appear at the end of the block in a motorcar, which would make its way over the time-worn cobblestones, past the vendors selling sweetmeats and paper toys and the barbers cutting hair in the street and shaving their customers properly, without the silly water and lather that occidentals used.

Gou Sing had heard that this foreign devil known as Zephyr Davies was a very great man - mysterious, worldly, and fabulously wealthy. Some said he was a banker; others insisted he was a jewel thief. No one was sure how he got his money, just that he had a lot of it, and that he was ruthless in acquiring it. Gou Sing was eager to meet and study him, as it was his intention to make himself grand and mysterious in the years ahead.

The greatest man Gou Sing had been able to study so far was the grotesquely tall warlord, Chang Tsung-chang, who, like a number of Tuchuns before him, controlled much of Shanghai for a short time. Once Gou Sing had been lucky enough to actually see the tall, craggy-faced Chang disappearing into a brothel, carrying his treasure with him in a strong box that never left his sight.

Because Chang was realistic about the dangers of his profession, his most expensive possession was rumored to be a spectacular lacquer coffin. When a deadly rival moved in, threatening to break Chang's brief hold on the city, the Tuchun announced to the public, "I swear I will leave Shanghai only in my coffin." Gou Sing was deeply impressed by this heroic vow because most warlords sneaked away like cowards at the slightest hint of a conflict - even the cynical people of Shanghai were impressed. And the great Tuchun kept his word - abandoning the city, the huge Chang could be seen in his train car, sitting bolt upright in his splendid coffin, smoking a big Manila cigar.

As a child, Gou Sing had wondered what it would be like to be important and rich. Over the years, he'd seen many well-to-do residents of Shanghai and he'd speculated about their lives of comfort and privilege. He soon realized that such people weren't very different from his boss, Hong Fat, or even some of the neighboring boatmen he knew, they simply had more possessions. The fat matrons, swaddled in fur, and their sleepy-eyed, chinless husbands were curious, but failed to be fascinating. Perhaps once a year, however, he'd spot a wealthy member of Shanghai society who had a strangely magical presence, not unlike spying an exotic plumed bird. These rare individuals tended to be contradictions, radiating tremendous confidence, yet conducting their affairs politely, and frequently speaking with soft voices. What made them most intriguing to Gou Sing was that they seemed to be the keepers of secrets. He imagined that they'd been allowed to peek behind the curtain and see the great machine of life working. He felt certain that many of their guarded secrets were unpleasant, in fact, he'd be disappointed if several weren't shocking.

Perhaps he was wrong. Often, when he'd pointed out such an unusual human, he'd invariably hear his companion say, "You crazy? I wait on him last night, and he dull as dishwater." Maybe his friend was right, but Gou Sing was desperate to know what the lives of these fantastic people were truly like, and Zephyr Davies would give him his opportunity to find out.

He'd seen Zephyr Davies once before, perhaps a year earlier. The tall American had purchased a newspaper and was climbing into a marvelously solemn motorcar with drawn window shades. As the car hurried away to some extraordinary place, Gou Sing had wondered what kind of privileged troubles the man was grappling with. Chiji was the word that described the quality he'd seen in Davies. The Westerners had their own term for the phenomenon, they called it "charisma" - and it was a relief to know that what he sensed wasn't entirely of his own making.

However, he had a more practical reason for wanting to meet Zephyr Davies. Gou Sing had developed an excellent command of English, and, though he felt some loyalty to Hong Fat, it couldn't be a crime for a man to want to better himself - especially as Gou Sing was so tired of worrying now that Hong Fat had said that he might close his business. There was little comfort in the fact that carpenters had been laboring for days to install two great doors made of solid steel at the front of the shop. Yes, the doors' impressive appearance suggested permanence, but Hong Fat had only fed Gou Sing's insecurity by wringing his hands and moaning about how much the installation was costing.

For several nights, sleep had come to Gou Sing in fits and starts because he was so concerned about his fate - and the fate of his boss, of course. Fortunately, Gou Sing's youth helped to conceal the ravages of his weariness. Perhaps the fabulous American would be his salvation. He would be so impressed with Gou Sing's obvious skills that he'd offer him a job as a secretary; maybe even take him on as an apprentice jewel thief.

At the end of the hutung, a motorcar announced itself with a piercing, silver flash. This had to be it! As it came closer, Gou Sing could see that it was a great sparkling machine of polished metal with an open body made entirely of glistening wood sporting two tiny windshields, one for the driver and one for the passenger in back. If this car belonged to their customer, Gou Sing was very happily impressed, but what had he expected? Certainly not an orange limousine sporting pink curtains that so many wealthy Chinese favored; nor the likes of the light green sedan with a wide, gold stripe encircling its body that had been such an embarrassing hit at the auto show two years earlier.

The chauffeur lightly honked the horn as the machine ghosted its way through the throngs of coolies and rickshaw drivers. Automobiles rarely entered such narrow streets and many of the shopkeepers hurried out to look.

Gou Sing bounded forward and waved his arms, scattering the vendors and beggars. "Go! Go! Clear the way!" he barked in Chinese. The crowd parted, more in awe of the remarkable machine than as a result of his commands, but he dutifully remained in the street and proudly directed the gleaming automobile into the newly cleared area in front of Hong Fat's shop.

In the International Settlement he had seen many grand cars, but this machine was more dazzling than his previous favorite, an enormous, hearse-like Isotta-Fraschini.   He had learned to pronounce the name perfectly, after talking with the German chauffeur, while the owner's shroff, who happened to be present, babbled on about the fine "Scotta Fini" car. Gou Sing swore to himself that he would never appear so ridiculous - for now he was educated and well on his way to becoming a true "man of the world."

The stocky chauffeur, a great thick-necked Mongol with a flat yellow face and mashed ears, climbed out from behind the wheel and opened the rear door, then raised a panel that was like a ship's hatch with the second windshield bolted to it.

Gou Sing clasped his hands in front of him and bowed neatly as the white man stepped from the car's wooden passenger quarters.

Up close the American was not disappointing - he even matched his machine. Tall and aggressively handsome, he possessed a narrow nose and icy blue eyes that seemed to observe all things while looking at none of them. His face was unlined and youthful, suggesting he was in his twenties, yet experience shone in his eyes, hinting that he was older than he appeared, probably mid-thirties, and had seen things that even the hard-living beggars in the streets would find weird and frightening. It was a wonderfully disturbing combination. He held an ebony walking stick and wore a "camel's hair" jacket, which Gou Sing had learned was not made from the hair of camels - confusing and slightly annoying.

"Hispano-Suiza,"   Gou Sing said, reading the unfamiliar, elegant, silver scrawl across the front of the motorcar's radiator, and being careful to pronounce the words with the slightest hint of scorn. "My boss own Isotta-Fraschini," he lied, "a finer car than this one."

"Good for him," the handsome white face said with a soft, but still appropriately deep voice. "A Tipo Eight, or an Eight A?"

Caught in his own trap Gou Sin couldn't allow himself to look foolish. "Chauffeur will know." Then he added with exaggerated contempt, "I never talk to chauffeur." At least, this last statement wasn't a lie; Hong Fat had no chauffeur.

"I see."

The man's gentle and considerate voice didn't match his dangerous appearance - and his sparkling eyes made Gou Sing especially nervous; they seemed emotionless and probing, like the lens of a reporter's camera. These eyes looked at you and seemed to see too much.

Without further acknowledgment, Zephyr Davies strolled toward the proud steel doors at the front of the shop. Had the white face been secretly impressed by Hong Fat's imaginary motorcar, or was he merely indifferent? Inspired by the possibility that he'd made a favorable impression, Gou Sing followed the millionaire into the shop.

Once inside, Davies paused, seeming to note every object in the shop with a single glance. Gou Sing approached, using his most courteous voice. "Can you listen, please, as I am asked to lead you to a beautiful walking staff that is in this shop. This staff is so very valuable that three time already thieves try to steal it." This was untrue, of course, but it helped to make the artifact seem more precious.

Davies nodded, and Gou Sing continued, reciting his words as instructed. "This great staff was gift to the Emperor Ch'ien-lung of the Manchu's in your eighteenth century. The maker is unknown. It is treasure of greatest worth."

For some reason the white face began to smile. As they edged towards Hong Fat's office, he said, "It seems that every artifact in China that can't be identified once belonged to Ch'ien-lung, the 'catch-all' emperor." Gou Sing nodded his agreement, though he was not at all sure what the white face meant. "When did you acquire it?" the American asked.

Exactly the question that Gou Sing had hoped would not be asked. "What you mean? My boss have this staff for many year, long time."

"Precisely how long?"

Until the strange little man had appeared in their shop a day earlier, he hadn't known such a staff even existed. "Twelve year," Gou Sing replied.

"I see. Still, I will need particulars. I couldn't consider a purchase until the staff is authenticated. Can you tell me who sold it to you?"

"You ask my boss, okay?"

"I'll give you two dollars Mex if you tell me now."

Two dollars Mex was a very tempting sum - Mexican silver dollars were the favored currency in China, being especially popular with white faces. Centuries earlier, citizens and foreign devils used Spanish pieces of eight to trade amongst each other, and the tradition remained in a modern form. Though the idea of two fat, respectable silver dollars tucked away in his jacket pocket was appealing, if Hong Fat found out that his assistant had deviated from his instructions by admitting that they did not have the staff for a very long time, and were only now, reluctantly, parting with it, he could be fired. More important - would the American be inclined to consider Gou Sing for future employment if he was so easily bribed? Was it better to be accommodating, or to demonstrate a steadfast loyalty to his boss? The risk was too great, so Gou Sing stuck out his tongue and chopped a hand at his neck, pantomiming a decapitation.

Zephyr Davies stared at him, "I have absolutely no idea what you're getting at."

Gou Sing shook his head and reenacted the mock decapitation. "My boss will kill me if I tell you thing that he must tell you himself." With a polite smile, Gou Sing walked several paces, knocked lightly on the office door, then pushed it open, relieved that he could soon turn the whole matter over to Hong Fat.

As usual, Hong Fat's inner office was an embarrassment. The desk and chairs were scarred and dirty, the many file cabinets battered, scratched and of wildly different sizes and shapes. Gou Sing had spent the morning dusting and straightening, and he had cleaned and polished the shop's eight cuspidors - still, everything looked moldy and sad. The heat made matters worse; his skin felt so sticky under his cotton jacket that he wanted to rip it off his body and tear it into three hundred shreds.

Hong Fat was seated behind his desk; and he didn't even attempt to rise, which was exceptionally rude. Americans were prized commodities in the old Chinese city, and it was strange and out of character that his boss made no introductions, had not so much as bowed - a grave affront.

Entering behind Gou Sing, the handsome white face moved to the center of the room, not appearing to be bothered by Hong Fat's behavior. He sat on a heavy, antique chest, wisely ignoring a frayed armchair, which Gou Sing had a strong desire to burn.

"Please," Gou Sing said, stepping forward in attempt to demonstrate some civility, "can we offer you tea?"

Whenever a legitimate customer arrived he was to be graciously welcomed. Such a guest of honor was traditionally given, "the top of the wine jar," and "the bottom of the teapot," where the best cup lay. Outside the coolies drank from big earthenware jars set in the streets by a benevolent society, but in Hong Fat's office the finest tea available would be served in tiny cups and the best cup would be given to the customer. While they drank, they would discuss the weather, the quality of the tea, or perhaps the business of antiques. It would be unseemly to talk politics, or to get to the point too quickly. Americans were known to be annoyed with such politeness, but they were uncultured; pandering to them would be akin to a policeman curtailing a criminal investigation out of consideration for the thieves.

The American shook his head, his hands resting, unmoving, in his lap. This was a relief to Gou Sing who had little enthusiasm for fetching the tea pot on such a hot day.

Hong Fat cleared his throat, an indication that Gou Sing should leave. He was not happy with this request, but someone had to watch the shop.

Obediently, he went out into the hall and quietly shut the door behind him. Unable to quiet the hot rustling of anxiety in his chest, Gou Sing walked a few feet and entered a closet. A small crack where the wooden boards of the closet wall didn't quite meet allowed him to peek into his boss's office. Extremely careful movements were required because Hong Fat's mood was so disagreeable that Gou Sing's job would surely be in peril if he was found out. Still, he couldn't resist eavesdropping on his own future, and he had confidence that he could be very quiet.

No more than five seconds had passed when Hong Fat rose from his chair, like a large dog getting up from a nap, and made his way to a cabinet behind his desk. From it, he removed a long, securely padlocked, cedar box. As Gou Sing strained to see better, Hong Fat fumbled to unlock the box, finally opening it. Out of the box, he removed a shining, jewel encrusted walking stick.

Gou Sing let out a soft gasp – he'd heard about the staff, but had not actually seen it until this very moment. Even in the subdued light, a burst of fiery red and green and gold exploded from the artifact. It had a hilt of polished silver, trimmed in gold and ebony. The body was gloriously inlaid, crusted with glittering emeralds, rubies and sapphires. Intricate jade carvings, in elaborate patterns, wound their way downward from the hilt. He tilted on his haunches, causing the floorboards to creak as he risked a glance through the cracks at Zephyr Davies.

The American's face remained unchanged as his gaze moved slowly up and down the staff. Gou Sing expected the man to be like a desperate sailor admiring a presentable dance hall girl, but Zephyr Davies was more like a somber professor: clinical, emotionless.

Hong Fat spoke up impatiently. "You likee?"

"What price?" Davies responded, as if bored.

"Plenty, plenty money," Hong Fat proclaimed, lapsing into the contemptible Pidgin. "You see – you likee." He handed the staff to the white face.

"What price?" Davies repeated, giving the artifact a quick, indifferent glance.

Hong Fat's mouth formed a flabby sneer. "Too much for you."

The millionaire shrugged.

"Okay, you no wantchee." Hong Fat reached down and took the staff back from the American.

Gou Sing felt fear flash hot on his skin; had his boss changed his mind about staying in business?

Davies slapped his legs and rose. "No can do," he said, and jabbed at the jewels with his index finger. "This no b'long number one, savvy?"

"What fashion no can?" Hong Fat protested.

Davies shook his head, sadly. "No b'long number one."

A silence followed as Hong Fat watched Davies return to sit on the old chest, where he fidgeted, awaiting a response.

* * *

With a welcome sense of amusement, considering how troubled he'd felt all day due to the leech on his back, Davies thought that

Hong Fat matched his name. Roughly translated "Hong" meant "clan," and the antiques dealer was as big as one - at least, horizontally, if not vertically.

Employing a liberal amount of preposterous ceremony, Hong Fat had withdrawn the infamous "clouded twilight" from a padlocked cedar trunk and presented it to Davies. In person, the artifact was proof positive that bad taste was timeless.

After the required amount of haggling, where Hong Fat went so far as to "angrily" reclaim the artifact, real negotiations began. Following a long silence, the rotund merchant become fussy and gregarious, explaining that the artifact had been purchased years ago from a reputable antiques dealer, a man, whose name he could not recall.

Because of its age, and the tales he'd been told of the piece, Davies assumed that "the clouded twilight" was quite valuable. It was true that some of its jewels appeared to be paste, but a couple of others seemed genuine to his less than expert eyes. Under any circumstances, its history counted for a lot so he was anticipating an asking price of five or ten thousand pounds. He was astonished, therefore, when Hong Fat told him that he would part with the artifact for no less than, "three hundred dollars, Mex." Not that three hundred dollars wasn't a lot of money, four bespoke suits could be purchased for that amount - clearly, the Chinese tradesman had no idea of what had come into his possession.

Hong Fat's "unshakable" asking price was such a pittance for an important piece of Chinese history that, instead of requesting to think it over, or taking snaps to show to his client, Davies countered with "two hundred-and-fifty." When Hong Fat accepted, "the clouded twilight" had a new owner. Davies had no regrets - the cost was so easily absorbed that it was nice to pay up and get the whole business over with – and if the staff was as valuable as rumored he'd scored quite a coup. Besides, he was displeased with the gift he'd given to Madame Lin on her previous birthday; this would set matters right.

He did insist that the artifact be wrapped up in whatever had contained it when it had first arrived at the shop. There were protests and excuses, an insistence that wrappings, which were years old, would never be kept. Davies persisted, however, falling back on the role of wealthy eccentric - the role that he was actually playing was that of a thorough detective.

* * *

After a long period of negotiation, the American and Gou Sing's boss had fallen into another nerve-jittering silence. Finally, Zephyr Davies began to speak, but his voice was so low that Hong Fat was forced to lean forward to hear. Gou Sing suffered from the same problem, and very carefully he attempted to rearrange his position to favor his right ear. As he maneuvered about, his knee jarred a ceramic bowl filled with rags from off a shelf and it fell to the floor with a loud crash. "Oh no!" He swore under his breath, trying to remain as still as possible. *Why am I so stupid?* he thought, as he stood in the tiny broom closet hoping that he would be mistaken for a clumsy rodent. Perhaps he should make a little squealing sound so that the charade would be complete. This thought confirmed that his stupidity had no limits.

Torturous moments passed. The American was still speaking, but his utterances remained undecipherable. Perhaps Gou Sing had been spared, the gods had granted him one last moment of good luck.

Then he heard the words that he dreaded as Hong Fat abruptly shouted in Chinese, "Gou Sing, come in here at once!"

* * *

Wearing a sheepish expression, the Chinese boy reentered the office, exhibiting a forced nonchalance, which implied that he'd been doing something that he shouldn't - smoking in a corner perhaps. Brusquely, his boss directed him to go out and search through what Davies suspected was the recent trash. After about ten minutes, the lad returned with a wad of torn, stained butcher's paper, cut to contain an object that was long and narrow, and which had several luggage stickers attached to it. Davies knew that Madame Lin would demand to know who had sold "the clouded twilight" to Hong Fat, and the baggage tags would go a long ways towards settling the matter.

He only had himself to blame for the unfolding melodrama revolving around Madame Lin's family artifact.   Between the Junior and Senior years of high school, he'd spent his summer vacation working with the Pinkertons. The sojourn had horrified his mother, and rather amused his father.   Though Davies had never progressed beyond running errands and making deliveries, he'd gotten occasional tastes of real detective work, and one or two colorful stories told at parties had earned him a reputation as a society detective.   Now every couple of months some old friend called up to solicit his aid, usually on some business that turned out to be thoroughly trivial.

He bid good-bye to his Chinese hosts and returned to the street, where a crowd was still gathered around his Hispano.

Settling into the snake skin rear seat, he examined the large piece of torn, brown wrapping paper, retrieved from the trash. Written on it in English was the fragment of an address. He could make out, "Property Of:," but everything else was gone - except for the words, "teo, California, U.S.A."   He folded up the papers and turned his attention to the garish walking stick itself, thinking that, all and all, fulfilling his obligation to Madame Lin had been far easier than he'd expected.

III. THE MONOGRAMS

Seated comfortably in the back of the Hispano, Davies continued to examine his purchase. "What is that?" he asked, handing the walking stick forward to Max, and pointing to a small symbol, which was embossed on a decorative band of metal. The symbol, not easy to make out, was an odd, unfamiliar Chinese character with lines scratched through it. The workmanship on the character itself was neat and assured, while the lines were ugly, jagged scratches. They seemed to have been added later by another hand, and they implied anger.

Max peered at the symbol. "Name."

"Perhaps the maker's signature," Davies suggested. "But what of those odd scratches?"

Max made an uncharacteristically delicate wave of his hand. "Too old," he said flatly. "Who know?"

They drove several blocks and stopped across the street from where Madame Lin was seated in a rickshaw, waiting for him. Sitting stoically in another rickshaw, parked behind hers, was a weathered servant woman, who accompanied her mistress everywhere.

A severe and handsome woman, Madame Lin never looked quite real. She might be a mature thirty or a youthful fifty, it was hard to tell with many Chinese. Davies, however, knew for a fact that she was sixty. A pair of round spectacles seemed out of place on her smooth, mask-like face, and her hair was concealed by a headdress of metal and jade, which made a tinkling sound when she turned her head. She was perhaps the vainest woman he had ever met, and the most uncompromising; but oddly her bad traits were strangely lovable.

Madame Lin turned and stared expectantly at Davies as he got out of the Hispano and crossed the street, staff in hand. When he reached her side, he made a little bow and handed the artifact to the stern old woman - she took it eagerly. "My goodness - you actually have it? I thought you were only going to verify its authenticity."

Davies smiled. "I don't think the curio shop's owner knew what he had; he sold it to me for three hundred dollars Mex, such a bargain, from what you tell me, that I couldn't resist."

Madame Lin placed the walking stick in her lap, and took his hand, gripping it fiercely. Her skin was impossibly soft. "I don't know how to thank you. You are such a kind man, always there when I need you."

"Please," Davies replied, having none of this, "I'm not kind at all. I've got an abundance of free time and nothing better to do - not that your business is unimportant."

Madame Lin released his hand and gave him a sad smile, which made him ashamed of his flippant tendency to answer emotion with a casual line and a shrug. "I imagine you think this all trivial, but 'the clouded twilight' is history, Zephyr, it is China. Consider if the first American flag, sewn by Betsy Ross, should appear in a common pawnshop. It's insulting!" She picked up the artifact again and examined it carefully. "I don't remember it being this shabby. One would think it would have been shown more respect."

From his jacket pocket, Davies withdrew the scrap of wrapping paper, retrieved from the trash. This he handed to Madame Lin, pointing to the baggage tags that were still attached. One was from the American Mail Line and proclaimed "Cabin Class," but no incriminating passenger name was visible. "You might compare these with some of the other baggage tags on your niece's luggage. If they match we'll know that she brought the thing to China. Whether she actually sold it to Hong Fat, I can't say. You know, I'm eager to meet this niece of yours."

Madame Lin gave him an arched look. "Don't be too eager, she's a little devil." Evidently, the old woman didn't realize that these words were far from discouraging.

"Do you question her moral standing or something of that sort?" Davies asked. A Chinese woman with questionable morals always appealed to him.

Ignoring the question, Madame Lin popped a tamarind candy into her mouth. "Would you care for one?"

Davies shook his head.

"I have to hide these or my husband will eat them all. Take this for now." Reverently, she handed the staff back to Davies. "I'll drop by your villa tomorrow with the money to repay you."

"That's not necessary," Davies said, "consider this a gift."

"Nonsense," Madame Lin snorted. "No one can ever accuse me of not paying my bills. Besides, I'm indebted to you enough; I don't want to add to my obligations."

"If that pleases you," he said, eager to get home and into a cooling tub. "At least, you can rest easy knowing that your 'clouded twilight' is back in China." He shook her smooth, bony hand, and trudged back to the waiting Hispano. Behind him, he could hear Madame Lin's coolie grunt as he raised the handles of his rickshaw in preparation for scurrying away.

Under the great shade trees of Davies' fashionable suburban neighborhood the air seemed green; it was cooler and damper here. Davies' rented villa, just off the Avenue Haig, was the only Chinese-style home in the midst of sumptuous Italian mini-palazzos, great English Tudor mansions, and German rococo palaces. In China, the White Man's burden was extremely heavy - comfortable havens of escape were regarded as necessities by those who bore it.

Being mistrustful of his servants, Davies left "the clouded twilight" in a concealed compartment beneath the Hispano's rear floorboards, normally reserved for munitions.

He hurried inside, and, after a brief shower, he changed clothes, thinking again about the ghastly thing that he'd found on his back a full day earlier. The perverse gadget had been coated by some kind of glue on one side, and had apparently been designed to lodge on the skin. It could have been slipped down the back of his collar at the club, or on the street. This was the less troubling scenario; his servants might have attached it while he slept. That they may have played a hand in the affair was particularly disturbing.

The note must have referred to his attack on the German in the street. Though, if the incident had gained such notoriety, why hadn't he been contacted by the International Police? There couldn't be more than three Hispano-Suizas in Shanghai; tracking him down would be simple.

Perhaps the German was one of the unique sons of Shanghai and that's why he hadn't elected to press charges. If the German was a well-known confidence man, and not an upright citizen, appearing before the police would not be in his self-interest.

Could the German, or perhaps one of his friends, be behind the tiny beast placed on Davies' back? But was that Teutonic behavior? Wouldn't he or a crony be more likely to show up in Davies' front drive, reeking of beer, and try to attack him physically? And why would the note be phrased so poetically instead of saying something like, "You're going to pay, mit spades?"

If there was ever an omen that it was time to leave, this was it. He'd had enough adventuring and turmoil, wandering aimlessly in search of some noble pursuit that would bring purpose and passion to his life. Certainly running guns had proven to be one of the least intelligent ways he could have chosen to improve conditions in China. Now he'd been given plenty of motivation to go home and become respectable. As he snugged up his tie, in foolish defiance of the oppressive heat, he thought that it might be good to join the family lumber business and learn how things are done the proper way. Then, if he felt up to it, he could come back to China and build a hospital, or open an orphanage. All he wanted was a victory, just one. Something he could feel proud of, which proclaimed that he was a contributor and not the parasite that he'd, frankly, been for too much of his life.

Now in fresh clothes, he had Max drive him to the French Club where he often enjoyed a cocktail or two before returning home for supper.

It was half-past-four when Davies nodded to the stylishly dressed doorman and strolled through the French Club's tasteful lobby. There were clubs that only admitted whites and on whose steps one greeted a Chinese acquaintance coolly, as if he was your servant. A few blocks away there would be another club, patronized by everyone, where all social and racial barriers dissolved, and the same Chinese that you'd just snubbed was now your equal. The French Club was one of these more liberal establishments where everyone was your friend - though those with money made the best friends.

In the dining room, a string ensemble was playing a medley of the latest American songs. Davies climbed the grand stairway, smiling at passing acquaintances whose images faded from his mind almost immediately. He ordered a couple of drinks, thanking God that Prohibition had not plagued China. The subject of bootlegged spirits, preceded by his trip to the Chinese druggist the day before, caused him to contemplate the perverse things that found their way into liquor back home in the States. How lucky he was not to be there.

He considered making a night of it, but he quickly ran out of steam and left the French Club after barely an hour. He'd been too tired to socialize, yet he was still too wound up to relax.

He arrived home at a little before six in the evening, entering his bedroom through a side gate in the hope of avoiding any potential conversations with his servants.

He indulged in a long bath, and after toweling off he wandered across his bedroom to fetch clothes from a dark mahogany chest of drawers, a remnant of Imperial China. Opening the chest he removed a powder blue silk nightshirt. "What the,.." The words died in his throat as fear surged through his body, sickening him.

He dropped the shirt on the floor and frantically tore through the bureau, examining the twenty or so shirts that remained in the drawer, handling them gingerly as if they might sting him. It was literally beyond belief. All his clothes were neatly in place, exactly as he had left them, which only made things more disturbing. He pulled open a second drawer and fumbled through another handful of shirts. They were his shirts all right; he recognized a slightly frayed collar on one, a tiny wine stain on another. A little more than two hours earlier he had rummaged through the drawer and nothing had been amiss. Two hours, and his mind caught up with his emotions, the implications of what he now understood hitting him like a sledge hammer punch to the stomach. Weakly, he sat at the foot of his bed and looked down at the shirt that he held in his hand - like every one of the shirts, which made up his wardrobe, it had been subtly altered. Exquisitely embroidered above its breast pocket was the tiny Chinese character that had been etched on the base of "the clouded twilight." Even the jagged scratches had been reproduced.

IV. MOTHS TO THE FLAME

Davies threw on a dressing gown and walked outside, crossing to the east wing of the villa through the courtyard.

As Davies entered the home's kitchen, Lo-Chien looked up from his cooking and grinned. "Very handsome," he said, gesturing toward the embroidered shirt in his master's hand.

"Oh really? You savvy? What thing?" Angrily, Davies pointed to the embroidery.

The grin on Lo-Chien's fat, boxy face vanished.

"I suppose no one come house this afternoon?" Davies asked, his voice breaking, embarrassingly.

Lo-Chien shrugged and absorbed himself in making dinner.

"My room was broken into," he shouted, too furious to speak in the Pidgin English that Lo-Chien was likely to understand. "Don't deny it; a crime has been committed - and, if you had anything to do with it, I can have you arrested! You go to jail!"

Lo-Chien's chopping grew more determined.

"Lo-Chien, you fine helper, I fond of you and I fond of everybody, but I simply won't have this. No b'long plopper! Savvy? If you can't tell me anything, I'm afraid you go. You all go. You leave tomorrow. Now, what thing?" Once again he held up the shirt and pointed to the tiny symbol.

Lo-Chien didn't even look at him. Davies felt sure that the old man understood the significance of the symbol, but he preferred being fired, or even jailed, to telling what he knew. Now Davies felt his anger giving way to a sense of dread.

"All right, you gone tomorrow, five o'clock. This time. Everyone gone. All paid for whole month. Highly generous," he muttered as he stalked away.

The thing done to his wardrobe was preposterous and impossible, and the more he thought about it the more it scared the hell out of him. As he reentered his room and saw his clothes still strewn out on his bed, and on the floor, a nauseating wave of panic swept through his body again, making him sweat.

Twenty minutes later, Davies knew that he possessed fifty-four shirts, five smoking jackets, twelve sweaters, and fourteen pairs of silk pajamas, which he disliked wearing.   All were now monogrammed, and the work had been done in a little over two hours.   Eighty-five embroideries, not done in advance and glued on, but real embroideries whose threads penetrated his garments, each of which would have taken a skilled craftsman nearly an hour to complete. In lieu of a better explanation, forty-two and a half of China's finest tailors had invaded his house, done their work, and left without a trace while he had been at the French Club. Why had someone gone to extraordinary trouble simply to make an obscure impression on him? And who in China had the money, the power, or the sheer cleverness to carry out such an invasion? There had to be some trick, some simple but ingenious way that his clothes had been monogrammed in an impossibly short time that didn't require an invading army. If there was a trick, however, he sure as hell didn't know what it was - not yet, anyway. One thing was certain, Davies had better find out why someone had left such a cryptic message - and fast.

He made another phone call to Madame Lin and got the number of her friend, Dr. Sun. Dr. Sun had been contacted by Hong Fat earlier in the week to do an appraisal, and it was Dr. Sun who had alerted Madame Lin to the possibility that her family heirloom had unexpectedly been returned to China.

Calling the Shanghai museum, Davies learned that Dr. Sun was working late, so he made an appointment for seven-thirty. Then he poured himself a Scotch, and, with twenty minutes to kill, deposited himself in his garden. Detesting the lack of greenery found in traditional Chinese courtyards, he'd taken steps to insure that his was well-vegetated. Its lush beauty, however, provided no reassurance tonight.

What to do next? It was inconceivable that his servants were blind to the invasion of his bedroom; that made them accomplices - potentially as dangerous as the intruders themselves. He hated to dismiss his staff, though he didn't know any of them particularly well. Few of them spoke English, and he'd spent so much time traveling that a new group of faces, handpicked by an ever-fussy Lo-Chien, seemed to greet his every return. Interviewing their replacements would be a dreary affair, especially as it would leave him alone for several days, an unhappy thought. One thing was for sure, there was no longer any point in locking his door when he went to bed; the intruders were so skilled that he might as well be sleeping on the sidewalk in the worst part of town.

He stared at several large, unidentifiable insects attacking a Chinese lantern, which glowed red under one of the eaves of his home.   He was growing weary of a life that had been so astonishing that only recently had he grasped that it totally lacked purpose. Perhaps he should be grateful, because it had a purpose now. Fate smiles down in odd ways.

Was he up to the challenge - that was the real question. Even a man of privilege like himself couldn't weave his way happily through China like a practiced drunk at a cocktail party without ever having to confront the land's cruel realities. When his turn had finally come he'd discovered that he wasn't nearly as resilient as he'd assumed; but he'd have to be resilient to get through this latest outrage. Once again the memory started to play like a stuck record.

Six weeks ago Davies had met a fairly bookish looking Chinese, an engraver, while out betting on his favorite dogs and drinking at the Canidrome in the French District. The fellow was with his sweetheart, another equally homely Chinese, but together they seemed to glow. They weren't "huggy kissy icky sweet," actually they argued quite a bit, but in that good spirited, teasing way so common with two people who have a fierce affection for each other. Frankly, they had made him feel jealous and lonely, this unspectacular couple.

The man was a well-established member of the Kuomintang and Davies realized from talking to him that his girlfriend was more of a leftist, and this was causing friction between the engraver and his political friends. Still, the three of them had spent a grand evening together, ignoring their problems, drinking, laughing, "going to the dogs," and comparing notes on their separate business ventures.

The Chinese fellow had telephoned several times the following week, mostly asking questions of a business nature, but soon it became apparent that something was wrong. The Kuomintang had grown so intolerant of the man's leftist girlfriend that they were accusing the engraver of being a Communist sympathizer; it was obvious that some kind of showdown was in the works. The poor fellow was in a real state; he believed in China and its future, he was firmly committed to his cause, but he dearly loved his girlfriend and wanted to settle down and spend his life with her. "What should I do?" he'd kept asking. To Davies, the solution was elementary, politics was so much nonsense - take the girlfriend and run, he'd told him. Go to another city, go to America if need be, and have a good time.

Finally, the engraver had agreed, and Davies said that he'd front for train tickets to Canton. He'd even offered to come by at eight the next evening to drive the man and his lady friend to the station.

When he'd arrived the following night, he knew he was walking into a tragedy. The engraver's little house was ablaze with light, and, through a window, he could see that it was jammed with mid-level Kuomintang members and soldiers. His friend was standing in the center of the room looking completely wrung out, just nodding his head as his colleagues shouted at him. The girlfriend was on her knees with her hands tied behind her back. Someone put an ugly square revolver into the little man's hand as the jabbering din of advice went on and on. Finally, the girlfriend looked up and Davies could see the pleading in her eyes, he could see that close bond, that connection, that exists in the eyes of two people who deeply love each other; a kind of acceptance and understanding. The woman watched her lover as he placed the black gun against the side of her head. Then he pulled the trigger. Davies had to look away and he found himself focusing on the face of his friend instead. 'Till the end of his days he'd be willing to swear that in the second or two that followed he could actually see the little man's soul fade away, like a spark sputtering out. He had no idea what had happened to the fellow after that, but he could imagine that he was now one of the Kuomintang's best fighters.

A bit of Davies' own soul had slipped away after the experience, and his normal optimism had given way to despair.

He'd been on the verge of shaking his depression, when he'd found a ceramic leech on his back. Everything had gone downhill from there. Tonight was the capper.

V. THE CURSE

"It is indeed a valuable piece. It is associated with the fifth emperor of the Han dynasty."

"I thought the third," Davies said.

"No, the fifth." Dr. Sun's correction was emphatic. A shrunken man in his eighties, and so crippled with arthritis that he could hardly walk, Dr. Sun had taken Davies from the museum's front door to a dusty little sitting room. There, he warmed his hands over a small stove, despite the fact that it was a sultry night. Being a staff member, he was exempt from the regulation that forbid Chinese to visit the museum on any day but Saturday.

The museum itself was a dark old building with layers of cobwebs festooning its scattered treasures; ironically, much of its personnel was made up of the forbidden Chinese. As was the case in many fields, their intelligence and competence made the white man's burden an awkward one.

"The artifact known as 'the clouded twilight'," Dr. Sun continued, "is a very old and precious walking stick that was reputed to have been treasured by the fifth emperor of the Han dynasty. Are you familiar of Chinese history, Mr. Davies?"

Davies' knowledge of Chinese history was sketchy, but the Hans had been one of the earliest and most durable rulers of China. "Wouldn't he have ruled in the first or second century before the birth of Christ?"

As he waited for his teapot to boil, the old doctor smiled, apparently surprised by Davies' knowledge - most foreign devils took little interest in China's past. "In your calendar, the second. 'The clouded twilight' was originally of simple birch, and, according to a fanciful and not entirely reliable legend, the fifth emperor toured China on foot with it - an unprecedented act that allowed him to see what the lives of his subjects were truly like. When he returned to his palace he was worshiped by his people for his kindness and concern, and so the jealous nobles of the court secretly stole the staff and had it decorated with the most beautiful and precious of metals and jewels. Then they returned it to the emperor as a gift of tribute, and to curry his favor." Dr. Sun paused. He was breathing through his mouth, and although probably the result of some affliction, this tendency made him seem more meticulous and scholarly. "The emperor was so incensed by the nobles' bold act of ingratiation that he confiscated all their properties and ordered that the entire court be banished. He then executed the leader of the nobles as well as the staff's maker, who was a favorite of his, and announced that 'the clouded twilight,' 'painted like a courtesan,' should be destroyed. It never was. Though its fate was a mystery for many years. Not to the Lin family, however; for the past twenty odd years it has been the property of their house."

Davies was tempted to suggest that the old man finish his lecture lying down; he seemed on the verge of collapse after only a few minutes of talking.

"The artifact really had no history after the Han emperor disposed of it," Dr. Sun continued, apparently unconcerned by his own tenuous stamina. "That is until it resurfaced in 1782 as a gift from the King of Burma to Ch'ien-lung of the Manchu Dynasty. How it made its way to Burma, no one is certain. Ironically, the Emperor never took possession of his gift - nor did he ever see it. Perhaps he was fortunate in that respect."

"How's that?" Davies asked, squirming on the hard wooden chair, which had been provided for him.

"'The clouded twilight' has quite a bloody legacy, I'm afraid. Would you like some tea?" Slowly the old man began to pour himself tea from a clay pot that sat atop the small stove.

"No thanks." Every social visit in China revolved around tea and Davies dreaded the stuff. Especially, as his stomach had launched a rebellion upon the discovery of the leech, not to mention his monogrammed clothes.

Dr. Sun took a sip from his cup, then made his way to another wooden chair facing Davies - where he sat and closed his eyes. "Let me see, 'the clouded twilight' was to have been delivered from Rangoon to Peiping - we have to call it that now - by General Yang Su." He opened his eyes and stared hazily in Davies' direction. "While his boat was provisioning in Canton, however, the General was murdered and the staff stolen. Naturally, in his fury, the Emperor ordered all the General's envoys executed and their stomachs sliced so they could not join their ancestors." The old man paused, inadvertently adding dramatic emphasis to his tale. "The artifact did not reappear until almost a hundred years later in the hands of a northern warlord. Remember, in those times it still had all its jewels and was of considerable value. This warlord was accused of betraying his countrymen in the Opium Wars. He was found on a river bank, still alive, with his tongue and eyes neatly removed and placed in a rice bowl beside him. As you know, this is the traditional Chinese method of dealing with a, how would you put it? A 'squealer.'" He widened his eyes for emphasis. "There are certain Chinese gangsters who still practice this punishment."

With an internal shiver, Davies recollected that he'd encountered one or two thugs who still did.

Dr. Sun put both of his hands on the arms of his chair. "Would you excuse me for a moment?" He labored to rise from his hard little chair, and Davies rose to assist him. "I shall be right back."

"Right back" must mean sometime before Monday, Davies thought as Dr. Sun made for a side door with the speed of a leaf drifting in a pond. After the doctor had finally gone, Davies moved to reclaim his chair, then decided that standing would be more comfortable. Why had Dr. Sun left in the middle of his lecture? Had he revealed too much? Or was it something as simple as the old scholar falling victim to his eighty year old bladder? What a life the man must have had; to have even made it to eighty in a place like China was an amazing feat.

Davies now became aware of how exhausted he was himself. The events he'd experienced over the past forty-eight hours had left him so numb and depressed that, if permitted, he'd be in his bath right now, content to stay there for the rest of the week. After finding those monograms, however, he had no choice but to soldier on, which was hardly his style. He wasn't much of a stiff-upper-lip kind of fellow - his manner was to react to unpleasantness as an Oriental would. Orientals, he'd learned, weren't very good at extinguishing their emotions, their technique was to eliminate the source of whatever upset them. Ask an Oriental an awkward or pointed question and while his emotions surged and flared he'd pretend that he hadn't heard you: external suppression. An Occidental, on the other hand, would answer frankly, rationally, revealing thoughts and superficial feelings but never anything deep or substantial. His technique was internal suppression. Davies, however, wasn't allowed to use either evasion or suppression; he was forced to muster all his resources at a time when he'd never felt more spent.

The door creaked open and Dr. Sun returned, taking a full minute to settle back into his chair.

"Is everything all right?" Davies asked.

"Quite so," Dr. Sun replied, refusing to reveal a clue as to why he'd left in the first place. "Where were we? Ah yes, 'the clouded twilight.' Now, in 1875 it showed up in the city of Peiping. You see, my memory is one of the few things that hasn't failed me. There it was presented to the Emperor T'ung Chich by a conquered warlord from Chunking. Seven days later the Emperor died." He made a gentle smile. "Are you beginning to get the idea?"

Davies nodded, hardly relieved to be hearing a tale about death, death, and more death.

"It was concluded that 'the clouded twilight' was cursed, and the Empress Dowager, Tzu Hsi, ordered it destroyed. That was thought the end of it. Nonetheless, it reappeared four years later, showing up in the home of a prosperous Chinese merchant, and quite frankly nothing remarkable occurred. Except that the merchant was a boorish fellow who would talk on for hours about nothing and his neighbors secretly remarked that this was the true curse of the artifact."

Davies laughed, politely, causing the old man to give him a scolding frown. "It all stopped being funny several years later. The man's only son, merely nine years of age, determined to become blood brothers with a local playmate. The boy accidentally cut the main artery in his wrist and bled to death." He shook his head. "Children can be so foolish. It was claimed that the young man used a small dagger that he found concealed in the staff, but I sincerely doubt it."

"Why's that?"

Dr. Sun took another sip of tea and smacked his lips. "So often curios are rumored to have secret compartments and such, and the stories are always romanticized nonsense. Wishful thinking. Since the boy's death, it is claimed that everyone who comes into possession of 'the clouded twilight' will be visited by terrible events."

"Any idea how the Lin family got the thing?"

The old fellow smiled, wistfully. "I did not know they possessed it until I heard it was on display in a Chicago museum. I made inquiries and discovered that it was there on loan from the Lins. They are descended from a powerful Han faction, as you know. Are you well acquainted with them?"

"My mother attended Vassar with Madame Lin. I guess, I've known her most of my life."

"Your mother? I would hope so."

"No, Madame Lin. She taught me to read, in fact."

"Is that so? Yes, I could easily imagine her swatting you with a ruler."

Davies chuckled. "Actually, she was very patient. At the time, she was just learning English herself and needed my help as much as I needed hers. Though, I think it rather insulted her pride to be regarded as a 'mere student;' so she never let me be anything but a helpful pupil."

Dr. Sun stared into his cup of tea. "She's quite a character, isn't she? Madame Lin donated several pieces to the museum; but I haven't seen her in some time, dear woman. I suppose these past years have not been easy for people like the Lins. I heard that, like so many wealthy countrymen, they came to Shanghai escaping from somewhere." He stared, glassy-eyed, at a far wall. "One despairs for our future, I fear."

"You aren't impressed by Chiang?"

"I'm an historian. Few historians are optimists."

"Uh huh." Davies changed his position on the hard wooden chair, but it didn't help much. "You're right about the Lins. In fact, I was with them when they had to give up their home in Changsha. We came down the Yangtze, and I've got to say that after spending weeks hiding with the Lins in a cramped sampan I grew pretty fond of them."

"I'd expect the opposite. Old friends can become the objects of murder plots under such circumstances." The old man paused to take another, much needed, sip of tea.

"I owe my life to Madame Lin, so I'm not too inclined to complain."

"Really?" Dr. Sun moved his chair closer to the fire. Davies couldn't believe that he actually felt cold on such a hot night.

"In Nanking, I, well let's say I did something I shouldn't have. Chiang's soldiers didn't take kindly to it and came looking for me. Madame Lin got up on those little bound feet of hers and came right out to face them. It was amazing, this tiny old lady, chewing on her cigarette holder, and threatening these big soldiers with her cane. I guess they could have shot her on the spot, but she was so damned fierce. I think she actually scared them. She scares me half the time. When I asked her what in the world she'd said to get them to go away, what do you think she told me?" He laughed softly. "'Zephyr, I merely explained to them that I was a sorceress and if they didn't leave I would curse them to wander endlessly in the afterlife searching for their ancestors.'"

"In her case, a believable threat." Dr. Sun placed his hands in his lap, the image of contentment. How he could look so comfortable and relaxed on his own hard wooden chair was something else beyond Davies' understanding. "I met her husband once; he seemed quite pleasant. Though, I hear he has a temper. It was his hope that the staff might be reclaimed by the Chinese government and I agreed to help him. Unfortunately, China does not have any formal government that is fully recognized by foreign powers. I have sent letters to Chiang Kai-shek suggesting that he make a formal request for the staff, and other historical pieces. However, the Generalissimo is very busy with other problems. And from what you tell me, Mr. Davies, the question is now academic."

"I'd say so," Davies agreed.

"On the other hand," the old man made a gurgling chuckle, "perhaps the Generalissimo would be wiser not to pursue the matter. He has enough troubles without acquiring a cursed walking stick."

"Do you think the staff is cursed, Dr. Sun?"

The old man gazed into the fire. "The myth of curses surrounding inanimate objects is a very interesting phenomenon, Mr. Davies. I am inclined to think that objects, which are extremely valuable attract people who are both greedy and violent. Hence, violence will be a part of these peoples' lives. I assume that you do not believe in such things as curses."

"Quite the contrary," Davies replied, "two years ago I was hired to find a golden dragonfly with a similar reputation. Perhaps it was just coincidence, but the day after I took the job I cut myself shaving. I've another question, if you don't mind. This symbol, can you tell me what it means?" From his jacket, he removed some old snapshots of the staff that Madame Lin had provided him with and showed them to Dr. Sun.

The old man had to change glasses to examine the photographs, an act which consumed another three minutes. "It's the maker's signature, altered to indicate that the maker was put to death. More grim doings, I'm afraid. It's rumored that it was the maker himself who placed a curse on the staff."

"I see. If a person was presented with a note, say, and it had that symbol on it, would it be safe to assume that one was being threatened with death?"

Dr. Sun coughed, raspily. "This all sounds very melodramatic. However, that would be a fair interpretation. With a slight modification, I think."

"Yeah, what modification?"

The doctor put his reading glasses away and made himself comfortable again on the impossible wooden chair. "The artist who created the staff was a favorite of the Emperor. The poor fellow surely thought he was doing his Emperor a great tribute, yet the Emperor saw it differently. He viewed the artist as siding with the nobles against his wishes. The primary reason the Emperor executed the staff's maker was because he felt the man had betrayed him. So, if I were to receive this symbol, I'd take it as a threat of death that would only be carried out if I neglected my obligations to a friend or benefactor. I think the message wouldn't be so much 'death,' as it would be, 'obey or die.'"

"I see." He wasn't sure if this different interpretation was a relief - and at the moment, he couldn't think of any murderous benefactors. "But there's something else." He tried to retrieve a thought that had sped through his mind several minutes earlier. "Oh, yeah. You said that in the eighteenth century the staff still had all its jewels. You mean to say it doesn't now?"

"I thought that was fairly common knowledge," Dr. Sun replied. "The Lin family were probably the main culprits. From time to time, some of the staff's owners would be in need of ready cash - they would pick off jewels from the staff and sell them, replacing them with paste."

"How many of the original jewels are still on the staff?"

"Well, none. But for historical reasons, the staff is still quite valuable."

"How valuable?"

"In your country, or Europe, I would think that a seller could get five hundred, perhaps a thousand pounds. That's hardly insubstantial."

Nor was it a fortune. This was a bad day for Davies' stomach; the illogic of unseen forces clamoring to get their hands on an object worth about as much as a second hand Buick was weird. "Tell me, could 'the clouded twilight' have any other worth than as an artifact?"

"Do you mean as a treasure map? Perhaps a key to a secret door?" Dr. Sun's frown was now causing a dozen new creases to form on his face, it was hard to believe there was room for any more.

"Exactly," Davies responded, hopefully. "Is there another reason why it might be highly sought after?"

"Not that I know of. There was no fabled treasure associated with the fifth Han emperor, nor with any of the possessors of the staff. Ch'ien-lung had many beautiful things, of course, but he never even saw the staff. And my research indicates its design was not altered. 'The clouded twilight' could hardly have been made in the second century before Christ to point the way to a secret treasure amassed in the eighteenth century. Regardless, there are no legends or myths or folklore or anything I have ever heard of to indicate that the staff is tied to anything but itself."

"Could it be a pawn in a feud? A warlord wanting it to have more face than a rival?"

Dr. Sun squinted at him in a way that made Davies think of a veterinarian about to put down a cat. "How long have you lived in China?"

"About five years. Why?"

"Shame on you. And you still believe in those penny dreadful stories? Please, you must know we Chinese are a practical people. You would expect us to go to war over some old tree branch worth five hundred pounds for face or prestige or rivalry? What silliness. No, it's just an old artifact, not particularly unique. The only thing I have ever heard of that distinguishes it is the curse."

When the old fellow finally walked Davies to the front door, he was no longer angry. Smiling thoughtfully, he asked, "If you find this staff, Mr. Davies, what do you intend to do with it?"

Davies answered with a laugh. "I think I'll get rid of the damned thing as fast as I can."

Dr. Sun nodded. "You may be wise to do so. And where are you off to now?"

"Good question, I guess I ought to eat something."

"I can recommend a charming little cafe, not too far from here in the French Concession."

Davies noted Dr. Sun's dining suggestion, then he thanked the old man and left.

The evening was hotter than any in mid-August that he could remember; and the sultry air made him feel particularly tense. All around him, shirtless rickshaw coolies with glistening sweat-covered backs darted, with the nimbleness of insects, through a parade of black motorcars and bicyclists.

Before he realized it, the Hispano had entered the French Concession, home to the cities' best clubs; Chinese warlords and gangsters found a haven here, as had Dr. Sun Yat-sen and many young Communist revolutionaries.

He hadn't possessed much of an appetite since his home had been invaded, but he needed to eat. After Dr. Sun's tale of tragedy and blood, he didn't fancy more than soup; but maybe the French bistro the old man had recommended could revive some of his enthusiasm for dining. He signaled to his driver to turn right. Although a large part of him felt like fleeing China, logic told him that his only salvation lay in learning more.

Across the street, a beggar with a milky eye and no front teeth smiled at him and nodded his head. Davies nodded back, somewhat imperiously, assuming the man approved of the Hispano. Then he thought again, and what little appetite he had completely vanished.

VI. A NIGHT TO FORGET

Davies sat in a smoky, curio-choked French bistro on the Avenue Joffre staring again at photographs of "the clouded twilight" that Madame Lin had given him. The photographs were black and white, neither retouched nor hand-colored, but he could easily imagine the variety of sparkling hues the jewels must have once had. He released a heavy breath, slipped the pictures into a jacket pocket, and looked across the room to where the matronly wife of one of Shanghai's leading bankers was seated with several friends, evidently slumming.

Wearing a look of anger and astonishment, the matron was staring intently at another diner, evidently because she had been seated a mere table away from a girl who worked at Gracie Gale's well-known Number Fifty-two. Come on, what did the woman expect when she came seeking adventure in such a place? As Davies watched, the prim woman's comically open mouth slowly closed and her expression of contempt relaxed into one of careful scrutiny. Stealthily, she pulled eye liner from her purse and began to sketch the whore's dress on the back of her menu. The next day the sketch would surely be sent off to a Chinese tailor. For better or worse, Gracie's girls were the first in town with the latest American styles.

This reminded Davies of the week, several years back, when Gracie had sent engraved invitations to a select group of bachelors, himself included, announcing a reception. It was to be held at Gracie's Kiangsi Road establishment to unveil her latest arrivals from San Francisco. Somehow the notice had fallen into the hands of a Chinese reporter who put it into the society column of one of the city's leading newspapers. This caused a terrific stink amongst Shanghai's "better women," and he couldn't help wondering if the dowager at the next table and her friends had driven half way to Gracie's before realizing their error. Those days had hardly been carefree, but now he longed for their return. For the moment, things were calm, but it was the calm one finds in the eye of a hurricane. Was it coincidence that he'd been asked to find a cursed staff, and endured two home invasions within a forty-eight hour period? It had all begun after he'd battled with the German in the street. Was that somehow the catalyst? What moral lesson did that leave him with - don't beat fat Germans in front of witnesses?

The ugliest aspect of the intrusions into his home was the knowledge that a stranger had been through his personal things. They'd looked at his life, invaded his privacy, and had probably left joking about what they'd seen. He felt a terrible sense of violation.

Far worse, a person who could secretly alter eighty-five articles of his clothing would have no problem slitting his throat as he slept, or slipping a poisonous snake into one of the little cabinets built behind the Hispano's front seat. This possibility had occurred to him earlier in the day when the sight of one of his cigars had caused him to nearly jump out of the car.

He'd hoped that his interview with Dr. Sun would give him some insight as to who was behind it all, but he was now more confused then before. The list of entities capable of assembling the army of tailors needed to alter his clothes so quickly was a short one - there were the Communists and the Kuomintang. But to what purpose? Moreover, they lacked the imagination to concoct such a scheme. A local warlord wouldn't possess the necessary organizational skills. The only remaining person with the resources and cunning was Elder Brother, the head of the underworld and the most feared man in China. Indeed, he was famous for the kind of twisted acts that Davies had been subjected to with the ceramic leech and the monograms. But Elder Brother and Davies were actually on the best of terms. And why on earth would Elder Brother have an interest in "the clouded twilight?" Besides, if the monograms were a threat, advising Davies to hand over the artifact immediately, then why not say so in plain English - or plain Chinese, for that matter? Davies scowled, annoyed with himself. Why was he so sure that the invader was a Chinese? He was assuming again.

He took a tentative sip from his soup and thought about how ironic things had become. He'd traveled to China to experience life to its fullest, often romanticizing about undergoing "adventures" just like this one. The reality was far different than he'd expected. He now had an unshakable dull headache and practically no appetite. He couldn't concentrate as unpleasant images of his own demise kept playing in his head like a stuck record. His stomach churned so relentlessly that he dreaded eating or drinking, and was as concerned about public displays of belching and flatulence as he was about ducking daggers that might sail his way. Yes, it was great to feel so fully alive - but how could he complain? He was merely getting a taste of what the wretched Chinese living on the streets must feel every day of the year.

A waiter appeared with his chit. As Davies reached for his wallet, his hand freeze in mid-air. Resting on a small, lacquer tray, the chit had something extra written on it in a precise, elegant hand that had become all too familiar. His heart was racing but his hand was slow to respond - it took nearly a minute for him to muster the courage to reach for the thing. Even then, he used the tray as a tool, sliding it closer and taking care not to touch the chit itself.

In what was becoming a wretched ritual, his mouth went dry as he read the message scribbled beside the listed cost of his food: "A wise man honors those who serve him. A foolish man blames others for matters he must resolve himself."

God, not again. Davies felt physically ill. It was as if he had fallen into a hole on a moonless night finding himself in an underground pool of cold, black water. There was no way out, and he could either swim endlessly or drown in darkness. Another chill raced through his body. This is what he deserved.

VII. THE MONSTER

Saturday, August 11, 1928

Seven o'clock was nearing and Davies sat in his back garden awaiting the arrival of Madame Lin. He knew she would not be late. Above him, the thick, rich leaves of summer shimmered on the chestnut trees enclosing his garden, causing him to think of how certain hot afternoons give way to the kind of warm evenings that tempt the most cynical to consider the existence of a divine power.

A friend of his back in the states, a rather effete inheritor of garish wealth, claimed that beauty was the only thing worth living for. Davies had dismissed the theory as self-indulgent and shallow, but after years of fighting to make a mark on the world, only to see petty squabbling and ruthless selfishness wipe out painstakingly conceived and executed enterprises - as a toddler would gleefully destroy a castle of blocks - he had started to wonder if his friend wasn't right after all. These days his greatest ambition was to climb into a chilled martini and sit on the banks of a canal and study a fanciful crescent moon-shaped bridge, its centuries old stonework adorned with rich, green tufts of moss, as dappled light danced across the still, mirrored water beneath it.

But hours devoted to whimsical reflection, (pun intended,) were no longer possible - not after the appearance of the monograms on his clothes - not to mention the sinister chit. Why were so many strange dramas happening all at once? He still hadn't recovered from the incident with the ceramic leech, and now this peculiar new situation with Madame Lin.

Davies' thoughts were interrupted by the image of Lo-Chien making his way arthritically through the garden. The sun, which was an hour shy of setting, seemed to be progressing faster than Davies' sixty-year-old number one boy.

"Madame Lin friend bottom side," Lo-Chien muttered when he finally arrived, "you see?" He handed Davies a card - it was one of Madame Lin's with an introduction scribbled on the back. Lo-

Chien disapproved of most people who came calling at Davies' villa, it meant more work for him and less time for his mah-jongg games with the cook. Tonight he seemed particularly disgusted.

"A young woman, is she?" Davies asked, hopefully. He hadn't expected Madame Lin's wicked niece to come along with her aunt, but the idea certainly interested him.

The old Chinaman curled his lip. "Person," he spat. "Kind, my no savvy."

He looked sharply at the old man who was making a great clatter as he picked up dishes from the table. "What do you mean you don't know the kind of person?"

"My no savvy," the Chinaman repeated contemptuously.

Davies folded his newspaper, this was going to be interesting. Maybe the mysterious niece had feet for hands, or was some sort of goat girl - that would explain Madame Lin's hesitation to put her up. "I see person, now. Three piece man come supper."

"Hmph!" Lo-Chien snorted, and he shuffled off.

There was no doubt about the gender of the "person" escorted into the garden courtyard by his number-three boy; Davies had to force himself not to stare. Following behind the houseboy was an agonizingly beautiful Eurasian girl. Wearing a stylish, Western-style frock, simple, obviously tailor-made, she was thinner than most women, yet fuller in the places that mattered to men, himself included. The young woman was about twenty Davies guessed, the recipient of the best of two possible worlds. She had full, scornful lips contributing to a sensuous quality that defied her serious demeanor. Her high cheekbones and aquiline nose were elegant; her dark, almond eyes dead calm in a way that gave no clues as to her thoughts and made her seem unapproachable. Despite belonging to a scorned social class, there nothing subservient in her manner; she held her head high as she took in the gardens and the little reflecting pools with a sly, assessing glance. What a lovely item to have in his own back yard. Perhaps her skin was a little too olive in hue, her features a tad foreign for his taste, but his taste had been known to change.

He rose and extended his hand. "You must be Madame Lin's niece."

Giving him the same indifferent look that she'd used when appraising his garden, the girl presented her gloved left hand. The gesture was as cold as ice, the hand offered palm-down for him to do with as he wished. He gripped the smooth kid leather. "How nice to meet you." Getting no response, he couldn't think of anything else to say but, "Please be seated."

Gracefully, she sat in the chair he offered her. The reason for Lo-Chien's grumbling was now obvious - it was prompted by the traditional Chinese contempt for Eurasians. Such people were neither Chinese nor white, and thus were not people at all. When he had announced the young lady's arrival, it had probably strained the old man's sense of propriety to even refer to her as a "person."

"How long will you be staying with us in Shanghai?" Davies asked, taking his own seat and hoping that his attraction to her wasn't embarrassingly obvious. There was no reply. Strike one. Or maybe the triple threat was in play - a friend had once told him that "when you're rich, good-looking, and *interested* people don't trust you – they assume there's a catch." Nonetheless, this was no time to allow over-confidence, or its evil twin, self doubt, to cripple his resolve because, if Madame Lin's suspicions were correct, this young woman had brought the damnable "clouded twilight" to Shanghai. She alone may be able to tell him what the wretched artifact's illusive secret was.

As silence reigned, he regained some of his self-confidence and flashed his most effective, "mischievous little boy smile." "Now come on, I know you're not that shy."

"She's mute."

Startled, he looked across his lawn to see Madame Lin approaching, tipping back and forth like a drunk on her bound feet, a motion unsuited to her imperious manner. Accompanying her, as usual, was the weathered, middle-aged servant girl. Tonight, Madame Lin was dressed in a stiff, richly embroidered gown of emerald silk, which must have been like walking in an oven. "I must apologize for Monica, Zephyr," Madame Lin said as she hobbled closer. "She refuses to talk. I have no idea why."

"So she can talk?" This news, implying that the girl was waging a silent temper tantrum, subdued his embarrassment as he guided Madame Lin into her own chair. Her servant remained standing.

As Davies sat down again, Madame Lin said, "May I present my niece, Miss Marshall?" The word "niece" was given minimal emphasis.

Davies nodded. "Miss Marshall."

A a barely discernible smile of acknowledgment formed on the young woman's face, but there was something sad and distant about it, which reminded him of something that he couldn't quite put his finger on. He hated that. Davies turned to Madame Lin. "Now, let me understand, she was talking when she arrived?"

"I suppose. Regardless, she won't speak to me now."

"But why?" Davies asked, "don't you have any idea?" He turned toward the lovely, young Eurasian - was she angry - frightened? It was difficult to tell; the smile had faded and her face now completely lacked expression.

The sound of clattering heralded Lo-Chien's return with a tea tray. The old man made quick work of it. Teacups were set in front of Madame Lin and Davies, and a third cup was left on the silver tray; it appeared that the old man's efforts were aimed solely at insulting the young Eurasian woman. "Lo-Chien, no b'long plopper," Davies said sharply. "Wantchee supper, no tea." He pointed to the tea setting. "Away, chop, chop!"

The scowl on Lo-Chien's face intensified to a degree that implied the risk of permanent deformity as he put everything back on the tea tray and returned with it to the kitchen.

"I'm sorry," Davies said, "I'm having trouble with my servants." He glanced toward the door leading to his kitchen and saw, to his disgust, that his number-two and number-three boys were elongating their eyes with their fingers, ridiculing Monica's faintly oriental features.

Madame Lin appeared indifferent to the insults directed toward her niece. She turned to the young woman beside her and said sharply, "Is this what you want? To make me look foolish in front of my old friend?" Apparently feeling that she hadn't been abrasive enough, she hissed, "Sit up straight, Monica!"

The girl didn't so much as flinch.

Madame Lin leaned conspiratorially across the table. "Poor Monica, you can see now why I cannot invite her into my home. Just look at how she's behaving, this childish play-acting. I suppose I can't be surprised, as she is not Chinese."

So this was what it was all about; the woman had no more regard for her niece than did Lo-Chien. It was shocking that someone so intelligent would be capable of such third-rate thinking.   "She's not anything, is she?"   Davies remarked sarcastically.

Relaxing back into her chair, Madame Lin signaled for her servant to bring over her wooden purse, from which she extracted an ivory cigarette holder. "Please be kind, I did not say that. But, Zephyr, face it, we're all different, are we not? Some differences can be seen, your eyes and skin, for instance. So there must be other differences, unseen, that reflect themselves in behavior and thinking." She punctuated her theory with a raised eyebrow. "If Monica was full-blooded she would have been brought up with values and traditions, taught a respect for her ancestors, and this would have led her to moral behavior. Why would one ever steal or cheat knowing the disgrace it would cause to your family? But her mother dedicated her life to spurning these fine values, and you see the result."

It was extraordinary that Madame Lin was willing to launch into this diatribe in front of the girl as if she was nothing more than a piece of furniture.   "Can you be sure that she's all right, physically?"

"Believe me, she's perfectly capable of speaking. Aren't you, Monica?" Madame Lin leaned forward and smacked the young woman lightly on the face.

"That's enough," Davies said, astonished.

The niece maintained her defiant stare, but under the table, where her aunt could not see, she briefly took hold of Davies' sleeve. The gesture was so unexpected that he didn't know how to react; the display of vulnerability from one who'd appeared so haughty moments before was thrilling – but the cynical part of him couldn't help but wonder if it was also manipulative.

Madame Lin gave him a resigned smile. "You make me feel like a criminal, Zephyr, as if Monica's refusal to speak is because I've not allowed her to stay with her uncle and me. However, I'm not impressed - she's done it before." She waved an unlit cigarette in the air. "But perhaps you know better."

Again Davies turned to Monica. "Is that fair of her?" he asked softly, "Have you done this before?"

Not surprisingly, the young woman remained mute.

"Miss Marshall, try to understand that we're on your side. Even if you brought 'the clouded twilight' to Shanghai, it's now back in the fold, as it were. You aren't in any trouble and no harm has been done, save for the rift that seems to be growing between you and your aunt as long as you remain silent. Isn't family important to you? All your aunt wants is an explanation, is that so unreasonable?"

Despite the gentleness in his voice this approach got him nowhere as Monica continued to stare blankly forward. Was the young woman's silence punishment for her aunt's rudeness? She was such a striking beauty that she could easily have been pampered into childishness and tantrums - in America such things were not uncommon. Maybe the exact reverse was the case, she had grown so weary of being regarded as a lovely non-person that she was determined to act like one.

Still, he wasn't inclined to write her off as a faker. She had entered his garden seeming aloof and cool, but shyness often came off as arrogance, and coldness was frequently caused, literally, by paralyzing fear. The sad fact was that non-whites had to tread lightly in Shanghai, and the possibility that Miss Marshall had stumbled into the wrong place at the wrong time couldn't be discounted. Under her light make-up, there were no signs of cuts or bruises on the young niece's face, which was reassuring. Even the area around her lovely mouth was unmolested, suggesting that her tongue, which had not yet revealed itself, was completely intact. Yet an emotional trauma couldn't be ruled out; anything was possible now that there was such great unrest afoot in China.

Suddenly, he remembered a moment from his past that had eluded him, and with it came the realization as to why Monica's little smile was so unnerving. He turned back to Madame Lin. "You want my opinion? Something very serious has happened to her. I'm certain of it."

* * *

In the darkness of his tiny cabin in his father's sampan, Wong Gou Sing lit the sixth joss stick. The first two had been for him, the second two for his boss, Hong Fat, and the third for the wealthy American, Zephyr Davies. Most natives of China were adjusted to lives of frugality, misery, injustice and illness, while the white faces remained immune. Therefore, Gou Sing was still shocked that the men who had treated Hong Fat with such cruelty earlier that day had remarked that Zephyr Davies was the next on their list.

* * *

Color had left the sky. A cool breeze was causing the simple act of sitting to seem like a divine pleasure at the conclusion of such a hot, stagnant day.

Lighting a cigarette, Madame Lin merely shrugged in response to Davies' insistence that something truly awful had happened to her niece. "She hardly seems on the verge of a breakdown."

Giving Madame Lin a cursory glance, Davies said, "You're an expert, are you? I thought you were going to explain things to me, but all you're doing is making everything enormously confusing. Is she a mere trickster, or are you seriously concerned about her? You can't have it both ways."

"Please don't scold me."

He turned away and contemplated his garden of shadows. It wasn't that the woman's niece had greater appeal to him as someone sweet and innocent, quite the opposite. However, he rather liked the idea of proving the girl's goodness for the sole purpose of flinging it in his bigoted friend's face like an insult. Though her goodness was still unproved, the seriousness of the young woman's plight was something of which he was now convinced. The explanation might seem idiosyncratic, but to him it was conclusive. As a boy, he'd been fascinated by photographs of Teddy Roosevelt. He'd been unable to understand why Teddy's famous grin was so electric until a test paper had haphazardly dropped on a photo and covered everything but Roosevelt's eyes. The eyes were of a man who was crying, and though Miss Marshall wasn't grinning insanely, the sad, calm look in her eyes combined with the hint of a smile on her face had a similar unsettling quality. The resigned sorrow in her expression wasn't from a fleeting hurt, but something much deeper. It wasn't an act, because what made Miss Marshall's calm stare so dynamic was that she was trying to hide any trace of emotion, and she was failing.

A sense of urgency swept through Davies; he must find out for himself what had led to Miss Marshall's silence. Yet he felt powerless; with his current servant problem he'd be courting turmoil if he invited the girl to stay with him. Still, he despised the idea of her being left alone; though his home was no longer the safe haven that it might have been just twenty-four hours ago. For a few moments, he'd forgotten about the awful incident with the leech; sleep wouldn't come easily tonight. If he had to choose between problems to solve, he very much preferred the mystery of Monica's silence over who had violated the sanctity of his home.

A knowing smile formed on Madame Lin's face, as if she'd just gotten a peek at his thoughts; she was making him feel like a love-sick teenager. He glanced at his watch - a reliably adult gesture. "I'm feeling a bit hungry. We're getting nowhere with this. Maybe if we all go somewhere to grab a bite we'll be a little more charitable to each other."

With stiff grace Madame Lin rose. "I'm sorry, Zephyr, I still have many things to attend to. Monica is staying at the Astor House. I'm sure she can use my rickshaw to get back. And if it would not trouble you to drive me to my home, I mean, perhaps we could talk for a few moments more."

"No trouble at all." So Madame Lin wasn't even willing to be seen in the same car with her niece who was now studying her shoes, which were extremely clean and well polished - her preoccupation with them was a little odd.

The girl did another curious thing as they passed through the house to the front door. While Lo-Chien was leading the way, she lagged behind and touched Davies' elbow. When Davies glanced at her, she looked away as if nothing had happened. Madame Lin's icy stare suggested that she had also seen her niece's private overture.

Madame Lin directed her rickshaw coolie to take Monica back to the Astor House. Davies quickly intervened, however, insisting that they drive the girl to her hotel.

Max had already brought out the Hispano, and he was standing by it, dutifully holding the rear door open. Davies never tired of looking at this car. Yet Monica was no more impressed by the Hisso than she'd been with anything else she'd encountered that evening. Adding insult to injury, Davies noted a glinting drop of oil on the gravel beneath the car's engine – an occurrence that the Hispano factory had promised would never happen. God almighty, if he didn't have enough to worry about, he was now confronted by betrayal from the finest car in the world.

Monica and Madame Lin's servant somehow squeezed themselves into the front of the Hispano beside Max. Davies rode in the rear with Madame Lin.

As the car turned out of the drive and onto the street, Madame Lin stoically removed a silver case from her coat, withdrew an English Players, and maneuvered the cigarette into her ivory holder. Next came a platinum lighter. "Why won't this light in this absurd car?" she said as she tried to coax the cigarette into service.

The rear windscreen was little more than an ornament, and Davies shielded her from the wind.

The cigarette ignited, and after taking a triumphant puff through her holder, Madame Lin said, "Don't you wish your ears could swivel in the wind?"

"I'm sorry?"

She raised her hands to the side of her face. "When the wind is blowing right into your face, it hurts your ears. Don't you wish we could just take our ears and turn them around so the wind wouldn't bother them so?"

"Now that you mention it, I think God made a mistake."

"God makes many mistakes," Madame Lin said quietly.

When they arrived at the Astor House, Davies walked Monica to the lift. He'd liked to have escorted her to her room, but her hotel was too respectable to allow such familiarity among mere acquaintances of the opposite sex. It was a pity, because if they were alone for a moment she might open up. Besides, she was so damned pretty that he couldn't help but fantasize about the possibilities, despite the seriousness of her plight. He imagined her eyes brimming with grateful tears as she took his hand, pulling it shyly to her soft, full lips, caressing his fingers with the tip of her tongue. And that would be but the beginning.

The sliding door opened and Monica entered the lift. The elderly Caucasian who manned the contraption seemed to be half-asleep, and he remained silent as he waited patiently for instructions.

"Look, I hope you'll be okay," Davies said, and glanced at the lift operator who turned away, apparently to offer them the illusion of privacy. "Would you like my number?" he asked Monica, who remained as still and silent as a post. "No, perhaps not. But why don't I give it to you, just in case." He fumbled into his jacket and removed his card, which he pressed into the young woman's gloved hand, causing her to flinch slightly with pain. "Is there something wrong with your hand?" he asked in his most empathetic voice.

She studied him as if he was a new hat that she was considering buying. Then she gently extracted her gloved hand, allowing her fingertips to brush against the side of his wrist. She pointed upwards, and the lift operator shut the door in Davies' face.

As he left the hotel, Davies felt thoroughly deflated. When it came to flirting with women he usually had good luck, ironically the most sought-after often being the easiest for him to conquer. To be rejected by someone who wasn't even white was a minor outrage. More accurately, it was well earned comeuppance, because why was he even thinking of flirting with a young woman who was in real trouble?

Walking down the front steps and approaching the Hispano, he saw, to his astonishment, that Madame Lin was playing a hide and go seek game with a girl from the streets. The child must have been three or four, and from a secure nesting spot in her mother's arms, she reached toward the interior of the open Hispano as the normally stern Madame Lin teased her, saying in Chinese what was probably the equivalent of, "warmer, warmer." Finally, the child pried open Madame Lin's left hand and was rewarded with a piece of hard candy. Madame Lin ceremoniously placed the candy in the girl's fat hand, and the child squealed as she accepted the gift, then buried her face in her mother's chest. Madame Lin smiled at the girl, then she turned and stared accusingly at Davies. It was as if she had become another person in less than a second. She waited until he had climbed aboard and settled in, and when the car was rumbling toward the Bund, she said, "I see she's already snagged you."

"So you've made up your mind regardless of anything I might say?" Davies shot back, testily. "You know I cherish you as an old and dear friend, but frankly this is nonsense. You bring her around for my opinion, then tell me how to think. It's outrageous that you don't invite her to stay with you. So she's only half-Chinese, haven't you outgrown such silly prejudices after all these years?"

He glanced to his side and saw that Madame Lin was looking downward, resembling a chastised schoolgirl. "Are you attracted to my niece?" she asked quietly.

"Why does that matter?" Despite her pitiable appearance, he didn't feel that sorry for her.

"Answer my question, please."

"Yes, I suppose I am. What of it?"

"Here's the tally. I say she's bad because she's not of pure blood. You've determined she's good because you find her attractive. Are you any less prejudiced than I? I think you're being very unfair."

He had to put some thought into his reply. "My prejudice isn't hurtful."

"It hurts me. After all these years, you're willing to categorize me because I have different beliefs than you. I'm a backward Chinese with old-fashioned ways. Is that not prejudice?"

Davies was forced to smile. "I guess we're both guilty."

"Thank you. If I was unwilling to amend my prejudices about Monica I should not have consulted you in the first place. But I must warn you not to be taken in by those sad airs of hers - and the fact that she has beauty on her side. It's all an act, I realize that now. In fact, everything has suddenly become very clear to me."

"I'm so glad."

Madame Lin allowed the ash from her cigarette to be swept away by the wind. "Yes, bringing her to you has been a great help. For now I see how, ever so softly, and ever so gently, she weaves her web. Believe me, you mustn't get involved."

"Now really."

"I'm quite serious, Zephyr. She's a monster."

* * *

VIII. SLEEPING ON THE JOB

Sunday, August 12, 1928

After a wretched night, Davies gave up all hope of sleeping and literally rolled out of bed at the ungodly hour of eight-thirty a.m.

Stumbling through his courtyard, he found a servant patiently waiting for him with the news that an early morning visitor had arrived. His servants might admit potential burglars into the house, but still they had the good manners not to disturb his sleep.

Davies plodded into the kitchen where he was greeted by the sight of Hong Fat's youthful Chinese assistant. Standing in a corner, the lad clasped his hands together, bowed smartly, and announced that his employer was desperate to buy back "the clouded twilight." A strange set of affairs had just gotten stranger.

* * *

When he appeared amongst the hanging pots and pans, Gou Sing realized that Zephyr Davies was still grappling with some kind of "privileged trouble." Curiously, today the handsome American's anxious mood made him seem diminished and less charismatic.

After Davies had barely consumed enough food to nourish a beggar, he led Gou Sing out to the circular driveway where the great car was waiting. "Climb in, why don't you?" the millionaire invited, without offering a reassuring smile.

Despite the American's grumpiness, Gou Sing was so excited to experience a ride in such a momentous automobile that he didn't hesitate to reach for the handle to the back door, except that there wasn't one. The front door swung open and the Mongol grunted for Gou Sing to sit beside him. He would have far preferred the back seat, but he climbed in beside the driver as directed. The car's upholstery looked like heavy, stained parchment. "What is this?" Gou Sing asked, brushing his hand along the surprisingly slippery surface of the front seat.

"Water snake skin."

The idea of sitting on dead snakes was not very appealing, but Gou Sing couldn't let his uneasiness show - besides, the spirits of the snakes might give him wisdom and cunning. All the same, he felt sinful as he took his seat in such a rich, strange environment. He hoped that he wouldn't catch a disease from the exotic materials surrounding him.

In front of the chauffeur were many numbered dials under glass, and all the needles jumped and waved when the Mongol released the engine from its silence. The man's gloved hands darted expertly from one lever to another, while his feet touched mechanisms on the floor and they rolled forward with a low whine.

It was a warm, pretty day, the sort that usually made Gou Sing feel lucky and happy. As the car took to the road with a great roar, he looked over his shoulder, grinning with appreciation, and saw that Davies remained lost in thought behind the rear windscreen. This seemed like a bad time to begin a conversation, yet what other opportunity would he ever be given? "Mr. Davies," he said, forcing a business-like frown onto his face, and hoping that confidence would follow, "maybe you need me to do work for you. Maybe you need secretary, why don't you think that?"

Davies gave Gou Sing a slightly confused glance, as if he'd forgotten that he had a guest in his car. "Are you offering your services in that capacity?"

"I am very competent in everything I do. I good secretary, I good at cleaning, I good at calculating, very good with abacus, and I not afraid - not of things."

Davies looked even more puzzled; Gou Sing couldn't tell if this was good or bad. "All right, I don't know why you're pitching fearlessness, but let me think it over." The American started to say something more, then he turned away, settling back into his seat and watching the passing scenery.

Although such behavior could be considered rude, Gou Sing wasn't bothered. He admired the calm, serious and arrogant way that many Westerners conducted themselves. Their actions were more satisfactory than that of his fellow Chinese who often seemed like a pack of little girls, giggling and shrieking, with faces that were soft and delicate. Even those countrymen who were tough and stoic and did little more than grunt struck Gou Sing as being overly emotional and transparent. He had difficulty taking his countrymen seriously, but the foreign devils like Mr. Davies were very serious indeed.

It seemed best to allow Mr. Davies to continue thinking, so Gou Sing turned his attention to the great car's long, shining bonnet where a sleek, silver stork was perched on top of the radiator. Instead of soaring, the bird bobbed up and down in a very ungraceful way.

Had he been too forward just now? Yet, if Mr. Davies was truly a jewel thief, it wouldn't do to appear meek. On the other hand, he had heard from beggars at Soochow Creek that Zephyr Davies had recently beaten a fat white-face in the middle of the street. Why a great and famous man would thrash another white-face into unconsciousness because a lazy and ignorant coolie rickshaw driver was not doing his job properly would require serious thought to understand. Regardless, the incident was a warning that he should not anger his potential new benefactor.

They passed through the north gate of Nantao, where two large billboards partially concealed one of Gou Sing's secret, favorite spots. "Look, Mr. Davies," Gou Sing said, risking a scolding as he turned and pointed at a twenty foot pile of crumbling gray brick with weeds sprouting from its mortarless crevices.

"Huh? What?"

"You not know? You not hear old men say that Shanghai is city where the part swallow up the whole thing? That wall is all that left of the first Shanghai, the 'city above the sea,' that rise from earth five hundred years ago."

"Is that a fact?" The American didn't give so much as a glance in the wall's direction.

"Nobody pay attention to that wall no more. Not even those who know it there."

"I see."

Gou Sing settled into his seat again, hoping that his gamble had paid off and he'd made a satisfactory impression. When no words came from the back seat, he debated whether to continue to demonstrate the fruits of his education. He could reveal that eighty years ago Shanghai's Chinese fathers banished the first white settlers to the miserable swamp on the north bank of the river. But telling this story could prove treacherous. It might insult Mr. Davies to know that everyone laughed at the barbarians who thought themselves so superior - because who else but fools would be happy to live in a swamp? Even the flattering end to the story might be regarded as a veiled insult - that within fifty years the wretched place had become the foundation of China's greatest city, swallowing up the old Chinese settlement.

Behind the rear windscreen, the wealthy American removed a cigarette from his jacket and lit it – he didn't seem to welcome conversation, no matter how enlightening.

As they turned onto the narrow hutung that led to Hong Fat's shop, Gou Sing caught sight of a laundry man that he knew. He waved to be sure that Lu-sing was impressed by his young neighbor's position in the front seat of a grand and glorious motorcar. Lu-sing just stared back at him, expressionless, but Gou Sing could tell that he was deeply surprised.

They parked in the same location as the day before and got out of the car. Unable to think of more interesting things to say, Gou Sing led Zephyr Davies through the great steel doors, and into the comparatively cool display room.

He threaded his way amongst the dark, wooden display cases, climbed the small flight of stairs, and knocked on his boss's door. He'd expected that Hong Fat would have reclaimed his cheerful personality with the sale of the emperor's walking stick, however, the opposite had been the case, and Gou Sing's stomach felt "squeezy" as he knocked again. Getting no response, he gently turned the knob, finding that the door was locked. Cursing his boss's love of naps, he removed his key, twisted it in the lock, and pushed the heavy door open and entered the room beyond.

Dim light was coming from a small, green-shaded lamp on his boss's cluttered desk. Glowing softly beneath the weak cone of light, Hong Fat was asleep, his head resting on a blotter. How did he dare to doze off at such an important moment? Gou Sing started to speak, and then he saw the long streams of dark plumb red, which crisscrossed the desktop and dripped onto the floor, landing with soft "thuds." There, blood formed thick, browning puddles, which played around his boss's fingertips. Hong Fat's mouth and eyes were open, his gaze fixed vacantly on the wall to his side, his right arm dangling and touching the damp carpet. Gou Sing tried to swallow. His arms began to shake. He willed the motion to stop, but his body wouldn't listen.

Behind him, the American spoke in a voice, which was so calm and unemotional that it made Gou Sing feel like a weak and helpless child. "When were you last in here?"

How could Gou Sing reply when he felt as if someone had taken the top of his head off and his insides were beginning to float away? The sensation was making him sick. "Two hour ago, maybe." What had he just said? Had he answered a question?

"And he was alive, I assume?"

"Yes. He okay. Everything okay." Hong Fat had been upset, but Gou Sing never dreamed he would go this far. It was wrong. Not just wrong, unnecessary. "Is..is he..?"

"Dead?" As fearlessly as a movie hero, Davies walked to the desk and peered at Hong Fat. "He'd get my vote."

Gou Sing nodded; all that he wanted to do was flee.

"Anyone here with him?"

"No."

"Anybody come by you didn't like?"

Gou Sing felt dizzy; he shook his head.

"Any fights? Anybody threaten him?"

"I don't know. I not here. Everything okay." None of this was true. Why was he saying it?

"What about the staff? Once again, who sold it to you?"

"Sold?" Gou Sing couldn't remember what they were talking about. He was wondering if Hong Fat had felt pain.

"'The clouded twilight.' The jewel-covered walking stick! Who sold it to you?"

"Huh? Okay, I tell you. Some little man. Wore big hat. I not like him."

"A white man? A Chinese? Did he have a name?"

"White. No name. I not know."

"There wasn't a woman? A young woman?"

"No, I see no woman. Just tiny, little man."

"How old was this man?"

"He was old. He was fat. He don't smell good, pee yu."

"But no name?"

Why didn't the white face stop asking questions? Gou Sing leaned on the frayed armchair that he hated so much. "I don't know. What you ask?"

"Once again, did this bad smelling man have a name?"

Too many questions. Fighting back tears, Gou Sing said, "I don't know. I just let him into office, he show us that stick, then I go work. Sorry. I don't know what he and my boss talk about. I busy working. I work very hard, you know."

"Alright, you'd better run along. Being a Chinaman, it won't do you any good to be here when the police arrive."

In his mind Gou Sing saw a dozen fat, blue policemen racing about the shop, and it hit him again - fresh and terrible - Hong Fat was dead. Gou Sing had no job. He had no more life. He might as well be dead too. A tear scorched his cheek.

"Scat now. You weren't here. I dropped you off on the Bund, in front of Jardine's. Got it?"

Gou Sing couldn't stop shaking. Where was he to go? Back to be beaten by his father? Didn't he have an obligation to stay here, to look after Hong Fat? He had heard many stories about white-faced men murdering Chinese people so they could steal their eyes and use them for the inner workings of cameras. He could see that Hong Fat's eyes were still in his head and available. He had been unable to prevent Hong Fat's death - should he make restitution by staying to insure that his boss's eyeballs were not plundered?

Instead of greedily grabbing Hong Fat's head, however, the American removed a card from his jacket and forced it into Gou Sing's hand. "Call me tomorrow at three. I may have some questions for you. If you help out, I'll pay you."

Somehow Gou Sing's fingers folded around the card; he hoped the dampness of his palm wouldn't melt it.

Davies picked up a piece of paper from Hong Fat's desk. He gave Gou Sing a sharp look. "Well, get going, damn it! Or do you want to end up with your head hanging on a wall?"

Gou Sing did not want his head hanging on a wall. "Yes, yes, sir," he stammered, backing away. "Have a, a pleasant afternoon, sir." He moved toward a back door, which led to the alley, praying he wouldn't fall down, and hoping the gods would forgive him for running away.

"Just a minute."

Oh, no! Had the police arrived? Gou Sing turned, but saw that he was still alone with Davies. He watched as the stern white face walked to the side of the office and nodded toward the front of the shop. "How much are you paying for those new steel doors you're having installed?"

"Door?" Gou Sing was confused. "Oh! Fine door all right, all right. Very strong...four thousand American dollar."

The American had a strange, taunting look on his face. "Don't you think you're jumping the gun a bit?" With a lightning fast move, he drove his walking stick into the back office wall. There was a brief explosion of paper and plaster and then sunshine streamed in through a gaping hole, revealing the alley outside. Gou Sing stared at the hole, embarrassed by this oversight in his boss's attempts at security. Was the white-face finally blaming him? Would a better door and a better wall have saved Hong Fat's life? "We fix good, okay? We do next, all set."

Davies brushed a speck of dust from his jacket, and nodded toward the door. "You better get going."

With only a dim awareness of what he was doing, Gou Sing unlocked the door and bolted away.

* * *

Davies stared at the open doorway. Where the boy had just left, a tiny pink feather hovered in the air, stirred up by the lad's wake - it soon fluttered away into the mottled darkness of the alley.

Hong Fat's death was not what he had anticipated. He'd made a deliberate effort to stick to facts, which had helped to keep his emotions from overpowering him. But now that the boy was gone, he had to face the fact that he was left alone in a dingy office with a bleeding corpse. Staying on an even keel wouldn't be so easy now. *Just go back to the basics, one foot at a time, search the room, analyze, be scientific and you'll get through this* he advised himself. *The poor fellow is dead, he can't hurt you now, can he? At heart, you're a Pinkerton, this is standard fare.* He concentrated on this directive and felt the old instincts beginning to take hold. Good.

Where should he begin? What of the slender Chinese boy who had just left? He was amusing, wasn't he? Had he been dismissed too soon? Though his build was slight, even delicate, he was no wilting pansy. A strong-headed, somewhat manipulative lad who hadn't fainted or screamed, though he had seemed properly upset. He could be expected to make a quick recovery from the morning's shock. But had he been too resilient? Should he be counted as a suspect? Probably not. Even though he'd had a key to the office, it had taken the lad a good two hours to go to Davies' home, wait for him to wake up, then accompany him back to the shop. Yet the freshness of the blood oozing from Hong Fat's head suggested that he had been shot just moments before they'd come in through the door. To confirm this, Davies crossed and reluctantly touched the skin near Hong Fat's wrist; it was still warm.

Should Monica be added to the list of suspects? Probably. Though, even if Monica had sold Madame Lin's staff to Hong Fat, it didn't make the young woman a criminal - certainly not a murderess. Perhaps she had brought the thing to China under duress. Maybe the staff had been stolen en route, and the girl's silence was from the shame of allowing such a priceless family heirloom to be taken from her.

Was he making excuses for her? Would he be so convinced of her innocence if she wasn't so damnably attractive? What if she was a fat little pig-faced girl? With bad skin? Wouldn't he have already sized her up as guilty? He tried to imagine Monica as ugly, with drooping eyes and a drooling slack jaw, as he examined the hole that he'd just made in the wall with his walking stick.

His mind was racing and he knew it was to avoid the unpleasantness of his current situation. So let it race. What was it about Hong Fat's security measures, or lack of them, that bothered him? Although he had taken perverse pleasure in pointing out the flimsiness of Hong Fat's back wall, the oversight was inconsequential. Hong Fat would have turned to his Tong, or at least to a local warlord for security; it would be unthinkable for him to consider another course. With a Tong involved, the back wall of the shop could be made of dandelion blossoms and the place would be safe. Up front, the four thousand dollar doors were probably being installed for show, not security. But evidently Hong Fat hadn't gone to his Tong, for if he had he'd still be alive. Why hadn't he gone? Had his Tong been unwilling to help for some reason?

Davies turned and made a quick appraisal of the room. It was a woeful affair. Things appeared to be in their proper places, but there were too many things, and too many places - and so few of the things were attractive.

A thirty-two caliber revolver lay on the floor, less than a foot from where Hong Fat was slumped. Under different circumstances, it might have been just another artifact for sale.

Near the merchant's ash white hand, lightly coated with powdery gun residue, was a letter sprinkled with fresh blood. Davies crossed over and opened it - it was in Chinese and postmarked from Wenchow. He decided to pocket it, realizing as he did, that he was straining to be quiet. Who was he afraid of disturbing?

There was a small, black bullet hole, dusted with powder, in Hong Fat's right temple, but Davies could not immediately see any other wounds - not that he wanted to. The shopkeeper had been bleeding when Davies entered his office, a further indication that Hong Fat had been shot within the past few minutes. But a multitude of facial bruises and a couple of scabs at the corner of the mouth implied that Hong Fat had been beaten several hours earlier. Yet, oddly, there were no cuts on Hong Fat's pale hands, suggesting that he'd made no attempt at self-defense. Reinforcing this, the room was orderly. There were no signs of a struggle, or indications that the room had been ransacked.

Forty minutes later, Davies was hot and sticky from searching the shop aggressively. His nose was running and fouled with dust, but no important clues had been found.

It was time to pack up, and he didn't want to overlook anything. He returned to the desk, noting that all of the papers in or on it were written in Chinese. There was no obvious receipt for the staff, which might indicate the little fat man's name, so Davies took Hong Fat's ledgers for future perusal.

He could hear firecrackers going off down the street as he gave the room one last, quick examination. Satisfied with his search, he pulled the yellow handkerchief from his breast pocket. Unlike his skeptical Western contemporaries, the Chinese had turned to fingerprints centuries ago as a means of criminal detection, so he used the handkerchief to carefully pick the revolver up from off the floor. He examined the gun, aimed it, and fired two slugs into

Hong Fat's back. Then he put the gun back down on the carpet, some distance from Hong Fat's dead, white hand.

Exiting through the rear of the shop, Davies gave the alley a brief inspection. Immediately, he noticed that right outside Hong Fat's back door were several small, circular indentations made in the dirt. He crouched for a closer look, then crossed to where a hodgepodge of soiled boxes full of garbage had been tossed to the right side of the back door. He began sorting through the boxes, finding little more than discarded packing for antiques. Occasionally there were remnants of food, and scraps of paper written in Chinese, which he kept. Then he made his way out of the alley and to the waiting Hispano.

IX. A SIP OF CALVADOS

He was too emotionally exhausted to continue assessing what he'd just found; yet again his mind was too frantic too rest. He ordered Max to drive him home, and, once there, Davies took a quick bath to wash away the smell of death. After a change of clothes, they set off for the Shanghai Race Club.

Distractions helped Davies to think, and he was also curious to find out if he was being followed; but the sultry afternoon only netted him ten dollars in lucky bets and no insights of any kind. As five o'clock approached he had Max take him to the French Club.

Time was passing in chopped-up fragments as Davies made his way to one of the private business offices that the club maintained for members; eventually he sat down at a spindly Louis XV desk, not quite sure what day it was or how he'd gotten there. He managed to compose himself and dialed the number of an American attache that he knew. He utilized the man's private number, assuming that his friend was probably just getting home from an afternoon round of golf.

Initially, Davies had worried that Hong Fat's killing had been a setup. But he quickly realized that he was in no danger, even if he became a genuine suspect. An American or European who committed a crime, whether against another Westerner or a Chinese, could only be tried by a court administering the justice of his native land. As the case would be overseen by his consul, a man with whom he had shared drinks and jokes at parties, such unpleasant affairs were dealt with in a most gentlemanly manner, if they were attended to at all. Davies had often been protected by this pomposity known as *extraterritoriality*; someday he'd remember to feel guilty about accepting its care.

"Sorry to bother you, old man," Davies said, when his phone call was answered by a man with a meticulously cheerful voice - it was a safe guess that the fellow had won his golf game. "Zephyr Davies here. How are you doing?"

"Can't complain," the cheerful voice responded. "Though this heat isn't much fun."

"I despise it. Look, I happened across an ugly business in the Nantao District. Nothing pressing, just the murder of a Chinese, a shopkeeper. Perhaps you fellows should let them know."

"Very good," the voice said as if taking an order for luncheon.

"But, for heaven's sake, keep me out of it," Davies insisted. "When I'm sober, sometime tomorrow afternoon I expect, I'll stop by the embassy and give you a full report."

"Actually, old bean, for once, you don't sound like you've been drinking."

"A very temporary state of affairs that's about to be remedied."

After he'd provided more particulars, Davies hung up and drew a cigarette from his case. He eased back in his creaking chair as much as he dared and savored the rich, burning tobacco. He already knew who'd killed Hong Fat - what he needed was for word of Hong Fat's death to get out as as *inaccurately* as possible.

The irony of it all - the Chinese police would not solve the crime. Nonetheless, they would conduct an investigation into Hong Fat's death because he'd been a respected merchant. They would spend weeks sifting through clues and sooner or later, guilty or not, someone would be punished, all to protect the noble concept that a human life had value. Yet, by morning a hundred beggars would be dead in the streets of Nantao. The time and money invested to catch one killer could have as easily been expended to protect their lives. Why did the authorities bother to catch one murderer when so many starved? If you died one way you were worth something, if you died in a different way you had no worth at all. Only chance determined whether you would be mourned or forgotten.

Perhaps he was being too hard on the Chinese. Were they really more calloused than other races? It could be easily argued that they were simply less hypocritical. Despite "how do you do's" on the street, sentimental paeans to street orphans in the movies, and the social importance of funerals, how much did Westerners really care for each other? Ahh, the siren song of cynicism.

He rose from the elderly chair and made his way back to the stairs. As the muffled sound of music and laughter came up from the dance floor below, he thought that when he'd arisen this morning he hadn't expected his day to be so filled with death. It had been weeks since he'd enjoyed an evening at the French Club.

Perhaps the throaty, witless giggles of a Russian blond, the latest tunes, a dash of Calvados, and the fragrance of jasmine could blot out, for a few moments, the sadness of China.

* * *

The smell from the river was intruding through the half-open window, and the late afternoon pall of cooking smoke had begun to rise over the masses of junks and sampans packed along the Bund. The odor of frying fish and vegetables mixed with the constant stench of burning petroleum that smothered the city. There were other odd smells, the bitter fragrance of tea, a whiff of peanuts as they disappeared into a distant hold, the pungent rose petal scent of incense burning in Nantao's little shops and temples - all of it underscored by a sharp, sweet trace of night soil. Unpleasant as it was, Monica preferred to think it was night soil, otherwise the smell was of death. With the exception of the incense, these were not the aromas she had expected to encounter on her first trip to China.

She'd set a terrible set of events in motion, unleashed a pack of furies, and things were now far out of hand. Why did life build up your dreams then crush them like snail shells? This had been her last chance; this time she thought she'd finally broken the curse. Once again she'd failed.

The heavy air from outside was making her feel increasingly damp and dirty. If she pulled the window shut, would that make her room cooler or hotter? She took a sip of brandy. As the fumes tickled the inside of her nose, she decided to risk Malaria and leave the window open.

Abandoning her bed, Monica rose from the white, knobby bedspread, brushed aside the mosquito net, which was not provided merely for atmosphere, and crossed the room to the open window.

It was exhaustingly hot out, and though her hotel in the International District had been built by Westerners, its thick masonry walls provided as much insulation as crepe paper. Sitting on the concrete sill, she tried to find the hint of a breeze as she gazed at Shanghai's skyline, currently obscured by a yellow haze. She had imagined quaint buildings with mossy, tiled roofs and some grand, foreboding Emperor's palace lording over a misty cityscape.   Instead she'd been greeted by "The Paris Of The Orient," where bankers and real estate tycoons hobnobbed with gun-runners and drug smugglers in the most exciting, depraved, scandalous city in the world.

What was she doing in this place? She'd hoped that Shanghai would finally turn things around, but the whites here thought she was Chinese, common and contemptible, and the Chinese snubbed her because she was mixed. The worst of both worlds. If only she'd been born white - if only so many things. All she wanted was a home, a family, a place where people cared about her. More than anything she wanted to be worthy of being cared about. But the disasters of the past forty-eight hours guaranteed that would never happen. Now she was in a strange country alone. *Alone*, a state that would entomb her eternally.

Below, in the street, she could hear a coolie train approaching. She gazed downward to where a throng of chanting coolies, their muscular backs glistening under the light of the relentless sun, were pushing what looked like a motorized street car down the wide boulevard. Coolies were China's beasts of burden and she'd learned that their wages of a few cents a day were so low that they were a cheaper form of power than a horse, or any kind of machine. She felt no kinship with the Chinese, yet she longed to join the coolies, working endless hours, too exhausted to think or plan. If she became one of them, wouldn't she fade away, simply vanish into oblivion? It was such a pleasant thought.

X. FAMILY PRIDE

Monday, August 13, 1928

With the memory of Hong Fat's head lying in a pool of blood vivid in his mind, Gou Sing's heart resumed its swift pounding the moment his eyes opened to daylight. He pulled his thin blanket over his head and curled into a tight ball, trying to ignore the sounds drifting across the water from surrounding sampans. The bugles had awakened him. The first brassy rooster calls had come from the American gunboats anchored a hundred yards out in the river, followed by the distant echoes from the mighty British "greyhounds" a half mile away. The odd symphony of foreign devils rendering honors to each other inspired a chorus of off-key answers from hundreds of junk and sampan owners. At one time bugles, cymbals, and drums were used only by warlords to make face with the peasants in the countryside. Now everybody seemed to be in possession of such miserable noise-makers.

Once the bugle calls died, he could hear the chattering voices of a thousand neighboring sampan dwellers filling the air; people who were born, who grew up and married, tended to their families, and who died afloat. Gou Sing could think of one or two sampan people whom he was sure had never touched land.

What if the men came back? He hugged himself, remembering the four huge, ugly men who had come and asked him questions as he'd stepped out of Hong Fat's shop the previous day. At first, he'd thought they were the police, but they were worse. They'd searched him, then they'd followed him home and searched the sampan. Fortunately, only the women in his family had been present, and they would keep quiet. When the big men found nothing, they had left. He was lucky to be still breathing.

How he longed to go back to sleep, but his father would not permit it. Knowing he could not stop the day, Gou Sing slid off his narrow pallet and moved quietly through the doorway to his father's empty bedroom, being careful not to bump his head on the low ceiling. He reached beneath the mattress and removed the red lacquer box containing his father's prized package of Three Castles cigarettes. Keeping a nervous eye on the hatchway to the upper deck, he sneaked out a cigarette, lit it, and returned the box to its sacred hiding place. Then he stole back to his pallet. On the walls of the little cubicle where he slept he'd hung pictures of legendary Chinese heroes in order to inspire himself to be brave - along with advertisements cut out of magazines displaying glamorous women smoking cigarettes, which were meant to encourage him to be beautiful and haughty. As he puffed on the elegant white cylinder filled with tobacco, he reflected that he would need all of these qualities to survive this day, especially as his only choice was to face the inevitable.

It was not his fault that Hong Fat had been murdered, but his father would beat him, anyway. His father had paid much "squeeze money" to get Gou Sing the job with Hong Fat. Therefore, by his father's old-fashioned thinking, he would lose much face because of the shop owner's death. It would be a great dishonor for the family.

He had not wanted the job, and before his father took him by the ear and marched him over to Hong Fat's shop, Gou Sing had earned twice as much money on the Bund. He'd found that if he was extremely clever and aggressive, he could coax the British, American, and Japanese sailors coming ashore to pay him good money to be taken to places like "Blood Alley." Or to one of those wretched bars where they could fondle a fourteen year old Chinese girl behind a soiled curtain. The owners of such places paid adequately to have sailors brought to their establishments; and he always hung around until closing because drunken sailors paid even more money to be helped back to their ships without being seen by the shore patrol.

He'd made enough money providing these services to be a dutiful son and give "everything" to his father without revealing that he kept more than half of his earnings for himself. Still, his father had grumbled. The other boatmen sneered and laughed at Wing hsu and sometimes spat when he walked by. To have a son who worked for white-faced ocean devils was not honorable. Finally, his father had talked to Sun Cho-jen, the elder boatman, and "squeeze money" was passed on to a taipan who arranged to have Gou Sing become Hong Fat's number one boy. It was a job that brought much face to Gou Sing's father, but almost no money to Gou Sing. Except for what Hong Fat deducted to pay for his English lessons, all the money went directly to his father. The education was Gou Sing's idea.

Hong Fat was a widower with no heirs and he'd hinted that Gou Sing might take over the business some day, an idea that appealed to his father. Impressed with Gou Sing's cleverness, Hong Fat had personally trained him as his secretary and bookkeeper and was delighted that Gou Sing had learned to master the abacus so quickly. Gou Sing was, himself, surprised that learning came easily for him and he'd developed a secret plan to better himself. Someday, when Hong Fat's shop was his own, he would be the most popular antique broker in Shanghai. Again he'd trick his father and keep half the profits for himself. But now that Hong Fat was dead there would be no future and no money for anybody. There would be much loss of face for the Wong family.

As he took another puff from his cigarette he was forced to consider his own selfishness. Truly, his future was in peril, but at least he had a future. Hong Fat, on the other hand, had no future at all. How could Gou Sing think only of himself at such a time? Hong Fat had been good to him. When not in one of his moods, he had been funny and lively. Of greatest importance, Hong Fat had believed in him. If not for the portly antique broker, Gou Sing would never have been given a glimpse of what might be - he would have no hope of becoming anything more than a stupid coolie.

He smoked the cigarette until it burned his fingertips, then scrubbed it out and scattered the ashes over the plank floor. He searched for something purple to wear because today he needed the help of his lucky color. His purple cotton tunic was too warm for summer, but beneath his gray fedora he could wear a purple skull cap.

He went to the kitchen where a bowl of cold rice and fish was waiting for him. Still standing, he held the bowl close and shoveled in the food with chopsticks. Half way through, he was compelled to stop chewing and listen to the exchange of voices on the upper deck.

"Dead! Murdered! Assassinated! Four bullets in his head and five in his back. The police found him last night." There was no mistaking the whining voice - it was that of Chou Ho-pan, the boatman from the sampan two places away. Chou Ho-pan was the same man who had told his father about Gou Sing working for white-face ocean devils a year ago. He was an evil liar with foul breath whose wife refused to sleep with him, and whose children were opium smugglers and river pirates.

His father's voice was deep and angry. "You are a womanly liar, Ho-pan. It was some other man in some other shop. Somebody is making a fool of you, and you should keep your mouth shut so people don't see your rotting teeth!"

Ho-pan laughed gleefully and Gou Sing could hear him jumping up and down and slapping his legs. "You are the fool, Wing hsu. It's in the newspapers. If you could read, you could easily see the truth, the whole city is laughing at you. Everybody who can read knows it's the truth. Hee, hee."

A silence followed and Gou Sing knew what was coming. He gulped down the last of the rice before the angry shout echoed from above. "Gou Sing! Come up here!"

Gou Sing set the bowl aside and climbed the ladder. His brother's wife, Mai-li, was sitting at the front of the boat playing with her two-year-old son. For the hundredth time he reminded her that the leash, wisely tied to the little boy to prevent him from falling overboard, was loose. Mai-li flashed a frightened expression and turned away. This was not a good sign.

His father was standing at the back of the boat, legs apart, his fists closed at his side. A short, stocky man, he had powerful shoulders and a punch like a hurtled stone. Despite clothes that were poor and tattered, he had great pride and was easily the most stubborn person Gou Sing had ever encountered. Now his jaw was tight and his face dark with accusation. He pointed at the neighboring sampan. "This stupid Ho-pan says Hong Fat is dead. Tell him he is a fool and a liar!"

Gou Sing glanced at Ho-pan. The wrinkled old man was grinning, his black eyes dancing. Reluctantly, Gou Sing looked back in his father's direction and considered how to respond. Arguing, or attempting to be rational, would only make things worse.

Gou Sing stared listlessly at the deck. "Ho-pan is telling the truth, papa. Hong Fat is dead."

He could hear the sharp hiss as his father released a breath. "You idiot! How can he be dead?"

Gou Sing shrugged.

"And where were you when this happened? Cowering under your desk?" His father stared at him with blazing eyes, his face growing purple like a strangling man's. In the manner of an enraged demon, his father let out a deafening roar and his arms started flapping as if he was a bird. He raged about the deck, cursing all of his ancestors and all the white-face ocean devils who had turned Gou Sing into a filthy and worthless speck of bilge water scum. He suggested that Gou Sing was not his real son, but the bastard child of some passing Chekiang bandit with a foul disease; and he thanked the heavens that he had two other sons who were only partially as stupid as Gou Sing. Then he struck Gou Sing hard across the face. Before there was time to respond, Gou Sing was grabbed by the ear and pushed and dragged and kicked across the other sampans to the shore. Gou Sing didn't attempt to fight back, his father inflicted less harm when he wasn't challenged - nor would it be wise to run away because it would only encourage his older brothers to track him down and beat him for being disrespectful.

Where were they going? They passed the Hongkong & Shanghai Banking Corporation, guarded by two magnificent bronze lions whose paws and tails were slick and shiny from being petted by a hundred thousand Chinamen who thought that after touching the statues one received the strength of lions. Unfortunately, Gou Sing couldn't reach either of the glistening paws on today's journey.

They passed six more blocks and turned into a narrow street in the Native City, and only then did Gou Sing realize that Hong Fat's shop was on the next block.

As they raced toward their destination, he caught sight of the familiar money changer locked into his cage on the corner. Then he spied a handful of small girls squinting painfully at the handkerchiefs they'd been hired to embroider. No one was about to help him, certainly not little girls.

On a nearby wall, three freshly severed human heads dangled by their hair, not the best of omens. He found himself staring at one of the disembodied faces, which still looked alive. He almost expected it to blink, despite the flies crawling along the darkened lips and around the ears. Someone had possessed that face, had often been comforted to see a familiar image staring back from a mirror - an image that was now an object of horror and ridicule as it hung with a curious nakedness, because how could a thing without a body be naked?

Near to the shop, traffic had come to a standstill. Mobs of eerily quiet people were pressed attentively against wooden police barriers. Their numbers did not discourage Wing hsu. His voice was fierce with indignation as he demanded passage, and the people stepped aside with barely a grumble.

A chair and a small table had been brought into the street. An important looking police official sat in the chair, flanked by two other officers. On the table were stacks of Hong Fat's papers and documents. The official was examining each of the documents, frowning thoughtfully as he held them up to the sunlight. He was an evil-looking man, a great fleshy creature with two wiggling chins, and fat fingers that were home to ugly, battered fingernails.

Halting before the official, Wing hsu made an elaborate bow. "I beg you to excuse my impertinence," he said.

The official ignored him, lifting another document, then looking down at the table as a ring of gold and jade tumbled from the papers. The official picked up the ring and examined it with narrowed eyes; he resembled a curious pig. He dropped the ring into the pocket of his tunic, and Gou Sing was sickened; last night the ring had been on the little finger of Hong Fat's left hand. The official gave Gou Sing's father an annoyed glance, then continued examining the papers. "Yes," he said, "what is it?"

Wing hsu pushed Gou Sing forward. "This is my ungrateful turtle of a son," he announced. "He is the employee of the honorable Hong Fat, whom you have found murdered in his shop. That my son has allowed the revered Hong Fat to be murdered in his own shop is a barbarous neglect of duty that casts the shadow of dishonor on the Wong family. It disgraces my ancestors. I am an unfit father, and this goat-turd of a boy is an unfit son. I will be honored, Magistrate, if you arrest us both and subject us to the vilest of punishments."

The official let out a long sigh. He studied Wing hsu, then he shifted his gaze to Gou Sing, but there was no revealing hint of his thoughts reflecting in the cold, black eyes.

Gou Sing smiled. What his father was doing was crazy. Even a hundred years ago it would have been considered old-fashioned. It was a stupid thing based on a very old and stupid belief that a father is at fault if his son does something improper. The impropriety in this case was the fact that Gou Sing had failed to work a miracle. Though he had been miles away at the time, he was still responsible for Hong Fat's safety, simply because he worked for him. The official certainly knew such beliefs made no sense. To be an important Chinese official, the man had to be wise and generous and have no use for the silly ways of old China. Soon his father would, once again, be an object of ridicule.

The official did not return Gou Sing's smile; instead he nodded at a nearby officer and went back to examining papers.

The officer drew out handcuffs and came forward. Wing hsu bowed and offered his wrists and Gou Sing felt a shameful satisfaction; his father was finally being taught the lesson he so fully deserved. Another policeman stepped forward to assist, but then he altered his course unexpectedly. Gou Sing's knees buckled as he understood what was happening. "I wasn't even there!" he protested, trying to back away, "you cannot do this!"

"Be silent!" his father barked.

Roughly, the second policeman yanked Gou Sing's wrist and clamped on a handcuff, which pinched sharply. Then he forced Gou Sing's other wrist behind his back.

"My father is crazy!" Gou Sing blurted out, feeling sick as he realized that nobody cared what he said.

The crowds behind the barricades jeered as Gou Sing and his father were marched away. When Gou Sing protested, he was struck with a wooden baton - it hit the side of his head with such force that he feared he would find his ear gone if he touched that area of his skull. This thought seemed to last barely a second, but as he blinked away tears, he realized that, somehow, he was three blocks away from where he had been struck - and his shoulder was warm and damp with his own blood.

* * *

XI. UP TOO EARLY

Tuesday, August 14, 1928

The kitchen already smelled of frying bacon as Davies groggily staggered in and muttered, "Bring me some juice, I'll be outside."

A grunt emanated from Lo-Chien's sagging, boxy face.

Satisfied with this response, Davies plodded out to the center of the garden courtyard where four weathered, wooden chairs were huddled around a slightly cockeyed table. Resting on a white linen tablecloth were some scones and an ironed newspaper.

Breakfast was usually at noon, but today's early morning business had miserably begun at nine. God, he hated the morning. Morning meant mothers and teachers scolding you for not living life their way. Why were early risers so heavily into recruitment - like Christian missionaries? As he sat, it occurred to him that the decline of civilization could be attributed to the noxious practice of early rising. Executions occurred at dawn, likewise most heart attacks. And how often in history books had he read the words, "the battle began at dawn?" If he was forced to rise regularly at sunrise he too would be inclined towards slaughtering his fellow man. Those who clung to the dubious virtues of morning were rewarded with itching eyes and the piercing shrieks of a dozen off-key birds. The whole rotten business masqueraded as something brisk and cheerful, but, in truth, the sun was rudely bright and intrusive while it failed to warm cold, damp air.

In contrast, the best things in life occurred late in the day: romantic candlelit dinners, cocktails, hours spent at plays or the cinema, dancing, symphonies, most people's sexual relations, nightcaps, cozy dinner parties, and the piece de resistance - sleep.

As he debated what annoying thing to dwell on next, his sixty-year-old number one boy came shuffling across the flagstone walk. Wearing his usual sour face, Lo-Chien presented Davies with several Chinese newspapers. The North China Daily News had taken little notice of Hong Fat's death. A small "filler" story at the bottom of page twelve stated that a merchant in the Nantao District had been found dead in his shop and that the native police were investigating. No doubt, there was a larger story in the Hua Mei Wan Pao, but Davies was not a subscriber. He had asked Lo-Chien to fetch a copy of Hua Mei Wan Pao and the Shun Pao and translate them for him, but, as it turned out, their stories were also brief.

"Shopman dead," Lo-Chien told him with poorly suppressed amusement. "Bullets headside. Big, bloody mess. Hole in wallshop, plum fixee." Apparently, the body had been found too close to the newspaper deadlines for them to get many details.

Davies dismissed the old man, then, from his jacket pocket, he removed the letter he'd found on Hong Fat's body. His Chinese was sketchy, but he could make out that unspecified cargo had been confiscated from a ship docked in Wenchow. The name of the ship was hard to decipher, as the handwriting was not good - something like a "Splendid Princess." The letter was signed,...actually it wasn't signed - there was just a scribble that resembled the character for "horse." A nick-name, perhaps. Davies took a bite of scone and thought that the deliberate vagueness of the letter implied that the shipment must have been of something that Hong Fat didn't want mentioned, probably something illegal. It followed that its being seized would have landed the late shopkeeper in the soup.

Davies had barely been up an hour, and already his thinking process felt squishy from "over-exertion," so he turned his attention to his English paper, hoping that his brain might relax if it ran in place for a spell. His best revelations often came to him this way, when he least expected them.

The rest of the news was very much like the news of the previous day. The taipans were indifferent to the Japanese, who were rattling their swords at Manchuria, and they were breathing easier now that Chiang Kai-shek had betrayed the communists. Hadn't that been a nasty business? During the previous winter the Kuomintang had ordered the slaughter of hundreds of Chinese civilians thought to have communist sympathies. Plenty of people had been shot, and a number of unfortunate souls had been roped together and thrown into the Pearl River to drown. For weeks, Davies had seen dark, leathery bodies littering roadsides in the country, many of them beheaded. As long as money was to be made, however, no one was very concerned about Chiang's brutality.

Meanwhile, in the United States, tall, country clubish Herbert Hoover had been nominated to run for president against the noisy Catholic, Al Smith. Hoover would win, he looked the more presidential, and it was hard to imagine a president named Al.

Sadly, the paper contained no entertaining gaffes like the article about dissent in the local Presbyterian Church, which had run several years ago containing the rather unchristian sentence: "What in 'ell has happened to the beer I ordered?" Davies had theorized that a note from a white reporter, meant to be sent to a bar, had been intercepted by a Chinese printer and mistakenly added to the day's news. Chinese printers, though diligent and highly skilled, rarely understood English. Some newspaper men considered this a plus because otherwise a typesetter might try to "improve" the copy. Davies had been highly entertained, imagining how distressing the note was likely to be to members of the religious community.

"Juice," a guttural voice said from a few feet away.

Davies' heart rate nearly doubled. He looked up and saw his number-three materializing from the garden's shadowy vegetation. A glass of orange juice was placed before him and before he could say, "thanks," the man silently retreated, like a lure being pulled through dark water to an unseen shore.

Leaning back in his creaking chair, Davies began to take a sip of his orange juice, then thought better of it. Last night he'd fired his servants, and this morning, because of a note on his chit, he'd rehired them. Maybe he was a weakling. But if he could be murdered anywhere in Shanghai, as the note had made clear, it might as well be at home - it was far cozier. Still, if a poisoning at the hands of his servants was inevitable, he didn't intend to be unduly cooperative. He pushed the juice away, reaching instead for a glass of water. It occurred to him that his servants might have deliberately neglected to boil the water so he abandoned it as well.

"Shirt."

Davies glanced up again. His number-four-boy was trying to hand him what he'd worn yesterday, now washed and ironed. He remembered that he'd ordered Lo-Chien to launder the unmonogrammed shirt he'd worn on the previous day, and summon a tailor to make up a dozen more, as parading around in sinisterly-embroidered clothes was completely out of the question. Finally comprehending that the man standing before him was only carrying out his own instructions, Davies rose, took off his dressing gown, and slipped on the shirt. It was still uncomfortably damp.

Almost immediately, Lo-Chien appeared like an ill-mannered ghost; the morning was turning into a Charlie Chaplin movie. "Car ready. You go Madame Linside."

"Oh, yes, I remember. Thanks." Davies tucked in his shirt and made his way through the garden, trying to adopt the manner of a man who knew what he was doing. The day was already starting to get hot

As he passed through his hall, he noticed that lying on a sideboard was a small envelope with no stamp, addressed simply to, "Mr. Davies."

"When did this come?" he asked, picking up the envelope.

"Ten minute," his number-three replied. "We forget, sorry."

Annoyed, Davies opened the envelope. The note inside was most direct, and rendered in handwriting that was small, neat, and pleasing to the eye; the work of a good student from a fine school who'd spent long hours practicing her pen strokes. "You're a kind man," the note read, "whose concern and attention to me is quite flattering. But I'm afraid I'm not at all drawn to you. So, please, you must leave me alone. Sincerely, Monica Marshall."

Davies refolded the note and called out for Lo-Chien to fetch him the telephone, he'd have to delay his visit to Madame Lin's.

XII. THE BAD SEED

Davies' attempt to rendezvous with Monica Marshall in the late morning was not successful. He asked to be allowed to visit the occupant of room four-fourteen, deliberately avoiding a mention of Monica's name. As a gentleman caller, he was forbidden to go upstairs and knock on her door. This ploy didn't work, however, and the desk clerks at the Astor House responded, chidingly, that *the woman* in four-fourteen was not to be disturbed. He nodded with understanding while studying the mail in the slots behind the desk. Spying a useful name, he claimed that he'd gotten the room number wrong and was actually visiting a male friend. Astonishingly, this did the trick.

Having made his way past the clerks, we went up to Monica's room and knocked forcefully on her door. Eventually, the door cracked open, and it was a great relief to see her drowsy, reddened eyeball staring at him. He began to speak, and she promptly slammed the door in his face. What the hell? This was not a very good way to win his sympathy. He vigorously banged on the door causing a number of angry faces to peer out from rooms down the hall. A hasty retreat was in order.

He went down the stairs, leaving Monica to enjoy her solitude. Maybe Madame Lin was right about the young woman's character. However, as he reached the lobby he began to wonder if Monica had been threatened to not talk to him. Worried about this, he tracked down a pay telephone and rang up a fellow who often performed unpleasant tasks for him.

Nathan Leibowitz was a would-be inventor, one of many dreamers attracted to Shanghai and the way it offered a brand-new blueprint for living. A perfect spy, he had the kind of features that no one noticed: slight, balding, bespectacled. Leibowitz had created some clever tools that aided him in surveillance, and these convinced him that he was truly an inventor. Sadly, he was only good at creating things that went with a job that he held in contempt. It was a tragedy when a man had a talent for something that barely interested him, and not much talent for the thing that stirred his passions. Davies offered twenty dollars a day for the job of keeping tabs on Monica, and Leibowitz promised to be over to the Astor House within an hour.

On the drive to Madame Lin's, Davies thought again of the sinister note on his chit. At least, he had a pretty good idea as to why Dr. Sun had mysteriously excused himself the previous evening - he must have been receiving telephoned instructions to direct Davies to the little French Bistro. Would the museum be willing to disclose Dr. Sun's home address? Under pressure, the not so good doctor might be persuaded to reveal who had given him his malevolent directive.

Because of Monica's infuriating unwillingness to open up, Davies wasn't nearly as late arriving at Madame Lin's as he had anticipated. As the Hispano rounded a bend and her house came into view, it was hard to believe that the heart of Shanghai was so close by. Although Chinese in design, Madame Lin's home had the feel of a whitewashed cottage in the English countryside. With its rich shaded lawn sloping gently to the banks of the Whangpoo River, and her meticulously tended rose garden, he was again reminded of the terribly underestimated importance of beauty in life.

The Hispano came to a stop, the deep whir of its engine fading and being replaced by a strange jumble of bugle music emanating from distant warships, which were rendering honors to each other. The easily romanticized sound confirmed that it was exactly twelve, a barely acceptable hour to be awake.

He got out of the car and spotted his friend, tilting on her bound feet, as she supervised her gardener in the pruning of a rose bush. Seeing Davies, she excused herself and made her way precariously to his side.

As she took his arm for stability, Madame Lin said, "There's that bad squirrel." She nodded toward an innocuous animal that was scampering across the lawn. Again, she'd felt no need to greet him in a traditional manner.

"There's a moral hierarchy that applies to squirrels? How do you know which one is good?"

"Such things are obvious. She's always chasing the birds off of the trees; she thinks she owns them. I know she regards me as a trespasser. Such a selfish little thing."

"How do you know she's a 'she?'"

"What else could she be?"

Once inside the pleasant, wood-paneled entry hall of Madame Lin's home, his friend paused to place the roses in a vase, while a cigarette holder dangled perilously from her mouth.

In short order, Davies found himself in the upstairs sitting room of her villa, pointed toward Madame Lin who sat primly on a flowered divan, a fragile teacup balanced on her thigh. Here, the smell from the nearby river was overpowered by the perfumed aroma of old wood and fresh flowers. The clutter of paintings, vases, and tapestries gave the room the appearance of an over-stocked museum. Even the teacup in Madame Lin's hand looked as if it had been exhumed. In contrast, his glass of Haig and Haig, served neat as he liked it, was fully alive as it encouraged him to savor the sensation of melting into the heat of the day.

As usual, she got right to the point. "I am sorry that I am a rude and insufferably anxious person," she said, "but I don't see 'the clouded twilight.' You did bring it with you, didn't you?" Madame Lin's heavily jeweled hand glinted as she removed a pair of spectacles from a handy side table and put them on, apparently to confirm that he'd been remiss in his duties.

Avoiding her question, he told her about the monograms, and of Hong Fat's violent demise, hoping that she could shed some light as to why her artifact was at the center of so much turmoil.

"If you say this is true, than I am obligated to believe you," she said, implying that she didn't believe him at all.

In order to validate his admittedly far-fetched tale, he'd come equipped with a copy of the Shun Pao, which he extracted from his jacket and slid over to her. As she read, he said, "You'll note that Hong Fat's death is suspected to be the result of a robbery."

"My gracious."

"I'm still sorting it all out. I don't buy the robbery angle - there was no evidence of a struggle, nor was there any indication of forced entry."

"Let me understand. You were there? You actually saw his dead body? The shopkeeper's?"

Davies nodded.

She regarded him over her glasses. "It must have been dreadful for you."

"I don't know, one sees bodies all the time in the streets."

"But one never looks at them. To think of what people will do to other people. It's really frightening."

"That's exactly why I'm going to hold on to your heirloom for the time being. If I bring 'the clouded twilight' here, your house may be the next one broken into. I can't have that."

For the first time, a look of concern formed on her face. "Let me emphasize that if this is all becoming too much, you are very welcome to tell me to 'take my business elsewhere.'" He assumed this was a polite dismissal, but she surprised him by reaching across the coffee table, taking his hand, gripping it with great strength, and saying, "Believe me, Zephyr, our friendship is far more important than this silly business."

"Out of curiosity," he said, sidestepping her display of emotion and guiding the conversation back to the safe harbor of business, "what will you do if you find that Monica is guilty of bringing this thing to China?"

Appearing disappointed with his officious behavior, she released his hand. "That is my concern, Zephyr. Part of me is angry, that's true. But can't you see that, despite all my complainings, I'm worried about this girl? And you share my concerns, I know that. Tell me, what made you feel so sure that she is in real trouble?"

"A look in her eyes I guess."

"That means nothing."

"Maybe. But it's something that you notice more and more amongst the Chinese, the soldiers in particular. It's a look that comes from seeing too much of life. That's why I don't believe she's playing some child's game. Back to 'the clouded twilight,'" Davies continued, "yesterday you told me that it was last in your sister's possession."

"Yes," Madame Lin said. "'The clouded twilight' is supposed to be in your country, on loan to a museum in Chicago. My sister presented it to the museum five years ago. Yet, somehow it seems to have shown up here – along with Monica."

"Still, I'm not sure we should jump to conclusions," Davies countered, anemically.

"Don't tell me you don't find it strange that 'the clouded twilight' should appear at the same time that Monica has arrived in Shanghai?" Madame Lin's face hardened, suggesting her true years. With stiff, barely moving lips she said bitterly, "We should be grateful that the thief, Mr. Hong Fat, was very anxious to dispose of his stolen property. If he had not asked my friend, Dr. Sun, to appraise it, we'd know nothing of this travesty. Once Dr. Sun suspected it was 'the clouded twilight' he came directly to me."

"I understand that you think that Monica stole the staff,.."

"And sold it to Hong Fat."

"All right, she sold it to Hong Fat. But why sell it here where its price would be far lower than what she could get in either America or Europe?"

"Perhaps she ran out of money and was forced to sell it. How else would she be able to afford a room at Shanghai's finest hotel? I think she's the commonest of thieves! Please excuse my unkind words. 'Yes' I have not invited her into my home, but now you know I have some cause."

Davies sighed; family dramas wore him out. "Mightn't your sister have simply sold it in the States, and Monica has nothing to do with it showing up here?"

She went through the familiar ritual of placing a cigarette in her holder and lighting it. "No, because there's another strange piece to this puzzle. You see, Monica wired me from San Francisco. She told us that she was bringing 'the clouded twilight' home to us, but she wanted us to pay for it! The idea! And she wanted some tremendous sum. Granted, for years, it has been my husband's most fervent wish that this great piece be returned to China - but that doesn't mean he would buy something that he already owns." She thrust the cigarette out of her mouth for emphasis. "It's ludicrous!"

Davies nodded and sipped his Scotch, thoughtfully. "Perhaps you should write to your sister and ask her exactly what happened."

She lowered her eyes. "We haven't communicated in years. And I'd prefer to leave it that way."

Of course, things couldn't be simple. Davies brought his fingertips lightly together and recalled that the chief reason why Madame Lin despised her sister was because the younger sibling, "imitates everything I do." It was rivalry that had prompted the younger sister to move stateside and to also enter an American university. He disliked involving himself in what was clearly a family matter. Madame Lin wanted him to settle some dispute, right some wrong that probably had little to do with either Monica or this legendary staff, and everything to do with her hatred for her sister. A good deal of what Madame Lin had told him was truth of a very subjective nature. The Chinese were noted for their reliability when they conducted business - but they were also noted for their delicacy, and the line between delicacy and deceit was a fine one; the trick was to find the truth in the highly polished chaff. "I'd be interested in knowing more about Monica. I have to concur that her behavior is odd. What I'd like to know is if her behavior has always been so odd?"

She took a deep breath, which transmitted reluctance. "I'll leave it to you to decide. I told you that I only met Monica once, when she was a little girl. Years ago, I was visiting her mother in the United States; she had taken a home by a lake. Monica had no father, none who was willing to appear, at any rate, but she did have a younger brother. The boy was only four, but Monica was always slapping him, and poking him with sticks, and hiding things he wanted. She'd be sweet and kiss him and call him her darling, and then push him down the next moment and laugh. She loved to see him cry. Her mother never noticed. The only thing her mother ever noticed was when her highball glass needed to be refilled. My sister had no business having children."

In Davies' opinion, hardly anyone on the planet had any business having children.

"I had given Monica a little white blouse as a gift from China, very frilly and very pretty - but she wouldn't wear it and told me, to my face, that she hated it because it was 'Chinese, and too old fashioned.' But she made her brother wear it; he didn't know any better, and she thought that was so funny. I had a little scene, I confess, where I forced her to put it on and keep it on - and just like now, she refused to speak for two full days."

"Yes, but, remember, she was just a little girl."

Madame Lin took a defiant puff from her cigarette "On the last day of my visit I came out for lunch and was incensed to see that she had thrown the little blouse in the lake. When I went out to fetch it," Madame Lin abruptly stopped and glanced out a window, "I could see a little white hand sticking out of the sleeve.

It seems her little brother was in the blouse once again, he'd been in the water for several hours they told me."

Davies watched a single tear roll down Madame Lin's stoic face, a display of emotion, which he'd not expected. "It must have been terrible for you," he said, softly, "to have discovered such a horrible accident."

"Yes it was. And, of course, we did all assume it was an accident." She swatted the tear away with irritation. "But there was a gardener who worked at a home across the lake. He came to me and told me that he had seen Monica pushing at something in the water with a big stick. He thought she was playing some sort of game."

"I can't believe that Monica,.." his voice trailed off.

"Well, I have to tell you, at the time her conduct was odd." She studied something on her mantle, continuing to avoid contact with his eyes. "She hid. It took a full day to find her. Rather than displaying surprise at the news of her brother's death, she carried on in the most awful, angry, spoiled way as if the whole affair was an affront to her."

"Yes, but,.." Davies persisted, "it's still very hard to believe that a child could have committed such an act." He enjoyed the idea of Monica being wicked, but not in this way.

"You've never heard of such a thing in your travels?"

"Occasional silly folklore of demons and possessions - never of a child being a cold-blooded killer."

"And you don't think there's such a thing as a 'bad seed'? A person who is simply born bad and can never be redeemed?" Perhaps smarting from their recent tiffs, she added in the cautious tone of a diplomat, "After all, Zephyr, when the races are allowed to mix do we really know what can result?"

"I wouldn't know about that. I agree some people may be born bad, but it takes time for them to become dangerous. Granted, some kids are little monsters, but murder is something else. It's simply against a child's nature."

"I agree. And that's the only reason I was willing to meet with Monica at all. The whole thing is too preposterous. Children don't kill. I know the gardener saw - whatever he saw. But he was a simple man of lowly birth - sincere, but hardly reliable." Looking very put upon she said, "You see, you aren't fair to me. With all this, I'm still willing to give Monica the benefit of the doubt. But now, after all that you've told me,.." Her voice faded. "The important thing is, if Monica is not right in her mind...if she did kill this shopkeeper, I have a responsibility to protect others."

"Hong Fat wasn't murdered," he said, emphatically.

"But just a few moments ago you told me,.."

"The door was locked from the inside. The gun was held at close range, and there were powder burns on his hands and about the wound. What do think that means?"

"I don't hardly,.."

"It means he killed himself."

"But the paper said he was shot five times."

"Three times. I should know, I shot him. Or rather I shot his body."

"Why? Why would you?" She was looking at him like he was the crazy one.

"I'm sure he was driven to suicide. I shot him because I want those responsible to be confused; I want to draw them out - see what they do next."

"Who, what people?"

"I don't know, powerful people."

"What powerful people?"

"I can't answer that now. I don't know enough. There are too many pieces that don't fit."

"But what makes you think he was *driven* to suicide?"

Davies rose and began to pace the room. "Little things. He was badly beaten, for instance. There were simply too many things happening to him at once for it to all go uninvestigated."

"But this is preposterous," she said looking up at him from her comfortable sofa. "If he really did kill himself, driven to it or not, isn't it a remarkable coincidence to have occurred at the same time as this thing with Monica? That's why, sorry to say, it's most logical that Monica is to blame." Madame Lin's gaze drifted out the window again - and to the river. "I must tell you something," she said, removing her spectacles. "Several days ago, a disagreeable man came to my door; he was short and unkempt, and very drunk."

"A white man?"

Yes. He made me uneasy. He demanded to see Monica, and when I told him that she wasn't staying with me he became belligerent. I finally threatened to call the police. At that moment, he gave me a note and he left. I have it here."

She extracted the note from a pocket and handed it to him. The sloppily written message said: "Monica, meet me at the Willow Pattern Tea House at five-thirty sharp. If you're a good girl maybe I'll tell you where you can find what you're looking for. 'Your best friend.'"

The Willow Pattern Tea House was in the old Chinese city. At one point, it had been quite charming, but lately it had become a haven for tourists and was much the worse for wear. The note suggested a rather unintelligent hand who was unwilling to give Monica credit for having even rudimentary common sense.

Davies returned the note to Madame Lin. "Did you show this to your niece?"

"I did, but she gave no response whatsoever. A woman called for her too. So many strange people all at once. Do you think I may be in danger at this time?"

Not wishing to add to her worries, Davies said, "What did the woman want?"

"Only to know if Monica was staying with me. She was polite, but I put her off. And 'no' she did not give her name, nor did that drunk."

Davies rubbed his jaw. "I suppose they could all be ruthless criminals. More likely they're just people she met on the boat over." He felt a twinge of guilt for not revealing that the belligerent drunk sounded just like the man who'd sold the staff to Hong Fat. "That little man who visited you and asked for Monica, did he wear a large hat, and have an unpleasant odor about him?"

"You know him?"

"I know that he sold the staff to Hong Fat."

"Then it's obvious Monica's to blame. He must have been her go-between."

"Frankly," Davies said, "you've no evidence whatsoever to back up such an assumption."

"But it is the obvious conclusion. One thing that I don't think you understand, I am worried about her. Of course, I'd prefer that she be happy and well – but, the truth of the matter is, she frightens me - especially after all of this - that's why I haven't asked her here - I wouldn't feel safe with her under the same roof."

"I know she's troubled," he said, more forcefully than he intended, "but that only makes her in greater want of your help. Does family mean so little to you? Sometimes the needs of others must take precedence over our own fears."

XIII. GONE DRINKING

They motored back to the heart of Shanghai where Madame Lin had contrived to meet her niece. Unlike their previous journey together, his old friend brooded in silence until the chauffeur brought the car to a stop in front of the great shrine-like Astor House Hotel. Davies had a feeling that Madame Lin's unwillingness to talk was caused by more than hurt feelings, he sensed that she was withholding information. Equally troubling was a bit of evidence that he was, himself, withholding. For reasons of instinct as much as logic, he felt sure that Hong Fat had killed himself. But in the dirt of the alley outside Hong Fat's shop he'd seen those small, circular indentations. In his mind only one thing could have made them, the spiked heel of a woman's shoe. That particular alley would rarely have been used by a woman who wore high heels, but he didn't want to give Madame Lin any more ammunition to use against Monica. Poor Monica, what monstrous drama had she blundered into?

As they pulled up in front of the Astor House, the Russian doorman hurried forward, the gilt and brass of his imperial uniform glinting in the sunlight. "Madame Lin," Davies said with tight lips as he got out and helped her from his car. "I'll call you later tonight, if you don't mind."

He was startled to realize that Monica was standing beside him on the sidewalk, how had she gotten there? Turning toward her, he could see that the look in her eyes hadn't changed, the deep sadness was still present.

Unexpectedly, a modest smile infected the girl's face as she presented her gloved hand. The gesture was richly bizarre, considering that she had slammed a door in his face a couple of hours earlier. Feeling very strange, he took her small hand, being careful not to squeeze it too hard and cause her to, once again, flinch in pain. In return, she seemed truly grateful, as if no man had given her the time of day before - at least no man devoid of lascivious intent. Not that he didn't qualify, which made him wonder if he was slipping. "I have to admit, I'm a little confused, this morning,.."

Before an answer could come, Madame Lin pulled Monica away. "Thank you for the ride, please do call." Monica resembled a naughty pupil being marched off to detention by an angry principal as she was all but dragged up the steps of the busy hotel, though the stern Madame Lin looked almost comical, teetering back and forth on her bound feet. So much for subtlety; Davies thought, it would seem that Madame Lin was about to compare baggage tags.

A slight man in a gray suit followed lazily after them, and it took Davies a moment to realize that it was Leibowitz. Good for him, unremarkable to a fault, worth every penny he was being paid.

"A saucy mouse, what?" a voice behind Davies boomed, theatrically.

He turned. It was John Crockwood, his appreciative gaze fixed on Monica as she disappeared into the hotel.

"I should have known," Davies muttered. "Well, everyone's luck has to run out sometime. And she's not a mouse." Short on wit, at least, his words were pointed.

John Crockwood was in his late fifties, somewhat emaciated, with heavy, purplish bags under his eyes. He was the senior commercial attache at the British Embassy, and, as always, he was smartly dressed, today in a homburg, gray tweeds and a pleasant green tie. Despite his natty wardrobe, Crockwood always looked to Davies like a mad bomber. "I dare say she hasn't much to say, has she?" Caressing his tie in a disturbing way, Crockwood added, "but then you wouldn't want her to say anything."

"You're unspeakably coarse, old boy."

The Englishman sighed dreamily. "Now that little girl would really be something if she was white."

Davies dismissed his chauffeur and he and Crockwood walked to the Shanghai Club, discussing Chiang Kai-shek's latest edicts and the prospects of business ever returning to normal. Though Chiang was friendly toward the treaty powers, politics prevented him from openly embracing them. Nobody was certain how the situation would resolve itself, but the taipans were guardedly optimistic, if uncomfortable.

Once they had passed through the fat, stone columns falsely supporting the front of the Shanghai Club, then caught their reflections in the bronze plaque that proclaimed that dogs and Chinese were not allowed, they might have been in the heart of London. The rooms were darkly paneled, with the smell of roast lamb drifting in from the kitchen and mingling with the heavy scent of tobacco. It wasn't much of a trick finding an unoccupied space at what was officially the longest bar in the world. Their bartender, a bewhiskered Scotsman wearing a tam, was slowly "racing" back and forth to keep up with orders.

"So," Crockwood proclaimed when their drinks arrived, "I trust you've mucked about with your Chinese friend's problem satisfactorily?"

"I suppose." Davies sipped his martini and wondered what sort of voice Madame Lin's niece had when she chose to talk. He also wondered why she had slammed a door in his face earlier that day, then changed her mood as effortlessly as she might change her shoes.

"Tell me about the little mouse," Crockwood said. "Is she Madame Lin's daughter? Or perhaps a companion?" Crockwood's eyebrow lifted, suggesting a less than wholesome relationship between the two women.

"Her niece," Davies replied. "She's visiting from America and Madame Lin refused to take her in - put her up at the Astor House."

"Hardly a penal institution," Crockwood pointed out.

"But less than hospitable on Madame Lin's part, wouldn't you say? The girl hasn't spoken a word since."

"Since what?"

"Since being snubbed by her aunt." Davies blew out a sharp breath of frustration, reminding himself of his own father who was a master of using sound effects to indicate his displeasure. "Dear God, John, I believe I'm speaking English."

Crockwood chuckled and sipped his orange gin and seltzer. "You're smitten with the little trollop, aren't you?"

"What makes you think that?"

"The signs are embarrassingly evident Davies; the faraway look, a bit of brooding..."

"I'm never embarrassing." He hadn't realized his preoccupations were so apparent. "You'll have to admit, John, treating the girl like some jungle African come to visit is unfair."

"Umm, perhaps. But honestly, Zephyr, you really ought to stop this sort of thing. Maybe I'm out of place, but do you think that, just once, you could muster an interest in a girl closer to your own age? And your own race, for that matter? Your lust for the slopes does not flatter you. It's an embarrassment, frankly." Lowering his voice for effect, Crockwood asked, "Is she in trouble?"

This question prompted an accusing stare from the red-faced Englishman seated beside Crockwood.

"Not in the way you mean," Davies said, taking a sip of his drink as he entertained the possibilities. "But I have faith in her ability to make my life an even greater mess."

"Well, you know my position, and I suppose I can't stop you from making a fool of yourself, so I'll not belabor it. But remember, you're not as clever as you think you are."

"Yes I am."

"I've a nose for these things, and I'm telling you that girl is real trouble. I've seen several of your little playmates, but this one is different. I'd run the other way as fast as I could if I were you."

"You don't even know her, John."

"I don't have to know her. One glance is all I need, and I'm telling you,..."

"John," Davies protested sharply.

"I'm telling you that there's something very off with her."

"Based on what?"

"Based on the fact that I just know! Wasn't I right about that one last year? You know, the one who lived on the 'yacht.' Wasn't I? So tell, did Madame Lin engage you to discover why this niece of hers isn't speaking?" He let out a snort for emphasis. "What childish rot."

"Partly. Madame Lin's family owns a historical artifact, an Emperor's staff that was in the possession of a Nantao merchant, sadly deceased, as of last night. The family wants the thing back."

Crockwood's scarlet-splotched, deeply creased face relaxed into seriousness. "I think I heard about that. Fellow was shot three times. The thieves left everything neat as a pin. But they cleaned him out - even stole his ledgers."

"That's it," Davies said.

"Afraid you're a bit late, old boy. The Chinese arrested the culprit this morning. The poor fellow's secretary."

"What?" An image of Hong Fat's cocky helper, swinging around in the Hispano's front seat as he tried to teach Davies history, flashed through his mind. That such an innocent would be arrested made him sick to his stomach. "You're joking! Oh, that's fine!"

Crockwood dabbed at his mustache with a napkin. "The boy's father turned him in to the police this morning. Dishonor to the family and all that."

Davies winced and signaled for another drink. "What a bloody mess."

"Not much hope for the poor chap. Chinese justice and all. Remember a few years back? That Yank gunboat stationed up river a few li? The one that lost their flag?"

"No. remind me."

Crockwood looked distressed. "Davies, I worry about you. You told me this story."

"I did?"

"Of course. Remember, it turned out a local Chinaman was seen around town wearing short pants made from your stars and stripes."

"Vaguely."

"You must remember this. The Yanks called the Chinese authorities and said, 'look we aren't mad, we don't want the fellow arrested - just please give us our flag back so we can burn it.' 'So solly,' the Chinese told them, 'we already cut his head off.' And so they did. Coming back to you now?"

"No."

"Maybe you better not have that." Crockwood pointed to Davies' second martini, which now arrived. Ignoring him, Davies took a burning swallow of gin.

"Since your heart's set on inebriation, I suggest you try that with a splash of bitters next go around, everybody's doing it."

"Then I shan't."

"Don't be such a petulant child, Davies. This is one time when the masses have it right. A dash of bitters gives a martini that extra oomph we all yearn for."

"John, don't assume that everyone is a hopeless dipsomaniac like yourself, yearning for more oomph so that one can be rendered incapacitated in just half the time, and at half the budget. For the record, Hong Fat's secretary didn't do it."

Crockwood gave a deep, gurgling rendition of chuckle. "Don't be so sure. It wouldn't be the first case of 'employercide.'"

"Yeah, but the boy was with me."

"Ah, I see. Well, I'm afraid your testimony would do nothing more than annoy the Chinese authorities. They've got a neat case now - they won't appreciate interference from any white devils."

Crockwood was right. Davies had seen appalling evidence of Chinese "justice" and its prompt administration before. What a conflict. He certainly didn't want to abandon Monica in her speechless state, but the Chinese boy's plight was far more dire. It would do to put first things first. "Any suggestions how I might get him out of jail?"

Crockwood shook his head. "Good luck."

"Where's your British sense of outrage, John? I rather hoped you'd volunteer, and we'd trade you for the boy."

"I'd rather volunteer to parade around town in a little pink party dress. With a girdle, I fear."

An emphatic bang came from behind Crockwood. The red-faced Englishman had returned his glass to the bar and he glared at the back of Crockwood's head; then he wheeled around and strode off into the crowd. Crockwood watched him go. "I suppose the chap's right, I have no color sense. Pale blue would go better with my eyes."

Davies couldn't help but smile. One of the reasons why they were friends was because, despite his conservative, British exterior, Crockwood was, at heart, a subversive. And his knowledge of China had been invaluable. Over the years, Crockwood had been immeasurably helpful in supplying inside information about the military situation in China, and who might be prospective customers for Davies' "imports." He also kept at arm's length from Davies' business, insisting that he wanted to know nothing about what his American friend did with the information. Because of his knowledge, it was safe to assume that Crockwood's abbreviated account of what the Chinese police had found at Hong Fat's shop was impeccably accurate. "You'd think that after five years in this miserable place, I'd know how to get a Chinaman out of jail."

"You've been here for five years? The Shanghai Club? But, Zephyr, I have seen you step outside from time to time."

"I mean China, you dullard. I love it and I'm sick to death of it. I must tell you, it's almost a relief that Chiang seems to be in control of things, as I'll be out of business in no time."

"Your arms business? Or your business with lost waifs?"

Davies winced. "Please, John, try not to be frank and loud all at the same time. And you know very well that I've never become involved with anyone who wasn't of legal age."

"It's not my fault, it's the alcohol. Usually, I'm the soul of discretion, but this business does distress me." Crockwood toyed with something floating in his drink. "I know you're not a bad person, Zephyr, and you have inherently noble, though misguided, reasons for doing what you do. But you should never have been allowed to sell to the Chinese in the first place. How richly ironic that the 'war to end all wars' would be a bonanza for gun runners and small time arms merchants, parasites,.."

"Like myself?"

Crockwood grinned like a Cheshire cat. "I'm not naming names."

"You can argue I'm guilty of stupidity, but not of being mercenary. I never sold for profit, and *only* sold to warlords who I thought had a real chance of making China a finer, more democratic place," Davies countered, defensively. "Besides if anyone's to be blamed it's the knuckleheads who created the embargo."

Crockwood scowled, emphasizing his unfortunate resemblance to a gargoyle. "Bloody stupid either way, I agree. Explain the logic of the participants of the Great War decreeing not to sell arms to China, who was barely involved in the whole mess, by the by, until she has a stable central government? Marvelous little maneuver, creating a situation where China's forming a government becomes damned near impossible. And look at the suffering it's brought these wretched folk, with a new warlord in charge every week. I have to live with it, don't forget - whereas, you live by it." Crockwood waved his palm with a floppy grace. "However, if Chiang is recognized as the true strong man of China,

I needn't tell you that certain parties will be shut down, and not a moment too soon."

"The wars will continue, John. Resuming normal arms sales by the Western powers won't stop that."

"They might."

Davies shook his head. "No, it's just that they'll no longer be fought by warlords and bandits, they'll be respectable wars between governments. Warms the heart, doesn't it, old bean?"

"What a sad, sad country. As long as we're being frank, we've done our share to muck things up, haven't we?"

"My point exactly."

"Well, if the Japanese have their way and take over, at least they'll run things efficiently. Marvelous race, really."

Davies ran a coarse hand through his hair. "Not a very kindly one. The Japanese are far from the answer, John. Your affection for them mystifies me. Perhaps it's because you're such a stickler for tradition, and that sort of rot."

"Well I'm quite well connected with them and if they do take over, I'll be sure to put in a bad word for you. You know what I like about drinking? It brings out the true me."

"And what, exactly, is the 'true you?'"

Crockwood's eyebrows raised in unison, somewhat remarkable as his wasn't the kind of face that seemed capable of much coordination. "A revolutionary and a poet. A man who speaks the plain truth. And you know what I don't like about drinking?"

"No, but you'll tell me."

"It brings out the true you."

"Don't stop now." Davies added, not especially eager to hear the rest.

"Alright, the true you is a boor."

Davies took a hefty swig from his drink. "I'm sorry I've burdened you all these years."

"No, do go on. I love to hear other people's problems. It cheers me to know that others are more miserable than I."

Davies stared into the rich gloom of mahogany and smoke.

"Seriously, Zephyr, go on. Come now, don't pout like a misunderstood little child. You might fall in love with yourself, then where would your little urchins be?"

He had to smile. "I don't know, John. It was fun, I'll admit, to meet warlords and gangsters. And I felt pretty safe going to them as a purveyor of arms. Some, indeed, were colorful, intelligent, and well-meaning patriots as I assumed they would all be when I was young and green. But too many are simple thugs. Having a colorful story to tell at the club isn't worth its toll in human suffering. This adventure has made me a sleepwalker, walking around, not caring much about anything anymore."

"You needn't be so cheerful. You're driving me to another of these dreadful orange coolers." He frowned. "No, I shall take my own advice, a martini with bitters." Crockwood signaled for the waiter as Davies scrutinized his own glass of uncorrupted gin and vermouth.

"John, I'm still searching for a sign that soldiering on is worth it. But yesterday,.."

"Have another drink," Crockwood said, cutting him off again, "it will help you to take yourself more seriously."

Davies nodded with a wry smile. Since moving to Shanghai, his life had become a sort of strange, extended afternoon nap. China had cast a spell on him. There was a tantalizing sense of impending doom, of distant storm clouds rising, and a tension in the air that made the place hard to leave. Yet, his spirit had been slowly poisoned as he waited for the big show to begin.

Crockwood was right, he was taking himself too seriously, but sadly with good cause. Just what sort of adversaries was he dealing with? He was like a kid attending an adult party, hearing stories and finding himself laughing when everyone else laughed, but without understanding any of the jokes. His considerable knowledge of China didn't extend to the current situation with the monograms. He didn't know what he was up against, or understand the implications of his own actions. "When will the boy go to trial?" he wondered out loud as he contemplated the oily trails in his gin.

Crockwood huffed out a laugh. "It certainly won't resemble anything you or I would recognize as a trial. There'll be a brief court proceeding in a week or so, and he'll be declared guilty. If not for murder and theft, certainly for something else. And that will be the end of him, poor blighter."

Davies turned his glass slowly in his hand. In China, the administration of justice was as much a business as smuggling opium or selling tea. No distinct governmental bodies existed in Chinese Shanghai, no clear cut lines of authority. It was a broad patchwork of battling powers with the jurisdictions constantly shifting back and forth between the police, the military, the underworld, various taipans, neighboring warlords, and local bandits. Force and cunning were the only reliable instruments of justice, and sadly, for the secretary of an insignificant curio dealer, there was very little to bargain with. Davies had pulled off some remarkable con jobs in his munitions dealings upriver, but his was still an amateur status. On the other hand, as possibly the largest importer of arms and ammunition in Shanghai, his customers were not without influence. Dear God, how could he be so thick-headed? Perhaps it was the cold light of several martinis now illuminating the darker, more twisted alleys of his brain that made him feel like he should seek out the nearest sledgehammer and apply it gingerly to the side of his skull. It was obvious who had monogrammed his clothes, and he'd written the suspect off simply because acknowledging the truth offended his vanity. Instead, Davies had convinced himself that he was on such good terms with the fellow that the man should be rejected as a suspect. Yet, hadn't Dr. Sun advised him to look to an ally or benefactor? With typical arrogance, he'd ignored this advice, feeling that he was too special to be subjected to such humiliation.

And how had his benefactor managed to monogram eighty-five articles of his clothing in only two and a half hours? Simple; fifty tailors *had* invaded his house en masse. There was no trickery involved, the event had been an exercise in raw power - that was the telling clue.

Davies signed the mercifully untampered-with chit; then he and Crockwood swung off of their bar stools, and strolled out of the club and into the glaring afternoon sunlight. "Something might be done," Davies murmured, squinting as his unprepared eyes adjusted to the bright light.

Crockwood lifted a dubious eyebrow. "Oh? What do you have in mind?"

"Manipulation," Davies replied.

The Englishman shook his head. "Not in a Chinese court, Davies. Pride and all. They'll cut off your sorry secretary's head just knowing he has a white friend."

"What I had in mind," Davies said, "was going to visit my 'Elder Brother.'"

Crockwood came to a sudden halt and every trace of merriment vanished from his face. He took out his handkerchief and nervously patted his mustache. "Good lord, man, are you serious?"

Like sex and the amount of one's personal salary, Elder Brother was not discussed in polite British society. "Why not?" Davies asked.

Crockwood glanced about to be certain he was not being overheard. "Do you know the man?" he asked. "I mean, would he see you?"

Davies smiled. "Don't be coy, John, I know him. In fact, I rather think he's expecting to hear from me."

Crockwood would have preferred to believe that all of Davies' customers were missionaries and tea shop owners - he stared at Davies as if mortified to hear otherwise. "Your business is your own, I've always said that, Davies."

A tiny Chinese boy, no more than eight years old, sprang up beside Davies' shin and thrust out an empty palm. "Please sir," he said, "no momma, no papa, no cumshaw, no chow chow, no whiskey, no soda. Please sir." Clearly they were on this lad's turf. Though he knew the meaning of none of his English words, standing in front of the Shanghai Club day in and day out he had learned that whiskey and soda was something very important to foreign devils - a staple, no doubt, like rice. Before Davies could act, Crockwood gave the boy a stern look, then tossed him a few coppers.

"I think you ought to come along, John. To Elder Brother's."

"Me? Are you serious? Preposterous. Why, for God's sake? So I can be murdered too?"

"To lend the dignity and power of the great and feared British Empire."

"Bosh! And what if I were seen? Wouldn't that be something? The senior British attache calling on the ungodly Elder Brother. Where does the fellow live?"

"On the Rue Wagner, in the French District."

"Oh, well, he would live there. The French don't care who they sleep with."

"Are you game?"

Crockwood brushed at his mustache and glanced surreptitiously from side to side. "Nobody must know about this, Davies. I want your assurance of that. It's bad enough I'm seen talking to you all the time."

XIV. DEAL WITH THE DEVIL

Wednesday, August 15, 1928

As a child, Gou Sing had once come across a jabbering crowd of people taunting a half-naked man who was standing inside a bamboo cage. The man was perched on his tiptoes, straining to hold himself up. While the spectators jeered and laughed, the man spat and cursed at them. At the time, Gou Sing thought he was witnessing some sort of street performance. His father, however, explained that the man was a criminal whose neck was secured in a tight noose, and when he grew tired of standing on his tiptoes, the act of relaxation would cause him to be slowly strangled. Hearing this, Gou Sing tried not to look at the man, knowing that soon he would be dead and covered with flies. Afterwards he became afraid to watch acrobats or jugglers, and avoided any small crowd gathered in the street.

It would be wonderful to think that he had fallen prey to a fantasy story told by his father to make him behave - because that would reduce the possibility that he was about to become that man.

Gou Sing's hands were tightly bound and tied to a wooden stake behind his back. All around him were awful smells, terrible moans, and occasional screams. From the return of ambient light outside his door, he calculated that he'd spent seventeen hours kneeling on hard ground that had been sprinkled with pounded glass, sand, and salt. Fortunately, his legs were too numb to feel anything.

On his way in, he'd seen fellow prisoners hunkered down in their cells. They were mostly tough, hardened men, looking to be far stronger and braver than he was. Yet so many of them whimpered and cried out. Despite his misery, he had barely made a sound since arriving in this place, but how long could he remain quiet? What awaited him? What would cause him to add his voice to the symphony of terror?

* * *

"I don't know how I talked myself into this," Crockwood whispered as their car entered the French Concession. "And why, for God's sake, must we bring along these hoodlums?"

The hoodlums Crockwood objected to were brothers, two strapping Danish longshoremen with shaven heads who made themselves available when Davies needed bodyguards. They claimed to be specialists with knives, but this was likely bluster as they both carried revolvers in their belts. Davies had given them their instructions, emphasizing that there was to be no violence except in self-defense.

"If you're intending to start a war, Davies, perhaps you'd best drop me at the next corner."

"But, John, that's precisely why I brought you along. With the celebrated British attache present, I'm sure Elder Brother won't molest us." Davies paused, recalling a couple of unpleasant rumors about their host. "Fairly sure."

"Never again, Davies. And all for the sake of a bloody shopkeeper's secretary."

"Well, consider this, old boy. If we don't get out alive, I hear that Elder Brother gives marvelous funerals, absolutely first cabin. 'Gangster's remorse' and all that. People who you've never met will cry over you, and your family won't have to pay a dime."

"That's a bloody comfort."

He felt less jovial as the chauffeur turned onto the Rue Wagner and they rumbled up the broad tree-lined street. In truth, he was no more certain about their reception than Crockwood was. He had never met Elder Brother in person, and if he hadn't seen the gangster's photo once in a Chinese newspaper he wouldn't even know who to say "hello" to.

Davies' contacts with Elder Brother had been through intermediaries, usually one or more Chinese thugs meeting in dark, waterfront bars, or in the muddy alleyways of the Native City. Deals were made on the telephone or through hand-delivered notes, and then the money and merchandise exchanged in the middle of the Whangpoo River, with both sides armed to the teeth and ready for a double-cross. So far, their transactions had been handled to everyone's satisfaction; but this was the first time either of them had asked for anything more than a standard dollars-and-cents business deal.

Davies had telephoned from the club, making a series of tedious calls that resulted in his being given another number to call. Finally, a Chinese voice had asked in perfectly manicured English, "Can you pop by around ten o'clock tomorrow morning?" Under different circumstances, he might have been amused by such a pleasant invitation, a facade as thick as a fading sing-song girl's make-up.

"Ten o'clock will be satisfactory," he'd said. "But I must bring my associates."

The voice answered back briskly, "I'm quite sorry, but that is not acceptable to us. Please come alone."

"If it is not acceptable, I will be unable to deliver merchandise to Elder Brother in the future." Davies was glad the man couldn't see him wince.

That brought a long silence – then: "Will you wait, please?"

Five minutes later the man was back. "How many associates do you wish to bring?"

"Three," Davies replied. He had no illusions about protecting himself, no matter how many men he brought along - they could never save him in the event of an altercation, but their presence might discourage one from breaking out in the first place. Besides, it would be a loss of face to arrive without an entourage.

"Three associates and no more," the man conceded. "Ten o'clock, then. You will stop at the gate and wait there." And the phone clicked off.

They had been expecting his call, he could tell by the rehearsed cordiality in the man's voice. This confirmed Davies' begrudging conclusion that Elder Brother had ordered the monograms placed on his clothes, and the leech dropped down his back. He was in as much danger as ever, but he felt slightly relieved knowing who he was up against. It was no surprise that the servants in his own household had played a part - in Shanghai every Chinese worked for Elder Brother; it was considered almost patriotic to do so. Rounding up fifty tailors on short notice would have been easy for a man who was the unofficial leader of all China.

Elder Brother headed the dreaded Blue and Green societies, which had been created during the Manchu Dynasty as a secret brotherhood of freedom fighters. Now the societies formed the backbone of the underworld - still vaguely respectable, even Chiang Kai-shek could be claimed as a member. In fact, it was because of Generalissimo Chiang Kai-shek, and Davies' desire to help support the Northern Expedition, which was organized to finally rid China of warlords, that Davies had initially sold arms to Elder Brother. At the time, he mistakenly assumed he was selling his weapons directly to Chiang's generals - not to the head of the Chinese underworld, who was the Generalissimo's unofficial enforcer. Had he known he probably wouldn't have gotten involved. When later, he discovered who his true customer was, it was too late back out – and ever since he'd been trapped into being one of underworld king's major suppliers of munitions.

Still, there was no reason for Elder Brother to harm him. Their arm's length relationship had been cordial enough. After Davies' last shipment of guns, in fact, he had received a note from Chiang's enforcer stating that he was highly pleased with the quality of the merchandise, and with Davies' professionalism; soon he would be placing another order - it was a veritable testimonial. But there were enough stories about Elder Brother's mercurial temper to make Davies uneasy.

When one of his top lieutenants had been arrested and shot in Kiangsu Province, Elder Brother executed all three of the man's bodyguards and set fire to their homes. He did the same to an entire block of shopkeepers who reported his extortion attempts to the police. It was Elder Brother's army that had recently slaughtered five thousand Communists. And, of course, there was the story of the French Admiral.

On a lazy fall afternoon, the day before he was to sail for home, the Admiral of the French Far Eastern Fleet sat down to an elaborate dinner hosted by the French Consul General. A celebrated French lawyer was the first to die. Then, one by one, the remaining guests mysteriously passed away. Only an old Chief of Police stubbornly hung on and eventually recovered. Rumors went out that black smallpox germs had been planted in the fine damask napkins used at the table, and it was instantly assumed that Elder Brother had punished the dignitaries for some unknown slight. Such was the potency of Elder Brother's fearsome reputation that no one in Shanghai, not even the authorities, bothered to consider the obvious theory: the men had all succumbed to ordinary food poisoning.

Risky as it may be, Davies had a surprise of his own. Elder Brother probably assumed that his American arms supplier had asked for a meeting as a panicked response to finding eight-five articles of his clothing mysteriously monogrammed, but Davies would mention neither the incident nor the staff - instead, he would ask a favor. Such impertinence was risky, but it would put Elder Brother off his game, making it easier, hopefully, for Davies to press his own agenda.

His reluctance to play by Elder Brother's rules was partially due to his being more than a little tee'd off. He could only pray that anger wouldn't be his downfall - nor would it bring harm to Crockwood. He was torn about allowing the British attache to come along, there was potential for real danger. He'd spent all night and half the morning agonizingly weighing the pros and cons, finally deciding that Crockwood should accompany him.

With any luck, he wouldn't be pushed to a confrontation. It's one thing to resolve to do something in your head, it's something else to actually go through with it. If it came down to that, better to be shot dead on the spot and dragged away in a pool of his own blood, then spend more sleepless nights wondering when and how his end would come.

The chauffeur pulled to a stop in front of Elder Brother's gate precisely at ten. Despite its fierce-looking exposed manifolds, their hired model K Mercedes was a rather agricultural machine and its brakes had to be applied a full block in advance. His Hispano was so far superior, he wondered why the Germans didn't just give up and turn their Stuttgart works into a brewery.

The Danes lumbered out of their jump seats and Davies followed them onto the sidewalk. Nothing was visible from the street. On either side of a massive wooden gate, stone walls rose twelve feet from the ground and were crowned with broken glass and tangles of barbed wire. Nothing short of ten-inch guns were likely to penetrate such a fortress - and a fortress it clearly was - no one would ever have regarded this place as just another large home in the neighborhood; Elder Brother's compound radiated all the warmth and coziness of a maximum security prison.

"I suppose you're determined to go in there, Davies," Crockwood croaked from the back seat. Despite his wrinkles and receded hair, he seemed like a small child afraid to knock on the door of the neighborhood's ghostliest house on Halloween.

"Why not?" Davies called back. "Did you think he lived in a rice paddy?"

A small peephole opened in the gate. An eye contemplated them. The hole closed, there was the sound of clanging metal, and the gate groaned open. Ten men came marching out to the street. They were the largest and ugliest Chinese Davies had ever seen; drugged, soulless fellows who had taken pains to poorly conceal the Mausers that bulged beneath their long, blue cotton gowns. They fanned out, surrounding Davies and his men.

The Danes came quickly forward to flank Davies. Crockwood, who had remained in the Mercedes, gulped air like a fish, and stepped out of the car to join them.

Moving from the street, through the gate, and into the villa was a choreographed dance. One of Elder Brother's men went first - next came Davies and his "associates," each with a Chinese guard at his shoulder. Behind them, the gate scraped shut with a heavy, grating thud.

They crossed through an immaculately clipped garden to the front door of a big fieldstone house. Davies reflected that gangsters had the same taste the world over.

Once through the door, they entered a long stone corridor with crates of rifles, mortars, and ammunition stacked shoulder-high on either side. At the corridor's end they marched up a short flight of stairs, and, a moment later, they were ushered into an opulent, wildly over-decorated sitting room with marble pillars and potted palms - it looked like a hotel lobby complete with little nests of tables and arm-chairs for private conversations. One table was surrounded by a group of Chinese businessmen who were courteously arguing amongst themselves.

"Good Lord," Crockwood murmured, evidently distressed by the garish decor. Overhead, the gridiron of beams was decorated with gilt dragons, all with glittering eyes and ferocious talons. There were many priceless Chinese antiques on display, but most were neglected. The metal objects were badly tarnished, while other pieces were in great need of dusting. Definitely, this was a man's haven; it would seem that there was no Mrs. Elder Brother.

They only had to wait about ten minutes. At the far end of the room a door opened. Davies' escorts stiffened and the businessmen abruptly stopped their chat and rose, respectfully.

Elder Brother came out of the shadows; he couldn't have stood more than five feet tall, nor weighed more than eighty pounds. Despite a delicate chin and huge bat-like ears, he had a proud gait and an almost aristocratic face. It was a fascinating face, reptilian, exceptionally intelligent, stoically calm; and with eyes that looked at you once and saw your deepest secrets. In his presence one felt completely understood, almost appreciated - yet this man was willing to use his understanding of you in any cavalier way that he chose. The gray cotton gown that Elder Brother wore was very simple, and well pressed. But his front teeth were yellow and black with decay, and within his skull-like face were eyes so dark that they seemed to have no pupils. It was an extraordinary sight; for here was the most powerful man in China, shuffling forward in bedroom slippers and looking simultaneously as fragile as a paper bird, and as deadly as a cobra. Davies wondered if Elder Brother's enemies had any idea of what a physically delicate creature he was. Yet, if they were both locked in a room alone, Davies wouldn't dare to take him on.

Elder Brother's bony, claw-like fingers were tipped with the telltale brown of the opium addict. He lifted one of the gnarled hands like the Pope blessing a petitioner. "Zephyr Davies," he whispered in a scratching, wail. Apparently that was the extent of the great man's English.

Davies bowed low, the gesture of utmost respect, as Elder Brother fixed a vacant smile on his face, studying him for a long minute. The dull eyes then drifted to Crockwood, seeming to note the mustache, the necktie, the tweed suit, and polished shoes. Then he grunted, moved to a chair, and sat down as if the meeting had already exhausted him.

A middle-aged Chinese man gestured to a nearby sofa. He was so nondescript that only now did Davies realize that he'd been in the room all along. Davies was instantly transported back to prep school where he'd learned, through bitter experience, that, ironically, the best way to be invisible was to hope to stand out.

Because such a desire was extremely self-focused, fussing over your appearance, and wondering whether or not you were being witty or interesting was a guarantee that you would disappear in public. Not until he was well into his thirties did he learn that the best way to command attention was to be aware of other people and to be legitimately interested in them. A step beyond was *seeing* - those who looked at others and truly saw them were always the most charismatic. For this reason alone, Elder Brother, despite his tiny, homely demeanor, would have been the center of attention at any gathering - while his interpreter, with his carefully selected clothes and immaculate English, was doomed to obscurity. "Please sit and be comfortable," the interpreter suggested in polished English.

The Danes remained standing while Davies and Crockwood sank into a soft, flowered, over-stuffed sofa. The couch made Davies think simultaneously of his grandmother and of a carnivorous plant.

From somewhere deep in the shadows, two young boys appeared carrying tea trays. Elder Brother was served first. His pot was carefully unwrapped from a silken cloth and set before him. He did not use a cup, but rather drank directly from the spout of the pot. The pot had a locked lid and its spout was carefully coiled so that poisons could not be inserted in it.

For Davies and Crockwood, tea was poured into cups from a separate pot. Crockwood's hands were shaking so badly that his teacup banged noticeably against its saucer.

In contrast, Elder Brother sipped noiselessly, then smacked his lips and gazed downward with half-closed eyes. He spoke in a soft voice to the characterless interpreter hovering at his side. The interpreter nodded and looked at Davies. "Elder Brother hopes you are in good health, and wishes to know if you approve of the display of your boxes in the entrance hall?"

"I am very pleased," Davies responded.

The message was relayed. Elder Brother murmured something to his interpreter who in turn asked, "To what good fortune do we owe this happy visit?"

Davies studied the black eyes and wondered if Elder Brother was going to sleep - or maybe he was just waking up. "First, allow me to state what a profound honor it is to finally meet the great

Elder Brother in person," he said, hoping to temper his coming effrontery with flattery. "Knowing of his wise benevolence, I have come, humbly, to ask Elder Brother a trifling favor."

His statement was punctuated by the sudden clatter of the teacup slipping from Crockwood's hand and smashing, with a loud pop, against the stone floor. Immediately, Mausers whipped out from under the coats of all the men surrounding the table - even the interpreter and the four businessmen in the corner had leaped to their feet and were displaying weapons. All eyes were fixed on John Crockwood's reddening face.

"Sorry," Crockwood stammered, and weakly he gestured toward the smashed cup on the floor. "Not armed, just tea."

The interpreter grinned; even the hardened bodyguards laughed. Davies let out a sigh, grateful that Elder Brother's men were well trained professionals and had not fired.

Elder Brother gazed curiously at Crockwood as the guards stepped back and replaced the weapons under their gowns. The boys swiftly entered, mopped up the mess, and brought in a new teacup for Crockwood. When he adamantly refused it, the room was again filled with laughter, Crockwood nodding and grinning back at his amused hosts. Finally everyone settled down, and the conversation continued on as before.

The interpreter gave Davies a thin smile. "What is the favor you so humbly ask, Mr. Davies?"

"I seek to prevent a miscarriage of justice. I have a friend who has been wrongly accused in a Chinese court."

"I see," the interpreter replied; if he was surprised he didn't show it. "What is the charge?"

"He is charged with murdering the shopkeeper, Hong Fat."

The interpreter conferred with Elder Brother who still seemed bored by the whole thing. "What is your friend's name?" the interpreter inquired.

"Frankly, I don't know," Davies answered, realizing how foolish this must sound.

"The charge is murder and you don't know the accused's name?" The interpreter smiled, wryly. "This, truly, is a beneficent act." He paused for dramatic effect and then asked, "If your friend has been falsely accused, does that mean that you know who actually killed Hong Fat?"

Davies had anticipated this question and he was determined to answer before a flush of color in his face betrayed him. "Yes. Hong Fat killed Hong Fat."

"Oh really? Then why, Mr. Davies, did the newspapers report that he was murdered? In fact, I am at a loss to explain how he managed to shoot himself twice in the back."

His ploy had come back to bite him. He had enacted it to frustrate and confuse the one responsible for Hong Fat's death, not realizing that Elder Brother was the culprit. The gangster couldn't be pleased to know this. Davies had planned for the consequences of his actions with all the foresight of a prankish college student. "I am to blame. I was hoping to confuse an individual, an obscure, petty thief, I assume, whom had attempted to rob Hong Fat. I wanted him to think that he had competitors and be alarmed into careless actions." This was a tactical lie. He'd never thought that a common thief had orchestrated Hong Fat's suicide, but it sounded reasonable enough, and implied that Elder Brother was never thought to be involved. The question was, would Elder Brother be convinced?

The interpreter gazed blandly at Davies, then he relayed the information to his employer. After Elder Brother's mercifully amused response, the interpreter fixed Davies with a hard gaze. "Elder Brother wishes a favor in return, Mr. Davies."

"He has only to ask," Davies said, dreading what was about to come, "I am honored to grant it."

"An artifact is missing from the shop of Hong Fat, and some of our friends believe that you visited the shop on several occasions, even being present on the day of the suicide. We are led to believe that you must fancy this artifact, as your clothes are embroidered with a replica of the maker's signature. Can you please tell us who has taken this artifact, Mr. Davies?"

Finally he had confirmation that Elder Brother had ordered his clothes to be monogrammed.

Elder Brother lifted his gaze to study Davies' reaction.

"I may be able to locate the artifact for you," Davies answered. Then he pressed his luck. "But if I was observed visiting the shop, the boy accompanying me must have also been observed. Thus you know the boy is innocent."

Davies crossed his fingers as the interpreter conferred with Elder Brother again. "Why are you concerned about this boy?" the interpreter asked, turning again to Davies. "He is only a secretary."

It was a good question, which Davies hadn't even considered. For the first time, it dawned on him that an actual human life was at stake, and he realized that he was operating on the same level as an animal lover who was fighting to get a stray dog away from the pound, or a cat out of a sewer pipe. "He committed no crime, isn't that enough reason for me to be concerned?" Davies responded. "It is well known that the people of China love and respect Elder Brother because he is merciful, and he protects the people from the oppressions and injustices of a corrupt police force, and the atrocities of the armies. Saving Hong Fat's secretary will be another example of Elder Brother's well known kindness and beneficence." He heard a soft groan from Crockwood, and crossed the fingers on both hands, hoping Elder Brother's interpreter would repeat the entire speech. While he jabbered through it, Elder Brother frowned as if he had never heard such nonsense. Then a broad smile lighted his face. He nodded and made a brief reply to the interpreter.

"Elder Brother wishes you to find the artifact that was taken from Hong Fat," the man said.

Elder Brother cut in, angrily. With a blushing face, the characterless underling hastily added, "Elder Brother is unhappy that Hong Fat, now deceased, was not a patriot. It was most unseemly that such a traitor would be in possession of, for even a few moments, a treasure of such importance to the good people of China. He wants you to help rectify this maddening injustice and bring the artifact here to him." He looked Davies straight in the eyes. "We assume that you do not presently have it."

The bland little man was being as blunt and direct as a Westerner and Davies' face again felt very hot. "Of course, I will be honored to help. I assume he wants it for his collection."

"Why he wants it is not open to speculation." The sudden edge in the interpreter's voice indicated that Davies had overstepped his bounds. "And the staff must be delivered in its entirety, unmolested, uninspected and in its proper carrying case. Is that satisfactorily clear?"

As a bit of emotional punctuation, Elder Brother turned and gave Davies a piercing look of annoyance. Such a look from a man who was as comfortable committing atrocities as Lo-Chien was laundering clothes had somewhat more impact than a peeved glower from an under-tipped bellboy.

"Tell me, Mr. Davies," the interpreter asked, as, behind him, Elder Brother continued to direct a bitter stare at his American guest, "is it not true that you are presently planning a trip back to the United States?"

What the hell? Was Elder Brother actually capable of reading his thoughts? "I've given it some consideration."

"That is excellent. Because there is something else that you could do for Elder Brother, which would bring great honor to yourself. However, it requires an immediate journey to San Francisco."

"My word. And what would be required of me?"

"An associate of ours can give you the particulars."

"Let me understand, I won't know my mission until I meet with this associate in San Francisco? By nature, I'm a curious fellow. I'd be most grateful if you could tell me what to expect." Grateful was an understatement. Elder Brother wouldn't have gone to so much trouble to frighten him unless he had something extremely demanding in mind, and Davies would like to know what the hell it was.

"That is never our policy," The interpreter answered with none of his previous cordiality.

The time had come to utter the simple sentence that might send Davies and his "associates" into the Whangpoo with their hands tied to their feet. He didn't dare to hesitate or he might lose heart. "Excuse me if I sound disrespectful, but what if your associate asks me to do something that I don't want to do?"

Silence overtook the room. The businessmen, who'd been sporadically watching the conversation, looked away. When the interpreter replied it was unnecessary for him speak above a whisper. "Are you telling Elder Brother that you have no loyalty to him?" Beneath the interpreter's measured tone was an anger so intense that Davies could feel it - the man was no longer invisible.

Davies swallowed hard. "I'm a selfish man. I'm only loyal to myself, and to the things I value."

The interpreter's eyes grew small. "And so Elder Brother has no value in your estimation?"

"I'm saying that you don't have to insist on my loyalty if your cause is worthy."

"But who are you to decide what is worthy? How dare you!" the man's lip curled. "Are you loyal, or are you not? That is all that matters."

Davies' heart was beating so powerfully that he wondered if they could see his shirt moving. He willed his voice to remain strong and certain. "As I said, I am loyal only to my own judgment. If I can't rely on myself, then I am such a weak and useless person that I can be of no service to anyone, certainly not to Elder Brother."

The interpreter stared impassively at Davies, then he relayed this response to Elder Brother in an uncharacteristically clipped, guttural Chinese. Davies risked a quick glance at John, whose face was now nearly the same color as his starched collar.

The interpreter looked sharply at Davies. "Your line of thinking is not acceptable to Elder Brother. He suggests that you reconsider your position."

Elder Brother made a small gesture with his hand, which caused his bodyguards to become noticeably more alert. Davies could hear John's breaths coming quicker and harder. Personally, he felt so gutted that he wondered if he still had the energy to protest. But if he backed down he'd be a slave for the rest of his life, never knowing a moment without fear. He wasn't even sure who was speaking as he heard words flowing out from his mouth, "My mind is made up. I will not rethink my position."

"Are you quite sure? You have a responsibility to your friend, after all."

"You certainly do," John whispered.

"If something happens to him, I won't help you. I promise that."

The interpreter smiled, it was the smile of a sadist who was about to be entertained.

Elder Brother made another gesture; with ragged hands his bodyguards reached into their tunics. They would follow any command, so long as they were provided with enough opium.

Davies tried to ignore the fast, stifling voice of desperation clawing out from somewhere in his chest. "Mr. Crockwood is a very influential official whose government will take grave notice if anything should happen to him." He took a breath, telling himself that he was doing it for emphasis, and knowing that this was a lie. "If Elder Brother wants the respect and assistance of the British Empire, he must demonstrate that he is a statesman and not a common thug."

Dear God, how could he have said something so insulting? Apparently Elder Brother understood the slur, and he raised a hand giving some cryptic instruction to his bodyguards. The interpreter began to relay Davies' statement, but his employer cut him off, spitting out words in a voice that was loud and coarse, each word sounding like a jab from a fighter's glove.

The interpreter waited for Elder Brother to conclude his tirade - then he turned toward Davies and smiled again, coldly. "Mr. Davies, you have made it unerringly clear that you are a not a flatterer - and Elder Brother reminds me that he can never trust flatterers. The service that Elder Brother wishes for you to perform is a just one - and he trusts that you will come to the same conclusion. If you do not," he sneered in a way intended to have a comic effect, "he understands that you will not hesitate to relay your objections to him. Now then," the interpreter said, resurrecting his polite demeanor, "as to the other matter - the boy whose name escapes you is called Wong Gou Sing. Do you know who the judge is?"

"No I don't," Davies replied, not quite believing that he'd carried the day, and not even sure how he'd done it. Nonetheless, he was deeply relieved that the interpreter had returned to his false civility. Feeling almost guilty, Davies added, "I assume the case will be tried in the Native City."

The interpreter nodded. "That will be Chang Wo-tin."

At the mention of this name, Elder Brother banged a hand down on the table. Again his dead eyes had come to life, shimmering with fury and cruel intelligence. He shouted out a tirade and when he'd finished he glared at the interpreter, challenging him to relay the message with the same fervor.

"Elder Brother says that Chang Wo-tin is a wicked man," the interpreter said forcefully. "He has been nothing but trouble to the good people of Shanghai. Elder Brother is the President of the Chung Wai Bank. He is the Director of the Hua Feng Paper Mill. He is the President of the Shanghai Emergency Hospital, and the head of the Opium Suppression Commission.   Yet this Judge, Chang Wo-tin, refuses to respect Elder Brother in his attempts to assist Chinese justice. Elder Brother has always been a champion of justice and an enemy of oppression. He is well known to be the protector of the people!" The man straightened and looked Davies square in the face. "Chang Wo-tin is not a true patriot. Chang Wo-tin has gone too far!"

Davies nodded. "My sentiments exactly."

XV. SEMANTICS LOST

"**I**f you will excuse me, old boy," Crockwood wheezed when they were safely into the car again, "I think I may vomit."

"Not on the pleasant upholstery, John. Please wait until you get back to your embassy."

With skin as white and greasy as a corpse's, Crockwood had not fully recovered from the morning's entertainment. "Do you realize they nearly shot me? Dear God! And you just had to press our luck! I should kill you myself!"

"I'm so sorry, John. I never expected it to get this bad."

"Then why, for heaven's sake, did you let me come along?"

"Because, well, perhaps it was stupid. But, John, I strongly believe that Elder Brother knows more about us than we'd like to think. I hate to say it, but if you hadn't come you still would have been in danger, simply because you associate with me. I didn't think that you'd want to learn that ugly truth some night when you're all alone. I thought you should know who you were up against, and have the opportunity to look him in the eyes and plead your case. Now, at least, you know that the matter is put to rest."

"Is it?"

"I believe so. Elder Brother may still contact you but I think in an orthodox way."

"He'll invite me to tea, I suppose."

"Just keep a firm grip on your cup."

Crockwood shook his head. "Don't remind me. I suppose we're damned lucky. Frankly, I still don't know how you pulled it off."

"Coming out of there alive?" Davies rubbed his chin, its unmarred condition a happy reminder of, indeed, how lucky they'd been. "That's stumped me too - I've been trying to figure it out since we left. What the magic words were. And I think I know."

"You will enlighten me."

"I asked him to choose between being a statesman and a common thug. That should have cooked our goose, except that Elder Brother wants to be regarded as a statesman more than anything in the world, and he acted accordingly. From here on, if you treat him like one you'll do just fine.

"Let us pray so. Good lord, the cheek of that man. Did you catch that comment - 'the head of Chiang's Opium Suppression Committee?' He's China's leading opium smuggler! His police break into the dens and confiscate his own drugs!"

Davies shrugged. "At least he's half public spirited, which is more than can be said for most of us."

"What I don't understand is why your Elder Brother wants the staff at all. Did you note the condition of his antiques?"

"Yes, but it's not so much the staff he wants as it is me. I expect that Elder Brother is looking to expand and he wants me as a go-between. Elder Brother cannot easily pass into the moneyed, white business circles of Shanghai - but evidently that's where he wants to go."

"How do you conclude that?"

"John, I'm merely speculating. I've no evidence, but I'm unique in that I can easily travel between the two worlds. I'm as well known to the Chinese underworld as I am to the bankers and the country club set. Wouldn't that be an advantage to him?"

"Contracting you would be an advantage to no one."

"I wonder if getting me to retrieve the staff is nothing but a test of my loyalty? If he really does spring this Chinaman for me, truly, I will be in his debt. I've done my best to sell myself into slavery."

"Well, it's your business."

Davies nodded absently. He'd out-negotiated Elder Brother, winning the right to refuse his next assignment - as well as gaining a pledge from the gangster to free the Chinese lad. But, despite some extremely tense moments, had it been too easy? Something else was bothering him, as well, something that Elder Brother had said. It kept rattling around in his head and he couldn't shake it, like an annoying piece of food stuck between his teeth. Maddeningly, the exact words eluded him, he could only remember having thought to himself at the time, *now that's odd.* Unfortunately, he could no longer recall what Elder Brother had actually stated to prompt his response.

As he tried to reenact the meeting in his mind, he speculated on what might be asked of him in San Francisco. He urgently wished that he knew Elder Brother's game. Was he to assassinate Governor Young, perhaps foreclose on an orphanage housing the son of a murdered rival? Maybe encourage the local authorities to look the other way when a shipment of drugs, or a number of teenage companions for elderly Chinese, were sailed through the Golden Gate. Just how far was he willing to play along? Was it illusion to think that, should he refuse to cooperate, he'd be any safer from Elder Brother and his men back home in the States? If he stopped to think about it he was scared as hell.

Crockwood seemed to be irritated by Davies' long silence. "Look at him. Thinking about his Chinese mouse, feeding her cheese I'll wager."

"Such pettiness, John," Davies murmured, jolted from his meditation. "Remember yourself, be English."

* * *

As he climbed out of Davies' limousine, his legs shaking and his hands still trembling, Crockwood realized that his run-in with Elder Brother had left him weirdly inspired. When guns had been pulled on him and he'd survived, he'd felt an exhilaration and sense of power that, quite strangely, made him want more. Those emotions were now compelling him to take actions with his life that he would have been too timid to even consider mere days earlier. Ironically, Zephyr Davies, a man whom he envied, had made him feel important. Elder Brother, a man whom he feared, had made him feel brave. Life was a peculiar business all around.

* * *

After dropping Crockwood at his embassy, Davies had the driver swing around to the Astor House. He'd yet to run into Monica on any of these sojourns, which concerned him. Hopefully, Leibowitz could assure him of the girl's well-being.

Indeed, his hireling confirmed that Monica had sequestered herself in her room for some reason. She'd had food sent up, and left half-empty trays outside her door; so it was a reasonable bet that she was still alive – and in possession of some appetite.

Davies arrived at his villa late in the afternoon and bellowed for Lo-Chien to make him a drink.

"Madame Lin call." Lo-Chien bellowed back.

Sorting through his mail, Davies walked into a neighboring study and immediately phoned his old friend. Mercifully, she was home; for the past few days, Madame Lin had been impossible to reach - perhaps she was spending extra hours at the dog races making her traditional two dollar bets.

"Sorry to have been out of touch," Davies said. "But I did try to reach you. How are things?"

"I fear my attempted luncheon meeting with Monica at the Astor House must be regarded as a disaster." As usual, Madame Lin had gone directly to the point; she could be so remarkably non-Chinese. "I started by asking her about her strange friends, and the result was that Monica threw a fit and stalked out. I followed her upstairs, but she locked herself in her room, and that was the end of the whole business."

"So you never got a chance to compare baggage tags?" Davies asked, relieved that Madame Lin had inadvertently given him an explanation for Monica having become a recluse.

"No. That will have to wait for another day."

"Perhaps it's just as well. Give the girl some time to calm down. So she is all right?"

"Except for being a little fool. Have you discovered anything I should know about?" Madame Lin asked eagerly.

"I'm afraid I've been distracted by another matter. One that couldn't wait, I might add." Davies didn't elaborate, and arranged to meet with her the following evening. "But perhaps you should consider donating 'the clouded twilight' to the Shanghai museum. The fact is, I can't guarantee your safety if you take possession of it. Will you think it over? At least, have Dr. Sun authenticate it while you make your decision."

Madame Lin agreed to think it over. After he rang off, he continued inspecting the day's mail. There were no new notes from Monica.

* * *

The door to Gou Sing's cell creaked open, letting in a faint shaft of gray light; a new jailer was about to enter with a surprise. Gou Sing had welcomed these surprises, because he was anxious about being forgotten and left alone in the cold and the dark. Also, each new person coming into his cell offered hope; perhaps they would take pity on him. But now he knew that none of the jailers had anything but hard cruelty in them. Being forgotten was better.

At first, time passed with unbearable slowness but his spirit eventually adjusted so that everything became like a dream. It helped to set simple goals, the main one being that he would remain silent. He flirted with the idea of playing for the jailer's sympathy, but the endless wails coming from other cells made it clear that exaggerating his misery would get him nowhere. Better to show how brave he was by remaining still and quiet – maybe then the jailer would be so impressed that he'd allow Gou Sing some privileges - simply out of respect.

He'd learned to sleep in a sitting position, but he had to find the perfect balancing posture because the slightest movement caused pain to shoot from unexpected places like his side or his jaw and jar him awake. Being in a dreamlike state was his only solace, but it never lasted for long. A sound would awaken him, or the sudden fear that rats were gnawing on his numbed legs drove him to wave his bound hands about feverishly to scatter them, as if this would accomplish anything.

A faceless form, nothing more than a breathing shadow, the jailer walked behind him. Gou Sing tensed, awaiting the next act. Strangely, his neck and shoulders hurt more than his bloodied knees because the unaltered position had put his legs to sleep many hours earlier. Gou Sing lifted his head slightly, and was immediately struck on the shoulder. He tried to remain still, but he had to swallow, and when he did the jailer struck him against the back of his head. The blow wasn't that hard, but slightly stronger than the first; how bad was it was going to get? If the jailer stayed away from Gou Sing's ear, which was oozing blood, being struck repeatedly might knock him unconscious. That would be good. But what would happen when he awoke? What would it be like when he was finally ordered to move, and the blood rushed back to his lower body awakening the searing pain that waited there? With any luck, they'd just shoot him through the head first. As the jailer stood behind him, making no noise at all, over and over Gou Sing repeated a silent chant to himself: *shoot me, shoot me, shoot me!*

* * *

XVI. CHINESE JUSTICE

Thursday, August 16, 1928

Davies enjoyed his first full night of rest in well over a week. Now that he was a member of Elder Brother's team, he embraced the illusion that he was somehow protected from harm. Even his servants fell into step, seeming more polite and gracious as they served him a remarkably bountiful breakfast that was more lovingly presented than normal.

After dining, Davies swung by to pick up Crockwood, who had agreed to witness the boy's trial that afternoon. The weather had become more civilized, and, on the way to the old Chinese city, they stopped and strolled in a small and neglected park that overlooked the river.

Crockwood was still fascinated by Hong Fat's demise, and wished to review what they'd learned. With the help of Mr. Chen, a Chinese business acquaintance of Crockwood's, they had managed to decipher some of the ledgers and notes that Davies had stolen from Hong Fat's office. These revealed that Hong Fat had taken out a loan against his shop to the tune of twenty-thousand pounds in order to invest in an opium shipment with a partner, probably a minor warlord.

"It all comes clear," Crockwood said with poorly suppressed glee, causing Davies to suspect that his friend had fallen prey to one of the guilty pleasures of playing detective: the opportunity to briefly lord over the mysteries of life and death and reduce them to neat little bromides that left the theorist the smug master of a normally rapacious universe. "We know that Elder Brother controls most of the opium that comes into Shanghai, and the little fellow is extremely intolerant of competitors. However, 'Pee wee' would never have noticed a small-time operator like Hong Fat, so the shop owner's profit was well assured."

"'Pee wee?'"

"He's a tiny fellow, isn't he? Our Elder Brother."

"Do you have a similar nick-name for me?" Davies asked as he paused to withdraw a cigarette from his coat pocket.

"I certainly couldn't repeat it in public," Crockwood sputtered. "Now then, Hong Fat felt secure because opium can be sold quickly."

"Right," Davies said, lighting up. "Hong Fat's loan was due in ten days, but for opium ten days is a pretty long period of time."

Crockwood adopted the look of a clergyman at a funeral. "However 'the cloudy sunset' put an end to it all."

"Are you concluding that 'the clouded twilight' put an end to Hong Fat as well?"

"Exactly. I'll wager that Madame Lin's friend, your Dr. Sun, is one of 'Pee wee's' men - and hearing about the staff from Dr. Sun, 'Pee wee' would have learned of Hong Fat." Crockwood drummed on his tie with his fingers, an irritating habit that apparently helped to prod the creaking cogs of his gin-soaked brain into turning. "I'll wager that Dr. Sun was instructed to make an offer for 'the cloudy thing' that was insultingly low. But feeling his warlord friend could protect him, Hong Fat may have refused 'Pee wee's offer - that was a fatal mistake."

It was Davies' turn to theorize. "One can imagine how incensed 'Pee wee', now you've got me saying it, Elder Brother would have been when he learned that he'd been turned down. So Elder Brother sent men around to insure that his offer was taken seriously. Sadly for Hong Fat the men arrived perhaps minutes after the staff had been sold to me."

Crockwood wiped his brow, and then nodded his agreement as they climbed back into the Hispano. Five minutes of walking was his limit and his lungs were already making alarming sounds.

"Anyway," Davies continued, as he settled into the back seat, "Elder Brother's men demanded that 'the clouded twilight' be reclaimed and turned over to them - so they threatened Hong Fat and beat him. The bruises on Hong Fat's face were one indication of Elder Brother's pique."

"Poor wretch."

"Perhaps Elder Brother's men told Hong Fat they'd be back later, and 'he'd better have that staff.' After they left, Hong Fat tidied up. He locked everything up tight..,"

Crockwood cut in. "And knowing he could never produce the damnable thing, killed himself."

"Not quite," Davies said. "Hong Fat was playing for time. I'll bet he told Elder Brother's men that he'd have the staff for them the next day. But staff or not, his time was up. Elder Brother must have found out about Hong Fat's operation and the opium ship waiting to pick up additional cargo in Wenchow."

Unable to restrain himself, Crockwood delicately brushed his drooping bottom lip. "Then 'Pee wee', using his authority as Opium Commissioner, confiscated the entire shipment."

Davies nodded his agreement. "With no opium, Hong Fat could not possibly repay his loan; he would lose his shop, and the kind of loan sharks who offer ten day deals wouldn't be very civil when it came to collecting. So that letter from Wenchow was the final straw, the one informing Hong Fat that his opium shipment had been seized."

Digesting Davies' theory, Crockwood brushed at one end of his mustache. Just who did the sagging old reprobate think he was making himself attractive for? Davies reminded himself that Crockwood had lived alone for years, and his self-fondling was probably the only human contact he ever received.

"Also there was conceivably a criminal indictment waiting for Hong Fat," Davies said, trying to take his mind off of Crockwood's weirdly sensual grooming habits, "and I wouldn't be surprised if the warlord friend slunk away in the night the moment he realized he'd been asked to protect Hong Fat's shop from the likes of Elder Brother."

"Indeed." Crockwood agreed, stroking his eyebrow for final emphasis.

"Damn it, John, will you stop caressing yourself? If you need to touch up your make-up, go find a washroom."

"I realize you resent the idea of maintaining proper grooming, Davies - but vanity is a public service and I'm merely performing my civic duty."

"Dear God." He searched his mind for some kind of wicked retort but finally settled on a simple, "hmmm," as he thought of Hong Fat's head lying in the pool of blood. Crockwood seemed to catch his mood and they both stared dourly to the north, and to the great buildings along the Bund, which looked to be less assembled than carved out of tremendous blocks of stone.

Suddenly, Crockwood appeared as if he'd been taken ill. "Uh, Zephyr, your man, the driver." He nodded in the direction of the front seat.

"Max?"

"Yes. Max the Mongol, he doesn't, I mean, he isn't, uh, does he work for..."

"'Pee wee?'"

"Not so loud! God, what have I done? Me and my big mouth."

"Don't worry, I can assure you that Max is not one of Elder Brother's men." Crockwood smudged at his brow with relief. "But don't forget that I am."

Crockwood looked apoplectic. "Zephyr, that isn't funny."

"I think it's hilarious. Why don't you go on with more theories while I decide whether or not you're worth saving."

"I'm in this mess because of you! You should be ashamed!"

"Incidentally, John, do you still own that bottle of Chateau d'Yquem, '18? The one you keep in that musty closet that you fantasize is a wine cellar?"

A look of unfettered outrage overcame Crockwood, causing him to almost appear alive. "Damn you, Davies, that's not cricket! Now, bother, I can't think."

"That's never stopped you." Davies glanced toward the river where he could make out the masts of the brooding hulks of four British warships anchored far out in the Whangpoo, their flags snapping briskly. Gathered around the closest man-of-war, like puppies snuggling against a mother dog, were several steam yachts with polished teak decks and gleaming brass rails. Their enormous "mother" drifted near the center of the river - its scale too large for Shanghai - as if some giant child had been playing with toys whose sizes didn't match. After the events of the week, just looking at Shanghai made him feel like a man who was sick from eating too much of a special dessert. "What, indeed, should I do with the damned 'clouded twilight' now?"

Crockwood gave a gentlemanly cough. "Considering the thing's reputation, our Elder Brother is the most deserving to receive it. But I fail to understand why Elder Brother would have monogrammed your clothes, threatened your life, and driven Hong

Fat to suicide over an old Chinese relic worth a paltry five hundred pounds, at best."

A very telling point Davies thought. Why, indeed, was the head of the Chinese underworld so eager to get his hands on an antique walking stick that seemed to have little more true value than a fortnight at a second rate German health spa?

"The time has come for a showdown with your Madame Lin," Crockwood said as the Hispano motored into Nantao. "She must know this staff's real value, what makes it so intensely desired by powerful individuals. After all, a great many of your assumptions are based entirely on things Madame Lin has told you, Davies. Could this old friend be misleading you as part of some secret agenda?"

Davies had already considered this unhappy possibility. "It's not her style, John, she's impossibly frank. She even tells me when she's holding back information. Besides, I have no interest in living in a world where friends betray friends. If Madame Lin deceives me, and sets events in motion that kill me, so much the better. End of topic."

The court proceedings took place punctually at three o'clock that afternoon. A large crowd had gathered outside the impressive, but battered, stucco courthouse. A path was reluctantly cleared for Davies and Crockwood as they made their way up the short flight of steps in order to go inside.

The interior setting was a strange combination of grandeur and poverty. A unicorn was depicted on one wall of the lofty, main court room - the Chinese called it a Ki-lin - and all about the magistrate, Chang Wo-tin, hung colorful banners, many of them exhorting him to be merciful. But the large room was dirty and unswept, and, with the accumulation of dust and trash on the floor, the place looked as if it also served as a prison. The smells were horrific - like an overused school gymnasium with rotting food in the lockers.

An array of clerks and secretaries was scattered about, and arranged behind these officials was a platoon of lictors, the fierce looking torturers and executioners who would administer the punishments.

Davies and Crockwood were allowed no closer than the open doorway, where several dozen Chinese pushed forward to see inside. Some had their faces pressed against the court's filthy windows.

Presiding over the affair, Chang Wo-tin, scowling with practiced disdain, sat on an elevated platform. He was a thin, tired-looking man with greasy hair and a dramatically wrinkled face.

"What is he saying?" Davies asked Elder Brother's characterless interpreter, who had met them in front of the court building and accompanied them inside. As much as he was concerned about the boy, Davies kept thinking of Monica's note from several days back and her baffling behavior in front of the Astor House. Had someone forced her to write it? The possibilities were disturbing.

Before the interpreter could answer, Gou Sing was brought into the room, barely able to walk. Ugly purple and green bruises adorned the lad's face and back, one of his eyes had swollen shut and a long brown stream of dried blood criss-crossed his neck. Gou Sing was forced to kneel in front of the magistrate, and his blood-stained, bandaged legs revealed that he had been the recipient of the traditional means of obtaining a confession. Even witnesses received such brutal treatment, Davies had been told. China's unique system of justice dictated that they often be detained to prevent them from reneging on their testimony. The unfortunate witness found himself imprisoned, frequently being placed in the same cell with the person who was on trial. The case generally resolved itself then and there. When the jailer returned in the morning, both parties were dead.

The interpreter was listening carefully to the unfolding drama, his eyes fixed coldly on Chang Wo-tin. "In this court, the prisoners are not allowed counsel," he said, quietly. "Your friend has been informed of the charges, and he has submitted a written plea to the magistrate through a licensed notary. Chang Wo-tin has asked your friend if it is not true that he had confessed to the crime. Your friend has great audacity, most unusual. He actually wishes to rescind his confession. He argues that he was beaten and forced to write things that were untrue."

"Obviously he's been beaten," Crockwood muttered, mustering the required display of British outrage. "Look at the poor wretch. It's pure barbarism."

Though his breathing was so labored that he could barely speak, the boy was clearly protesting.

The magistrate snapped at him in Chinese, offended by the youth's attitude. He lifted his hand and slammed it down on the table. Whatever he was saying, his clerks and executioners seemed satisfied - this was how a judge was supposed to behave.

"Chang has learned that your friend speaks excellent English," the interpreter whispered to Davies. "He wishes to know how the lessons were paid for. Frankly, I do not like this turn of events."

The boy continued to speak in a strained whisper, apparently trying to explain his education; but the magistrate cut him short. He glowered at the exhausted young man and launched into another angry tirade - whatever he was saying, it got a strong reaction from Gou Sing. The color drained from the boy's face and he collapsed into a ball, burying his head in his hands. Suddenly his head sprang up; with tears in his eyes, he shouted hoarsely at the magistrate, prompting murmurs of disgust from the spectators.

Elder Brother's interpreter shook his head, disapprovingly. "Chang says your friend is disrespectful of the court. Apparently this boy was paid on fifty-six occasions. Each time a small sum was removed by the boy to further his own education. Chang regards these deductions as thefts, deliberately withheld from your friend's father. A thief can be executed if he has stolen three times - therefore Chang sentences your friend to death."

Davies felt fury rising inside himself. The whole proceeding was such a farce that he wondered why they bothered with it. The verdict was clearly predetermined, and if the boy hadn't been sentenced for theft no doubt the magistrate would have come up with another charge. Since justice wasn't the issue, the trial probably went on for the entertainment of the spectators who seemed to be greatly enjoying it. "How much time do we have until the sentence is discharged?" Davies asked.

The interpreter shrugged. "He will be executed immediately."

Two of the lictors, husky men in black robes, moved forward and roughly pulled Gou Sing to a standing position. A long wooden pole was brought in and the youth's hands and feet were bound to it. He was completely silent as the leather straps were pulled tight around his flesh, securing hands and feet that were trembling violently. The lictors hoisted the pole to their shoulders, and Gou Sing hung between them like a pig ready for roasting.

With a flat, dazed expression on his face, and a rapidly heaving chest, he resembled a field mouse held in the talons of a barn owl.

The magistrate rose and a clerk signaled that court was adjourned. The spectators were suddenly on their feet, most of them grinning. The outpouring of people pushed Davies and Crockwood and the interpreter into the courtyard.

"I don't understand," Crockwood said, "isn't a crime against a filial member not punishable in China? How can they convict him for stealing from his father?"

The interpreter gave Crockwood a wry smile, which must have been practiced in front of a mirror. "Excuse me, please, Mr. Crockwood, but are you going to go inside and tell them of their oversight? The fact is, the boy renounced his father and the judge complied."

"Let's not just stand here chatting," Davies said sharply.

The interpreter seemed unruffled. "Please. Matters are well in hand."

"Well in hand!" Crockwood scoffed. ""They're going to cut his bloody head off!"

"He is to be garroted," the interpreter corrected the portly Englishman. Then he gathered his robes and hurried off in pursuit of the grand procession, as if he didn't want to miss any of it himself.

* * *

XVII. A DECENT EXECUTION

Monica lay on the bed in her room at the Astor House with its own strange smell of food and overly sweet perfume. Maybe a Moroccan prince and his harem had crowded into her apartment the night before she'd arrived. Staring at the ceiling, she noticed how curious plays of light and shadow created a deformed man's face in the corner. He was grotesque but somehow likable. She wondered if she'd have a hooked nose and gnarled chin one day? Just how old would she be when her looks failed her? At twenty-one, she ought to have a little time left.

She felt like sliding off the mattress and curling up on the floor - a peculiar impulse considering that she was already in bed. She bitterly regretted being so unhelpful when Zephyr Davies had tried to contact her several days earlier. Now that she wanted him, he seemed to have vanished. Even her aunt didn't know where he was.

Margaret, the pleasant lady who'd shared a taxi with her when she'd left customs, had told her to call if she needed help. But, despite her dowdy, cheerful warmth, Margaret had been offering advice on sight-seeing, or finding a good restaurant - she certainly couldn't be of aid in the current situation.

Over the past three days, things seemed to have settled down. Though, there was always a vague feeling when she went out that someone was behind her. She never saw anybody, she simply had a sense of a shape, a disheveled, heavy, hulking thing that was never far away.

She'd shrugged it off as her imagination, until she'd heard the noises in the hall. Nothing distinct, just an occasional shuffling sound, something that might have been low breathing, a lingering shadow under the door across from hers.

Still, she'd tried to remain brave, she couldn't hole up forever; she had important things to do.

But twenty minutes ago, when she'd returned from tea, she'd realized in one jarring moment that her worst fears were true. As she'd approached her door, key in hand, her first impression was that someone had spilled milk - a simple accident that the hotel staff needed to be alerted to. But as she came closer, she saw that it wasn't milk and it wasn't an accident. Written on the outside of her door in messy, white globs of cold cream was the message, "I found you." *This can't be true*, she'd thought, and daring another peek at her door she saw that the cold cream was gone. *What?* Instead of cold cream, sharp fingers of sunlight slashed across the painted wood and gradually she understood that what she'd seen was nothing more than a play of natural light augmented by her cruel imagination.

In the hours that had passed since, she'd barely moved - instead of bowing to logic, the panic inside her grew stronger and more heartless with every breath. After what had happened several days ago, the very thought of cold cream was so perverse that it caused her to tremble.

She stared into her glass of brandy where a solitary bubble floated. From the smeared glass her gaze drifted to her fingers, two of them bandaged. Terrible images began to flood into her mind: a freshly cut onion, gleaming with liquid - dark water, black and foul - a child's, milky-white hand - the flat, doughy face of a customs officer as his moist, fleshy fingers squeezed hard on her arm. She felt breathless, she had to get out of this place. There was a great weight on her chest giving her a sense of being buried under heavy, damp earth. Was she dying? She must be - she'd earned it - God had finally caught up with her.

* * *

Davies had to fight his way through the crowd to catch up with the interpreter, who was quickly disappearing into the assembling procession of jailers and prisoners. "Does Elder Brother know they can move so quickly with these things?"

The interpreter smiled sweetly, like a sleeping child. "Do not worry. We have a fine plan." Then he turned on his heels and followed after the motley queue of prisoners. Davies and Crockwood pursued him, trying to stay clear of the festive mob.

The great wooden gates to the courtyard surrounding the hall of justice were pulled open and the newly formed procession marched out onto the congested street. Seven men, dangling from poles, were being carried to the execution grounds. Following after them on foot was a swarthy, stocky man whom the interpreter pointed out as Gou Sing's father - his ears had been cut and little flags thrust through them. A policeman proceeded Wing hsu, carrying a sign proclaiming the man's crimes and his assigned punishment: a flogging. A second policeman performed a preview performance, whipping Wing hsu lightly every time a third policeman banged a small gong. Near the end of the procession were twenty odd Chinese wearing the cangue. Their grimacing heads each protruded through a thirty pound slab of wood, shaped roughly like a ship's hatch. Written on each cangue was the prisoner's name and a list of the debts he had neglected to pay.

At the very rear of the procession was Chang Wo-tin. He rode in an ornate sedan chair supported by eight bearers in official uniform. Red tablets carried by a ninth man proclaimed Chang's rank. His lictors accompanied him, carrying whips and chains signifying the punishments they would inflict. The skinny judge was preceded by two gong bearers who struck the number of raps, which indicated their master's rank, and by two avant-couriers who howled out for all to make room.

The crowd was in a raucous mood, many of them taunting the prisoners and shouting obscenities. The only good thing that could be said about the whole horrifying spectacle, Davies thought, was that the Chinese held their executions at a decent hour.

"Barbaric!" Crockwood muttered. "I dare say you've lost your friend."

Davies nodded, unease festering in his stomach, as he tried to keep Elder Brother's man in sight.

As the procession turned onto a busy avenue, it intercepted a gaily decorated wedding ceremonial. The two processions merged, becoming one gaudy, unlikely pageant. The wedding party was splendid; brightly adorned bearers carried the bride in a palanquin draped with rippling bunting and red and gold banners. The families rode in lavishly adorned carriages drawn by horses that wore red nets and tasseled headgear. A full dress Chinese marching band followed along performing "Dixie" and "The Camptown Races" and "There'll Be A Hot Time In The Old Town Tonight." These were standards used at all important occasions, including funerals, and the Chinese always performed them slowly, with great pomp and seriousness. Today their melodies mixed disturbingly with the sinister gong beats of the criminal procession.

Chang and his criminals made a long, regal turn, breaking away from the wedding and heading for a broad, empty field surrounded by a high wall. The gates to the execution grounds were pulled open; the procession filed inside and the throngs of spectators quietly took their places.

In England Davies had visited the sights of famous battles, broad fields whose grassy plains had witnessed so much killing that the elderly oaks had literally been nourished on human blood. Those locales had always been so pastoral that it was hard to imagine that any tragedies had ever occurred there - but not this austere field; in the strange, gray, dusty light, broken up by the gnarled shapes of a few barren trees, there was no doubt that this was a place of execution. The air here reeked of fear.

As the seven prisoners were untied from their poles, several of the condemned collapsed from emotion and had to be carried the last few feet to where they were roughly bound to wooden posts, after which their heads were covered with cloth sacks. One prisoner was sobbing and crying "Huyin" in a most terrible, mournful way. Davies believed Huyin to be a woman's name, and he wondered who she was – or had been.

Chang Wo-tin sat serenely in his sedan chair, the crowds and petitioners held back by his official entourage. Chang's hands were folded in his lap as he gazed out at the spectacle in seeming anticipation of a pleasant afternoon of song and dance.

His serenity was shattered when four large men came out of the crowd and walked briskly to the magistrate's sedan chair. Davies recognized two of the stone-faced giants as having escorted him into Elder Brother's villa earlier in the week. The judge's guards made no attempt to stop the four; it was well known whom they represented. The thugs bowed low and thrust their heads into Chang's private sanctuary. The man on the left presented Chang with a small, beautifully wrapped package. Chang glanced apprehensively at each of them, as, with a weak smile, he accepted their gift. With the thugs staring at him and refusing to leave, the judge reluctantly tore off the wrappings. He gazed silently into a small box and studied the attached card, presumably signed by Elder Brother. Slowly, he lifted his head and thanked the men.

They bowed in return. One of the thugs spoke several sentences; Chang nodded and tried again to smile, but smiling wasn't his forte. Still, he seemed eager to repay Elder Brother for his charming and thoughtful gesture. The thugs smiled back, and walked briskly away - their job done.

"What is it?" Davies eagerly asked the interpreter.

"Ahhh, a most appropriate gift, a miniature coffin - delicately carved of teak - truly beautiful." The interpreter smiled. "The coffin is Chang's - and the gift is the fact that Chang is not in it."

"It did seem a little small for him," Crockwood remarked, dourly.

"Don't worry, we'd make him fit." The interpreter lifted a warning finger to Davies. "Do not forget 'the clouded twilight,' Mr. Davies. Elder Brother has many more gifts for people who practice obstinacy." With that, he moved off and disappeared into the undulating mass of spectators.

A roar came from the crowd; the executioners had stepped forward and were being received like star athletes. Each prisoner had his own executioner, and a coarse rope was slipped over every one of the sack-covered heads. All seven executioners methodically checked their garrotes; and after receiving a nod from Chang, they slowly began to tighten them.

With bizarre timing, the tea dance started up at the Majestic a number of blocks away. The faint sound of a jazz band could be heard, pounding out a cheerful foxtrot. What kind of crazy town was this, Davies thought, where people danced and carried on with giddy abandon while a grim death scene was occurring practically next door? Even more perversely, one of the criminals was jerking his right leg in an awful death spasm, and the motion seemed to be in perfect syncopation with the distant music. Davies didn't know if he should laugh or cry. But he worried that he was committing some kind of sin for even noticing the man's well-timed kicks.

Davies' heart pumped a bit faster as he stared at the man behind the Chinese boy. Because of the distance, he couldn't see the rope clearly, but the executioner had begun to twist, going through all the motions of a first-rate strangling. Nauseatingly, his youthful prey was struggling and kicking with agony.

Davies glanced at Chang, the judge wasn't even looking at the boy's executioner. Had Chang already given some discreet signal

instructing him to spare the lad? If so, had the executioner seen it?
Or was it possible that there had been no sign and Chang had
bravely decided to defy Elder Brother? It looked very bad.

Even worse, could Elder Brother have tricked him? This
thought caused the beats of his heart to accelerate, rapidly. He
struggled to recollect accurately what had happened just moments
earlier. Had the interpreter misrepresented the meaning of the tiny
coffin – was it not a warning to the skinny judge, but to Davies
himself? Was the boy's killing to be the ultimate test of Davies'
loyalty? Had Davies overplayed his hand? Had he offended Elder
Brother, and his arrogance was now resulting in the young man's
death?

* * *

XVIII. DEFIANCE

Madame Lin crumpled the telegram and tossed it to the floor. How many of these things was the man going to send her? He wanted to know everything; she was surprised that he hadn't asked for the ratio of earth to night soil that she used on her roses. He felt the need to advise her of everything; it was getting tiresome. But were any of the fellow's warnings about Monica actually true? Was it time to share these telegrams with Zephyr Davies? She was afraid of over-burdening him, as he wasn't charging her. But how much could one impose on a friend? He'd complained about being kept in the dark, and maybe it should stay that way. Perhaps she should send Monica to a good doctor, forget about "the clouded twilight," and ask Zephyr Davies to go back to his normal routine of sleeping late and drinking. All right, she'd call him just once more. If he didn't answer she'd contrive some other way of dealing with her current problems. She went to the telephone and made her final call.

* * *

The other six prisoners had definitely not been spared. Muffled, gasping cries came from the cloth sacks. Bodies twitched and thrashed; one man had soiled himself as the crowed yelled with delight. The cries of the man who'd been wailing "Huyin" became desperate child-like shrieks until they were transformed into choked-off gurgles.

Who had these men been? What had they done? Maybe they were all brutes and cut-throats who deserved to die. But without a knowledge of their pasts, they all registered as victims. They were simply frightened, unlucky souls and all Davies could think as he silently nodded to each one was "Godspeed." One by one the life was slowly squeezed out of the men. Some died in ugly paroxysms of protest. Others seemed to go with nothing more than a feeble whimper.

Ten minutes later the dead had lost their futile struggle and there was nothing more worth looking at. Like a bonfire that had burned itself to ashes, there was no longer anything to fascinate. The crowds turned and filed through the gates, well-mannered, smiling happily, satisfied with the afternoon's entertainment. It was as if they were leaving a football game and their team had won.

The magistrate's chair was hoisted high and carried off; the only remaining people were the executioners and the friends and relatives of the dead.

Lazily, the executioners untied their victims, who were now slumped at their wooden posts, and laid them flat on the ground. The executioners pulled the sacks from the bodies, revealing swollen, purplish faces and matted hair. The man who'd screamed "Huyin" still looked tortured, death hadn't calmed his expression in the slightest.

The mourners came forward. Most were grim and dignified; several were wailing and sobbing miserably. Some of the victims, including the man who'd cried a woman's name, had no mourners.

Davies and Crockwood hurried forward to where the boy was lying on the ground, as still as a stone. As he ran, Davies prayed that Elder Brother hadn't betrayed him. Perhaps the boy had fainted, and some small movement would show at any moment. As he got closer, however, there was nothing to distinguish the slight figure from the other rigid bodies sprawled in the dust.

* * *

Zephyr Davies had not answered, nor had he left any message for her. Now Madame Lin was left with little choice but to mention her growing uneasiness to her husband.

Fortunately, no more strange people had come to her door. Yet, she sensed that they were still close by, observing her, planning something of which she would surely disapprove. If only Davies would answer his phone, or return just one of her numerous calls. He'd mentioned that he was having trouble with his servants; could they be deliberately keeping information from him?

Consulting with her husband was a last resort. It wasn't because she wished to spare his feelings, sweet little man that he was. No Mr. Lin would want to take charge, he would have a strong opinion of what should be done and how to proceed. He would not allow her to do things her way, and that was why he hadn't been brought into the situation. But she was being left with no alternative. Would he agree that Monica should be placed in a mental institution? As the young woman's auntie, she had the power, and had already drawn up the commitment papers. The hospital she'd visited the day before might be a little dirty, but the doctors had seemed competent enough.

Why were the wicked forces that created trouble in life so adamant? Why didn't happiness and contentment knock relentlessly on one's door like an intrusive neighbor? Why was it always a gnarled branch that smashed the window during a storm, and not a week's supply of delicacies - fresh oysters, weightless tea cakes adorned with orange blossoms, and, of course, cigarettes?

* * *

IXX. A SHORT DRIVE TO A NEW LIFE

Gou Sing tried not to breathe as he squeezed his eyes shut and prayed that they wouldn't be seen flickering. The executioner had placed the rope around Gou Sing's chin, surprising him. He'd quickly taken advantage of his good luck by putting great effort into "dying" dramatically, hoping that the large man would not realize his mistake. Now the man was bent over and carefully lifting Gou Sing to his feet. Terrified, he tried hard to slump and play dead, but the executioner was whispering to him not to worry. What was this trick? Gou Sing's survival depended on continuing his charade, so he never saw the executioner laugh, only heard him. But he felt the friendly pat, after which the big man coiled his rope and walked away. Gou Sing lay on the ground for a long time, more frightened than when he had been trussed on a pole. His stomach ached and his muscles burned from forcing himself not to move or breathe. Then he heard Zephyr Davies' voice. He let out a gasp and blinked at the yellow-gray sky above him. He looked from side to side, seeing no one moving close by, and forced himself into a sitting position, using up nearly all of his remaining energy. After brushing the dust from his clothes, he turned and stared at the row of lifeless bodies beside him; everything was so peaceful and quiet, it was as if he was in a temple. Then he glanced at Zephyr Davies and a silver-haired white man who were quickly coming his way.

Rising, Gou Sing hobbled across the field toward them, grimacing with every step. He thought that his pain would force him to concentrate, helping him to maintain his composure, but his hands had begun to shake and he couldn't stop them. The smell of dry grass was so powerful and intoxicating that burning tears swept down his cheeks without his permission. "What are you doing here?" he demanded of Davies. Instead of being elated, he was puzzled and a little annoyed - did the great white man think it would be amusing to come and watch him die?

Davies slapped him on the back and then led him toward the Hispano-Suiza, where the chauffeur was waiting with the rear door open. "Thank God, you're okay. You gave us quite a scare."

Was this arrogant man presuming to take credit for the executioner's mistake? "That okay," Gou Sing said. "What you talking about?"

Across the field, some of Chang's lictors were staring directly at him. Gou Sing froze, and his heart began to pound wildly. He pulled free of Davies and lurched toward the gate; but just as he feared, his legs collapsed beneath him and he fell to the ground - hard. He felt a wrenching pain in his knees and shins so intense that it shot through his entire body and almost caused him to lose consciousness. As the horrible, sickening sensation subsided, he saw that the lictors had turned away as if they had no interest in him at all. What was going on?

Now Zephyr Davies was helping him back on to his feet. It was the firm gentleness of the white man's touch that made it all suddenly clear. "You help me?" Gou Sing asked.

"Forget it," Davies mumbled. "I think you've earned a ride in the back seat. We'll make John sit up front."

When they reached the car, Gou Sing slid gracelessly onto the slippery snake skin. Such an emotional day had heightened his senses, and the sweet, perfumed aromas of snake skin and wood made him feel queasy. Davies joined him, and the chauffeur latched the cowl and closed the door. As the hulking driver somehow squeezed into the cramped space behind the wheel, Gou Sing saw the silver-haired white friend sigh with resignation and climb in front.

Gou Sing tried not to move very much on the soft cushions, the sensation of the snake skin against his skin being so unsettling. It all still seemed like a dream.

*   *   *

As the Hispano pulled away and motored toward the waterfront, Davies observed that the Chinese boy's bruised and swollen face was nearly unrecognizable. Still, beneath the grotesque swelling, it was clear that he was thinking about something very intensely.

"Where we go?" the youth asked suspiciously.

"I suppose I'll drop you at your home," Davies answered.

"What home?"

"Don't you..."

The boy cut him off. "My father is a turtle! He is terrible man. I am bad son, and should not criticize him, but he is terrible man!" In China, a turtle was the worst insult one could hurl at another. Turtles were slow and not industrious. "You take me to Soochow Creek, fine! I live on street - I don't care. I dead now, anyway. This was my time - I play game and lose. Now I just practice; make no difference what I do. A man who does not exist is free to do anything. What did you...?"

"How did I get you free?" The boy nodded. "Do you know who Elder Brother is?"

The boy looked at him with astonishment. "You go to Elder Brother? You go for me?"

"Yeah, I..."

"What he look like? He very fierce, right? And very tall."

"Well, he's certainly fierce. But actually, you're a bit taller."

"Really? Me? Oh." The lad contemplated this revelation; it apparently had great significance for him. "His men come and talk to me, you know."

"Oh?"

"Yes, they want to know if I have that walking stick. They visit Hong Fat too."

"Did they harm you?"

"Oh, no. They were nice. But scary. And I was very brave, Mr. Davies, I must thank you. Thank you. Thank you." He repeated his thanks several more times, each time with a little bow of his head and his hands clasped in front of him. "You want me to come live with you, okay? I do whatever you want. I am dead, I have nothing to lose. We go to your house, okay?"

Davies smiled with resignation. He was aware of the traditional Chinese belief that if you saved a man's life he was more or less your property from that moment on. He had anticipated this turn, and he hoped the boy wouldn't be too offended to be handed back his freedom. "Listen, you really don't owe me anything. If you can answer a few questions we'll be all square. Is that okay with you? Uh, I'm sorry, I don't even know your name."

"Oh. It is Wong Gou Sing."

"Sing, uh, what? Come again? I'm not very good at catching Chinese, I'm afraid."

"Wong Gou Sing."

"Wong, 'ow', or 'o'? Is it 'o' Sing?"

"No!"

"No? So, it's 'No Sing?'"

"No!"

Davies laughed. "What's your brother's name? 'No Sun?'"

"I don't understand," the boy said.

"I'll just call you 'Sin'? Okay? 'No Sin', how's that?"

The boy shrugged. "Why not? I'm dead."

"So, Sin, don't you have a mother? I mean, you must have some family that cares about you."

"We go to your house, okay?"

"Well, I think it's best if we take you to your home, where they can care for you. Your wounds obviously need tending."

No Sin laughed bitterly. "Okay, that okay; you drop me any place. Nobody want me now."

As they motored past Hongkew Park a gaily dressed Filipino band was performing for a small crowd of Japanese. The European waltz music was oddly comforting - there being something cheerful about its lush, complex sound. Davies reached into his coat pocket. "Look, I can give you a little cash."

No Sin shook his head. "No, you already do too much for me. I be fine."

"Well, take some money, anyway. I wouldn't want anything to happen; I mean, we wouldn't want you to end up in one of your silly courts again."

No Sin gave him a startled look. "Oh no!" he exclaimed, shaking his head. "They are great courts, Mr. Davies. They are best courts of all. You do not understand. I read about your courts; they are much more silly. Maybe they fair, okay. But they are not practical."

Crockwood had been listening in silence, frowning occasionally at Davies. Now he shook his head and stared out at the passing buildings.

"I have always been under the impression," Davies replied, "that fairness is what counts."

No Sin shifted on the seat. "Listen," he said, warming to the subject, but still shaking uncontrollably. He had been shaking on and off since getting into the car, and now that his tone was stronger and more relaxed, his body was rebelling, slowly deteriorating into ever more violent spasms. "In time of the Emperor Kang-hsi there was a complaint by the people that the courts were very corrupt. The Emperor investigated and decided that the people were right. Therefore he set down a very wise official, what you call it? 'Decree.' In future, great efforts would be taken to insure that the courts remained as corrupt as possible, as a protection for all citizens."

Crockwood gazed upward as if appealing for divine intervention.

Despite an occasional wobble, No Sin's voice was as flat as the expression on his face, but tears swept down his cheeks as he spoke. "See, if courts become too fair they would be jammed with the affairs of troublemakers, and clogged with lawsuits. Everything would take so long that no one would ever be prosecuted. Instead, let the good citizens settle their differences among themselves like brothers - in civilized manner, referring to help of some old man. For those who are obstinate and quarrelsome, let them be ruined by expense and injustice of the law courts - it will be good lesson to them."

Davies shot Crockwood a brief, fraternal smile. "We have the same system in America - it's just that nobody cares to admit it."

"Why not? Americans always very honest." Forty-five minutes earlier the kid had been a shattered lump of flesh on the verge of being strangled to death. Now he was the proud defender of Chinese justice and culture - and maybe he was right. Despite a population of four hundred million, despite warlords and poverty, and a complete lack of central government, the Chinese had one of the most orderly and crime free societies on earth. It was not the law that did it, it was fear of the law.

Beside Davies, No Sin settled back, satisfied that his arguments had carried the day; though he was shaking more violently than ever. "There are many things I can teach you, Mr. Davies," he proclaimed, his teeth chattering. "Many wise ways of China."

There was an innocent charm about this battered lump of flesh - there was also an impish side that suggested a budding swindler and confidence man. He was concerned, though, about the boy's shaking. Perhaps a shot of whiskey would help, but as Davies reached beneath his jacket it occurred to him that the lad might be carrying disease and he'd have to be sure that his flask was sterilized before he drank from it himself. "Listen, if you won't go home, I think we need to take you to the hospital. I'll be happy to pay the bills."

"No!" the boy shouted with surprising energy. "I no go hospital."

"Yes, but you've been through a terrible ordeal, your legs are badly cut - infection can set in."

"That my problem. Don't worry, I use Chinese drugs, they the best. I know where to get them." Bitterly, he added, "I be fine."

It was obvious that Davies was being punished for not opening his home to the newly christened No Sin. Certainly, he could offer the boy a job of some sort - what was one more servant, more or less? But Lo-Chien traditionally chose the household staff and he would be furious to have his authority usurped. Davies had seen the unhappy repercussions of choosing his own helpers before. He knew that No Sin's life would become a living hell if he was added to the servant pool - he'd be given the worst jobs and be subjected to a brutal reign of intimidation. Frankly, his days would be more pleasant on the streets. Under different circumstances, he'd have no reservations about giving Lo-Chien his walking papers, but now that Davies had entered Elder Brother's fold, that option was completely out of the question.

The boy's fate was sealed when Davies realized that the chauffeur had parked the car on the Bund where Soochow Creek emptied into the Whangpoo; perhaps No Sin didn't need any whiskey after all, and he removed his absently placed hand from the pocket that held the flask. "Let me think over your previous offer, Sin. Can you write?"

"I am very fine writer, Mr. Davies. There are many things I can teach you about writing."

Davies laughed. "I'll look forward to that. Take this and don't argue." He handed the boy some coppers and a Mex dollar - then he nodded to the chauffeur, "Help the lad out, will you?"

No Sin was still in great pain as he struggled to maneuver himself through the door. He moved more like an old man than a youth of nineteen, and the look in his eyes had changed. There was still some fire and sparkle, but also a sad and lost quality; he seemed fully ten years older. Max helped No Sin to the sidewalk where he supported himself with the aid of a lamppost. He stared into space with a dead expression, something inside him was gone forever and it wasn't yet clear what had replaced it. Mechanically, the boy waved as the car pulled away from the curb.

"You aren't honestly considering hiring him?" Crockwood asked wearily.

Davies shrugged. "I suppose not. Still, I feel like a heel just leaving him there."

"Why don't you have all China come and move in with you? His isn't the saddest case." Crockwood shook his head. "You could be getting yourself in serious trouble to even consider taking on a boy like that. I've never seen a white man get mixed up with these people without being sorry."

XX. THE FLICKERING LIGHT

Friday, August 17, 1928

The following afternoon, Davies and Crockwood found Dr. Sun waiting stoically for them in his cozy office at the Shanghai museum. If "the clouded twilight" turned out to be real, it would be the doctor's responsibility to hand it over to Elder Brother - assuming that Madame Lin agreed.

Crockwood was excited to see the artifact "in the flesh," and Davies coyly unwrapped a section of bleached wood and phony jewels from the neat paper sheaf, as if he was revealing one of Sally Rand's thighs. Unimpressed with Davies' performance, Crockwood rolled his eyes, then pointed to a torn section of the outer wrapping. "What happened there?"

"A present for Madame Lin," Davies answered. "I removed all the baggage tags so she could determine if her niece wickedly brought this thing to China."

"Will you be speaking to her later today? Doesn't she have a little house by the river?"

"Charming place, don't you remember? No, I intend to play hooky this afternoon, and Madame Lin will have to get by without my obvious charms."

After Crockwood had been allowed to fondle "the clouded twilight," and the cursed artifact had been left in Dr. Sun's care, Davies and his eccentric friend returned to the waiting Hispano. Not unlike a long distance runner pacing himself, Crockwood was sobering up for a marathon of out-of-town cocktail parties - a train would whisk him away to his revelries in an hour. For his part, Davies felt lucky. He'd saved a Chinese boy, and it was a huge relief not to feel obligated to search his car or his bedroom before entering. He would celebrate by inviting Miss Marshall to dinner. If he was able to convince the alluring mute to stammer a syllable or two, she might give him a clue as to why Elder Brother was so eager to get his yellowed claws on "the clouded twilight." Then Davies could put the whole dirty business to rest, once and for all.

After all he'd been through, what a coup to have the week end on a triumphant note. Perhaps Leibowitz would even let it slip that he'd caught sight of Monica staring dreamily at Davies' business card for hours on end.

Unfortunately, when Davies mentioned his optimistic supper plans, he was swiftly brought back down to earth. Empathy was not Crockwood's specialty, and he took glee in emphasizing that Monica, nonspeaking, ostracized by her aunt, was still in a pickle. As they neared the car, he argued that Davies' attempts to save all the lost souls of China wouldn't change anything in the grand scheme of things. "You've plucked one soul from the abyss this week," he wheezed as he climbed into the back of the Hispano. "That's more than any of us can lay claim to, don't press your luck with 'silent Sal.'" Settling into the snake skin seat, Crockwood curled his lip scornfully and added, "Just like the frogs to render the sublime into the ridiculous. How can you stand to be seen in this gaudy bus?"

Davies made a point of not answering as he also boarded and sat beside his irascible friend. They rode in silence for a several blocks before Davies allowed himself to descend to the level of pettiness that Crockwood favored. "As for gaudy buses, thank God, I didn't allow that pompous ass of a salesman in Singapore to bamboozle me into buying a new Phantom Rolls-Royce." One of Davies' favorite rituals was to twist Crockwood's nose by ridiculing anything English.

"We Brits are hopeless lot, aren't we?" Crockwood grumbled, yet with a trace of relief in his voice because their conversation had been allowed to return to its normal tone of foolishness.

"Well, John, one can't ignore the Derby works' peculiar engineering, so typical of your race. If a part is prone to failure, their demented solution is to provide two versions of it. Whereas the poor Hispano,.."

"Poor Hispano! This damn contraption costs, what, six-thousand pounds? You can buy a fully staffed villa for that."

"Exactly. For six thousand pounds you expect perfection, and you get it - so one takes the poor thing for granted, and soon it suffers the same fate as the model husband who becomes remarkably annoying to his wife if he slips up even once. While the Royce, for five thousand pounds, is like the handsome gigolo who regularly beats his lover and is regarded as an absolute saint on those rare occasions when he repents and acts like a normal human being. It follows, absurdly, that when Rolls-Royces achieve average performance they're deified."

Crockwood slipped Davies a caustic look. "Does that mean I should expect your canonization when you demonstrate the characteristics of an average intellect?"

Once Crockwood had been deposited at the Shanghai South Station, where he was to catch a train to the resort town of Hangchow, Davies instructed Max to drive on to a marvelous shop in the old Chinese city that specialized in candies. There, he selected sweets that were traditionally Chinese, as well as a few of a European caste - Belgium chocolates and such. He had these wrapped for Monica, then spent the better part of an hour strolling around and consuming a few of his purchases.

Once he'd completed his walk, he returned to the car. Max fired up the Hispano, and they wound their way painfully through the crowded, narrow streets cutting through the ramshackle Chinese buildings of Nantao, the traditional Chinese section of Shanghai. The streets here were so constricted that the nagging sunlight had only a small chance of sneaking in and nipping at the back of his neck. Being able to travel almost exclusively in shadow was a small relief on what had become another sultry afternoon. It was nice to let the warm wind buffet his face; to look up at the passing gray and red tiled roofs and the colorful silk banners embroidered with dragons and Chinese characters. The charming flags competed with fliers for Japanese liver pills, and macabre warnings about the danger of crossing railroad tracks, which depicted chubby, jolly-looking Chinamen being torn into neat, bloody pieces by a passing train. Here in China there was no Western compulsion to sanitize the unpleasant.

Spying a drab assembly of unfortunates gathered at a street corner, and feeling the full measure of being a "champion of the oppressed," Davies pitched out a handful of coins. Conscience money, he thought - when the whole place finally exploded it might buy him a few moments of good luck.

He felt the familiar rush of guilt as a half-dozen beggars scrambled for the cash that he'd tossed. What must it be like to beg for one's subsidence, and sleep in filthy alleys, while regarding cold slop from a garbage pail as a stroke of good fortune? He lived so comfortably that poverty was, for him, the kind of mysterious dreamscape that wealth was for most other people. How much longer would the Chinese put up with the arrogance of foreign devils like himself who only concerned themselves with matters like their motorcars oozing lubricant? Yet, irrationally, even the poorest beggars smiled when they saw his ostentatious machine - perhaps because they didn't notice it leaking oil.

* * *

No Sin had spent most of his new leisure time searching for Zephyr Davies. He'd decided to keep his new name, it seemed lucky, and he hoped that it would lead him to a new life. He couldn't stop himself from imaging that, upon reflection, the American had come to the wise conclusion that a talented Chinese would make a valuable assistant of some kind. Especially, as spending the rest of his days hiding from his father and brothers was not his concept of a promising new life. To tell the truth, he was becoming desperate. What lay ahead for him - begging and hiding with no place to sleep, while spending weeks, maybe months, in the clothes he now wore? It would be better if he had died on the dusty field of execution. So, when, not far from Da Ching, the Temple for the God of War, he saw Davies' marvelous sparkling motor car stopped for cross traffic, he grabbed his fedora and ran to where the millionaire could see him. "Mr. Davies," he shouted and waved his hat in the air.

The American glanced in his direction. No Sin waved his hat again - but the white face turned away and No Sin felt his heart sink as a Chinese policeman waved traffic forward and the Hispano moved on. With it went every hope that No Sin had for a new life. All that was left him now was a silly name dreamed up by an uncaring American.

* * *

As the fading sun assaulted Davies' squinting eyes, creating around him a flurry of undecipherable activity, the Hispano maneuvered past several ox-carts, and made its way through the old city gates and onto crowded Du Ma Lu, or Great Horse Road. His fellow foreign devils, lacking in poetry, called it "Nanking Road" because it eventually made its way to the city of Nanking.

The Hispano's ride became smoother as it moved from cobblestone to concrete, and Max accelerated, aiming for a Chinaman who stood in the middle of the road, blocking their path. This fellow had undoubtedly concluded that a demon was following him about causing misfortune to enter his life. A wily Chinamen had ways of tricking demons, and this man could be expected to leap out of the way at the last moment, hoping that his demon would be less agile and run down. The practice had seemed charming when Davies first arrived five years earlier - now it was a damned nuisance.

Davies liked the Chinese, even if he did not like China. Few cultures demanded so much conformity, yet the average Chinaman struck him as being more of an individual than most Americans or Europeans. It was one of those paradoxes that contented him that there was order in the universe.

They entered the International Settlement where automobiles replaced ox-carts, and traffic was regulated by electric signals and uniformed policemen. Here the streets were broad and clean and smelled of exhaust and electricity. Davies' gaze drifted upward to the proud, heavily ornamented skyline that was as crooked as the city itself, figuratively and literally. So many of the buildings had been constructed on unstable ground that every year sidewalks had to be torn up and rebuilt, and lifts cleverly realigned. The whole damn place was a grand fraud whose charm was wearing thin.

In the settlement, throngs of Chinese had been replaced by colorless treaty power men, cluttering up the well-swept sidewalks, wearing tailored suits complimented by neatly pressed gray slacks. Strolling in and out of handsome office buildings, they fooled no one with a slow-moving ease that was false and contrived, knowing that their prosperity was built on trickery and oppression. For the first time in a month, however, he found his cynical observations to be more of a source of a amusement than ennui. Things really were turning around.

It was nearly dusk, and Max rose up in his seat and pointed to something ahead. They were approaching the Astor House and an unusually large crowd was milling about. Sikh policemen were trying to turn traffic away, and it seemed that some sort of incident had occurred. "Pull over," Davies commanded.

As soon as the car stopped, he fumbled with the latches to the rear cowl and bounded out into the crowd All around him gentlemen in soiled evening clothes hurried to and fro. Shanghai's volunteer fire department was made up almost exclusively of wealthy Britishers, the cream of Shanghai society, and apparently this emergency had caught them in the midst of some grand social event.

All the commotion was centered around the portico over the Hotel's front entrance - had a light illuminating the Astor House sign exploded and sparked a fire? As he got closer, he could see that a body was snagged in the metal structure, twenty feet above the sidewalk – some poor, clumsy maintenance man had probably fallen during the discharge of his duties, what a shame. Then Davies' breath froze in his throat, for he could see that it wasn't a man but a woman's body, cruelly mangled. A flickering streetlight nearby caused the lifeless face to glow an eerie, pale green. *Dear God, don't let it be Monica.*

"Bring the bloody ladder here, for pity's sake," an Englishman demanded, with typically restrained annoyance.

Getting close enough to make out the features of the hideously contorted body, Davies heard his own voice cry out as he realized that the lifeless face staring back at him belonged to Madame Lin.

Elder Brother's threats, the recent execution, the death of his Chinese friend by the hand of her lover, even the confrontation with the arrogant German - it had all, finally, become too much. Davies slumped to the sidewalk, buried his head in his hands, and wept for the first time since his childhood.

XXI. BROKEN GLASS

Mercifully, no one disturbed him as he sobbed on the sidewalk. The citizens of Shanghai were so accustomed to dramas enacted on the streets of their city that they were comfortable to let them play themselves out.

After a full five minutes had passed, Davies rose and made his way toward the entrance of the hotel. Then he saw her. On the far side of the crowd, hurrying toward the street, was Madame Lin's niece. Her head was down as if she was trying to avoid being seen. Davies circled around, and as she was about to slip into a cab he strode forward and took hold of her slender wrist. The girl was so disoriented that she hardly responded. Her face was pale, the artery on the side of her neck throbbing rapidly.

"Monica, do you know what happened? Is that your window back there that she...?" Davies gestured toward the hotel and saw that somebody had found a ladder and was trying to pry the hanging body loose from the portico.

As a fireman hurried past them, Monica turned and caught sight of the body. Her mouth dropped open with the best rendition of surprise Davies had seen in a long time. She covered her mouth with her free hand and began to wilt. Quickly, he helped her into the back of the cab. Maybe she was acting, but Davies was no longer sure; it appeared that she really had no idea that her aunt had died until she had just now seen her. So why had she been hurrying in the first place? "Driver, let's go."

The cab took off with a jerk and a whine. Davies turned back toward the young woman who appeared to be drifting into a state of shock. He took her thin hands and rubbed them briskly. "Monica, I'm very sorry, but if you can talk I need to know what happened."

She remained expressionless.

"All right," Davies said as soothingly as he could, "give me your purse."

She drew the purse tightly to her breast.

"This is for your own good, Monica. Come on, I don't have all night." He snatched the purse from her, then slid open the dividing glass window. "Driver!" he called out, "pull over!"

The thin-faced, large-nosed taxi driver swung to the curb. With puzzled hostility, he stared into the rear view mirror. Davies scribbled a note on a business card and handed it to the cabbie. "Meet me at this address in three hours. Just drive around in the meantime, and don't let her out of your sight. Do you understand?"

The cab driver acted as if he didn't.

"Here," Davies gave the cabbie ten Mex dollars. "I'll pay you twice that when get back with her. Can you look after her? She's quite distraught."

"This is not a problem," the driver said in a thick Russian accent - his feigned disapproval having vanished at the prospect of being lavishly overpaid.

Davies pushed the door open and slid out. The young woman's eyes widened and she reached out and tried to reclaim the handbag, but he jerked it out of reach. "I'm sorry, Monica, but I'll keep the purse - I'm afraid I can't afford to be stood up." As he slammed the door, and the taxi drove off, a fleeting shaft of light fell upon a narrow section of the rear compartment and revealed that there was blood on Monica's dress. He signaled for the taxi to stop, but he was too late.

Had the red smudge come from Madame Lin? Monica had seemed genuinely astonished when she'd caught sight of her aunt on the portico, yet what other explanation could there be?

The red stain shimmered in his imagination, a terrible reminder of what had just happened. My God, Madame Lin of all people - a difficult, obstinate woman, often cold and petty - but a woman of character; always struggling with herself, trying to be the best she could, refusing to cower in the light of truth. A woman, despite her aloof manner, who could sense feelings and respond to another's pain with an ease and a strength far beyond what his clumsy, selfish emotions were capable of.

He thought of her vanity, the beautiful dresses, the perfect hair and porcelain face, everything groomed to a level of perfection that became surreal. Then the bitter irony of having everything she put so much effort into hideously ridiculed by the manner in which she had died. The ultimate insult, dealt by a sadistic universe.

Despite these disturbing thoughts, a part of him felt an odd relief that he now had a crystal clear mission: to find Madame Lin's killer. If a trail of clues pointed directly to Monica, she could be pretty and sad and have a wonderful explanation for everything, but she would be punished harshly, no two ways about it. All that mattered was seeing Madame Lin's death avenged.

A distinguished-looking gentleman, out for a stroll with his wife, was staring at him oddly. Davies remembered the purse under his arm and blew the man a kiss – such flippancy was probably inappropriate under the circumstances – but Madame Lin's death was far more inappropriate and he was angry – grief would have to wait its turn.

He walked to the Hispano and locked the purse securely in a rear cabinet, then continued on to the hotel. He wasn't worried about Monica disappearing - she had no luggage with her when he'd intercepted her, and her passport and visa had both been in her handbag; clearly her options for escape were limited.

Davies walked through the busy lobby and glanced at the front desk; nobody was checking out. Fine, he could look into that later. He took advantage of the general state of confusion to make for the stairwell, noting that the English firemen must have gone back to their party. Taking two stairs at a time, he checked each floor until he reached the fourth. He stepped out onto a long, elegantly flowered carpet, entering a hallway, which smelled of perfume and cigarettes. He was hoping to run into his hireling, but Leibowitz was nowhere to be seen.

Ahead, two uniformed policemen stood outside a room that was directly over the portico. The policemen would try to keep him out, but he went right up to them, hoping to spy a familiar face through the open doorway. He was in luck. "Ah, Inspector Singletone," Davies said as the coppers roughly grabbed him by the shoulders. "It's reassuring to see this investigation will be in good hands."

"Just happened to be on the premises, did you?" Singletone muttered, not bothering to look up from his examination of Madame Lin's wooden purse. "Really, what are you doing here,

Davies?" He gave the cops a quick glance. "Let the bloke through, he'll make us look good as he tries to play detective."

"Inspector," Davies said, entering. Though he'd sparred with Singletone in the past, the man was a dedicated professional, as capable as anyone in Shanghai of finding Madame Lin's killer; it was good that he was aboard.

Inspector Singletone was a relentlessly average-looking man, average height and average build, with a ruddy complexion, a clover field of freckles on his pale forehead, and a weed patch of thinning, reddish blond hair. His tone was ever-serious, but he was a master of gallows humor and it took one no short while to realize that a great deal of what he said was in jest - especially since he looked the part of humorless policeman. Davies was always amused by people who looked the way they were expected to look, and apparently Singletone was too, using his own appearance as a way of quietly kidding everyone he encountered.

"If you're wondering if she jumped," Singletone said dryly, "she knocked over a table, broke a lamp and smashed several window panes doing it. Possibly in training for a new Olympic event. Don't touch anything, Davies."

He knew that Singletone had only allowed him to enter because he was regarded as a suspect. Nodding toward the purse, Davies asked, "Find anything?"

Singleton had spread the contents of the wooden purse out on the table before him. There was some make-up, a few pieces of Madame Lin's prized tamarind candy, an address book, some cigarettes, and several more unimportant odds and ends. "Someone took all her cash, can't imagine why."

Davies moved in for a closer look. The scrap of brown paper with the baggage tag didn't seem to be present. "Looks like there must have been a real brawl in here. Did anyone hear anything?"

"Not a peep. Bit of a surprise."

A neat, young plainclothes policeman came through the door, breathing hard. "She registered under the name of Norma Stirling, Inspector. Apparently the victim was her aunt. We've five people who saw her going down the stairs and out the building just after it happened."

"No sign of the girl?" Singletone asked wearily.

"It appears that she gave us the slip."

The inspector stared pointedly at Davies. "You know anything about this, old sport?"

'A little," Davies replied, wondering why Monica had registered under an alias. "I was acquainted with the victim - her name was Madame Lin, or did you know?"

"We're being awfully cooperative, aren't we?"

"Madame Lin was a very dear friend. I want to see her killer brought to justice just as much as you do."

"Ah, yes, I recall that you are rather fond of the slopes." Singletone took out a small note book. "May I ask where you've been during the past hour?"

Davies laughed. "I do have a criminal look about me."

The inspector gazed at him coldly - waiting.

"I was driving along the Bund in an open car until twenty minutes ago, Inspector. I'm sure four or five hundred people saw me."

"We'll check with all of them. Were you acquainted with this Miss Marshall, the woman staying in this room?"

Davies hoped to heaven nobody had seen him in the taxi with Monica. "I thought her name was 'Norma Stirling.'"

"Well then, she'd better change the lettering on her luggage, and the labels on her clothes. They all say 'Monica Marshall.' If you're going to play games with me, Davies, I'll gladly ask you down to the station where we can be alone, just the two of us."

Davies gave a cooperative nod. "I believe 'Monica Marshall' is correct. I don't know her that well, Inspector. But still, I can't imagine the girl doing something like this. Must have run away because she was frightened by the man who did it."

Evasively, Davies moved to the bedroom door. A small Chinese coin lay in the doorway. - it was a rare piece of copper cash, the kind used in the previous century. As he remembered it, this commonest of coins bore, for centuries, the impression of a woman's thumbnail. Supposedly Yang Kwei-fei, the courtesan of Hsuan Tsung, the "Lustrous Emperor," had made a "moon mark" with her nail on the clay mold, 1,200 years before. Davies picked up the coin, it was worn but the mark was there - extraordinary. He handed the coin to a frowning Detective Singletone, and peered into the bedroom.

The bedroom was neat and orderly, and Davies thought of how a mood alters perceptions so dramatically. It was a pretty room, nicely decorated - but tonight nothing seemed pretty. This room, the hotel, Shanghai, and the dark sky above it were all part of a universe that had become disfigured and depraved.

* * *

Nicolai adored Shanghai. There was always so much going on. It was easy to make money here, much easier than it had been in Leningrad.

His favorite thing was the music. The Chinese music, of course, was strange and annoying; but jazz was everywhere. He could even get it on the car radio he'd mounted and wired himself. It had taken him over a year to save up for that radio, but it was worth it. He'd just asked the woman in the back of his taxi if she minded the music, but all she'd done was look out the window. He took this as a sign of her approval - which was good because his favorite song had just begun to play: "Yes We Have No Bananas": a celebration of his own special way of speaking - what could be more wonderful?

He was curious about the young woman in the back seat. After the man had left, she'd stopped her crying so fast that Nicolai was sure that her tears had been an act. But now he wasn't so sure. He knew fragments of many languages and had tried to strike up a conversation first in English, then in Chinese, then in French, then in German, and finally in Russian - but she'd refused to answer in any tongue. Her silence was more troubling than her tears; her emotions seemed very genuine, and very heavy. She would make a good Russian heroine - brooding like a thunderhead.

He didn't care much for Russian women, too stocky, too melodramatic. He liked the little Chinese girls, just like this one. They were always sweet and funny. Nobody bothered him here if he had a Chinese girlfriend, just as long as he didn't flaunt her. Another reason why he was starting to think that he might stay in Shanghai awhile. Originally he'd viewed it as a stepping stone to America. But what did America have that Shanghai didn't have? A stupid prohibition against liquor, that's what.

He hoped he'd be able to see what happened when the man came back. With any luck the well-dressed fellow would also want to take a long ride in Nicolai's cab. It would be interesting to see if his hunch was right - though he knew it was. The man was going back to his wife, that was obvious. But would the tears return? Would there be a scene - a good and proper brawl in the street? Torn clothes and finally a young woman left alone needing a broad Georgian shoulder to cry on? Sometimes he thought he had the best job in the world.

* * *

XXII. TREES

Glancing out the window, Davies could see that two policemen had climbed onto the portico and were struggling to dislodge Madame Lin's body. He couldn't avoid noticing that her clothes were quite bloody. God, it was awful.

In Westerns one regularly saw fighting cowboys sail through a picture window and land on a dusty street, where they resumed their brawl without missing a beat. In fact, broken glass could be lethal; many who had blundered through windows found themselves bleeding profusely from a dozen sources - the lucky ones escaped with multiple stitches, the unlucky died from blood loss within minutes of lightheadedly joking about what a mess they'd made. There was enough blood on Madame Lin's body to suggest she had perished this way; the coroner would have the final verdict.

Davies turned again to face the ravaged interior. The room was making him dizzy, or perhaps it was his mood that forced him to sit down on the window sill. There was something indescribable at play, like one of those roadside mystery spots where gravity was a bit off.

Now that was odd - the table that supported a lamp and the phone had toppled over, depositing both on the carpet. Yet a nearby wastebasket, which should have been knocked over by the table, was intact. Davies moved to the wastebasket and realized, from the debris *beside* it, that it had been overturned, then righted and put neatly back in place.

"I wouldn't touch that."

"Come look at this."

"What ever did you find? Evidence that our killer was remorseful and decided to tidy up a bit?" Singletone remarked laconically, as he came to Davies' side.

"Tell me what you make of this." Davies pointed to two lonely scraps of crumpled paper lying at the bottom of the wastebasket.

"I said don't touch!" Singletone squatted, inelegantly, removed the papers with his gloved hands, and carefully unfolded them.

One scrap was blank, the other was the tail end of a telegram, which was signed "H.W." Both scraps were smeared with dried blood. "Hello? What's that?" Singletone said, taking a last item from the wastebasket. "It looks like a cigarette holder."

"It must be Madame Lin's. What the hell was it doing in there? Which begs the next question - where's the rest of the bloody telegram?"

"Literally bloody." Singletone rose and began to read the words on the printed scrap of paper.

"Do you mind if I take a look?" Davies asked, peering over the inspector's shoulder. "I found it, after all."

"Finders keepers doesn't apply to police business." Singletone put the two bloody pieces of torn paper in his jacket pocket, then shouted orders to his men to begin a search for the rest of the telegram. This only made Davies more curious to know what had been in the confiscated fragment.

"There's bloodstains here on this chair," Smixon, the burly constable, yelled with rosy-faced enthusiasm.

"I'm well aware of that, constable," Singletone hollered back. "It's the fragment of a telegram we're after, remember?" He turned to look disapprovingly at Davies. "What would you bet that we find the rest of it on your absent lady friend?"

"How should I know? You didn't allow me to read so much as a word of the thing."

"I will grant you one thing," Singletone said as he looked around the room, "whoever we're dealing with - they're damaged goods, that's plain enough."

"Wouldn't that be true of any murderer?"

Singletone continued to gaze into space. "I don't know, I've been doing this for years and one gets a feeling. This is something else - a cut above, if you will. Or should I say, 'a cut below.'"

Davies moved to the door, wondering why the inspector felt the need to drop hints about information he was unwilling to divulge. "An interesting theory, but I need to look after my car. I'll be back."

"Davies," Singletone yelled after him like a mother pleading with her son to wear his galoshes, "would you mind popping around my office in the morning? Say tennish?"

Damn these early risers. "Certainly, Inspector. Is there anything in particular you want to chat about?"

"No, it will simply cheer me to see your face in the morning. If you run into Miss Marshall, perhaps you could bring her along with you."

"Ahh. Well, in that case, I too will very much be looking forward to it."

Davies hurried down to the lobby and walked straight up to the front desk. He tried to appear official as he addressed the forbidding, thick-faced, seemingly humorless desk clerk. "I'm with the investigation upstairs."

"Yes, dreadful business, isn't it?" the man said in a tone far more friendly and genuinely concerned than Davies had anticipated. "Have they found much?"

"I can't say. But you can help me. Has anyone checked out within the past hour?"

"Yes, I'm afraid this business sent them packing. Mr. and Mrs. Trees, just across the hall, you know. They were quite distraught."

"I see. What room exactly?"

"Four-seventeen."

Logic dictated that this room was, indeed, right across from Monica's. "Ah, right. And where can I post a cable?"

"They can help you at the end of the desk there."

"Thanks." Frankly, Davies was surprised that his hunch had paid off so quickly.

At the end of the desk, the youthful clerks in attendance were painfully sincere. "May I help you?" the younger-looking of the two asked. He was English, thin and officious, with a schoolboy pink complexion - obviously starting at the bottom rung on his way up the hotel management ladder.

"I'm interested in any telegrams that Mr. and Mrs. Trees may have sent out or received. Particularly recent ones."

"Well, that information is confidential, you understand."

"I understand, but I'm with the investigation."

"Very good, sir. But if you don't mind my being forward, might I see some identification?"

Davies handed the lad a five pound note. Awkwardly, the young fellow pocketed it - this sort of thing was new for him, but not unappreciated. "Well, uh, uh," he stammered, "two radiograms came in within this afternoon, actually. I think Mr. Trees retrieved them about two hours ago."

Davies nodded. "I see. Did he give you anything to send out?"

"Well, yes. It's still here, the courier's due to pick it up any minute now."

Davies stared at the clerk who was refusing to take the hint. "You've been very helpful so far." Davies slipped the Englishman another pound.

The thin Englishman looked very put upon. Nonetheless, he took the money and returned with an envelope, which he slid over to Davies, hoping that nobody would notice.

Fortunately, Tree's penmanship was as neat as the young English clerk's well-starched shirt and carefully knotted bow tie. The note read simply, "Reserve suite with ocean view for Trees, September 8 - 11." The cable was addressed to the Moana Hotel in Honolulu.

"How would you describe Mr. and Mrs. Trees?" Davies asked, returning the telegram.

"Well, in truth, I never saw them."

"But weren't you here when they sent this radiogram?"

"No, actually. I mean, I was. But they sent the draft down with the bellman."

"Then who checked them out? I understand they left less than an hour ago."

The Englishman began to turn an even more flattering shade of pink. He quickly conferred with his assistant, who seemed equally flustered. In short order, the first young clerk returned his attention to Davies. "You see, sir, they phoned to have their bags brought down, and asked that their bill be sent up to their room. They left payment in an envelope with their bellman."

"Let me speak to the bellman."

The bellhop was summoned and quizzed, as were various other clerks, maids and elevator operators. When the proverbial smoke had cleared, memos had been left on tables, commanding voices had come out of closed bathroom doors, and no one had actually seen either of the Trees. This development was strange in and of itself, and certainly suspicious. Davies felt increasingly confident that he had blundered onto Madame Lin's true killer. However, aside from the name Trees, and a reservation at the Moana Hotel, the only thing that he was able to call a lead was the revelation that the mysterious room-holders had been traveling with a maroon steamer trunk.

"Just one trunk for two people?" Davies asked.

"Now that you mention it, that is odd, isn't it?" The young clerk replied.

"So the only reason you think they're a couple is because they checked in as one? I wonder if we're dealing with just one person?"

The clerk's expression remained blank, this all seemed over his head. If Trees was an individual, and not a couple, his, or her sex, remained unknown - the voice heard on the house phone was described as soft and deep, not definitively masculine or feminine.

"Did the Trees ever make any inquiries about Miss Marshall?"

"Miss who?"

"The woman in room four-fourteen, where the investigation is being conducted."

"Oh, Miss Stirling. I can't say. As we told you, none of us ever saw either of them. There was one thing, though, a bit odd."

"Yes?" Davies asked, his voice brightening with expectation.

"Right before checking out, they asked that a large, empty fruit jar with a good strong lid be sent up from the kitchen. I was instructed to leave it outside the door."

"Strange."

Davies contributed another pound, and was able to get a peek at Monica's registration card. Her address was listed only as: "San Francisco, U.S.A.," and she spelled Stirling with an "i."

He returned to the other side of the desk, and had little difficulty getting the key to room four-seventeen from the falsely stern man, who now seemed even more eager to help.

Unfortunately, the Astor House's housekeeping staff was far too efficient. If there were any tell-tale blood smears on any of the door knobs or cabinet handles in Trees' recently vacated rooms, they had already been wiped clean. With a limited command of English, the busy fleet of Chinese maids were difficult to communicate with. Nonetheless, Davies had a go at it. "Can I look?" he asked, pointing to a bag of laundry lying near the front door. Before the maids could answer, he peered into the laundry bag; disappointingly it contained ordinary sheets.

He proceeded to the bathroom where all the towel racks were empty. "What happened to the towels? Towels," Davies repeated, carefully.

"No towels," the leader of the maids answered back.

"Already laundry?"

"No towels." She smiled, demurely. "Steal."

He grappled with her meaning. "Guest steal?"

She nodded with enthusiasm. "Yes, guest. No towel here."

If Trees was a souvenir hunter it was curious that he'd taken the towels and left the ashtrays, which Davies could see were still present. Things were starting to add up. Trees had used the towels to clean up the blood on his hands and clothes. He might have tossed them somewhere, but more likely he'd packed them in his luggage. There was a small chance that another approach could help Davies tell for sure if Trees was their killer. Removing his handkerchief from his breast pocket he returned to the bathroom. As he suspected, the sink looked pristine. With the handkerchief, he carefully wiped around the base of each nickeled fixture.

Between the tiled bathroom wall and the free standing sink was a two-inch gap. Now he jammed the cloth into this gap and moved it about, picking up whatever he could from the back of the sink. Withdrawing the handkerchief he saw that marks of red and pink were clearly evident on it. He'd be willing to bet his Bugatti that a test would show the stains to be of Madame Lin's blood type.

This discovery inspired him to give the room a second going over. The Chinese help must have thought him eccentric as he peered under the bed, and beneath furniture. Nothing more was found, however. No matter, he already had enough. And it made sense, he realized, that no one had heard a struggle in Monica's apartment. Most of the other rooms on the floor were rather distant, while the guest who was closest, and most likely to report strange sounds, was Trees himself, (or herself.)

As Davies left the room, which had recently harbored Trees, he felt a grim satisfaction that came from knowing he was on the right track, and that someone was going to pay dearly for butchering Madame Lin - additionally, that his faith in Monica was not misplaced. There was order in the Universe after all, a reassurance born of a very strange set of circumstances.

He decided to share his discoveries with Singletone, despite the peril involved. The evidence about the Trees was circumstantial, and Singletone would be furious with Davies' "interference" in his investigation. Across the hall, Singletone's second in command, the burly sergeant named Smixon, stared at Davies, threateningly. Nonetheless, Davies persevered. He soon regretted his decision.

"A tidy little tale," Singletone said as if surmising a magazine serial, "which casts Miss Marshall as a hapless innocent threatened by sinister forces. Of course, I only have your word for it. And even if this handkerchief is found to contain someone's blood, from a shaving mishap no doubt, you've had a good forty minutes to weave a story that wraps everything up neatly and gives you a reason to skip town with your lady friend. Are you hoping for a sailing gift?"

"This is exactly why people don't assist the police."

"But you can assist, Davies - by being in my office tomorrow at ten with Miss Marshall."

It seemed like a good time to leave. Davies was grateful that Singletone allowed him to do so.

Before abandoning the hotel altogether, Davies made a search for Leibowitz; however, his hired spy was nowhere to be found - maybe he was out following Monica's taxi.

Returning to the Hispano, Davies instructed Max to drive him to the French Club.

Once inside the club, he sat at the same spindly desk, telephoned Lo-Chien, and instructed him to have one of the servants drive over in the Model T suburban sedan that the staff used for shopping, and park it behind the club.

After a half-hour had passed, Davies strolled out of the rear of the French Club, found the suburban, and instructed the waiting servant to take the night off, giving the man a wad of cash along with a directive to make his way home, either by taxi or rickshaw, sometime before the close of the weekend. Davies then climbed into the Ford and used it to motor to his meeting place with Monica. Confident that he was unobserved, because Singletone's men were watching the Hispano, he parked, switched off the trembling engine, and made a thorough inspection of the girl's purse, which he'd brought with him.

Her wallet contained five hundred and forty-three American dollars, a little disturbing considering that Madame Lin had been robbed. There was a passport and a visa identifying Monica as a twenty-one-year-old American citizen residing in San Mateo, California. Damn it, "San Mateo!" The interrupted address on the scrap of brown paper he'd found at Hong Fat's had said, "teo, California." That made a pretty solid connection between Monica, the missing staff, and Hong Fat.

He continued his search, finding the usual feminine accouterments: lipstick, a compact, eye shadow, a small bottle of expensive French perfume, a handkerchief, a silk scarf, a pair of dark glasses, a small, dirty Kewpie doll, and loose change. A piece of hard tamarind candy, still wrapped, caught his attention; it was the kind that Madame Lin favored. Had it been given to Monica as a peace offering? He placed the candy in his pocket, and went on with his search, finding a note on a napkin that said, "Call me if you need a friend," signed, "M," and then a local phone number. Otherwise, there was nothing out of the ordinary. Mercifully, there was no sign of the missing telegram.

Had the slaughter of Madame Lin been happenstance or premeditated? Had money been taken from Madame Lin's purse for appearances only, by someone other than Monica? Somehow he knew Singletone was right, this wasn't a simple crime, there was much more to it.

His imagination was taking off at a full gallop, so it was time to calm it down by putting his mother's hat on. Davies' mother was good Midwestern pioneer stock, and her practicality and skepticism had kept his father from going off the deep end. Davies' father was a dreamer and adventurer who'd made a fortune doing a lot of remarkably stupid things. This had been the secret of his success, trying what others never thought of, frankly, because others were more sensible. But his mother had tempered his father's wild enthusiasm with cold logic and preached, as if it were hell fire and brimstone, that one should "never assume." So whenever Davies felt especially cocky and sure of himself and like his father, he had trained himself to think like his mother. What would she make of these new clues? His mother would be unimpressed he realized, a little sadly. She'd scold him for even thinking of sailing off to Honolulu because a mysterious individual had been staying across the hall from Monica, and had happened to check out right after the murder. "I would have too," he could hear her insisting. Perhaps the name, "Trees," which screamed *alias*, had been chosen because the husband and wife, who really existed, had an unpronounceable Eastern European name and liked to go by something that people could remember and spell. As for missing towels and the blood, perhaps Trees had been a good Samaritan who'd tried to help Madame Lin, then fled realizing that he, or she, might be held as a suspect. He remembered the blood on Monica's dress, and suddenly things weren't adding up at all nicely. Sometimes he really hated his mother.

Drumming on Monica's purse, resting beside him on the passenger seat, he gazed out at the river, which sparkled with the lights of a hundred boats and ships, as his mind began to flood with new questions. Had Madame Lin been the killer's target? Or had Monica? Was it a case of mistaken identity? Could Madame Lin have walked in on a botched robbery? If so, what had the killer been after? The missing, bloody telegram? Something Davies hadn't learned of yet? Or "the clouded twilight" itself, believing, incorrectly, that Monica still had it? And why, after all was said and done, had Trees left so quickly for Honolulu? Was his mission accomplished - or incomplete? Dammit, it was monstrously inconvenient of Leibowitz to have disappeared at this time; he might have seen everything - he'd better report in soon.

However, even if Leibowitz came through with vital information, Davies had a feeling that the answer was out there, somewhere beyond Shanghai. To hell with his mother, and her cautious thinking. In his gut he knew that it was time to leave.

XXIII. DARK URGES

The Model T was parked in front of the Hongkong & Shanghai Banking Corporation, No. 12, the Bund. Davies checked his watch for the sixth time in twenty minutes, ten-forty-three and no sign of Monica. He was getting anxious. No more than three dozen autos had passed since he had arrived, so he couldn't have missed her. Besides, most of the traffic at this late hour was of the quaint variety: rickshaws, pedestrian water carriers and coolies collecting night soil, all of them passing silently, like bats flitting through the darkness.

Davies exhaled heavily, and removed the handkerchief from his jacket. The pink and red stains had already turned brown, more indications that what he'd found in the crevasses of the sink was blood.

Putting the cloth back into his pocket, he fixed his gaze on the dark street, mentally going down the list of things that needed to be done.

In deference to his mother, Davies would do a little more snooping before discharging his servants and closing his villa. If no new clues contradicted his theories, he'd send a registered letter to John Crockwood authorizing him to sell the place, deposit the proceeds in Davies' bank, and pocket a nice commission for himself.

At the bank, he would secure a letter of credit from Mr. Chen and withdraw five thousand dollars in cash.

He would arrange for his last shipment of arms to be sold to his number-two boy at a fifty-per-cent discount.

The Hispano-Suiza, and his cute little Bugatti that never ran, would be stored at Mitchell's on Edinburgh Road. He'd decide later whether to sell them or have them shipped to the States.

He had considered buying tickets on a night train, and then reserving a room at the Grand Hotel in Peiping for the benefit of Elder Brother, but the man was too resourceful - honesty would be the best policy. He'd still buy tickets on the night train, but they'd be for the benefit of the police.

He took the piece of tamarind candy from his pocket and rolled it around in his hand.   Could Elder Brother have ordered an underling to murder Madame Lin, then plant evidence suggesting that the killer had fled towards America - all to provide Davies with an extra incentive to travel to San Francisco and fulfill his obligation to the gangster? Was he being played for a sucker?

There were a couple of notable flaws in this theory: if Trees worked for Elder Brother, the trail he or she had left behind was far too subtle.   Why not leave bloody towels in plain sight, for instance, if the whole affair was a ruse?   Besides, it was inconceivable that the most powerful man in China would resort to cheap trickery, it would be an admission of weakness.

With one puzzle unfolding to reveal another, Davies still had been unable to find Trees booked out of Shanghai on any mode of transportation.   As an afterthought, he'd called the airport from the French Club.   Flights had only been leaving Shanghai for a couple of years, but established routes to several Chinese cities already existed. A plane for Hong Kong had left Lunghua Field roughly an hour after Madame Lin had been murdered.   This created a troubling scenario.   The Nippon Yusen Kaisha company had a steamer sailing from Hong Kong for San Francisco via Honolulu in eighteen hours.   It was too late for Davies to reach this ship before it sailed, even using an airplane.   However, if Trees had managed to catch the earlier flight, he had a fair chance of boarding the Japanese liner in Hong Kong.

Davies found it astonishing that he had managed to work any of these scenarios out in his head, because he was only thinking at half-speed.   Every idea that he mulled over was brought to a thudding halt by the memory of Madame Lin's ugly death, rather like a car being made to stop at a railroad intersection.   He'd finally forced himself to make a list, which featured big gaps in its text, caused when he'd paused and stared mindlessly at the paper for minutes at a time.

Despite his sympathy for her, many of the facts did point to Monica as the killer.   He knew that Madame Lin's own instinct had been to avoid Monica because she was a "danger to others."   Davies had ridiculed her for mistrusting her niece, insisting that Monica was perfectly sane – but had Madame Lin been right all along?   Had Davies' completely unsubstantiated assurances about

Monica caused his dear old friend to go to her own death? He realized that he was developing a desperate need to prove that Monica had not killed Madame Lin, simply to clear his own conscience.

He rubbed at a distracting smudge on the glass of the Model T's lone instrument, an ammeter, and something else occurred to him. One steamer trunk for two people couldn't be overlooked - nor could the fact that no one had actually seen Trees. But why would one individual check into a hotel and masquerade as a couple? He remembered his mother's words, "never assume," and suddenly the answer wasn't so difficult to construe - it had everything to do with Shanghai's wicked character.

He was led to think of a friend of John's, another resident of this outrageous city where long traditions of depravity had become virtually institutionalized. The friend was an elderly bachelor, very wealthy, who would leave two dollars on his mantle every Saturday after dinner, and then go out for an hour's stroll. On his return, his resourceful oriental servants were expected to have a Chinese girl waiting for him. When the bachelor's Chinese friends found out about this, they were mortified - two dollars was the sailor's price and it was a serious loss of face that their friend would be content with such a cheap whore - after all, this reflected badly on them. Therefore, every Saturday, the Chinese merchants banded together and procured for their thrifty neighbor a girl from Soochow, a nearby city known for its lovely women.   This woman's companionship cost ten or twenty times what the elderly bachelor was willing to pay, but the old man never found out, and his neighbors were happy. Perhaps Trees was just such a man - a lonely visitor to Shanghai, he had taken rooms across from Monica's for the sole purpose of spying on her, and stalking Madame Lin. But out of the numerous less than upright choices in Shanghai, Monica had selected a respectable hotel.   If Trees wanted to invite a sing-song girl back to his room, he would have been asked to leave. However, if Mr. Trees had registered as a couple, telling the desk that his wife was to join him shortly from an outing in the country, he could bring at least one girl masquerading as his wife up to his rooms without protest - or several wearing proper clothes and a heavy veil. The more Davies thought about it, the more it seemed to click; there was no Mrs.

Trees, only a strange man with dark urges to be satisfied as he carried out his darker mission.

A set of slow moving headlights reflected in his rear view mirror. Davies turned as a car approached from behind, the driver apparently checking addresses - then the taxi pulled to the curb in front of him and the lights went off. Thank goodness, she was finally here. Davies quickly unlatched the door and stepped out. He crossed to the taxi and paid the Russian the handsome bonus he'd been promised. The man smiled broadly, but hesitated to leave. Davies decided to ignore him, leaving him parked at the curb, softly whistling "The Sheik Of Araby."

As Monica stepped out of the taxi, Davies was again struck by how pretty she was - mis-colored and excessively exotic perhaps, but frankly, more beautiful - definitely more voluptuous. Her high heels clicked on the pavement as he took her arm and escorted her to the Model T. She clung to his sleeve in a flattering way, her eyes darting about.

"I've come down in the world," he said as they reached the car. "Incidentally, your aunt was pushed out of your bedroom window about six-thirty. At least five witnesses claim to have seen you both before and after the crime." It was a fine "how-do-you-do," he was a true master of charm.

Davies noted a fleeting expression of anxiety on her face. Damn! If she would only speak. "There was someone staying across the hall from you. Do you remember seeing him?"

She glanced downward as if she was examining the pinstripe on one of the wooden spokes on the Model T's rear wheel - it was a telling reaction.

"Monica?"

She didn't respond - standing so still and expressionless that he fantasized that he could leave and return in two hours and find her in the same spot, holding the same pose.

He was of two minds: on one hand he felt so frustrated, powerless, and guilty that he had a strong desire to throttle her. On the other hand, he'd concluded that her maddening silence was due to real trauma, and the bloodstain on her dress might not brand her as a murderess as much as it represented another emotional assault on an innocent who had, once again, found herself in the wrong place at the wrong time. Considering the sadness rather than the horror of what had happened to Madame Lin a couple of hours earlier his violent urge faded. "Monica, please, I'm trying to help you!"

Her pretty little mouth remained set in a determined frown - a trembling at the edge of the lips offered the only hope that he'd made some kind of impression.

"All right, now listen, can't you muster a little courage and speak? I believe your aunt's killer was staying across from you, right under your nose. I believe that her killer has already left for Honolulu. I'm sailing within the next twenty-four hours to go after him."

She looked up at him with surprise; apparently she hadn't expected him to take such bold steps.

"You don't know me, I can't promise you anything, and my whole trip may be a waste of time. You can come with me - or you can stay. But consider that you're the prime suspect, and the police will find you and charge you with your aunt's murder. So what's it to be? Stay or go?"

Her blank expression morphed into one of suspicion. She studied him, unwilling to make a move toward the car's open door. Could he blame her? Though a part of him was ready to bust her in the chops, he had to remind himself that she'd also been through hell and didn't know him from Adam.

"Monica," he said, gently taking her arm, "can't you comprehend that a wonderful woman is dead. I advised her to be kind to you - was that a horrible mistake? The police think you did it, and frankly your behavior goes a long way to persuade me that they are right. If you saw something, and can point me in the right direction, now is the time to speak up."

She pulled her arm free of his grip, walked to his car and climbed in. There, she sat primly in the passenger seat, waiting for him to join her.

Now he was the one who wouldn't respond. Who was she, really? A murderess – or a victim? This was a moment of decision, it wouldn't be so hard to drag her out of the car and leave her in the street. Yet, if she had killed her aunt, wasn't it better to have her with him? The last thing he wanted was to go all the way to Honolulu - only to learn that Trees was innocent and Monica was guilty - then be forced to sail back to Shanghai and try and find the childish mute.

"I don't know why I'm doing this," he muttered as he climbed in beside her, slamming the door with either an appropriate or an inappropriate bang, depending on which of his conflicted moods he decided to favor. "As the Chinese say, 'we go Ningpo more far.'"

XXIV. THE NEW ELDER BROTHER

No Sin was not so easy to find. Davies left Monica in the Model T, again without her purse. Starting where he'd dropped the Chinese lad the previous day, he searched along the banks of Soochow Creek, then in the small park near the waterfront. Hundreds of beggars and derelicts were huddled in little groups, gambling, talking, cooking rice over tiny fires - so many that, on a clear summer night, the park was shrouded in a yellowish brown fog that stung the eyes. The smell of cooking vegetables, boiling oil, and unwashed bodies was overwhelming.

He had handed out dozens of coins before a tiny boy with a swollen stomach led him by the hand to a bench at the far end of the park. There, beneath an improvised blanket of newspaper and straw lay "No Sin," looking like a lumpy bag of produce. Somehow Davies wasn't surprised that Sin was curled beneath the bench, rather than lying on it; a choice that was so consistent with the lad's peculiar style of defiance. Davies gave him a gentle kick. The boy rolled over, vanishing behind the bench in an apparently defensive maneuver. A moment later his head cautiously appeared behind the back rest, apprising his attacker. Recognizing Davies, he rose and bowed, an enormous grin enveloping his battered face.

"Mr. Davies, I am very surprising."

"Sin, you said you wanted to repay me."

"Yes, yes. I do something you want."

"Very good, I'm ready to give you your chance. I have to leave town. Right away. Okay?"

"Okay," the lad echoed, and he took Davies by the elbow and guided him through the park as if he were a gracious host leading a guest to the sitting room. He moved stiffly and his face was still puffy, giving him a slightly piggish look. "I have friends. It good you come to me. They don't charge too much. Where you want to go?"

"Foochow."

"Ahhh," the boy nodded.

"And, Sin, a young lady will be coming along with us."

No Sin gave him a disapproving glance through all the swollen flesh. "A white-faced lady?"

"No," Davies said.

The boy appeared concerned. "A Chinese lady?"

"Partly. She's a little of both."

No Sin came to an abrupt halt and stared at him. "I do not understand. How can she be both?"

"It happens."

No Sin shook his head. "I do not think it should happen. You should not associate with such a person, Mr. Davies. No. You can lose face. I think you know better."

"'Face' doesn't concern me, Sin."

"You the boss," he said with resignation.

"If it's consolation," Davies added, wondering why he was trying to justify himself to an adolescent Chinese upstart, "the reason I'm leaving Shanghai is to find a very bad person. Tell me again, did anyone suspicious visit Hong Fat's shop within the past two weeks?"

No Sin nodded.

"Who?"

"I tell you already. - who you think he bought the emperor stick from? That stinky little guy."

"So you didn't have the staff for twelve years?" Davies smiled.

No Sin responded with a pained look. "Why, you believe that stuff? Come on. I know you smart."

"Don't worry, I didn't believe you." That seemed to please the boy. "And you never saw anyone else who troubled you?"

The boy nodded again.

"Is that 'yes' or 'no'?"

"'Yes', I never saw no one else who bother me - don't you pay attention?"

"Tell me again, what did the suspicious man look like?"

"Well, he was little man." The boy indicated a height of about three feet, which Davies assumed was an exaggeration. "Wore glasses and big hat. Talk too much. Could never get him to shut up."

"Anything else?"

"No."

The boy had led Davies onto a wharf lined with the shadowy outlines of junks. Now he stopped next to a squatty, barrel-chested sailor with dark, oily skin and opium-stained teeth who was coiling ropes at the side of his boat. While No Sin talked, the sailor continued his work, spitting occasionally, as he shifted positions and glanced off at other junks. When No Sin finished, the man straightened and took a long, contemptuous look at Davies - then he spat again and walked off, disappearing below deck.

"Do not worry, please, Mr. Davies," No Sin said, "he will come back chop, chop."

"What's he doing?"

No Sin shrugged. "Burning joss sticks. Maybe smoking opium. Maybe he lies down with his wife for a little whiles."

Davies smiled at the lad's continuously inventive grammatical choices, and noted that the junk was not one of the better ones he had seen. It had the usual eyes painted on its bow so that it might "see its course." But Davies doubted that the eyes would do much to prevent it from crashing into practically anything and sinking. The junk was painted five mis-matching colors, and its squared sails were a patchwork of old red and orange canvas scraps - colorful, but hardly reassuring. The decks and spars were worn and gouged by countless years of hard sailing. Under the circumstances, however, where slipping away unnoticed was critical, it might prove the safest means of travel - certainly the humblest.

Five minutes later, the barrel-chested sailor reappeared, but he seemed to have other things on his mind. He moved along to the far side of the ship, checking lines, throwing bits of trash over the side and squinting up at the masts. When he finally circled back, he looked at Davies and No Sin as if surprised to find them still waiting.

A heated exchange followed with No Sin shaking his head. The man threw up his hands and walked away, muttering to himself. The boy smiled. "Everything fine, Mr. Davies. He will take you to Foochow. I get you very good price. You go get young lady, and your bags. I will see that cabins are proper."

Davies chuckled inwardly; his appraisal of the youth as a budding confidence man was right on the mark. He wondered if he wasn't traveling with the next Elder Brother. "I can't leave until tomorrow night, Sin. I'll see you then. Oh, by the way, could you. uh, well, I don't know any other way to put it, could you buy me a nice little dress?" Davies fished a couple bills from his pocket and handed them to the boy who was staring at him with great concern. "Uh, I think a size two. The sizes are the same here as anywhere, I believe, aren't they?"

The boy seemed unsure.

"I know, just so there'll be no confusion, why don't you buy something that you can fit into?"

"You want to buy me a dress?"   No Sin had a strange, unblinking stare on his face.

"Of course not. It's for my lady friend, she's about your build, so just have them fit it to you. And get something pretty, will you?"

"You say 'pretty,' what you mean – flowers - or elegant style? Or what?"

"More elegant, I suppose. I don't know, just get something you'd like - I mean, if you were a woman. And get some other things women like, rouge, lipstick, stockings, you know." The boy continued to stare at Davies; he had looked less frightened at his own execution. "It shouldn't be hard, just think like a woman. You have a sister?"

No sin nodded a slow, "yes," then shook his head, "no".

"Well ask the shop clerk what women like. And you can say you're buying it all for your girlfriend, that sounds better doesn't it?"

Tentatively, No Sin nodded again.

"I thought you told me that you were never afraid of things."

"When?" the boy asked.

"In my car, on the way to Hong Fat's."

"Oh, yes," No Sin replied - but he still looked mildly terrified. Of course, Davies had never worn a dress, and though posing in one was not generally life-threatening, he didn't envy the collision of emotions contained within the boy's slender frame.

"Will I get paid?" No Sin extended his hand. "You offer me ten dollar, Mex, remember?"

"I suppose nothing is going to come easy today." Davies dug into his pocket. "All right you little pirate, five dollars in advance." He handed No Sin some silver dollars, enough to buy a month's worth of decent meals.

"We shake, okay?" Again, No Sin offered his hand.

Davies took it and shook. The deal was sealed.

XXV. CAUSE OF DEATH

Motoring away from the park, Davies returned to the French Club. With Monica riding on the floor, he drove past Max who was still parked out front in the Hispano. As they had planned, Max started up the big car and followed. When they neared Davies' villa, Max passed them, heading for the front gate. In the meantime, Davies parked a few blocks away. He was counting on the police to flag Max down and demand to know why he was returning home without his employer. While Max explained that his master had hitched a ride with a party-mad friend, Davies and Monica would be climbing over the wall that separated Davies' home from his neighbors'.

The ruse worked beautifully, and, once safely nestled inside the compound, it was decided that Monica should bunk in Max's quarters above the garage.

Although it wasn't requested of him, Max elected to sleep in the Hispano so that Monica could have his room to herself.

Davies was not surprised, for Max, the Mongol, was a gentle, honorable man. He largely kept to himself, and had little to do with Lo-Chien and the rest of Davies' household staff, whose constant gossiping and intrigues disturbed him. Monica's presence had to be kept a secret from them above all others - they would gladly turn her in to collect the ample reward that Davies learned was being offered by Mr. Lin.

Monica accepted her situation with typical silence. She seemed relaxed, almost happy to have the little room above the garage to herself. Davies took advantage of her seeming change in mood to try, once more, to coax her to talk. After speaking a few words to buck her up, he asked if she was supposed to meet her aunt earlier that evening - and was rewarded with an affirmative nod. He pressed his luck and asked if she had seen Madame Lin's killer. Unfortunately, this shut the girl up completely. Finally, feeling the lateness of the hour, he made for the door. As he did so, Monica crossed to Max's nightstand and began a search of its cluttered top. Not finding what she wanted, she rummaged through a drawer.

Puzzled, Davies crossed over to Monica who had found a stubby pencil and was scribbling out a note on a matchbook, which she handed to Davies. It read: "Thank you. I am innocent."

He nodded, noncommittally.

She raised up on tiptoes and gave him a quick, soft kiss on the lips. Then she disappeared into the bathroom. He was so startled that he simply stood stupidly in the center of the room forgetting how to breathe. Boy, she was confusing - and exasperating - and lovely to contemplate.

Saturday, August 18, 1928

When Davies finally attempted to rest at a little past four in the morning, it was with his old service revolver under his pillow, a poor sleeping companion. As expected, the night was wretched and sleepless as his mind raced in circles; while the hot, damp air in the room refused to budge. Adding to his anxiety was the question of what had happened to the man he'd hired to watch Monica? Leibowitz was a true professional who wouldn't forget to report in, but he hadn't. Why was that? Had he stumbled onto something?

And what about Monica? How would he ever get her transported to the junk without being detected? The best scheme he could come up with was to sneak back to the Ford that evening, have Monica get down on the floor again, and head to the junk. The police were only watching the front and rear of his villa – he saw no evidence that they were paying any attention to his neighbors' yards, or had any idea that the old Model T, parked a few blocks away, belonged to him. As for his servants wondering what had happened to their primary mode of transportation, he'd simply tell them that the old Model T had broken down and wouldn't be back home for several days.

Despite these nighttime anxieties, his mind kept replaying images of Monica's gentle kiss. Had it been a simple expression of gratitude, as its quickness suggested - or did the fact that she had chosen to kiss his lips instead of his cheek constitute a sexual overture? It was absurd - here he was facing one of the greatest crises of his life, and he had again fallen into the role of a desperate, love-starved adolescent.

Departing turned out to be more than the normal mucking about one endures when traveling overseas. The big, important matters had been handled, but Davies no longer had time to go back to the Astor House to learn if anyone else had actually seen Trees, or to check for discarded bloody clothes or towels. Nor was he able to pack much. Important papers and personal items were placed in several, small suitcases and given to Max, with instructions as to their handling. If Lo-Chien became suspicious of luggage leaving the house, he'd be reminded of the fictional business trip to Peiping.

The authorities had inadvertently helped out. There was no question that the police were watching the villa, ready to pounce should Davies try to make a run for it. But they wouldn't be suspicious of Davies' ten o'clock meeting with Singletone. While Davies was at the police station, Max could slip down to the waterfront, leave the luggage and a few other odds and ends with No Sin, and quickly return to fetch his employer.

As for Davies' wardrobe, the monograms had added another bit of serendipity. Because of them, he'd already ordered a tailor to make up a dozen new shirts. He'd expand the order to include several suits - the tailor would know his measurements. These clothes would also be delivered directly to the junk, with neither the police nor his household staff any the wiser. He could rest now, knowing that the transportation of his wardrobe and luggage was handled.

His rest didn't last more than twenty minutes; he was jarred awake by the sound of the old Model T chugging through his gate and coming to a sputtering halt in the garage. Hurrying out to investigate, he encountered the servant who he'd paid to have a night on the town. Apparently, the fellow didn't have a celebratory bone in his body and had come home early. He'd spotted the Model T parked down the street, and decided to investigate. He was surprised to find that it started right up, so he drove it home. He was quite proud of himself – Davies was forced to thank him for his conscientiousness. Now what? How on earth was he going to smuggle Monica out of his home?

Just before dawn, Davies crept out of the compound, utilizing several of his neighbors' yards to reach a street corner a block away. Monica remained behind, hopefully still sleeping. It was too risky to sneak her out with him and put her in a cab. The morning papers would undoubtedly have a description of her, and though there were plenty of Eurasians in Shanghai, one who refused to speak would arouse suspicion. Once out on the sidewalk, he walked back to his villa, swaying slightly to reinforce the idea that he'd been out all night drinking. As anticipated, the police questioned him as he approached his driveway, and he explained that a foolhardy, (and imaginary,) friend from the club had driven him home, or had, at least, attempted to. Still inebriated, the debauched friend had gotten lost, and his motoring skills had deteriorated so dramatically that Davies had ordered the man to pull over – insisting that he'd prefer to walk the remaining five blocks.

Falling for this tripe, the police allowed Davies back inside to bathe and change clothes - and shortly after half past nine he set out for his appointment with Singletone, discovering, as he had expected, that the police had issued an arrest warrant for Monica. This was made abundantly clear when they stopped his car as it attempted to leave his drive.

"I'll be requirin' a look at your motor, sir," the large, ruddy-faced constable named Smixon said, after presenting Davies with the necessary papers. "Mind steppin' out, then, guv?" Davies sensed real hostility beneath the man's humorless facade.

If things didn't go perfectly within the next few seconds, both Davies and Monica would be spending their leisure time in a Shanghai jail. Only two things were on his side, his ability to bluff, and the fact that he was riding in a dual cowl phaeton. The conceit of this body style was that its purpose was to mimic a modern biplane so that rear passengers could imagine themselves soaring about town as fearless aviators. When everything was properly battened down, those riding in back resembled barnstorming pilots where only their heads and shoulders could be seen, even by someone standing right next to the car. If Davies could keep Smixon from raising the rear cowl, a long prison stretch would be avoided – for the time being anyway.

"Didn't you hear me?" Smixon bellowed, "Step out!"

"I'd rather not."

"What was that?"

"I believe you heard me. Now, if you want to press the matter, I'll leave it to you to explain to your superior officer why I was late for my appointment with him." Under different circumstances, Davies would have relished playing such a trump card. The fact that Monica Marshall was curled on the floor at his feet, barely concealed by the rear cowl, tempered his glee.

"How's that, now?"

God, the man was slow. "I mean that it's nine forty-seven, and I have a ten o'clock appointment with Inspector Singletone. If I leave right now, and my man drives like a demon, I just might make it."

"Very well, we'll make it on time, don't you worry." Smixon signaled to another officer. "Hold the fort, I'm off to headquarters." He reached out, trying to find the non-existent outside handle for the rear door.

"In front, if you don't mind," Davies said firmly.

"Not good enough for the likes of you, am I?"

"In a nutshell. I paid a fortune for this car - I intend to get my money's worth; especially as I may be spending the rest of my days in prison. So allow me a last indulgence, won't you?"

"Still gotta see what's inside."

Davies hesitated, then unlatched the rear door and pushed it open. The cowl with the rear windscreen bolted to it remained closed, but Smixon was allowed to peer through the doorway and into the rear compartment where he had a view of Davies' legs and his polished shoes resting serenely on a padded footrest.

Smixon grunted his approval and Davies pulled the door shut.

"Shall we be off?"

Smixon spat onto the gravel road, and climbed in beside Max, who was holding a front door open for him. That was certainly close, Davies thought as the car gathered speed and Monica curled up again at his feet. She was a clever girl and had silently opened the other rear door, climbed out, and, with Davies' discreet assistance, shut it soundlessly behind her, crouching down outside the car as Smixon performed his inspection. Because of the cowl being in place, Smixon was unable to see the far door open and close, nor was he able to see Monica reverse the process as she scrambled back inside just before they took off. Clever Max, anticipating the search, had stopped the Hispano and angled it in just such a way that the view from the street of Monica's maneuver was blocked by the pillar supporting Davies' front gate. That way, none of Smixon's cohorts were able to catch wise, either. Unfortunately, there was still the matter of Davies getting out of the car without Monica being seen.

They pulled up to the sidewalk in front of the Police Station in the British Concession precisely at ten. Davies unlatched the cowl, raised it, threw open the rear door, climbed out, then battened everything down so quickly that he was standing on the sidewalk before Smixon could find his way out of the front seat. It was a minor blessing that the Hispano had unusual inside latches to compliment the lack of exterior door handles, adding to the constable's befuddlement. "Come back for me in forty minutes, Max." Davies said as he watched Smixon finally exit the car and lumber into the street. "If I've been detained, I'm sure the constable here will come down and let you know."

Apparently, Smixon felt a mighty need to demonstrate his position of power, grabbing Davies forcefully by the arm, and escorting him into the building.

Once inside, Davies found himself squaring off with Singletone, who was even less cordial than usual - a minor feat. "As I recall, I asked you to come with Miss Marshall," the policeman said coldly.

"Surely, your men have already informed you that I haven't seen her. They have been spying on me, after all."

Singletone gave Davies his proper British rendition of the evil eye. "I need a small favor from you." Instead of explaining, he made a smart turn and walked briskly down the hall, with the expectation that Davies would follow.

As the hard, clacking sound of their footsteps bounced off the walls, they went to the far end of the building, down a flight of stairs, and into the only cool room that Davies had experienced in months. The room had a high ceiling, and a handsome simplicity of design. A criss-cross of heavy, wooden beams provided a touch of unexpected elegance, contrasting with slick green walls, a worn linoleum floor, and gurneys draped with white sheets concealing ominous lumps, which gave away that they'd entered the morgue. Without ceremony, Singletone walked to one of the lumps and pulled back a sheet. "Any body you know?" he asked.

Davies ignored the tasteless pun. He assumed that Singletone was trying to force him to look at Madame Lin's corpse, a task he wasn't up for. However, the phrasing of Singletone's question made him unsure. Not wishing to appear squeamish, he approached the gurney and gazed at the face of the cadaver beneath the sheet. He felt the sick and angry sensation of recognition, and retreated to the edge of a metal counter, on which he leaned, numbly.

"Found him last night in the alley behind the Astor House," Singletone said. "Shot once in the back from close range. The bullet snapped a rib and lodged in the heart they tell me." The Inspector looked at Davies, accusingly. "Well?"

"I know him." Davies said, feeling like his torso was so empty that the sound of a hard swallow would cause echoes. "His name's Leibowitz; I hire him on occasion."

"On this occasion?"

Davies nodded. "I asked him to keep an eye on Monica Marshall. I was worried about her."

"I'd say your worries were misplaced."

XXVI. THE SECRET OF THE JAR

Singletone led Davies back upstairs, demanding, as he walked, to know what Leibowitz had learned. When Davies said that the poor man hadn't filed a report before dying, the dour policeman harrumphed in a traditional English manner.

They entered the Inspector's office, another sober, yet peculiarly handsome room with an unusually high ceiling. As the blotchy-faced Inspector took a standing position behind his desk, he chastised Davies all over again for showing up alone. Unable to get his mind off of Leibowitz's killing, Davies promised to do his best to bring Monica along next time; then he fell silent as Singletone recited his reasons for making the young Eurasian woman his prime suspect. At the top of the list was the fact that no key to Monica's room had been found in her apartment, or amongst Madame Lin's things. Singletone, who had mercifully calmed down, wondered how Madame Lin had gotten in.

Davies shrugged, knowing that any theory he offered would be bitingly rejected.

Singletone's explanation was that Monica had simply admitted her aunt when she'd heard a knock on the door. "A further indication," he proclaimed, "of the girl's guilt" – "because who else would be in that room, other than its registered occupant?"

This, however, was the least of several new, troubling discoveries. Madame Lin had been seen entering the hotel at about six-twenty in the evening. At approximately six-forty-five she had phoned down to the front desk from Monica's "digs" and asked if they knew where her niece was. As it turned out, Monica had left a message saying that she'd gone downstairs to dinner, and Madame Lin was welcome to look for her there. When Davies pointed out that this contradicted Singletone's previous statement and would surely clear Monica, the inspector insisted, stubbornly, that it struck him as too obvious an attempt by the girl to contrive an alibi. He imagined her holding a gun on her aunt and ordering her to place the call.

"But Monica would have been seen having dinner at the time of the killing," Davies insisted.

"She was seen," Singletone agreed from behind his worn, Georgian-style desk. "But before the killing. At the time of the murder, she'd left the dining room and was unaccounted for."

"Maybe she was taking a walk, or posting a cable."

"How well acquainted are you with Miss Marshall?" Singletone asked, ignoring Davies' theory.

"I hardly know her."

"I suppose you'd be interested to know what was contained in the telegram we found."

"You're finally going to tell me? Though, I'd be surprised if it had any significance at all."

"And why's that?"

"Because the killer regarded it as nothing more than a rag to be used for wiping blood off his hands. I'd certainly check for fingerprints." In fact, the police force in the International District was one of the few in the world readily willing to check for fingerprints, influenced by their Chinese hosts.

Again ignoring Davies' advice, Singletone removed the shred of telegram from his desk and held it up for Davies' inspection. "You make anything of the signature?"

"The initials 'H.W.'?" Davies shook his head.

"It seems this cable was from a family member."

"A well-heeled family member."

Singletone tapped his chin. "How in the world do you deduce he's 'well-heeled?'"

"Look at all the words," Davies said, pleasantly, trying not to launch an argument. "Awfully talky for a telegram. That much babble wouldn't come cheap."

"Perhaps," Singletone conceded. "However, as you can see, this fragment of the telegram warns of Miss Marshall being mentally unstable, and it implies that she is dangerous."

"But then it's even less likely that Miss Marshall committed the crime."

"I hardly follow."

"She would have cared dearly about this little bit of text because it mentions her name - and in such an unflattering way. She wouldn't have left it in the trash for us to find. However, if the murderer was someone else, why not leave behind a scrap that would seem to incriminate another person?"

Singletone made a sly smile. "You described the actions of a rational person, forgetting that the telegram questions the girl's mental stability. No, I'm convinced that Monica Marshall is our killer."

"It's incredible the tortured contortions the police will subject logic to in order to prove a pet theory."

"Oh, really?" Singletone remarked, dismissively. "Then consider that Madame Lin took the telegram so seriously that she'd begun proceedings to have your friend, Miss Marshall, committed to an asylum for the insane here in Shanghai. Now, is that motive enough for you?"

"How do you know?"

"The asylum confirmed it."

Davies felt like he'd been kicked in the stomach - but with Madame Lin's foot.

Singletone sat casually on the edge of his desk, emphasizing his having the upper hand. "If that's not enough, I received a report from the coroner; and the cause of death certainly suggests an assailant lacking mental stability. Your friend was shot once through the head with a twenty-two caliber bullet. The sound was probably muffled by a pillow. However, this was not the cause of death. Some people survive gun shots to the head, and your Madame Lin was one of these. She was finished off in a rather disagreeable way. Before we removed the bullet, we encountered another object lodged in the skull, blocking the path, as it were."

"Do you intend to enlighten me?" Though, in truth, he'd prefer not to hear more.

"We found a cigarette butt."

"What?" The sickened emotion hit before the comprehension.

"Didn't she use a holder?" Singletone asked. "We found one in that wastebasket - and a spare was in her purse."

"That's right," Davies answered faintly.

"It seems that when the bullet failed to kill her, the murderer took Madame Lin's cigarette holder and jammed it through the wound, deep into the brain, and then twisted it around as if they were whipping cream. The butt dislodged and remained in the brain when the holder was removed."

From this point on, Davies remembered little - having only a vague recollection of Singletone droning on about how this revised sequence of events suggested that Madame Lin had conversed quietly, even cordially, with her murderer for a full twenty minutes before death concluded their encounter at around seven. These revelations were far from comforting, if Madame Lin had been so relaxed with her killer maybe Singletone was right about Monica.

"By the way, there was something else," Singletone said. Davies braced himself, he didn't imagine the Inspector was about to add something gay and amusing.

"Her right foot was removed - rather neatly."

"I beg your pardon?"

"It was cut off. Savvy? The foot remains at large. After being mutilated, the body was shoved out the window, where it lodged in the portico."

"That makes no sense," Davies said, again feeling light-headed and nauseated. "Even a maniac wouldn't want to call such attention to his crime."

"It may have been an accident. Corpses can be unwieldy, particularly when one is attempting a dismemberment." Singletone shook his head. "I must say it's a damned nuisance when these Orientals insist on dying, so exotically, in our territory."

The tactless remark brought Davies back to the moment. "A woman is dead, Inspector."

"A Chinese is dead. Don't forget, I only have so many men - and this nonsense takes them away from important matters."

Davies rose from his chair.

"Oh, do settle down." Singletone said with false exasperation, "I'm aware she was a friend of yours."

"She most certainly was. And what a ghastly way to die, you must concede that." Almost as ghastly was the fact that, despite their thoroughness, the police didn't care about Madame Lin. *Where* she'd been killed was all that mattered; already it was being called "the Astor House murder." Such a hotel was considered a safe haven in a wicked, Godless place like Shanghai, and the reputation of a reassuring, Western sanctuary couldn't be sullied.

Despite his outrage at Singletone's callousness, Davies felt grateful to the Inspector. The terrible revelation of Madame Lin's severed, bound foot banished any doubts about leaving for Honolulu. The question of why Trees had requested a fruit jar with a good, strong lid was now answered - what better vessel in which to transport a decomposing limb? Why Trees had done it remained a puzzle, but there was no longer any question that the deranged creature had killed Madame Lin. Equally clear was the fact that Trees was a monster - a mad dog that must be hunted down.

Davies was allowed to make his "good-byes," and he somehow managed to leave without being arrested - probably because the police expected him to lead them to Monica.

He was half-way home before he realized that he was riding in the back of his car without any recollection as to how he'd gotten there. All he knew was that his outrage was fading into energy-sapping despair as he took in the pageant of pre-luncheon Shanghai. Thinking about the events and forces swirling around him, the unjust free-for-all of China, Madame Lin's hideous death, his own culpability - his fevered mind dealt with the overload of thoughts and emotions by reducing everything to a simple, repetitive chant: *It's not right, it must stop.*

Once he got home, he made his way to his quarters, where he sat on the edge of his bed, rubbed his greasy forehead, and continued to ponder the way that Madame Lin had been killed. Could a cigarette holder thrust into the brain, and a foot removal, be symbolic of something - a weird, Chinese ritualistic exercise like the removal of a squealer's tongue?

After five minutes spent lapsing into a vegetative trance, Davies mustered the energy to rise and cross to the phone on his dresser, from which he rang up the not so good, but certainly helpful Dr. Sun.

The old curator was so horrified by what had happened to Madame Lin that Davies worried that the poor fellow might drop dead on the spot - every silence on the other end of the line made him anxious. Fortunately, Dr. Sun rallied himself, and, wheezing noticeably, said that he could find no significance in the choice of a cigarette holder as a murder weapon - nor of a foot removal. All that it indicated to him was that the killer was completely out of his or her mind.

As an afterthought, Dr. Sun confirmed that the object that Davies and Crockwood had left with him was indeed the fabled and cursed "clouded twilight." The old man felt certain that Elder Brother would be pleased. With Madame Lin no longer in any condition to object, Davies didn't protest when told that a courier was due to arrive at any moment to take "the clouded twilight" to the head of the Chinese underworld. That, at least, was one less thing to worry about.

Ringing off, Davies sat again on the edge of his bed and gazed out at his garden. The events of the day caused him to recollect that, at the age of seven, he'd swam with friends out to a wooden float in the middle of a lake. On the way back, he'd suddenly run out of energy and began to drown. The accompanying sense of supercharged panic was not easily forgotten. His mind screaming *this can not happen* was all that kept him from going under, despite having no energy, and seeming to sink deeper with every stroke. This is how he now felt, helping Madame Lin had been like swimming to a nearby float, with no clue as to what perils lay ahead. Now with her death, with her foot removed, with Leibowitz's killing, Davies felt the old panic. It was a strange blessing that accompanying it was a desperate refusal to give in to forces that had all the ruthless, uncaring power of nature behind them.

Later, as evening approached, Davies packed up the Hispano and left for the waterfront. He couldn't remember ever feeling so nervous - and he knew that he was on his own because his consul hadn't rung up with a friendly warning that the police might be watching. That meant that "extraterritoriality" wasn't going to protect him this time; the reputation of the Astor House rated higher than his immunity from prosecution - regardless of how many friendly drinks he'd poured over the years.

He didn't get further than his own front gate. Again, the police were waiting for him and they flagged him down.

XXVII. ON THE RUN

"**S**tep out, please," Smixon said as if the morning's drama had never occurred. This time Davies obliged, waiting while the constable and two policemen inspected every square inch of the Hispano. They even lifted the bonnet, apparently in hope of finding Monica draped over a valve cover.

"We intend to search the house, then." Smixon's frustration was showing. "You'd like to wait in the courtyard, I expect."

"Search away," Davies replied, "but I'm in a great hurry. Since it's not me you're after, I assume I can be on my way. I trust you not to break anything."

"Now just,.."

"You aren't arresting me are you?"

"Not yet,.."

"So there you have it. Enjoy yourselves, the house is yours." Davies climbed back into the Hispano, signaled to Max and the car lurched forward leaving Smixon and his men standing like fools by the front gate.

"Follow him, damn you!" Smixon shouted to the closest officer.

* * *

Smixon knew it was a sham; no Austin Seven built was going to catch one of those seven thousand pound frogmobiles. It didn't matter, though - it was the girl they were after, and soon they'd have her. The rich sop was a bloody decoy and his servants were probably trying to sneak her out a back gate at this very moment. Not if Smixon had anything to do with it.

Forty minutes later, Smixon had seen enough of Davies' weird, pretend Chinese Emperor's palace to know that the girl wasn't there. The back yard didn't even have a gate, and, for hours, officers had been positioned so that every square inch of the villa's perimeters was under observation; as a result her escape was a bloody mystery. Smixon had been tricked, simple as that. Davies' Chink servants were wailing and carrying on like little children. At least, he could teach them a wee bit of respect for authority without risking a reprimand.

* * *

Thank God it had worked, Davies thought as he took a much needed gulp of Scotch from his flask. But it wasn't time to celebrate - they still had to make it to the waterfront, using a variety of circuitous routes in order to lose any spies the police may have sent after him. And he wasn't only concerned about Singletone's men - tonight every Chinaman in Shanghai had taken on a sinister caste.

An earlier phone call to Elder Brother had contributed, mightily, to Davies' uneasiness. He'd agreed to meet with a Mr. Kaneshiro in San Francisco on the first of October - a telephone number was provided. Elder Brother had been almost grandfatherly, but the parting words uttered by the head of the Chinese underworld had sent a chill streaking through Davies' body. It wasn't just the phrase, it was the sincerity in the voices of both Elder Brother and his interpreter. Having been briefed on nearly everything, including Singletone's suspicions of Monica, and the discovery of the cigarette butt in Madame Lin's brain, Elder Brother had said, "Be careful," in a tone that sounded as if he really meant it. Who could cause the most feared man in China to show such concern?

XXVIII. TOO MUCH TALK

When Zephyr Davies had not arrived at the appointed time, No Sin became worried that his own behavior was to blame. He had been given a chance to escape his horrible existence, and he'd spoiled it by being angry and arrogant - now he would be punished.

It had all started with the search for the lady friend's dress, where everything went very badly. On the way to a small dress shop, a sudden gust of wind had blown No Sin's prized fedora off his head, causing it to roll and bounce across the sidewalk and right into the entrance of the fancy Shanghai Club. As he ran after the Stetson, he'd been tackled by a burly Russian doorman, and shoved, harshly, back into the street.

"My hat," No Sin wailed, nearly out of breath, "it blow inside!"

Like a teacher scolding a disobedient pupil, the doorman pointed to the small plaque by the front door that read: "Dogs and Chinese Not Allowed." "Savvy?" he asked with a contemptuous sneer, as if not expecting No Sin to understand written English.

No Sin was forced to answer back, politely. "Please, sir, can you fetch my hat?"

The Russian walked inside. A moment later he came back and tossed No Sin's hat into the street.

On the next block, weaving his way through a pulsating crowd, his luck got even worse when he'd stumbled into the path of ten, laughing Japanese soldiers. No Sin bowed, apologetically, and hurried on, greatly relieved that the soldiers were in a benevolent mood.

At the clothing shop, no one could understand why No Sin wanted to buy a dress that he could fit into. Finally, the transaction became such an ordeal that he picked the cheapest and ugliest dress that qualified, and used the change to buy himself several packs of cigarettes and a handful of paper candy; he was entitled to some compensation after such a wretched afternoon.

On the way back he'd enjoyed a final indulgence, a ride on a coolie train. Once aboard, No Sin pretended, as was his custom, that he was an emperor. He looked down on the coolies and imagined that the bright blue umbrella hats that he saw bobbing back and forth signified his official color. Indeed, at one time only royalty had been allowed human bearers, so the fantasy was not an irrational one. Unfortunately, the luxury of riding on a coolie train hadn't cheered him for long. Thirty seconds after he'd gotten off at the river front, he was again sad and angry.

He was greeted by the sight of many bags and suitcases waiting on the dock, watched over by a tiny and exquisite young woman. Baggage and person had all been left there by Mr. Davies' driver at a quarter past ten that morning. No Sin made sure that the luggage was all properly placed in Mr. Davies' cabin, and he showed the woman to a cabin of her own. She wasn't very friendly, refusing to make small talk of any kind. Of course, her appearance was troubling. Why had Zephyr Davies humiliated himself and No Sin by taking along to Foochow a young woman who was of no race or nation, and who did not speak?

After showing her to her cabin, he returned topside and helped with the ropes and the sails, staying as far away from the woman as possible.

Eleven hours later, No Sin had given up all hope, and decided to see if the Laota would hire him as a crew member for some future trip. Then, magically, Zephyr Davies had appeared, running down the wooden planking that led to the junk, shouting apologies and asking after the girl.

They cast off in such a blur of confusion that No Sin forgot entirely that his dream had been returned to him. Sails unfurled, the junk steadily gathered speed as the crew clamored back and forth, shouting obscenities at other junks, and at each other. It was a warm August night, and finally they were moving out into the Whangpoo on their way to the sea.

After helping with the sails, No Sin went to the rail at the very rear of the junk and watched the stocky merchant palaces of Shanghai slowly recede as a full moon sparkled giddily on the water. He clutched the rail, and breathed in the exhilarating, salty air of freedom, as the sails popped and fluttered inches from his shoulder. Although he'd lived on a boat, he'd never actually traveled on one. The sense of motion, along with the knowledge that he was really going somewhere, made him euphoric. To his right were the great battleships of the English, the Americans, and the French, their huge guns plugged and silent, their sentry lights casting angular shadows over their decks.   The ships, three and four abreast, stretched in a line that seemed to go on for miles.   It was like passing beside another great city, a strange, quiet city made of gray metal.   Behind him, Shanghai and its masses of sampans were now slipping into the distance - somewhere among them was his father's boat.   Up ahead, the silent armada of warships stretched, seemingly, forever.   Bathed in soft, white moonlight their majesty was indescribable and beautifully sinister.

Soon they'd reach the sea, the first ocean No Sin had ever seen. Beyond it waited a wonderful new life.   He was happy with everything, even his new name; a name invented by the whim of a white man, a name that meant nothing.   It was good to be nothing and to have a name that matched; everything was brand new, he'd been reborn and his old name and the traditions that had created it were from a lost land that, behind him, was sinking beneath the horizon forever.

No Sin was jolted from his enjoyable thoughts by the machine gun popping of firecrackers on the forward deck of the junk.   This was followed by the frenzied shouting of the crew members - then came the noisy clanging of cymbals.   No Sin leaned as far over the mast as he dared and saw that they were beside another junk, close enough to shake hands with its crew; and they were overtaking the slower craft at great speed.   On the other junk, another round of fire-crackers and cymbals answered the popping and clattering on their own boat.   The sailors on the slower vessel were frantically hoisting sails and trying to gain speed - but they were too late.   The screeching and banging and popping continued while No Sin's junk took the lead.   The Laota swung the rudder and their craft made an agitated, but not unexpected turn.   The sails fluttered and snapped, the boom tilted heavily to the side, nearly banging into No Sin, who ducked just in time.   Swiftly they veered sharply toward the other boat, almost smashing into its side.   Their stern missed the slower junk's bow by less than a foot, and a great cheer rose from the deck below.   No Sin gave his own shout of victory as he looked behind him.   They would have good luck on their voyage now - the devils who attached themselves and then held hands at the backs of all Chinese junks had been scraped off and transferred to the other boat. No Sin's junk was free of evil spirits, while the other sailors would have very bad luck from now on.

He remained at the rail, thinking that fifty hours earlier he had been tied to a post with a sack over his head, waiting for the moment when a rope would encircle his neck and squeeze the life out of his battered body. With all his soreness and pain he had almost been looking forward to it. And now he was free, with the wind whipping at his face and the lights of Shanghai slowly drifting away into the darkness. It was incredible how quickly and completely the elements of life could change.

A sudden chill in the air announced that the ocean was not far away. A moment later, the junk rounded a bend, and the Whangpoo carried it into a suddenly vast expanse of muddy water - this had to be the broad mouth of the Yangtze River, and the moon reflected spectacularly on the open sea a few miles further on. No Sin had heard stories that the sea was a howling demon that swallowed up whole ships for sport. He'd heard wonderful stories too, about its beauty and vastness - but now that it was truly coming closer, the frightening stories had more power over him than the pleasant ones.

He climbed down to a lower deck and headed for the comfort of the galley. On his way, he caught sight of Zephyr Davies and his woman, sitting on boxes twenty feet away, looking at the fire lights of passing villages. Her hands were placed neatly in her lap and her face was as empty as the darkness. Her appearance continued to be fascinating. She had very smooth skin, like a young Chinese lady. Her cheekbones were high and sharp; her eyes neither those of a Chinese or a white-face. But of what use was she with her long, smooth legs and extremely small waist? It was like a mixture of a goat and a deer. The result was an interesting creature that one could not help staring at if it were in a zoo. But could it run swiftly, or give milk? Could one breed it with another animal and have any certainty of what sort of beast would come out? He suddenly felt ashamed of himself as he contemplated the strange being - undoubtedly the illustrious white man had his reasons for bringing the woman along - just as he had his reasons for striking a German, and saving No Sin from execution. And undoubtedly the millionaire would be pleased if No Sin treated the woman in a civil manner. It was a sacrifice he must make in a life destined to be full of sacrifices.

* * *

On the midship deck, Zephyr Davies leaned forward, elbows on his knees, his heavy mink greatcoat draped around him. He glanced at the view of the tranquil, shimmering water, and pulled a flask out of his pocket, taking a long gulp of smoky, burning liquor. "A man can stand just so much beauty," he muttered. Then he tried, once again, to find out from Monica what had happened at the Astor House. "You knew your aunt was coming to visit you?"

The young woman's gaze remained fixed on the open sea. Even after such a traumatic evening, she maintained the haughty look of a princess; the regal arrogance that, dismally, he found hard to resist - perhaps because sexual attraction was, in his view, not a form of affection, but of hostility. There was nothing more exciting than lovemaking with someone unimpressed and unapproachable, and seeing them become suddenly vulnerable. The greater their arrogance, the greater the satisfaction of controlling them, often with nothing more than a touch - and the reverse was perhaps more exciting.

"You know, Monica, it would make things a good deal easier if you would just speak." He punctuated his remark with an exasperated look.

Her lower lip came out, and she twisted the sleeve of her wrap in her hands. Even her sulking had a sensuality to it.

He took solace in another long drink from the silver flask, aware of the sound of water slapping against the hull as the junk slowly rose and fell. She watched him drink, her eyes narrowing with suspicion as if she was contemplating whether or not he was a practiced drunkard. "It's good for you," Davies said, "try some."

Like a child who had been ordered to down some abominable medicine, she took the flask, gritted her teeth, closed her eyes, and lifted it to her mouth. She held it there for three painful seconds, then lowered it, blinking and gasping for air.

"Feel better?" he asked.

She handed the flask back, and looked glassy-eyed at the floor.

Behind them, No Sin emerged from the galley. Davies could see that the boy was carrying a tray filled with sweets and little cakes, probably made by the captain's wife. No Sin stopped en route to rearrange the cakes slightly so they looked even more inviting.

Monica took no notice of the lad as he padded across the deck and came up behind her. He thrust his offering forward, brushing lightly against her shoulder.

As if she had been jolted by an electric current, Monica leaped to her feet. "Hey!" she cried. Seeing No Sin, she slapped him hard across the face, sending the tray of cookies and cakes clattering across the deck.

Davies was so stunned that a moment passed before it occurred to him that she had recovered her voice. He looked sternly at No Sin. Too angry to speak, the youth knelt on the deck and gathered up his offerings - then he rose and returned to the galley.

Monica retreated to the rail where she focused her anger on the ocean.

Davies went to her and tried to put his arms around her.

She shook him off. "Can't everybody leave me the hell alone?"

Surprised again, this time by her sailor's mouth, he backed away.

"I'm sorry," Monica whispered, "I suppose I've been a perfect little idiot." With unsettling swiftness, the calm look returned to her eyes, masking whatever emotion was inside, like the curtain going down after the last act of a play. Almost hoping that her facade would shatter, Davies handed her his handkerchief. "Thank you," she said flatly, "but I don't need that." Her voice was deeper than he had expected, huskier, throatier.

Davies folded the handkerchief and returned it to his pocket. "I see you've learned to talk."

"I started when I was one," she said, avoiding eye contact, "I think my first word was Lilliputian." She bit her lower lip and gave him a coy smile. "I really am sorry for all this." She was like a naughty little girl who knew she was not going to be punished.

She was right; though Davies felt obligated to scold her, his flirtatious side wouldn't allow it. "You have some explaining to do."

"Must we talk about it now? I'm awfully tired."

"I think I have a right to know why you spent so much time refusing to speak." He felt like adding that it was an incredibly selfish, puerile thing to do, but he didn't want to shut her up again.

"I'm sorry. I know not talking was childish, but I wasn't up to Auntie interrogating me with endless questions."

"Not talking hardly made things easier for me."

"Didn't I just admit it was silly?"

He was tempted to demonstrate his own rendition of silliness by turning her over his knee, but despite her cool demeanor, he could see that her body was noticeably trembling. A measured approach seemed more appropriate. "I assume you were afraid to tell your aunt that you had brought 'the clouded twilight' to Shanghai."

She nodded, her black hair swirling in the wind.

"And you sold it to Hong Fat?"

"You're not one for tact, are you? Couldn't you at least say how nice it is to finally hear my voice or tell me how lovely my hair looks in the moonlight?"

"I've indulged your behavior for the past week, I'd think you could indulge mine for several more minutes."

She sighed. "No, it was stolen from me, crossing over on the steamer. Mother asked me to return it to the Lins..."

"And when it was stolen you simply kept everything to yourself?"

She nodded, her eyes again averted. "I tried to find it secretly."

"Why not lie about the theft of the staff? Wouldn't that have been easier than all the drama of not speaking?"

She gave a small, choked off laugh. "You don't know my aunt. She'd pounce like a, I don't know, a ravenous weasel if I gave her the slightest opening, believe me. And then she'd never stop."

Her trembling was lessening and the chance of getting an emotional reaction out of her was slipping away. "It's with Elder Brother now, by the way. 'The clouded twilight.'"

Her eyes widened, her lips parted; he had her full attention.

"He's the head of the Chinese under,..."

"I know who he is. Dear God! You can't be serious! Oh, that's just fine." She turned and scowled again at the ocean.

"Incidentally, did you send this to me?" From his pocket he withdrew the note asking him to leave her alone.

She gave it a cursory glance. "Of course."

Her quick admission was another surprise. "Did someone instruct you to send it?"

"Certainly not," she snapped, revealing nothing except mild irritation. "I wanted you to follow me - isn't that obvious?"

"No, it's not obvious at all. It says to leave you alone."

She turned and looked at him like a teacher who was disappointed with her prize pupil. "Men hate rejection, you think I don't know that? I imagined you'd think to yourself, 'poor little thing, she doesn't mean it. Someone must have forced her to write it.' I needed your protection, but what would you have me do, write a note that said 'please help me,' and then refuse to talk when you came rushing to my side? I'm not that ridiculous. I was a little worried, and I wanted you to keep an eye on me, but I didn't want to have to explain myself to you."

Madame Lin's words of warning suddenly made far more sense. He wasn't ready to classify her as a monster, but she was certainly a masterful weaver of webs. "You're quite sure of yourself."

She shrugged. "What can I say? I'm very manipulative."

And brutally frank. "Who was I to protect you from?"

"You tell me. You're very clever, I'm sure you uncovered someone."

"Oh, for Pete's sake. Are you always this evasive?"

She leaned against the rail. "You have a lot of money, don't you?"

"Another evasion, and not exactly a polite question."

"Oh, I see. All right, let's go back to who I've been involved with, who I've been lying to, who I killed, but we mustn't discuss your finances. Is it your family's, or did you make it yourself?" The woman who showed up in his garden seemingly unable to talk was now the star of the debate team.

"What difference does it make to you?"

"I'm scheming."

"It's my family's. We've built up a dynasty selling monkeys to organ grinders. I run the business now and I'm always on the lookout for talented simians."

"You must have a special rapport with them."

He smiled, conceding defeat. It was astounding what a difficult, evasive, childish little vixen she was tuning out to be. Yet, an idiotic part of himself was still searching for any opportunity to take her by her delicate shoulders and begin kissing her on her lovely, scornful lips.

"It's getting awfully chilly, do you mind if I borrow your coat pocket?" Before he could answer, her hands were inside his jacket and her small body was pressed against him.

Now, quite unexpectedly, he had his opportunity, but instead of obliging his desires, his body went rigid. "As to Madame Lin,.."

"You don't give up, do you?"

"Monica, we're talking about your aunt."

He felt her tiny body slump. "I know. But I'm tired, and I'm freezing. Can we please do all our fighting tomorrow?"

"But if you're in such a state, I have the clear advantage. Why should I waste it?"

She pushed away from him. "You're going to have to, because I'm going below. I'd stay, but I'm not nearly as interested in you as you obviously are in me."

Unsteadily, she began to cross to the stairs, which led below deck. He moved to assist her. "Can you handle yourself?"

"Perfectly." She disappeared into the darkness of the stairwell that led below. A moment later a resounding banging and crashing came from a lower deck.

"Are you okay?" he called down to her.

"No."

"Good." He returned to the rail to stare at the dancing moonlight, taking in the faint smells of damp rope and fish. What was he was doing on this ship with such a spoiled brat? It was all so frustrating, as he grew older the world seemed to fall into two camps: those who were interesting, lively, creative, and stimulating were also invariably selfish, neurotic, and nightmarish to deal with - while those who were reasonable, considerate, and honest tended to be impossibly dull. He was still trying to find some middle ground, but it was proving to be damned illusive.

* * *

Sunday, August 19, 1928

Monica surveyed her tiny cabin. The room was certainly quaint, and cleaner than she had expected; there was even a small vase of flowers on a table near her bed - but the steep curve of the ship's hull, which comprised one wall, made her feel queasy and disoriented. As the junk rocked back and forth, the curved section of the hull suggested that the thing was ready to tip over.

Zephyr Davies was exasperating and intelligent to a fault, and he was sort of fun - especially to torment. He was exactly the kind of man she was always a sucker for - her teenage fantasy come to life. When younger, she guessed he'd possessed the kind of athletic, handsome perfection that seemed the birthright of children of wealth, and whose sheer beauty, unjustly kept them from being thoroughly unbearable. But this prep school brat turned adventurer now came across as more substantial in the way that the beauty was long gone, but one sensed that the adventures had been real. The face was sadder than in her fantasy, more thoughtful, and oddly, in her opinion, more attractive. There was still a spoiled quality, but it now appeared to have been earned.

Just her luck - wasn't it perversely appropriate that the very real encounter she'd longed for had finally happened at a time when love was the last thing in the world that interested her? All that really mattered was whether or not he could protect her. She needed him, and she was already starting to hate him for it. Dear God, she was doing it again. When was she going to stop searching for a hero to save her? Didn't she know by now that all she had, all she'd ever have, was herself?

Assuming that Davies could be believed, the emperor's walking stick was gone forever. What was it called? 'The purple twilight,' 'the dawn's early light'? She never wanted to see the damn thing again, and apparently she never would, which changed everything. The whole purpose of her trip, her whole life, actually, had just been flushed down the crapper. Maybe it was just as well. But what on earth was she to do now? She brushed away a renegade tear, and cursed herself for being so moronically willing to put her trust in someone simply because he resembled an adolescent fantasy. On the other hand, maybe, *just maybe* Davies could be her ticket out of this mess. He was rich, after all. He seemed to like her. If she played her cards right, things might be merely tragic instead of disastrous.

Back in Shanghai he'd said that her mind was injured, or something like that. If he only knew. What would the smug and handsome Mr. Davies think if he knew that she had been the cause of the event that had traumatized her the most? Once again, she imagined the surprised open mouth, the pleading eyes, and heard the hideous cries. Actually, there hadn't been any screams, only weird gurgles, and, if truth be known, she'd been unable to see either the eyes or the mouth. Her thoughts were getting far too morbid, let's not think about that, Monica - and for God's sake, let's not cry, you've spent enough time today fussing with your make-up as it is.

Tentatively, she sat on the bed, which surprised her by being quite comfortable. Was sleep at all possible? She was profoundly exhausted, but she was afraid of having another nightmare.

There was a bang as her cabin plummeted downward, the sound and the motion scaring her. Marvelous, the waters were getting rough.

Back in Shanghai, he'd asked if she'd seen her aunt's killer. Even if she'd been talking at the time, how could she possibly have answered that question? She'd seen something all right, but the only thing she knew for sure was that it had been staying in the room right across the hall from her's at the Astor House. She shuddered as she remembered the unspeakable, shambling *thing*, grateful that it would never be able to find her on a ragged junk in the middle of the China Seas.

IXXX. THE BLACK JUNK

Monday, August 20, 1928

The black junk had been following them all day. Other boats passed them, or turned away on different routes, but the black junk remained a stubborn dot on the horizon. When the captain stopped to repair the forward sail, the black junk tacked into shore, and then circled back into position when they were underway again.

They were sailing southward, about three miles off the coast, a stiff breeze carrying them along at a steady clip. The weather was clear, and the waves gave off long wisps of white spray. With its orange and red sails unfurled, their junk slipped gracefully through a boisterous sea. Close by, the rugged, mountainous coastline was broken up by deep canyons, wondrous rock formations, and an occasional village basking in the bright sunlight.

For the fifth time in four hours, Davies moved to the back of the boat and carefully focused his binoculars, trying to get a better look at the suspicious vessel stalking them. The rolling and pitching of the ocean made his task nearly impossible. "Damn! Why can't these waves hold still?" he muttered as he lowered the glasses.

* * *

The scenery was some consolation to No Sin. He still hadn't forgiven the white man and his unsavory companion for ruining his introduction to the sea. He had timed the serving of the tray of sweets perfectly, badgering the Laota's wife to hurry up with her cooking, for he wanted there to be a little celebration marking the exact moment that the junk left the mouth of the river and entered the open sea. Such a celebration might appease the spirits of the ocean and give them a comfortable journey - it would mark an important event in his life, as well. But the white man's mongrel whore had spoiled the moment, casting their course into spiritual uncertainty. He wished she would fall overboard.

By mid-afternoon, however, his mood was better. It had been a glorious day. At first, the tossing of the ship made him feel ill and frightened; he'd never expected the waves to be so big. It didn't help that ever since he was a small child he'd been afraid of water. But the Laota had given him a little plum wine, and he'd felt fine ever since. Now he marveled at the sights all around, never imagining that such things could really exist. The color of the water, for instance. It was so much bluer than he thought possible. The water in Shanghai was a muddy, yellowish brown and he assumed that the descriptions of the deep blue sea that he had read in books were nothing more than poetic fancy. Similarly, he'd seen drawings and even photographs of mountains and great valleys but he thought that they were grandly exaggerated. Of course, photographs don't lie, but a photograph could make a small mound of dirt look like a soaring peak. Since the land was flat around Shanghai, with no real geography to speak of, he expected the outside world to be the same - but the trees and occasional flowers along the shore, the long stretches of tan beach, and, most extraordinary, the mountains had turned his assumptions on their head. These mountains, with their cloud-shrouded peaks and an endless expanse of mysterious, purplish land behind them, were even more colorful and vivid, and startlingly immense than he'd thought possible. How much he had missed, even living in an exciting and famous place like Shanghai. Perhaps he really had died and was on a long journey to the afterlife. If so, he was thoroughly enjoying it. If only the white man's young lady friend would be swept away by a great wave, everything would be perfect.

* * *

As Davies watched the progress of the pursuing junk, Monica appeared on deck, climbing over the ropes and deck gear, barefooted now, wearing the yellow frock that No Sin had purchased for her. What was going on in her "scheming" head, Davies wondered? She had told him nothing since last night. After consigning him to burn in hell, when he'd checked on her a little past midnight, she'd remained locked in her cabin. She had risen at noon, and quickly returned to her quarters looking like a puppy dog that had choked on its favorite bone. Now her hair was tangled and her face was pale green. "Lord, you look awful," Davies observed.

Monica transversed the junk's last nautical barrier and leaned heavily on the railing, appearing very sorry she had come. "I think I should go back to my cabin." She swatted at her hair, only making it messier.

"Why did you even come out?"

"It's stuffy down there, everyone smokes." She glanced accusingly at No Sin who was striding along the deck, bounding easily over obstacles.

When the boy saw Monica, he stopped short. "Mr. Davies," he said as if they were all late for an appointment, "we go to shore now."

"Why?" Davies asked. At the moment the coastline consisted of nothing more than rocks and empty coves.

"Very important," No Sin answered in the manner of a self-important government official, "today is third birthday this year of Kwan Yin, Goddess of Mercy. She always celebrate birthday with big storm. We must take shelter."

Davies glanced at the sky and back at the boy. "That's ridiculous. Typhoon season has barely started. And look, there's not a cloud in the sky. Besides, Kwan Yin's third birthday isn't for another month."

"Big storm. You see." No Sin pivoted crisply and walked off.

Monica sighed with relief. "Anything to get off this boat."

Davies chased after No Sin, catching up to the youth as he was about to go below. "Sin, a dark sail's been out there on the edge of the horizon for the past day. I think we're being followed, and it would be extremely dangerous for us to stop now. Maybe you'd better tell the captain."

"Captain? Oh, you mean Laota." No Sin descended into the hold. "Okay, I tell him. We go into shore now."

Within moments, their junk began to turn and head for the protection of a narrow cove. Davies looked up at the sky. "Kwan Yin," he muttered sourly, "the Goddess of Mercy."

They anchored in a pretty spot, rocky cliffs dropping sharply into the water, a slender waterfall tumbling down mossy stones. The weather was perfect, a beautiful, warm end to an afternoon.

Despite the potential for danger, it was nice to anchor on still water and get a respite from the pitching of the sea. The crew appeared less stoic and more playful, as if they'd all clocked out after a full shift. Davies found this to be a relief since the sailors that he'd hired seemed to be more surly and hostile then most. With at least one exception. A small sailor with a slight limp had gone out of his way to stop and bow with both of his hands clasped together whenever he encountered Davies. It wasn't clear if the gesture was sarcastic or one of true respect, but the twinkle in the man's eye, and the playful warmth that radiated from him, made either motivation endearing. It was curious how you could feel an immediate kinship with someone after an encounter that lasted seconds, and how you could both quickly fall into the role of best friends, even though neither had spoken a word to the other and had no understanding of each others' respective spoken languages.

After an excellent meal of rice and fish, the Laota and his hired crew settled into a corner of the deck to smoke and play cards. The fish had been caught earlier in the day and was prepared with exquisite simplicity, just a trace of ginger and a spice Davies couldn't identify subtly complementing the natural flavor. Happily, his supper wasn't still moving.

Even on their battered junk, the service and accommodations had been charming. By nature, the Chinese were superb hosts - they concocted gourmet delights out of the simplest ingredients, and made sure that there were always flowers, usually Chinese lilies, set in a pretty blue and white vase in each of the cabins.

Up and down the rivers, and in the ports, there were Cook boats providing all manner of foods and delicacies, which were invariably served with fresh damask and fine quality silver and crystal. How so many poor Chinese came by these things was a mystery. Still, frog's legs, breasts of pheasants and guineas, caviar and pancakes, all were readily available in the most unlikely places.

Hearing an odd muttering, Davies looked to where the Laota's immense wife sat near the bow praying and burning joss sticks.

Several yards away, No Sin sat by the railing reading a Chinese magazine through Davies' binoculars.

Sitting beside Davies, Monica had gobbled up three bowls of fish and rice. The natural color had returned to her face, and the natural fire had reclaimed her personality. Monica put down her bowl and glanced up at the waterfall. "Could you be imagining things, Mr. Davies? All junks look alike."

"Like Chinamen?" Davies asked.

"Yes," she replied without a hint of sarcasm, which he found moderately alarming.

"You know, Miss Marshall, I'm wondering if I didn't like you better when you didn't talk." He lit a cigarette and inhaled deeply, the aroma mixing nicely in his mind with Monica's perfume. "One thing you never cleared up, were you supposed to meet your aunt when she was killed?"

She smiled with resignation and shook her head. "Here we go again. It wasn't cleared up because I was being evasive."

"But that's so out of character."

At least, his sarcasm was still functioning and it was answered by narrowed, scolding eyes. He liked that about her; even when she'd feigned being mute she had expressed a powerful attitude of one sort or another - it caused her to be very much present. "My excuse is that I was so damned tired that night. However, the answer is 'yes' I was supposed to meet her. Typically, she insisted on six-thirty, which happens to be my dinner time. I was starving, and sick of room service, so I went downstairs to eat. I left word for her, though."

"You weren't in the restaurant at the time of the killing."

"Is that a crime?"

"It leaves you without an alibi."

"No it doesn't," she answered readily, then took a gracefully executed bite of rice. "I was posting a telegram, the clerk will remember."

"Who were you contacting?"

"Just a telegram home - 'every thing's fine' - that sort of nonsense."

"I see." The explanation was plausible, perhaps the killer had been watching Monica, and simply took advantage of an unplanned opportunity to ransack the young woman's room.

"How'd she get in, by the way? Your aunt. Did you give her a key?"

She looked up from her food as if the engine of his brain had just thrown a rod. "Are you daft? I didn't want her snooping around."

"But that's been bothering me. Would someone break into your room, and leave the door *unlocked* behind them? And if your aunt had no key, then it suggests that the killer heard her knocking and chose to let her in. Why?"

Her eyes sparkled with a curious delight. "You're accusing me, aren't you?"

"No, but how did you get blood on your dress?"

"Yes," she said, unfazed, "that must have looked rather incriminating. Here's what happened: I went up to my room, and, well it was a mess. I probably brushed against something; oh yes, I think there was blood on one of the chairs." She smiled, mischievously. "Is that a good enough story for you?"

By feigning guilt with a cavalier attitude, she was coming off as innocent. It was a good trick, and he was adequately entertained to let her get away with it. All the same, he pressed on. "Didn't you realize that something had happened to your aunt?"

"Why should I? She wasn't in the room."

"Yeah, but the broken window and the overturned lamp. Not to mention the blood."

"You're really all business, aren't you? Don't you ever have fun?"

This familiar criticism left him stumped for a quick response. It didn't help that she was awfully pretty when her face wasn't green. "These aren't exactly fun circumstances. It seems that your aunt's death means a lot more to me than it does to you."

"You can't expect a half-breed to have human feelings," she said coolly.

"You're the most evasive person I've ever met."

She looked heavenward. "Oh, dear God. I wish I had a car like you, I could always count on it to start. All right, what's the next question?"

Branded as "all business," he was more than happy to accommodate her. "Is there any chance that your uncle killed your aunt? That sounds horribly cozy, doesn't it?"

Monica paused to consider this; her sudden willingness to cooperate was a relief, and Davies took it as a small gift. "It's possible. Uncle has a fearful temper. I only saw him get really furious once," her voice descended to a whisper, "and it made me believe in the supernatural."

"I think you need another drink." Davies drew out his flask and unscrewed the cap.

She was less demure about accepting his liquor this time, throwing her head back and gulping down a good jigger full. She'd be a full-fledged alcoholic in no time, and as he watched her take a second swig Davies realized that he'd failed to consider Mr. Lin a suspect. Certainly, jamming a cigarette holder into someone's head and pushing them out a window was consistent with a violent temper. Also, Madame Lin had been comfortable with her killer. Mr. Lin might have known of his wife's intent to commit her niece. If he had wanted to do away with Madame Lin for some reason, a visiting relative of questionable sanity would be perfect to pin the crime on. Severing Madame Lin's bound foot, however, seemed overkill - literally. "You didn't see your uncle that night, did you?"

She shook her head. Still clutching his flask, she looked downward, her glistening black bangs concealing her eyes. "I'm sorry if I was flippant just now. About my auntie, I mean."

He couldn't see her face, but he could feel her sadness and regret. It wasn't that he was unusually sensitive, rather that she had a unique ability to project her emotions. It seemed too much to hope for that she was finally experiencing the gravity of Madame Lin's death, yet clearly she was. "I won't hold it against you," he said gently, retrieving his flask and taking a swig of his own

"You like to drink, don't you?" The words were said without judgment.

Perhaps it was just as well that he give his policeman side the afternoon off. "Only until I feel a little glow, then I stop. I'm very scientific."

He offered her another sip, which she accepted. She rose and walked to the rail, leaning back and facing him, as if putting herself on display. "What else do you like to do? I'm crazy for jazz." She started to hum something, moving her shoulders back and forth.

He puffed out a couple of smoke rings. "Me too."

"You're just saying that."

"No, I love jazz. Also symphonies. But weren't we talking about something?"

"Of course, but I'm bored now. You read much?"

He fixed his gaze on the fading blue of the sky so she wouldn't think he was leering at her provocatively posed figure. "Sure - science, philosophy, history."

"Mysteries?"

"Rarely."

He heard her take a deep, appreciative breath. "Don't you wish we could stay here for the next week or so?"

The notion was appealing. It would be marvelous to forget about all their troubles and relax indefinitely in this place of beauty. She was humming "Who" and tapping her feet. He'd just endured one of the worst weeks of his life, and enough was enough. He walked to where she stood and took both of her hands in his. She caught on right away. For the next few minutes they danced across the deck, hopping nimbly over coiled ropes and empty burlap sacks, and she smiled the first real smile he'd seen on her face.

When they returned to the rail, he was content to be at a loss for words. Out of the corner of his eye, Davies noticed that No Sin was approaching, possibly with the intent of returning the binoculars. When he was a few feet away, the youth came to a stop and lingered.

"That Chinese boy," Monica said, also apparently noticing that No Sin was spying on them, "he doesn't like me very much."

"I wouldn't worry, I'm sure he's forgotten last night."

"No, it's not that. Just look as this dress." She tugged at the material. "It makes me look like a sing-song girl. One nicknamed 'last chance.' It's obvious he hates me."

"I'm sure he tried his best."

"That's a sad thought." She turned away from him and focused her attention on the mouth of the cove. "Zephyr." Something interesting seemed to have sparked her curiosity.

Davies followed her gaze, expecting to see a school of frolicking porpoises, or a distant whale spout. Instead, the black junk was drifting silently into the cove like a ghost - its hull dark and battered, its torn sails giving it the appearance of something disfigured. No lights could be seen on board, nor any signs of life as it crept closer, silhouetted against the glowing dusk. "Laota!" Davies yelled.

All talking and laughter stopped. The Laota and his crew swiftly rose to their feet and scurried in all directions, dousing lanterns, grabbing anything that might be used as a weapon. The Laota's mongrel ku started to bark loudly. The Laota's wife snatched the affronted animal, hurried to scoop up her prayer materials, then lumbered back to the main deck and went below.

Who in hell are they, Davies wondered - his heart rattling about like a broken part in a failing machine. Had Elder Brother's paternal cordiality been nothing more than a bluff? Or were these pirates? Which was actually the more unpleasant proposition.

XXX. THE SMILING SANTA

The black junk crept closer; with no signs of life aboard, it could be an abandoned derelict.

The Laota and his crew hid in various places as the sinister ship drifted nearer. If pirates were on the black junk, they'd have guns. Davies checked the Colt forty-five in his coat pocket, then escorted Monica to the stairs that led to the galley.

With Monica safely below deck, Davies ran back to join the others. Kneeling behind a gunwale, he surveyed his men. Crouched down and barely breathing, they looked like silly children playing hide and seek. A few of his comrades had produced knives, which glinted in the fading light - but did his crew really have any idea how to use their weapons?

The moist, warm air was still. He could hear the creaking of the approaching ship's hull, and its bow suddenly pierced the random patch of fading sky, which had been his focal point. The intruding junk was larger than theirs, only an arm's length away.

Characteristically a strange, sleepy calm overtook him when his life was threatened. In the past, when he had found himself punching it out with some thug he'd want to laugh - it all seemed like childish play acting. But today was different, too many recent frights and jolts had torn at his nerves.

He rose to get a better look.

A man screamed.

Like frightened birds rising from a marsh, two dozen figures filled the air as a flying wall of yelling attackers landed with thuds on their deck. They had guns and the sickening "pop, pop, popping" began almost immediately.

Darting to the protection of a mast, Davies couldn't tell the attackers from his own crew - he was surrounded by scrawny, wiry men flashing missing teeth, making it hard for his mind to take the danger seriously. His heart wasn't so aloof, his chest felt like it had horses' hooves pounding inside it.

A nearby Chinaman had a gun - his face was long and mean, and Davies knew he was one of the enemy. It was a blessing that the trigger on his Colt was so sensitive; Davies fired before he realized what he was doing, and a chunk of flesh and hair spun off in crazy circles from the side of the man's head. Like a rush of wind, two slugs whizzed by. Davies hid behind a hold, banging his knee. He swore to himself, aware of a nauseating roaring in his ears.

* * *

No Sin could hear guns being fired, but no one around him seemed to have one. Where he stood on an upper deck there were quick flurries of awkward movement, with more threatening posturing than actual fighting. He could see arms flailing, an erratic kick, and then one of the men would retreat - or be left groaning on his hands and knees. There was no elegance or technique, just lots of running, scrambling, wild kicking, heavy, exhausted panting, flailing about, and plenty of fear. He sensed the fear, but didn't feel it - it was like a disease, which he had grown immune to. After life with his father and brothers, fighting only aroused fury in him.

* * *

Another bullet whizzed by Davies' head, sounding like a ferocious bumblebee. What the hell had happened to his characteristic calm? *Just slow down, relax your breathing,* but his body wasn't listening. He hated this. He heard a thump. His body sprung up, saw a looming figure, and his hand fired the Colt over and over. His arm wanted to get into the act, making him punch as he shot. The attacker swatted at his shoulder, then crumpled. Davies ducked down. Could he have just shot one of his own crew? *Jesus.*

Every inch a fool, he'd left his ammunition in his cabin. He crouched down and checked - there was one bullet left. How could he be so out of breath - and so damp with sweat? An image of Monica, flashed through his consciousness - her clothes torn and bloodied, tears streaming down her face as hulking invaders circled her.

Was the man he shot still alive, ready to attack? He needed to check and fumbled onto one knee, told himself "now" and did nothing. *Hell.* Again, his body made the decision for him and he sprung up, not even bothering to look at the fallen opponent, which was the whole point of springing up in the first place.

Instantly he was slammed backwards onto the deck and smothered under a huge, flabby, foul smelling body. Davies' arm was thrown back and the gun fired its last bullet, hitting nothing. He squirmed beneath the behemoth, who was exuding the oniony smell of dirty sweat. As hard as he tried, he couldn't move beneath the man's soft girth. Rough, fat fingers clamped around his neck inflicting awful pain. His lungs burned and he was unable to suck anything in. *I can't let this happen* his mind screamed.

Using his pistol as a club, he knocked the man on the head, over and over, terror surging in him as he realized that his blows had no effect. Fading into blackness, he reached out and found the man's flat nose, which he twisted with all his might. This drew blood, he could feel it hot and sticky dripping on him, but there was no let up on the pressure around his neck. Then, at once, the man shifted slightly to one side, Davies going with him, and he saw, in the flurry of motion, that a pair of arms was wrapped around the giant's head, gouging at his eyes. It was No Sin.

Davies' left arm was now free. As hard as he could, he smashed the man in the face - but, with a tiny amount of punching space, his blows were feeble. Maybe repetition would prove effective, and he aimed for the man's already naturally flattened nose, hitting it with a staccato rhythm, and doing his best to stay clear of No Sin who still clung to the big man's head. Finally, the giant became annoyed. Trying to get away, he rose up just enough to free Davies, who clasped both hands together and struck the huge Chinese against the side of his skull using all the force he could muster. The man was knocked off balance and he fell over with No Sin clinging to him. Rising, Davies repeatedly kicked the big man in the head.

* * *

Below deck, in the junk's galley, Monica listened to the sounds of battle on the floor above. She was grateful not to be alone - she didn't think she could stop herself from becoming a shivering, sobbing child if forced to wait by herself in her cabin, wondering who was about to come through the door. In the galley, the captain's wife seemed to be even more frightened than she was, forcing Monica into the role of brave comforter, which was a strange blessing.   She murmured words that the older woman couldn't understand, in a tone that she could, as she petted her hair. Clinging to each other, and flinching with each pop from a gun, Monica concentrated on a pan of boiling water, which was sending a white cloud of steam into the air.   She had a good-sized knife in one hand - if someone came down the stairs, her free hand was ready to dart to the handle of the pan, then fling the scalding liquid into the intruder's face - all as a prelude to going to work with her knife.   Knives were something she'd had some experience with, which made the fantasy currently playing in her mind sickening to contemplate.

*   *   *

Apparently no one had brought enough bullets. All around Davies now were hand-to-hand scuffles. The fighting style was different than in the West, but still a brawl was a brawl. Skirmishes had deteriorated into exhausted embraces, clothes-tearing, and clumsy kicks. Most of the men who'd started out as boxers were now tired wrestlers on their way to becoming ballroom dancers.

Davies and No Sin had separated after leaving the giant moaning on the deck – he hoped the boy was okay.

A member of the crew was propped against a nearby gunwale, staring upward, a tooth dangling at the end of a bloody spit trail coming from his open mouth. Leaning down to help, Davies saw a vertical gash beneath the left eye, marking the spot where a knife had been driven deep into the man's brain. Davies recoiled, feeling dangerously light-headed. *Don't you dare get sick*, he ordered himself.

Toward the far side of the deck, No Sin was defending himself against two large attackers. Davies could see the seasoned fury of a boy who had spent his youth being beaten by older children. As Davies moved forward to help he caught sight of a dark, muscular Chinese with the sleek face of a snake, and wearing a pair of large hoop earrings, sneaking toward the entrance to the galley. A knife flashed in the man's hand, and an image of Monica flashed through Davies' consciousness - her clothes torn and bloodied, tears streaming down her face as the sinuous invader circled her, a lascivious grin broadening his face. Davies ran to cut the man off, back-stepping quickly, as the Chinese lunged at him. Looking desperately for a weapon, all he could find was a length of heavy rope, which he grabbed and swung at the man as violently as he could, using it as a whip, and aiming for the eyes. The knife wielding attacker retreated, shielding his face - but Davies was knocked off balance by his own enthusiasm, and he smashed into a wall. Looking up, he saw that the man was already coming at him. Davies hadn't the time to right himself - feeling that his heart was about to explode, he imagined the awful bite of the blade as it punched hard into his body.

There was a blur and some shuffling sounds; No Sin had hold of the knife, which was still in the far more muscular attacker's hand. There was a studious look on the young man's face as he grappled with the shining weapon - it may be as close as No Sin came to expressing fear, this flat, calm expression, as he and his adversary performed a weird, jerky dance, finally falling to the deck and rolling about.

Davies felt afraid for No Sin, and he kicked the muscular man hard, aiming for the head, but connecting accidentally with No Sin who grunted with pain. Suddenly both combatants lurched upward violently, then toppled over again, disappearing behind several barrels. No Sin and his opponent were now wedged between the barrels and the junk's hull so that all that Davies could see was their flailing feet. A glistening, richly veined arm, a knife securely held in its clenched fist, raised from where the mostly unseen battle was taking place, and another arm, far more delicate, grabbed onto it, struggling to hold it back. The muscular attacker had the advantage and in mere seconds his knife would plunge into No Sin. With miserable timing, a tangle of rope was jarred loose by the fracas and it fell with a loud thud and tented the fighters, so that Davies could not easily grab onto the snake faced man's arm and wrench the knife from his grip.

Aided by the clarity of desperation, Davies grabbed one of the man's exposed legs and, utilizing a strength that he didn't realize he possessed, he dragged both No Sin and the attacker out from the tight space behind the barrels. In the disorienting swirl of motion,

Davies felt a cold knife blade brushing against his neck, then pulling away with a sting.

Recoiling, he realized that warm moisture was streaming down his chest. Dear God, had his jugular been hit? The attacker was already back on his feet, and instinctively Davies lurched forward, head-butting the dark-skinned man, who fell crashing to a lower deck, landing on his back like a helpless insect, and making a sickening crunching sound. From out of nowhere, one of their crew dashed over and made a small quick movement, as if he wanted to slap the man on the shoulder. Davies heard a "thwak thwack" sound suggestive of a mosquito being swatted, and the snake face man's leg sprang up for some reason. Then he groaned, his mouth opening and retracting like a fish's, gasping for air. Davies saw the dark red slit in the center of the attacker's chest, which had been made by a knife blade. Like a wounded animal, the snake faced man was still alive, but only half there. Seconds passed before the mouth stopped its contortions, and the glazed eyes rolled up.

No Sin stared down at the body, his own dull eyes and open mouth superficially mimicking his adversary's. The boy was an excellent target, so Davies forced him to kneel behind a hatch.

In the blur of motion, Davies glanced up at the enemy boat and saw a white man who resembled a demented Santa Claus with white stubble in lieu of a full beard; his arms outspread on the railing. He looked to be fifty, with a face that was fat and red. He was smiling an ugly smile, and wore round spectacles and a large, white cowboy hat. It was such a bizarre and unexpected sight that Davies feared he was hallucinating.

The remaining attackers were now scrambling over the rail and leaping to the safety of the black junk. Realizing that they'd carried the day, his battered and wounded crew began to pick themselves up from the deck. Those who were able, shouted obscenities at the departing attackers. Those who were able shouted obscenities at the departing attackers.

Davies felt trapped in a strange white mist that was swirling about him; he was dizzy and exhausted, and the roaring in his ears wouldn't go away. His shirt was damp with blood, but he was still alive. Feeling the mercifully small wound on his neck, he realized that the muscular fighter's blade had missed his jugular by less than half an inch.

Across the deck, Monica was peeking out from a hatch and she seemed to be physically sick; No Sin was dazed and pale.

Davies' hand stung. Glancing down, he saw that it was bleeding and filled with slivers. How had that happened?

Of the twenty or so men who had attacked, half were scrambling back to the enemy junk - but the fight was out of them. They scampered around their ship, hoisting sails, screaming at each other. Davies smiled, though he didn't know why, and felt for his revolver, surprised to find that it was already back in its holster. As he watched, the black junk began to sail away.

XXXI. THE WATER DEMONS

Feeling an awful sense of triumph, Davies placed his good hand on the rail for support, and thought that he was a member of a small, exclusive club - those who've killed. He had a knowledge and power denied to others. Immediately, he felt guilty and ashamed, and dirty to be experiencing such a dark pride. His emotions began to twist around inside him, a sense of weary satisfaction, of bloated importance, being replaced by instant shame for allowing himself to feel even a flicker of gratification.

Frightened shouts were coming from the water. Davies, who'd been on his way to check on Monica, returned to the rail. Four men were flailing about, screaming for help. Three of them were crew members from their own ship, one of them being the sweet, limping man with the twinkle in his eye. Their voices were shrill; none of them could swim. Davies stripped off his bloody coat.

A sailor with a gold tooth crossed the wooden deck and grabbed him. Davies tried to pull free, but the sailor had an incredibly strong grip. Now other crew members were swarming around. Mustering all his remaining strength, he wrenched himself free from the sailor, and began to take off his shoes. Again the sailor grabbed him by the arm. "For the love of God!" Davies shouted. "Those men are drowning!"

A fist flew through the air and his jaw exploded with pain as his head snapped to one side.

No Sin had joined the crew, his hands were clenched, his eyes narrowed and burning with fury. "This all because of you! If you try help them," he spat out, "nobody will help you no more!"

Stunned, Davies looked at the boy, then at the malevolent faces of the other crewmen. It seemed incredible that they meant business, apparently subscribing to the old Chinese legends of water demons who dictated when it was time for a sailor to die. If the crew interfered, and the men were saved, the water demons would claim everyone in revenge. Perhaps it would happen later that night - the ridiculous storm that No Sin had predicted would capsize the boat with a huge wave.

There wasn't just anger on the faces of these men, but great pain. They cared about their comrades and hated to see them perish, but they had the grim determination of souls clinging fiercely to an unshakable set of beliefs. Perversely, the more they felt anguish and doubt, the stronger and more resolute they had to become in response. Davies had seen such looks before on the faces of zealots and soldiers carrying out street executions, men who took stoic pride in their ability to conquer any humanity inside themselves. Staring back at the members of his crew, he felt in greater danger than during the fight. "How can they live on a boat all their lives and not know how to swim?" he shouted futilely.

He made a final attempt to break free, but two more sailors came forward, one of them pressing a knife to his throat. There was nothing he could do but listen to the four shrieks echoing across the water. After an unbearable length of time, four screams became three, then three became two. The sound of thrashing arms grew faint, and the foreign words from pleading mouths turned into gurgles. Finally, one almost irritating pleading wail sounded as if it was the last note of a symphony. After a few moments, mercifully, all was silent.

"You've murdered them!" Davies said evenly, barely able to move his head.

Several sailors, including the one with the gold tooth, released him. The Laota and the crewmen quietly set about mopping up blood from the deck, and rolling bodies over the side. The splashes were ugly reminders that the events of the evening had been all too real.

Near the bow of the junk, one sailor was hunched over and sobbing; it was a safe bet that one of his closest friends had been in the water.

Transfixed, No Sin watched members of the crew drag corpses across the deck and toss them into the sea. The few members of their own crew who'd perished were carefully set aside, presumably to be disposed of later with a ceremony. Seeming to be lost in a dream, the slender youth broke away from the others and went to stand at his favorite rail near the stern. He stood alone, staring out at the ocean. Davies pulled on his coat and made his way to the bow of the ship where he did some sulking of his own.

XXXII. A BLOODY MOUTH

An hour after the fight, the men of the crew began a lengthy ceremony to appease the spirits of their departed comrades. It was a colorful ritual, which Davies wished to avoid, so he went down to the galley where Monica and the Laota's fat wife were drinking tea. The room was dimly lit by peanut oil lamps, which gave off an oddly welcoming smell.

"It's ridiculous," Davies said, still able to hear the low muttering of the crew praying over the dead. "If only I hadn't stopped to think! I should have jumped straight into the water, shoes be damned. By the time I figured that out, those men had drowned." He curled his upper lip contemptuously for emphasis. "I must remember never to think again."

"The crew would never have let you back on board," Monica said quietly.

"So what?"

"So where would you take them? There's no beach, just sheer cliffs and a fierce tide. You'd have drowned too." She took a sip of tea. "Which would have made me kind of sad, I hate to admit."

About the last thing Davies expected Monica to be was calm and supportive; it seemed entirely out of character - not that he knew what her character was.

The Laota's fat wife put a bowl of rice and vegetables in front of Davies. "Eat," she said.

Though the food smelled fresh and inviting, Davies pushed the bowl away. "I'm not hungry,"

"You eat," she grunted sternly, returning to her stove.

In contrast, Monica remained the image of pastoral warmth. "If you had angered the crew so they wouldn't help us, and we sat here, mightn't that other boat come back?"

"Not pirates," Davies said, "they'll go find an easier junk to plunder." Monica's gaze drifted to the floor, and Davies remembered the man in the cowboy hat. "What if they *weren't* pirates? Could they be bounty hunters - after you? Or maybe someone thinks you still have 'the clouded twilight.'" A logical theory, Davies thought, rubbing his sore hand. On the other hand, white men were known to collaborate with Chinese pirate bands - but their usual style was to book passage on a steamer, smuggle arms aboard, and commandeer the vessel at the right moment. Usually, the Chinese members of the gang would pose as part of the crew. "Monica, have you ever seen the fellow on that junk, the one wearing the cowboy hat?" He thought back to No Sin's description of the man who had sold the staff to Hong Fat.

Monica seemed irritated by his question. "I have no idea what you're talking about."

"I'm talking about that white man, baby...."

The Laota's wife turned from the stove. "Baby? You have baby? Ahh!" She wiggled a finger at him, scoldingly. "Naughty boy."

Davies chuckled, despite his frustration with Monica who'd cast aside compassion for more evasiveness. Thinking of all the little missteps that should have been nipped in the bud before they cascaded into disaster he felt his fury rising again. "I was insane to give that Chinaman credit for having more than a gnat's intelligence. We should never have stopped here! The Goddess of Mercy! Big Storm!"

"Yes, yes," the fat woman said, smiling and nodding, "big storm! I know!" She pointed to her heart.

"Grandmother," Davies said in measured tones, "if there's a big storm anywhere in China during the next month, I will kiss your enormous, lumbering, uh, never mind."

The woman's eyes brightened and twinkled. "You kiss? Ahhh, you sweet."

Three hours later, as the ceremony on the lower deck continued, Davies and Monica stood on the upper deck in the thick, hot air. They both felt a need to discuss the evening's battle, to find some meaning in the deaths, and to critique all that had occurred as if it was a play or a novel. Yet, certain events were avoided; they were too unpleasant. Finally, there was so little to say, and so much to feel.

A vivid flash of white lightning lit the sky. A sharp, boom of thunder followed, and below deck the dishes and pans rattled. A pattering of rain swept across the ocean toward them. The sound of the downpour grew steadily louder as rain pelted the ship in deafening, staccato sheets. Below them, the ceremony broke up as the deluge scattered the mourning sailors.

Holding his blue cotton jacket over his head, No Sin hurried up to Davies, a self-satisfied smile broadening his face. "Big storm," he said, looking upward, "I tell you. Always big storm on this birthday." He scurried away, victoriously.

As they watched the rain, standing under a furled sail for protection, Monica took his arm. Despite all her childish behavior, her silence and tantrums, Davies felt very close to Monica, and comfortable in her presence. Something had changed, perhaps it was everything they'd been through. In a peculiar way, they seemed to belong. The feeling was unspoken but mutually understood; there was no buildup, it just happened.

"I'm sorry about earlier," she whispered, "but I thought you would know better."

"What do you mean?"

"The man you asked me about. Of course, I know him. But I don't think I should have said so in front of the captain's wife."

"I don't follow."

"I thought you were the detective. If those were pirates, we were just unlucky. But if they were after me, then you and I would be blamed for the deaths of our crewmen - we're not terribly popular with them as it is."

"You're right," he said wearily, "I should have thought of that."

"You're tired. Besides, you're a man. Men aren't used to seeing things any way but their own. Women don't get to run the world, so they have to constantly put themselves in other people's shoes."

He *was* tired, and he responded defensively. "Actually, I'm very good at putting myself in another fellow's shoes."

"I'm sure you are. But have you considered putting *someone else* in the other fellow's shoes?"

"Huh?"

She seemed amused by his confusion, which made him feel even more hopeless. "Granted, you're the rare man who can imagine what it's like walking in someone else's shoes, but it's still *you* doing the walking - not everyone is you."

It was a good point, and one that surprised him; he hadn't expected someone whose behavior was often spiteful and childish to be so insightful. "So what about that man?"

She glanced downward, revealing a vulnerability that he'd not seen before. Previously, he'd assigned his own brand of vulnerability to her, one that flattered his self-image as a great protector. But the real thing was different, it didn't make him feel strong, it made him feel sad. "He's not nice." She turned away from him to look at the tattered, black sea.

"Can you tell me what happened between the two of you?"

She didn't answer right away. "I met him coming over from the States," she said, hesitantly. "He got me drunk one night aboard the ship,...." She stopped, the memory clearly wasn't a pleasant one.

"Did you mention the staff?"

"Probably, I'm an inexpensive drunk. I remember him carrying me into my cabin. The next thing I knew they were taking him away with a broken leg."

"*He* was the one who ended up with the broken leg? Boy, I'd better behave."

The slump of her shoulders indicated that his glib retort was not appreciated. "It's my guess that he stole the staff from me out of revenge."

"Or to cover his medical costs." What on earth was the matter with him?

She turned and looked up at him as if seeing him in a new and not very flattering light. "Your ability to wisecrack sure recovers quickly. Remarkable after everything that happened this afternoon."

He felt his face growing hot. They'd just come through a life-altering experience, but rather than being altered, he had reverted to behaving like a cocky-teenager, desperate to impress - an unshakable habit that overtook him whenever he was in the presence of a woman to whom he was attracted.

"So, when all this is over, what will you do?" She asked, thankfully changing the subject.

He didn't get the sense that she was being evasive, but rather making a peace offering. Relieved, he responded in kind. "I haven't decided. I own several thriving businesses in the United

States - though they're probably thriving because I'm not running them."

She brushed at his shoulder.

"What?"

"You've got a chip." A faint smile formed on her lovely face. "Just like me."

He had to smile in return. "Well, at least, I had the good sense to leave my younger brother in charge. I hate to admit that the kid I used to pick on proved to be a natural businessman."

"Exactly what did bring you to China, then? I know you don't need the money."

"Sheer adventurism. Having grown up in a rarefied, wealthy atmosphere I wanted to test myself against the harsh life that my parents tried to insulate me from. I must say, the life I exposed myself to turned out to be far harsher than I expected."

"You found your servants watering your liquor?" Her ability to wisecrack had also made a quick recovery.

"I think I'm telling you too much about me. It's ironic, I have a reputation in Shanghai as a kind of sinister xenophobe - like a von Krupp or a Zaharoff - when I still see myself as a spoiled rich kid who can't tie my own shoes."

She glanced at his feet. "They're fine. But next time try to find socks that match."

He looked down. "These socks match."

"Sometimes you just ask for it." She squeezed his arm.

Her sudden flirtation threw him off his game, causing him to counter with even greater seriousness. "I'm so sick of things like what happened earlier. I'm starting to see life as an unending barroom brawl. I've been globe trotting for decades, and I must tell you, the best that life has to offer is pale and flat. It hasn't a 'Chinaman's chance' against the worst that life can effortlessly conjure up, I know that now."

"Can we talk about something else?" she said softly.

"Sure." He took out a cigarette and leaned against the ship's closest mast.

She glanced up at him, regarding the cigarette with contempt. Remembering her complaint about everyone smoking on the junk, he put the cigarette back in its case.

"So what will you do when you get back to the States?" she asked.

"Interesting you should ask, I only just decided. When I was able to get No Sin out of prison it gave me a satisfaction - a kind I've never felt."

"I see. So you've decided to go about saving people whether they like it or not?"

The jab stung. "I know Sin wanted to be saved - I suspect you do. Helped anyway."

She rested her head on his shoulder. "Yeah, I do. And I'm grateful for what you've done."

Her display of affection was so appreciated, that it made him feel as if he was a perfect version of himself. He chuckled inwardly, thinking that his own mood swings were keeping pace with hers - their mutual exhaustion was probably to blame. In gratitude, he kissed her gently on the top of her head. "Maybe this sounds funny to you, but to answer your question, I thought I'd build homes - nice ones that just about anyone can afford. I'll help people to buy them, too. And definitely, no racial segregation - that's one thing I learned from Shanghai - the races should be together."

"So, is all this nobility really important to you? Or are you just trying to fight boredom?"

Again, he felt the sting of insight. "Look, it's not right," he said. "The way people suffer in China. The world over, for that matter. The poverty, the sickness - it's just not right."

"What a hopeless romantic. No, I shouldn't criticize, think of what a catch you are." She drew back and looked him up and down. "Rich, good-looking, and a moral crusader to boot. Women must throw themselves at you."

"They're more likely to throw things at me."

"Nonsense!" She gave him a knowing look. "Not with your money. I hate to say this, darling, but you talk too much."

Why did she have to end every pleasant encounter with an insult? She'd be lovely and affectionate one moment, and the next she was slicing him to pieces.

Monica let out a sigh, and again rested her head on his chest. "I have a confession to make."

Davies glanced down at her, hoping that she was about to reveal why she couldn't resist treating him like old finger-nail clippings - though a genuine soul purging was probably too much to hope for.

"Before Madame Lin's death, someone broke into my first hotel room, at the Sassoon House. Whoever they were, they filled up my cold cream and all my jars of facial cream with broken glass. I guess, I'm lucky that my fingers got sliced to pieces instead of my face."

"Jesus. Would he do something like that? The guy whose leg you broke?"

She laughed a bitter, throaty laugh, raised her head from his chest, and stared out at the rain. "Yeah, he'd do something like that. Except,..." She grew very still.

"Except what?" He glanced down at her. "Monica?"

She shook her head.

"Tell me."

"We better get some sleep."

"You brought it up. Now I won't be able to sleep unless you tell me."

She took a deep breath. "The night my auntie was killed I saw a man leave my room and go into the room across the hall."

"Oh really?"

"I wanted to know what the hell he was up to, so I knocked on his door. Well, he didn't answer - so I peeked through the keyhole." She shivered, certainly not from cold on this blistering night. "He was wearing a big heavy coat, and had very pale skin with dark circles around his eyes. There was blood all around his mouth, and he had awful, stringy gray hair. He didn't look human, Zephyr!"

His mind commanded him to remain skeptical, but it couldn't stop the hairs on the back of his neck from rising. Could she possibly know about the mutilations performed on Madame Lin? He knew he hadn't told her. "I don't believe that Lon Chaney is touring China."

Her eyes glinted with anger. "I'm not joking, Zephyr. I can't help it that it's true! After I saw that thing, I grabbed a bellboy and I told him to go get the hotel detective. Well, the bellboy was a moron, 'How do you know the guy broke into your room?' he kept saying."

"'I'm not going back in there,' I told him, 'maybe he's got an accomplice.' So finally we went into my room together, and of course the place was a wreck. Then I saw that thing leave from across the hall and go to the stairs - so I ran after it. God knows what I would have done if I'd caught it. I was chasing it when you came up to me by the taxi."

Despite this rich display of emotion, Davies couldn't dismiss the possibility that she was kidding him - or that she was truly crazy - or maybe the most manipulative person he'd ever encountered. On the other hand, it was easy to imagine a stringy-haired, black-eyed ghoul severing Madame Lin's foot and keeping it in a jar. He tried to sort it all out by putting Monica in Monica's shoes instead of himself. This exercise became so confusing that he quickly gave up.

"Zephyr?"

"Yeah?"

"How do you know that we're not on a wild goose chase?"

He pulled her close and stroked her hair. "I'm usually right about these things. I know that sounds smug, but look, at least, you're out of Shanghai"

"Yeah, but this time I almost wish that you're wrong, that we don't catch him. I'm not eager to see that thing again."

It was nearly four in the morning when the rain finally stopped. The patter of dripping water was hardly noticed by Davies, who stared out the open window in his cabin below deck and saw that a few brave stars were peeking through the steamy, white clouds. It was still quite warm, despite the rain, and his wool pants and white dress shirt felt damp.

Monica stirred in his arms; she had been cuddled there for over an hour. He had barely slept, but it hadn't mattered - though his joints ached from being so careful not to wake her. One of her eyes peeked open, and then the other. They closed immediately and she hugged his arm and gave him a little kiss on the lapel. "I missed you," she said drowsily.

Davies felt a startling jolt of happiness. "What do you mean? I've been right here all night."

She frowned like a child, her eyes still closed. "Yes, but I was asleep, you know." Her face grew calm, she was far away somewhere, dreaming.

XXXIII. DEATH IN THE HARBOR

Tuesday, August 21, 1928

Bearing no resemblance to Shanghai, Foochow was a postcard perfect Chinese port. Beyond the colorful patch-work of sails crowding the waterfront, the buildings were exclusively Chinese - old-fashioned with high, whitewashed stucco walls, winding narrow streets, and moss-covered orange and green tile roofs. The homes and shops glistened in the morning sun, and the harbor was surrounded by delicate islands and the forested slopes of mountains that rose into brooding, fog-shrouded peaks. The city was far cleaner than Shanghai, its traditional Chinese character uncorrupted by foreign invaders.

Standing on a creaking wooden dock, Davies paid up and bade farewell to his hired crew. Monica, with natural and genuine warmth, shook everyone's hand and smiled in her beautifully shy manner - but the Laota accepted her graciousness coldly, and the rest of the crew were equally surly.

No Sin carried Davies' luggage from the wharf to the shore, where an army of coolies pulling rickshaws and wheelbarrows swarmed down on them. In response, No Sin waved his arms and yelled threateningly, forcing the invaders to keep their distance.

"Hello, what's this?" Davies called out as he slipped into a rickshaw. The coolies were shaking their fists at No Sin.

"Please, I will carry all bags," the boy said forcefully. He grabbed four pieces of luggage, and, struggling beneath their weight, he marched toward the heart of the city.

"Hey! Hey!" Davies shouted after the defiant youth, then ordered the rickshaw driver to follow in pursuit.

"Where are we going?" Monica asked as she climbed into her own rickshaw.

"I don't know where Sin is going, but I intend to call on a shipping agent - we want a Japanese coast wise steamer that serves this port."

Foochow was very much like Venice; a maze of canals with quaint little bridges and heavy sampan traffic. When they finally caught up with No Sin he was in a square near the center of town, sitting on the luggage, panting and perspiring heavily.

"That's far enough, Sin. This is too big a load for you, and we can hire coolies to handle it from here." Davies stepped from the rickshaw and drew out his wallet.

"No!" No Sin said emphatically, "I carry bags!"

Davies had not expected the boy to come any further than Foochow, and he assumed that No Sin knew this. He counted out enough money to generously compensate the lad for his troubles and get him back home. "Sin, I appreciate what you've done, and I think we're square now. As you indicated the other night, you don't owe me anything."

The boy shook his head. "Mr. Davies, please, I go to America with you! I know I am bad son," his expression contorted, bitterly, "but I have bad family. I can make good, Mr. Davies." The pain on his face disappeared, and he smiled brightly. "I have fourteen dollar saved! I can pay my way on ship!"

A crowd had formed, several dozen people moving in close to look at the tall foreign devil and the argumentative boy. Others were frowning curiously at Monica, uncertain of what she was. No Sin pivoted sharply, picked up the luggage, and stumbled onward.

"Sin!" Davies shouted after him, "you can't just hop a boat to another country like a trip to the drugstore."

"Why not?" He turned abruptly, and with a smug smile he faced Davies. "Lookee here, you need someone to protect you - to teach you wise things. Last night you almost jump in water and give yourself to water demons, right? And you not know that bad storm was coming. You need protection from such not good thinking, Mr. Davies."

Davies did not need protection from his own thinking. "All your friends and family are here in China."

"I have no family! My mother - she dead. My father, what kind of father is he? He stink!" He smiled brightly. "I send him money from America - don't worry."

"No," Davies said, "it's out of the question."

Tears began streaming down the boy's cheeks. He sank to his knees and sobbed. Davies had not expected such an extreme reaction. He waited for the crying to subside, but it only grew more intense. The boy's despair was so absolute that, against his will, Davies began to feel his own heart breaking.

Not one to be outperformed, Monica grabbed Davies' sleeve. "For God's sake, Zephyr, do you let everybody boss you around? Let him go! I have no clothes, my auntie is dead, people are stalking me - if anyone should be throwing fits, I should! You don't see me giving you ultimatums."

A loud moan came from the spectators. An old man waved his walking stick menacingly at Davies and shouted something hostile in Chinese.

"Please, do I come with you?" No Sin cried desperately.

"Sin, I told you,.."

"Oh, brother!" Monica interjected.

"Both of you, shut up!" Davies shouted.

The boy wailed, "But you just leave me here!"

"Don't you see how he's playing you?" Monica called out, exasperated.

No Sin responded with a siren shriek of despair.

"Alright! Yes!" Davies said loudly and threw up his arms. "If you shut up you can go."

No Sin looked startled. "Really?"

Davies nodded.

A damp grin overwhelmed the boy's face. "I will shut up, Mr. Davies. If that what you wish, I will never speak again. I serve you in silence, forever. I will..."

"Please shut up, Sin."

Though Monica had also fallen silent, she was shaking her head with disgust. Irrationally, her disapproval caused Davies to feel a pang of shame – for what he didn't even know. "I'm sorry for yelling," she said as if she had been dealt a great injustice, "don't pay any attention to me." Despite her sarcastic attitude, her tangled hair and ugly dress gave her the appearance of an abandoned waif being subjected to the unconscionable treatment of a white faced brute.

Davies pulled out his wallet and gave her all the Chinese money he had. "Buy yourself some clothes, Monica. And for God's sake, get a brush for your hair."

Monica's eyes lit up like a child at Christmas. She grabbed the money and marched off, displaying only contempt for the well-entertained peasants.

Davies shouted after her. "Meet me over there at that little curio shop in two hours. Sin, you watch after her."

Unenthusiastically, No Sin shuffled off in pursuit of Monica.

Temporarily freed from his new "children," Davies located a hotel where he was able to telegram Crockwood, appraising him of his sailing plans. He asked his old friend to do a little snooping and see if Singletone had stumbled on to any new clues. He signed off, jokingly, asking his ex-drinking partner to be a liaison with Elder Brother.

A cocktail or two later, Davies rendezvoused with No Sin and Monica, who seemed to have bought out several local shops. Accompanying Monica were two coolies, who'd been recruited to assist with her things. No Sin had both hands free, and he used them to reach for the small package that Davies was holding; apparently he was loathe to help carry any of Monica's bundles.

Davies and his new traveling companions soon found the ship at the north end of the harbor, a rusty tramp steamer of Japanese registry. The chubby, smiling Japanese captain was polite in a way that made one feel immediately ill-at-ease and suspicious. At least, there were no tea boys allowed on his vessel. The awful tea boys would swarm around a passenger, pouring cups of tea at every hour of the day, whether the passenger wanted tea or not. If they were not tipped at the end of the voyage, their patronizing grins instantly vanished and one was lucky to disembark without a beating.

After Davies had settled into his stateroom, he joined No Sin up on the deck. They had plenty of time to stand around and admire the harbor because the ship was late in departing. "Is this satisfactory, Mr. Davies?" Monica asked as she made her entrance. "It's quaint, don't you think?"

"Perfectly satisfactory," Davies replied as he admired the new coat she'd purchased. It was Chinese, clearly handmade, but rather smart. The buttons had Chinese characters carved into them, and Davies fingered one. "I wonder what these mean? 'Open late Fridays?'"

Monica slapped his hand away. "They're good luck charms. And it's very warm, I adore it. Oh, and I got a new frock, see?" She pulled open the coat, revealing that she was wearing a dress of white silk that clung to her, caressing every inch of soft flesh beneath it.

Davies felt a sudden desire to commit an unspeakable act with her right there on the upper deck. He tempered his passion by giving her a quick nod of approval, then turning his gaze to the harbor.

"Did you notice the captain?" Monica asked, oblivious to his inner conflict.

"Briefly. Why?"

"You aren't bothered by the three small soiled spots on his lapel?"

"Not really. You're very observant, however."

"I'm not entirely comfortable entrusting our lives to a man who's so haphazard about his appearance." In response to Davies' chuckle, Monica added, "Don't laugh! Really, Zephyr, if we sink you won't find it so funny."

"I don't know, I might."

"We not going to sink," No Sin said in a soft, resolute voice.

"What's taking so long?" Monica demanded, proving that she could always be relied upon to jump to another subject without warning. "Shouldn't we have sailed by now?"

"Perhaps the captain is changing his uniform," Davies replied. "Actually, it looks like we're going to sit here until that man gets aboard." He pointed into the harbor where a sampan with a single yellow sail was making for them at great speed.

Monica peered at the little boat, then caught her breath. Standing in the middle of the small vessel, like Washington crossing the Delaware, was the fat, pink-faced man from the black junk - his cowboy hat pulled down low over his eyes. Behind the fat man's sampan was another that seemed to be in pursuit.

As the fleeing sampan quickly reached the side of their ship, the little fat man grabbed a single battered suitcase and fumbled his way up the Jacob's ladder.

Waiting on deck, the Japanese captain smiled and bowed, accepting a thick roll of bills.

"Where'd he get that money?" Monica whispered.

Davies didn't answer. He was wondering if the small man had found them intentionally, or if his arrival was just a ghastly coincidence. Whatever the fellow was up to, it would be better to remain calm and keep his concerns to himself - things would reveal themselves in time. After all, for the next day or so, as they sailed to their last Chinese ports, the little man wasn't going anywhere.

No Sin nudged Davies' shoulder and pointed at the fat man in the cowboy hat. "Why he here?"

"You know him?"

"Of course. He sell Hong Fat old walking stick."

Davies nodded, hardly surprised by this revelation.

Having pocketed his cash, the captain waved at the bridge. The ship's whistle let out a fat blast.

In the pursuing sampan, five or six coolies shouted angrily as they reached the side of the ship and the Jacob's ladder was pulled out of reach. Their crew consisted of a grandfatherly old man, a middle aged man who looked very patient, and whom Davies imagined had come along to offer a voice of reason, two tough-looking sailors, and two little boys who seemed to be enjoying it all. They could easily be members of the same family. A good-sized dog rounded out the crew; it barked loudly, apparently as offended as its masters.

"Someone forgot to pay his bills," Davies said, watching the fat little man shout insults and obscenities at the pursuing sampan, which were promptly returned. After making a final vulgar gesture, the little man turned away and made his way below, limping.

"That limp so fake," No Sin muttered. "I hope his other leg break so he match."

A second blast from the ship's horn caused Davies to jump. Within moments, a low rumble pulsed through the deck, and slowly the cargo ship began to move out into the harbor.

Behind them, the little sampan adjusted its sails and pursued the larger vessel as if it was a small dog yapping at the wheels of a bus. Inherently swifter and more nimble, the sampan caught a fine gust of wind and pulled ahead of them. As a fervent believer in the bitter laws of irony, Davies predicted what would happen next. The little sampan lost its wind, and its sails deflated. Helpless, the small boat sat placidly in the water as the larger craft bore down on it. The insults screamed by the Chinese crew swiftly became frenzied yells of panic and fear.

On deck, Monica grabbed Davies' arm. "They're going to hit it! Tell them to stop!" She waved feverishly at the bridge.

"I'm sure they know," Davies replied, reassuringly.

"Then why don't they turn?"

"They probably want to teach them a lesson, they'll turn at the last moment."

* * *

On the bridge, the smiling Japanese captain pointed out the sampan to a garrulous, heroically built, red-faced Englishman, a well-to-do China hand named Surgeon Major Devor-Hyde. "I say," the Surgeon Major exclaimed with sincere alarm, "those fellows seem to be in trouble."

"They just Chinaman." The captain turned to his mate and grunted. It would take some effort, but there was still time to turn and avoid the little sampan. The grunt meant that the captain did not wish to expend the effort.

* * *

The ensuing seconds seemed to drag on forever. As the Japanese freighter sailed over the little boat, it exploded into jagged fragments of splintered wood. Several of the Chinese sailors jumped off the sampan at the last minute, the patient-appearing man looking straight up at Davies, their eyes locking. He was quickly sucked underwater by the freighter's propellers, where he met a fate far worse than drowning. When the freighter's white wake churned out no more debris, they had lost their struggle with the water demons.

Not again! Davies felt as if his soul had also been torn to pieces by the propellers; tragedy and violence had been stalking him for a full two months now. Would it never stop?

Monica collapsed into Davies' arms. If she was a ruthless, cold-blooded killer she was way out of practice. Davies had to carry her to her cabin and put her to bed. She emphatically insisted on being left alone, "no ifs, ands or buts."   Despite this, she was still sobbing when he reluctantly shut her door behind him.   He felt guilty leaving her, but what else was he to do?

No Sin remained on deck, staring at the sea.   He stayed there until the sun went down, expressionless, unmoving.

Davies attempted a troubled nap until dinner time.   The effort was useless, all he did was lie on his bed and stare at the ceiling. His earlier, cheerful mood had been shattered; again the despair that he'd been fighting since his little engraver friend had shot his girlfriend in the head back in Shanghai six weeks earlier was overwhelming him.

He finally mustered the energy to rise and walk to a porthole, through which he watched the distant city of Foochow recede from view.   No longer was the port charming and quaint - all he could see was a world filled with useless, garish ornamentation - a hodgepodge of shoddy things that would only grow old and decay - meaningless things that, in ways he could no longer understand, tricked fools into thinking that life was worth living.   The sky, the sea, the forests, the reassuring beauties of nature that had always comforted and inspired him were nothing but faded light, empty space cluttered up with random and uninteresting shapes and textures – and once one left the realm of nature it was downhill from there.

After the battle of the previous day, he'd assumed that lightning wasn't going to strike twice, that he'd be rewarded with a long stretch of peace - but China did things its own way.   The afternoon's incident in the harbor was rare, but not unheard of. Coolies rated so low on the human scale that there would be no repercussions for their Japanese captain - it was conceivable that no one would even bother to register a complaint.

XXXIV. AN EVENING OF GAMES

Though neat and clean, Davies' stateroom was furnished with little more than the bare necessities: a bed, a dresser, a small desk, and a separate bathroom with a stall shower. The linoleum floor and faded blue curtains gave it a spartan atmosphere, like that of a cheap, Midwestern hotel room. Davies had finally fallen asleep thinking about a cursed walking staff encrusted with priceless jewels and how attractive it would look on the parlor wall of his home.

His dream-filled sleep didn't last for more than forty minutes. Nonetheless, he did muster the will to shamble out of bed when last call for dinner came at around eight pm. Thank God, he was starving, or he'd probably have blown his brains out on the spot.

Before eating he had an errand to run. He had little enthusiasm for pursuing the case after the tragedies of the past twenty-four hours, but soldiering on might help buck up his spirits. Therefore, he went first to the purser's door, knocked and entered.

The purser, a small, delicate Japanese, was not particularly helpful. His greatest service was to provide a manifest from which Davies was able to eliminate two-thirds of his fellow passengers because they were already on the ship when Madame Lin's killing had occurred back in Shanghai. He also determined that no one had brought a maroon steamer trunk aboard.

The ship's dining room was as banal as the cabins. It was painted a yellowed white with the same faded blue curtains. However, the six tables were covered with white linen, set with surprisingly good silver and crystal, and adorned with a charming arrangement of flowers done in the Japanese style. Unfortunately, the greasy meal of baked chicken and potatoes matched the faded curtains and linoleum, not the crystal. Davies speculated that the cook would try to make some kind of soup out of the gravy for lunch tomorrow.

Twenty odd, (very odd,) passengers were distributed amongst six tables. Most were Caucasians, and several gave him acerbic stares as he greeted Monica and pulled out her chair so that she could sit beside him.

At a solitary table in the far corner of the room, the pink-faced man, still wearing his cowboy hat, ate with revolting gusto, his jowls dripping with gravy. Davies sorely wished that there was some way he could get the man arrested for piracy, but he had no proof - nor did he have the energy for a confrontation. Maybe tomorrow. After the awful event in the harbor, his spirit wanted rest and calm.

With the conclusion of dinner, Monica and Davies retired to the ship's lounge and were recruited for a game of ma chiang by the ingratiating Surgeon Major Devor-Hyde. The fourth player was a thin, effete Chinese, impeccably dressed in an elegant, Western suit.

The lounge was formal, paneled in dark mahogany, and divided into two clearly defined sections. One area was dedicated to reading, while the other was set aside for more extroverted passengers. In this section, the "extroverts" on hand sat at small tables and ignored each other.

The game of ma chiang was fierce, and Monica played with surprising aggression. Davies felt that she seemed a bit too enthusiastic, and he suspected that she was doing all she could to blot out the memory of the afternoon's shocking "accident." The other players were equally energetic, perhaps for the same reason. Mindless relaxation was just what the doctor ordered, and the little tiles clicked and clacked noisily as the players picked them up and discarded them, muttering to themselves.

Davies looked up momentarily from his playing and saw that the jolly fat man with the cowboy hat, coffee cup in hand, was making his way out of the dining room. When he realized that he was being watched, he turned away so quickly that he collided with a chair, jarring the coffee cup so that its contents splattered over the front of his suit. "God damn!" he cried. A wet and messy sight, he brushed at his shirt and pants, then waddled into the more "introverted" section of the lounge.

"Boorish fellow," Surgeon Major Devor-Hyde said, and the game continued as if nothing had happened - but Davies noted that, for some reason, the effete Chinese shot the exiting man a look as venomous as any that Elder Brother could have mustered.

* * *

Still wiping coffee from his shirt, Huey Arnold stood glumly in the quieter section of the lounge: a comfortably worn room with overstuffed armchairs and shelves jammed with a disarray of books and outdated magazines. Muttering to himself, he made his way through the musty room, passed an unoccupied bar, and slumped into a sagging chair. He examined his shirt more closely. He had bought it a week ago in Shanghai, a beautiful four dollar silk shirt. He examined his pants - ruined. He crossed his leg and caught sight of a bruise he'd received climbing out of the sampan. Below the bruise, on his stocking, was a long run in the black silk. "God damn it," he muttered, staring at the run, "now I suppose I'll have to buy new clothes." He lowered his head and wriggled his foot nervously as he sulked about the injustices of the world. He should be a rich man by now. He should be a captain of high finance, wearing a natty bowler and strolling down Wall Street. Famous bankers should blanch with fear as he passed them; they should tip their hats respectfully, and spend the next twenty minutes of their time speaking about him in the most hushed of hushed tones. Or he should have listened to his mother who'd always advised him to follow in his father's footsteps and be a carnival barker.

That damned old Englishman playing tiles had given him a hell of a start. Some trick of the light made him seem like the other guy. Those saggy old limeys shouldn't be allowed to all look alike.

"Stop shaking your foot," a rasping female voice ordered.

Huey peered to his right. In the chair next to him, partially hidden behind a fat Japanese lamp, was a stout woman with sagging dewlaps and blue hair. Her mouth was a shriveled apricot, and her pale, blue chiffon dress looked like something from a Halloween costume party. The woman glowered at him. "I'll call the steward and tell him to put a ball and chain around it in another minute."

He stopped moving his foot and said, "Maybe I've had enough bossing for one night, mother."

"And maybe you haven't." The woman placed her hands on the arms of her chair as if ready for battle. "And why on earth don't you remove that ridiculous cowboy hat. Are you planning on lassoing a fish?"

He laughed. "Say, you're a bad egg. I'm going to have the captain throw you overboard."

She gave him a sympathetic smile. "I see you have a gift for comedy. It must come naturally to you, going through life as a clown. Are those brown stains on your shirt part of your routine?"

Huey looked down at his shirt and felt angry all over again. "There's a little tart on this ship did this. Jeez, they ought to keep you women on leashes." He leaned closer to the lamp, and whispered in a low, croaking voice, "She's done things that a man doesn't like to speak of. - not even to another man."

"I am not another man," the woman snapped.

"You coulda fooled me. Here, I'm going to show you something, mother." He pulled out his wallet and dug through a mass of business cards and papers. He held up several black and white photographs. "Look here, my wife and two daughters. Real lookers, aren't they?"

The woman gave them a brief glance. "They're grotesque."

"Hey now," He scolded, as he carefully unfolded a magazine clipping. "This is from a National Geographic Society monthly. December of nineteen hundred and twelve." He handed it across, keeping his voice low. "That Manchu walking staff is on this ship at this very moment."

The woman studied the creased picture. "Is it? And how do you know?"

"It was stolen from a shop in Shanghai last week, my darling. The little tart that spilled coffee on me took it. And you know what else?" He shifted in his chair and leaned closer. "She killed the shopkeeper. Then she killed her aunt, threw her out a window - an old lady - just like you."

The woman gave him a sour glance.

"You know how much that thing is worth?" He smiled, knowing how impressed she'd be.

"Fifty million dollars."

The over-packed baggage didn't believe him. He snatched the clipping and stuffed it back in his wallet. Why were women such pains in the ass? The less they had to offer, the more full of themselves they were. Well, they'd learn, learn that Huey Arnold was not someone to be toyed with. Leaning in close again, he whispered. "I'm going to tell on her to the captain of this ship. There's a reward, you know."

"Dear God, I've been stuck on this wretched ship for three hideous weeks, and just when I thought it couldn't possibly get any worse, you walked in. I think I shall give up traveling altogether."

"Maybe you should give up breathing." He pulled himself out of his chair. "Say, have we met before? What's your name, mother? I'm Huey Arnold."

The old lady lifted her chins as if she were announcing that she was a member of someone's royal family. "I am Mrs. Rosamund Kissler of Boston Massachusetts."

"That's too bad." He gave her the leering, sneering smile that she deserved, and strode out of the room.

When he reached his cabin, Huey Arnold locked the door behind him and flopped onto his bed. From under his pillow he drew out a paper bag filled with magazines he'd bought in Shanghai. He found the dog-eared page with a photo of a nude Russian girl on a messy bed, her arms resting across the headboard, her legs spread. She looked slightly drugged, poor thing. Huey removed a passport photo of Monica from his breast pocket. He placed Monica's picture over the head of the Russian girl and sighed. Monica had a pouting expression that was delightfully provocative with her nude Russian body. He loosened his belt and laid back on the pillow, listening to the steady throb of the ship's engines. "I must be an ill man," he said to himself, wondering where in hell the little bitch had hidden the stuff. Next time her cabin was empty he'd go through her things, even if her handsome, dumb-as-nails boyfriend was on the prowl. Jeez, when was she ever gonna learn about jerks like that?

An urgent knock sounded on his door. He set the magazines and photographs aside and tightened his belt. He slipped off his bed, forced the literature back into the paper bag, and slid it under his mattress. Walking to the cabin door he shouted, "Who's there?"

"You drop something," a youthful Chinese voice called back.

Huey opened his door a crack. The door catapulted inward, smashing him in the face. When he regained his balance, Zephyr Davies and some snippy little chink were inside his room.

* * *

"You don't look so good," Davies said to the little man, who appeared to be slightly dented after being hit in the face with a door - No Sin felt sorry for him. "Why don't you go into the loo and clean yourself up?"

"Maybe you should leave me the hell alone!"

"I think you've cut your lip."

"Well, that's your damn fault if I did."

To No Sin the little guy sounded like a "whimpery" child doing his best to stand up to a bully. If Davies was a bully, he had good reason to be - still, No Sin didn't like to see him act like one.

"Here, we'll help you." Davies grabbed the fat man by his damp armpits. No Sin came forward to assist, which allowed him a little control over his belligerent friend. They half-carried the fat man to the bathroom.

"Hey! Let go!" the fat guy yelped.

"No problem." Davies pushed the poor little man into the bathroom, slamming the door behind him. Davies nodded to No Sin who obeyed by holding the door shut.

"Hey! Hey, what are you doing?" a raspy voice bellowed as fists banged on the inside of the door. The little man's protests were mostly for show, and No Sin only had to apply a small bit of his strength to keep the door from popping open.

In the meantime, Davies had found some nasty girlie magazines beneath the mattress, and he slid them under the locked bathroom door. "Here. Keep yourself busy."

"What are these?" the little man shouted, "where did you find these filthy things?"

Davies paid no attention and began to rummage through the little man's room. Inside a bureau drawer he discovered six identical, small photographs of Monica, which he held up. "Obviously passport photos," he said, as if this should have great meaning for No Sin.

Davies then emptied the drawers of the fat man's dresser onto the floor; some scribbled papers seemed to interest him. "Hmmm, Monica's home address and room number at the Astor House Hotel. Also Madame Lin's address in the Nantao District."

This also meant nothing to No Sin, who watched passively as Davies went through the man's luggage. When he'd finished, he emptied the pockets of all the clothes hanging in the closet. Apparently there was nothing more of interest to be found, so he signaled for No Sin to open the bathroom door.

The little man was sitting on the closed toilet seat, and he threw the open magazines on the floor. "This is assault and kidnapping, sir," he said, rising and walking, duck-like, out of the bathroom, "a very serious crime on the high seas."

"Sorry," Davies replied as he sat on a built-in bureau. "I may have lost a toothpick in here - I was hoping to find it."

"You really think you're slick, don't you? My God! Look at this mess!"

"Sorry. Badly raised - no manners - send a complaint to my mother."

"Go to hell!" the little man spat. "You better stop riding me, fella. I can tell the captain."

Davies reached into his pocket and brought out a silver case. "Cigarette?"

The man blinked with surprise, falling for an old trick designed to make him drop his guard. After Davies lit the cigarette for him, the small man said, "I'll hand you a tip, keep your back to the wall when you're with her." Abruptly, the fat man turned and looked at No Sin. "Hey, don't I know you?"

"Of course," No Sin replied. "I am wicked."

"What the?" The little man was thinking so hard that it appeared to hurt. "But how do you two,...? This is strange."

"How did you meet Monica?" Davies asked casually. "Start at the beginning."

"What? Okay, I'll tell you what happened. A month ago she hires me in Seattle, right? We come out here, to Chinaland. I got my connections, and I find the thing she's looking for is at this Hong Fat's. - and I tell her so." He gave a short laugh and filled his lungs with smoke. No Sin had to turn away because the man's huge nose was pitted with blackheads and a residue of chicken fat still glistened on his bulging double chins. "So what does she do? Not only doesn't she pay me, she makes up a story and gets me arrested! Then she skips out. She takes all my money, my clothes, the works! I had to buy everything new! She even took my tooth powder!"

"Yeah, we could tell that you haven't been brushing." Davies leaned on the dresser and folded his arms. The ship swayed and creaked, which put the funny thought into No Sin's head that Davies' weight on the dresser was causing the ship to tip. "So you're claiming she never had the staff?"

"No, that's not what I said." He wiped his greasy chin. "Is that what you think I said? No, she had it all right."

"How could she have it, 'all right,' if she hired you to find it? Remember how you did a Herculean job of investigating and finally located it at Hong Fat's?"

"No, uh,..." the small man stammered.

"That what you say," No Sin pointed out.

"I mean, uh, that she had it *after* I found it for her."

"Well, I didn't hear it that way."

"Hah!" the man snorted, "What else would a liar tell you?"

"And what else would you tell me? Sorry, in a pinch, I always believe the one that's prettier."

The little man gazed moodily at his cigarette. "I was just trying to help you."

"Yeah. If she'd been arrested, you'd have loved watching them lob her head off back in China."

"I don't want to see her dead!" He grinned, showing off yellowed, gnarled teeth. "Just make her life hell on earth."

Davies pushed himself off the dresser, walked over to the little fellow, and grabbed him forcefully by the lapels, nearly lifting him off the ground. "You think you're funny? Nine men are dead, is that funny? There are laws against piracy in this part of the world."

"I don't know,..."

"I should think our captain would like to be informed of your recent escapades."

"You can't prove,..."

"I'll be more than happy to testify that I saw you on that junk,..."

"What junk?" The little man was speaking rapidly now, his face glowing like a tomato that was ripening before their eyes. "What makes you think you saw me?" He squirmed. "And how do you know I wasn't being held captive?"

Davies released the man and looked him square in the eyes. "You're lucky I want a little calm tonight. But don't think for a moment that your actions won't have consequences. Now, what about your visit to Madame Lin?"

"Who?"

"Don't kid me. Monica's aunt, she lived by the river - with a rose garden."

"Oh, the old Chink."

Davies grabbed the little fellow once more, causing No Sin to feel sick with anxiety. The small man raised his hands to protect his ugly face. "No, I didn't mean that! Sorry! I'm sorry, okay!"

Davies released the man, but his fists remained clenched. "Don't ever say anything like that again! She was a very good friend of mine."

"Okay, I'm sorry. I just wanted to know where Monica was. She cheated me, I told you that. Monica, I mean!"

"Got it. Once again, what were you doing on that junk?"

"What junk?"

Davies slapped the little man on his flabby cheek.

"Don't hit me!"

This plea only increased Davies' anger. He struck the small man again and again - it was as if he had been taken over by a demon – No Sin began to get frightened.

Yelping, the fat man tried to cover his face with his hands. "Help! Help!" he cried out."

Davies kept striking, even more violently, and No Sin couldn't take anymore. "Stop it!" he shouted, grabbing his friend's arm, "he littler than you! Don't be bully!"

No Sin immediately regretted being so blunt. What if Davies was so insulted that he sent No Sin back to China - or he became even more enraged and struck out at him, too? Instead, surprisingly, Davies stopped his attack and let his arms fall to his sides.

Greatly relieved, No Sin let go of Davies.

"I was hired to find her, okay?" the fat man said in a blubbery voice. "I didn't know those guys would actually attack you! My Chinese is no good; they must have misunderstood me."

"Who hired you?" Davies asked quietly, yet radiating an impatience that kept a knot tied in No Sin's stomach.

"The lady's husband, the lady who got killed." The little man was almost crying, and No Sin felt bad for him.

"Mr. Lin?"

The small man kept his hands in front of his face. "Yeah, that's the guy. He thought your friend, Miss Marshall, killed his wife. He offered a reward, and he was the one that chartered that junk, I swear."

"You were smiling. You saw all those people killed, and you were smiling."

"I smile when I'm nervous. See, I'm smiling now." He lowered his hands, revealing an unconvincing grimace.

Davies probably had more questions about the pirate attack, but he was so furious that no one could predict what might happen next. Davies seemed to understand this about himself, and he moved to the door and glanced around at the wrecked room with its clutter of strewn clothes and debris. "You know," he said, "I think your room is much better this way. It has a nice, lived-in look."

"I'll thank you not to call again," the small fellow said, jutting his chin in the air. Then he quickly lowered his head like a dog who knew it was unwise to provoke the leader of the pack.

Davies closed the door and walked with No Sin toward the rear of the ship, where the moon was making a long trail of sparkles on the waves. "That guy is a great suspect," he said, insincerely. "Trouble is, he has almost no money, and no pieces of a missing telegram - or a jar containing a severed, bound, human foot. There's nothing to link him to Madame Lin's death. Nothing at all."

No Sin didn't understand, but he nodded, and hoped that he'd be in bed and asleep before another half hour passed.

* * *

XXXV. AMOY

Wednesday, August 22, 1928

The power of time was astounding. After leaving the cabin of the little fat man Davies was dispirited and frustrated. By breakfast the following morning he was in a grand mood. His night, unexpectedly spent with Monica, had made all the difference, fulfilling fantasies he hadn't realized he had. He'd gone to check on her just before midnight and had been startled to hear cries coming from her cabin. He'd pounded on the door and she'd let him in. As it turned out, she'd been having a nightmare. He lingered at her bedside, tucking her in and comforting her, and one thing led to another. She'd surprised him by being the most sensuous and adventuresome lover he'd ever encountered. In the bargain, he'd learned something far more exhilarating and significant: Monica had an open heart. He'd been with plenty of lovers who could perform all manner of sexual acrobatics, foaming and groaning with frenzy and fury. Few, if any, of these had touched his heart. It wasn't something that could be explained, just that some people had something inside of them that sparked emotion in him, emotion that was deep and real. It was like a burst of sunlight that stung the eyes, it was either there or it wasn't. It wasn't illusion, and it couldn't be faked. With Monica he felt it from the moment they touched, he felt it at their moments of stillness, he felt it when her pelvis was thrust forward desiring to be part of him. That she had this quality was a shock, and answered one nagging doubt; it was simply impossible that she could be a cold-blooded killer - a hot-blooded killer, possibly. She behaved in bed as she behaved out, alternating between being coy, affectionate, flattering - and then cruel, ferocious and biting, (literally). The combination was so passionate and exciting that it eclipsed any encounters he'd had in the past. He'd never had complaints about his love-making, but with Monica he discovered that he had skills, desires, and abilities that he hadn't known were there.

What had sealed the deal for him, however, was the conversation that occurred when the love making was over. "Are prostitutes noble?" she'd asked as she'd run her fingertips gently over his chest.

To say the least, the question took him by surprise. "Are you about to ask for payment?"

She sat up in bed. "Perhaps I should. No, silly, I was just thinking that a street walker has to learn to like all physical sorts."

"Am I to take that as a criticism?"

"Only if you're insane." She pushed herself higher, getting comfortable. "No, listen now. Isn't that kind of enlightened, liking all physical types? I mean, isn't that what happens when people fall in love and grow old together? As their bodies change they still love each other, don't they? Don't they learn to appreciate each physical form their lover takes? And don't prostitutes have to do the same thing, only faster?"

He found a peculiar charm to her questions. "I don't think prostitutes learn to appreciate the different physical types they sleep with, so much as they simply tolerate them."

"But isn't that the same?"

"No. Tolerating something isn't appreciating it."

"But doesn't it bring you to the same place? You concentrate on who a person is, not what they look like. Aren't prostitutes really accepting? Can't a man go to one sometimes and be accepted and understood in a way no one else could offer?"

"How should I know?"

"Oh. I just thought. Never mind."

"So is this what *you* think?"

"No. I'm Catholic so I'm not permitted to entertain immorality. That's why I'm asking your opinion."

Her superstitious logic amused him. "Won't my opinion be just as immoral?"

"Probably. But it's interesting. And I can't get in trouble for listening to it. I mean, it wouldn't be my fault if I heard you ranting on a soapbox in the street - you'd be the sinner, not me. You know something, Wallace, I've decided I like you."

"Wallace?"

"You seem like a Wallace to me. I like it better than Zephyr, it's more substantial, more distinguished."

He was too tired to offer more than a weary smile.

"Don't worry, as long as I call you Wallace you'll know that I like you. Don't you want to know why I like you?"

"I hope it doesn't have anything to do with my socks."

"It's because you're a nut."

"I thought I was distinguished."

"No, I mean, you don't think like other people. Besides you put up with me." She studied him through squinted eyes. "On the other hand, I'm not entirely sure that I should put up with you. You can be a little hard to control, not that that's bad - it certainly wasn't a few minutes ago. But I'm a moody person, and there are times when all I'm going to want from you is blind obedience." She pressed her index finger to the center of his forehead. "Hmmm, I wonder what would happen if I gave you a little lobotomy with one of my hat pins." This was all it took for him to launch another bout of love making.

He was still too jaded to think that falling in love was possible. However, as he waited for breakfast to arrive, and recollected his last few hours with Monica, he realized that he was enjoying the best mood he'd experienced in months. He liked to think that they were both broken watches, which were starting to tick once again.

Despite the pleasant time they'd spent together, Monica had opted to pass the morning in bed; the events of the past few days had affected her powerfully - he'd look in on her after lunch.

As he sat alone at his breakfast table, he forced his mind back to grim matters and made another careful appraisal of the other eight passengers in the dining room. Each of them seemed capable of murder: the men were a seedy lot, looking to be the dregs of bitter, failed businessmen returning from the Orient. The three women were strikingly thuggish. Two of them could have passed as retired prison matrons who regretted having given up their jobs. Mrs. Kissler, the third woman, was an ancient dowager dressed in pale apricot chiffon, which matched her hair, and who was wearing as much make-up as a circus clown. She sat in a wheelchair manned by her handsome maid, a Negress, and seemed to take particular interest in Davies, chewing her food slowly and watching him like an owl circling a field mouse. Her stare caused him to feel an irrational guilt, as if he was being silently judged for having slept with a half-caste a few hours earlier.

Though all of his fellow diners were strange or sinister in some way, none of them looked adequately cadaverous to qualify as Monica's Astor House monster. Yet all of them would fit if dressed for the part.

He didn't have anything immediate on his plate for the day. Since the search of the small fat man's cabin had been so utterly fruitless, the fellow could no longer be cast in the role of Trees. The only thing to do was to wait, hoping that the real Trees would be discovered amongst the passengers - or be spotted boarding in Amoy, their next port of call. If Monica's description was to be believed, Davies could expect to see a gaunt figure wearing a tattered cape, clawing his way up the gangplank. In the meantime, was an aggressive approach preferable - or should Davies attempt to relax and enjoy himself while he waited, something he'd lost his knack for?

The aggressive approach came naturally, and was actually more relaxing to Davies n his current, anxious state, so he ran through a list in his head of all the people on board who could be Trees - someone who would have been in Shanghai at the time that Madame Lin was killed. That pointed the finger at Monica, and the little fat man. What of Surgeon-Major Devor-Hyde, or his aesthetic Chinese friend - had they come from Shanghai?

The nature of a coastwise steamer was to make a number of local stops along the Chinese Coast. Their freighter had originated in Yokohama a week and a half ago from where it had sailed to the island of Formosa, going on to visit ports on the Chinese mainland. Along the way, it had docked in Shanghai, then taken off on a criss-crossed route that was best described as whimsical. To be amongst them, Trees would have had to have made a fast, convoluted trip to one of the smaller ports, then boarded as Davies had done.

He spent an hour chatting with his more suspicious traveling companions. Most were evasive to one degree or another. Two inadvertently provided information that disqualified them as potential murderers. Surgeon-Major Devor-Hyde, and a saggy looking businessman, however, proved worthy of being kept on the list of possible suspects. The fey Chinese had also been to Shanghai recently.

Having gotten his fill of intrusive chit chat, Davies decided to call it a day. He returned to his cabin just before noon to drink and nap.

* * *

Thursday, August 23, 1928

They reached Amoy at around three in the morning. The slow throb of the ship's engines was suddenly absent, causing Huey Arnold to slip out of his troubled sleep. Without switching on his light, he crossed to his porthole to spy on the activity in the darkened harbor. Cargo was being unloaded onto various boats and barges as the ship lay at anchor. It was too cumbersome and time-consuming to tie up at a dock, especially with so many ports of call to be visited up and down the China coast.

Huey returned to his bed and switched on the table lamp. After swallowing a cozy wad of mucus, he studied his cabin's decorative molding and thought the unhappy thoughts that seemed to flourish in the dead of night. Why was someone like Zephyr Davies allowed to come into his room and push him around? Why had he been such a coward in response? He sighed, actually it was more of a wheeze; if there was one thing he could count on it was that he would always do the wrong thing at the wrong time. At least, he was consistent.

Sure as hell, he had a long history of mucking up - so many lost opportunities, so many dreams mangled. He would have made a great orator, a legendary big game hunter, the best dad any kid could hope for - he was wonderful around the little monsters, one of his rare skills. If only the photos he carried in his wallet were of people he knew, but he'd pirated the shots after he'd picked the owner's pocket. Now the chances of his ever having his own wife and kiddies was about zero. Plenty of women found unattractive jerks to be appealing, but they drew the line at him. Well, it was their loss.

Why did he bother at all? Why did he still harbor moronic illusions that eligible ladies could be muscled into regarding him as a wit? Face it, he tried too hard, and, for some reason, he couldn't stop himself from trying too hard. The fact was, everybody regarded him as a boor, and so be it.

What had caused his life to go so badly? Probably when he'd entered government service with idiotic notions of helping others. That job had seemed so promising, until he realized that not even a family of wetbacks could make ends meet on what it paid. Thanks to the stinginess of the almighty government, his goal of helping others had to be modified to simply helping himself. Not much, just enough to land in jail. After that disgrace, everything he touched turned to cow shit. Even his trademark cowboy hat was a reminder of a past disaster. Well, no point in dwelling on that.

He was jinxed, plain and simple - cursed with the ability to laugh at himself, which only gave him the strength to pick himself up and go on to bigger and more painful failures. It was almost funny, all that he had left was his faithful hat, and his own, mindless smile. No more self-esteem, no more dreams, and no hopes whatsoever for the future. His only companion: the hilarious assurance that things could only get worse, which they always did. One thing was sure, he had nothing to lose.

He switched off the lamp and stared up in the direction of the ceiling. What bothered him the most was that, when all was said and done, all he really wanted from Monica Marshall was that she be his friend. He had no illusions about his appearance - or her youth - but why couldn't she just like him? This sentence repeated in his mind until the words broke away, one by one, and he didn't know what he was thinking anymore - something about something. Then he was asleep and snoring loudly. Somewhere, lost in his dreams, he could tell that the sound was disgusting - even to him.

A little before seven in the morning there was a scratching sound outside Huey's cabin, which startled him out of an apprehensive slumber. He slipped off his bed and crept towards his cabin door. Carefully, he undid the latch and chain and cracked the door open; it was a big mistake.

* * *

Zephyr Davies was in bed when the sharp bang of a gunshot resounded through the steel passageway outside his door. Ironically, he'd awakened several moments before the shot, or maybe he'd only thought that.   Either way, the sound was unmistakable, and he was into his greatcoat and out the door in less than a minute.   No Sin intercepted him and they both bolted downstairs and into a corridor, rushing in the direction of the ugly noise. In the small recess outside the fat man's cabin, they found the little fellow on his knees, trying to crawl back inside. As they got closer, he collapsed and lay still.

XXXVI. THE HATMAN

Davies leaned down to feel the little man's pulse; as he did so the fellow moaned. "Let's get him inside," Davies said, not wanting to be a target himself.

No Sin helped him drag the fat man into his stateroom and onto the bed. "Are you hurt?"

"Oh, Dear God! Somebody shot me!"

"Are you sure?" Davies asked, seeing no sign of blood.

The fat man sat up, angrily. "I should know, damn it!"

"Where?"

"Well, well," he felt himself, then pointed to a section of his flabby midriff. "There."

Davies pulled up the man's shirt.

"Ouch! Damn it!" the man shrieked. "Be careful!"

The raised shirt revealed a lot of greasy, white skin, but no gunshot. "You're bruised a little, that's all. You may have bumped yourself when you fell."

"Let me see." The little man swung his head around and took a look for himself. "Someone did shoot at me." He began a sulk.

"I expect so. We heard the shot, as well. Any ideas who might have done it?"

"You, for starters - or your half-breed, tramp girlfriend."

Unlike Madame Lin, Monica did not yet hold a sacred place in Davies' heart, so it was easy to forgo a confrontation. "No one else?"

"Who else could there be?"

Davies went and inspected the door's outside molding, staying half way inside the room in case someone decided to take a shot at him, too. Sure enough, there was a slug embedded in the wood, and it would have missed the little man's head by about three inches. Davies pried the large slug out with his jack knife and pocketed it, thinking that Trees had used a twenty-two back in Shanghai.

A small crowd had gathered in the hall. The captain and several crew members had also arrived, and they reassured the agitated passengers that everything was fine. Very few people were convinced.

"What happened?" the captain demanded of Davies. "Is he all right?"

"See this here?" Davies pointed to where he had removed the bullet. "Somebody took a shot at him. Here's the slug - looks like a thirty-two." Davies handed the hefty chunk of lead to the captain.

"Thirty-two, all right," the captain concurred, holding the bullet up to a hall light. "When's he coming out? I want to talk to him."

"He's not hurt, only a little shook up. Don't you think we should be looking for the shooter?"

"Half the passengers carry guns," the captain said, shrugging off this suggestion.

"It still wouldn't hurt to check." Davies stepped out into the hall and, in the interest of getting the ball rolling, he walked over to the first groggy passenger he could find, and began quizzing him.

Not liking his position of authority usurped, the captain ordered several of his mates to fan out and gather information. Begrudgingly, the mates went and banged on nearby cabin doors, rousing whoever was inside.

Unfortunately the whole operation descended into chaos. The captain understood that the cabin search was to uncover the identity of the shooter, but most of his mates thought that it was to reassure the passengers. These mates went ahead on their own, inadvertently tipping off potential suspects, while taking no notice of suspicious behavior. Davies soon realized that the affair was a rout, so he let the captain and his crew go on without him, and returned to the corridor outside the fat man's cabin.

Determining the trajectory of the bullet, he estimated that the shooter had been standing about twenty feet away at the end of the hall. Unfortunately he'd chosen a spot next to the main stairway, which meant that he could have darted to an upper deck where there were a number of more expensive cabins, or raced one floor below to steerage. He might even be staying on the Hatman's deck. As a capper, there were no clues to be found - no damp footprints, no telltale fibers, no conveniently dropped cigarette lighter. All in all, Davies would have been better off if he'd stayed in bed.

After leaving the "crime scene," Davies stopped off at Monica's cabin to make sure she was okay. No Sin came with him.

Davies didn't suspect Monica of being the assailant. True, she had plenty of motive, but it didn't seem possible that she could have gotten her hands on a thirty-two revolver. He'd paid for her current wardrobe, even the suitcase that contained it. Her shopping spree in Foochow had been with his money, and she'd kept receipts and accounted for every penny spent.

"What happened?" she wanted to know as she let them in.

"Somebody took a shot at your little friend."

"I heard that. How is he?"

"I'm afraid they didn't get him. You were here?"

She pulled her robe tighter and snugged up the sash. "Why? You think I tried to kill him?"

"No, I can't imagine you missing."

"Do you have any idea who might have done it?" She looked at him like a teacher who was advising a pupil that he'd feel a whole lot better if he told the truth.

Davies laughed. "We have a lot of faith in each other."

"I wouldn't blame you if you did." She sat on the edge of her bed. "He's an abomination."

"He seems pretty harmless."

Her expression became serious. "He's like one of those poisonous toads - you think they're nothing more than ugly - you never imagine how dangerous they are."

"You're the one that broke his leg."

"I was terrified, thank you very much."

Davies helped himself to a small, wooden chair near her bunk, while No Sin remained standing. "So why is he so dangerous? What's his name, by the way? You wouldn't tell me before."

"Oh, right, his name is Huey Arnold, but he calls himself the 'Hatman.' That's because, well, he makes money forging things. Phony passports, and such. They're called 'hats.' You know, a cover." She seemed uneasy, and amplified it by winding her watch, which lay on an end table.

Davies tried to make himself comfortable on the hard little chair. "Did he help you with a passport? Don't you have one?"

She answered as if she felt she was being forced to explain something to someone who wasn't very bright. "Well, obviously he helped me with a passport. Why else would I deal with his kind? Look, you're welcome to stay here if you're still tired."

Though said casually, it was the kind of invitation that always registered. "Wouldn't that be a little scandalous?"

"Well, I meant that, you understand, uh, just in case you need me to protect you, that's all." She looked over at him and smiled demurely, her plump lips glistening and parted slightly. If the Hatman, wanting revenge, had poked a gun in through the porthole and shot him in the back at that very moment, it's unlikely he would have noticed. "Let's be frank, Zephyr," she said, her voice descending to a whisper, "what if that *thing* is aboard?"

"Okay, I understand." He took her hand and squeezed it.

Across the room, the ever-curious No Sin reached for the dirty Kewpie doll that had been in Monica's purse, and which was now reclining on her dresser. "Hey look at this!" he said, picking it up, "this is very adorable. Can I buy one in America? Very good luck, I betcha!"

Monica sprung up and bounded across the room. "Don't touch that!" She yanked the doll away and slapped No Sin across the face - the sharp sound echoing off of the shining, wooden walls of the cabin.

No Sin brought a hand to his reddened cheek and stared at her, blinking back tears. "You slap me again! You stupid, stupid, awful person! I hate you!"

"Get out of here!" she shrieked. "Don't you ever touch my things! Do you hear me? Ever!"

Davies had to step between them before they came to blows. "Sin," he said sternly, "I think you better go."

"I go," No Sin muttered, giving Monica a look that would melt steel as he marched to the door. "Witch," he grumbled under his breath, as he slammed the door behind him.

"What did you say?" Monica lurched for the door. Davies had to restrain her - he was astonished by her strength.

After calming Monica, and all but tucking her in, Davies was unable to finagle any explanation for her strange, violent behavior. He gave up and went out on deck where he found No Sin staring at the sea. "Sin, as much as you don't like her, we have to all get along. I'm a little concerned that this Hatman may try to assault her. I'd like you to watch her door for a bit - then I'll come and take over."

"Maybe not so good idea," No Sin said tightly, "maybe I kill her first."

Following a tense stare down, he left the boy outside Monica's cabin and headed to his cabin for a quick nap before breakfast. An hour earlier, he wouldn't have worried about the Hatman making a move against Monica. However, after witnessing her explosive temper, it wasn't so far-fetched to imagine that she'd somehow procured a gun and tried to assassinate the little forger. If the chubby fellow had come to the same conclusion, he might want revenge - or, at least, peace of mind.

As if things weren't already complicated enough, Davies was now troubled by the most recent source of controversy: the little Kewpie doll. Perhaps it was filled with opium or contraband or counterfeit bills. But dolls were sentimental things; more likely it was filled with memories. No Sin's handling of it had *not* solicited emotions of fear from Monica, rather of violation. That little doll meant a great deal to her, but why? What touching event from her past did it represent? Who had given it to her? A long lost beau? A grandmother? A special friend? Perhaps the strange little Hatman? Davies felt the burning whine of jealousy as he wondered exactly what Monica's relationship was with the small fellow. Where she was concerned, he was inclined to believe the worst - especially as her violent mood swings were getting harder to overlook or make excuses for.

XXXVII. HITTING THE DECK

Friday, August 24, 1928

Again, he wasn't able to sleep. At about nine in the morning, Davies gave up altogether and trudged off for breakfast like a respectable passenger drone.

Dining on cool, gray porridge, he glanced across the room and saw that Mrs. Kissler was sniffing everything before placing it in her mouth. He couldn't blame her. Thank God, they were due into their last Chinese port that afternoon and would take on some new food supplies. He took a last sip of stale coffee, then left the dining room and went down the stairs to the main deck.

The sea was calm, but a damp fog poured over the railings and drifted through the decks, as the foghorns moaned hoarsely. He had to move carefully, as whatever he brushed against was likely to leave a stain. Anything made of metal on a steamship was regularly washed down with kerosene to protect against rust. Such a bout of maintenance had recently struck their steamer, and he winced at the awful petroleum smell that so often gave modern ships an ugly, industrial character. Whoever said that an ocean voyage was glamorous?

Davies went to the radio room and was presented with a chatty telegram from Crockwood, which stated that he was extremely displeased to be a go-between with Elder Brother. The banal response was annoying, Crockwood had obviously made no attempt to speak with Singletone - it would seem that drinking took precedence over sleuthing - or loyalty to an old friend.

From the radio room, Davies entered the purser's office for another look at the passenger list. After boarding the freighter, Davies had counted twenty fellow travelers, either on deck, or in the dining room. Now there were twenty-three names on the purser's list. Nineteen of the names were occidental, four were oriental. Trees might very well have made his way to another ship, the one that had left from Hong Kong, for instance - but the attempted murder of the little man in the cowboy hat was a pretty strange coincidence if Trees was now on an entirely different vessel.

"Can you tell me who boarded last night in Amoy?" Davies asked.

"Two Christian missionaries, women - and Mr. Wen," the purser said, preoccupied with a manual that he was reading.

"Mr. Wen? Can you describe him?"

"No."

This was exasperating. "You don't care that someone extremely dangerous is now on this ship?"

Absorbed with his manual, the purser, a small man with a face vaguely like a weasel's, was thoroughly unimpressed with Davies' dire warning. "I cannot describe him because he covered his face while boarding."

"And you didn't find that suspicious?"

The purser shrugged. "We get all kinds."

"Was he tall, short, old, young?"

With his finger, the purser traced a selection in his manual. "His clothes were old, very worn. His hair was white, uncombed, his hands were skeletal, and that is all I'm going to tell you." He seemed to enjoy passing on such a provocative description.

"I would certainly like to talk to this Mr. Wen."

The purser finally looked up from his reading in order to wag a scolding finger at Davies. "He specifically asked to be left alone."

Davies wasn't about to take "no" for an answer, and through sheer nagging he managed to get Mr. Wen's cabin number - but to no avail. Though the description of Mr. Wen was tailor made for Trees, causing Davies great anticipation, the mysterious new passenger refused to respond to repeated knocks on his door. Adding to Davies' frustration was a faint rustling sound coming from inside. Dammit, he knew someone was in the cabin, laying low, and wishing he'd go away.

"It's the captain," Davies shouted, "I need to talk to you."

Not a word came from the cabin beyond. Whoever was inside was familiar enough with the captain's voice that they had not been fooled - or perhaps they were familiar with Davies' voice.

Davies went to the bridge and convinced the captain to return with him. The captain managed to talk to Mr. Wen through the door, speaking in Chinese. After several minutes, the captain thanked Mr. Wen, then turned to Davies and told him that the man inside cabin six should not be bothered. Davies was extremely dissatisfied with this outcome, but the captain was adamant. Davies decided that he would try again later, and adopting his most cordial manner, he announced that he was going to return to his own cabin. The captain accompanied him, evidently to insure that Davies kept his word.

By noontime the fog had been dispersed by a boisterous breeze from the west. The day was glistening and clear, and they had the sea to themselves with no other ships in sight.

Davies dropped by Monica's cabin, but she told him that she intended to stay in bed for the rest of the day, maybe the rest of her life. Not to worry, her health was fine, she just didn't want to get up. The traumas of the past few days had affected her powerfully. Davies said that he'd check back on her later that afternoon; perhaps she'd want a little food by then - not that he felt inclined to take any food, himself - he didn't feel well. He'd barely slept, and the headache that had come on at noon persisted. Hopefully, he wasn't coming down with something - there were so many interesting diseases in the Orient.

Momentarily refreshed by the brisk sea air, Davies wandered to the open area where the steerage passengers were sunning themselves. Mostly Chinese, they had no cabins and were more like campers than passengers. They slept in blankets, which were neatly laid-out on the wooden deck. Each blanket was like a tiny homestead, and scattered about it were the passenger's possessions - perhaps the only possessions they owned. There were no white-faces to be seen.

The more enterprising passengers had set up mini-bazaars, hawking items to each other - the Chinese, it seemed, could never forget business. In one corner, a few people were burning joss sticks and praying. Home-made banners with Chinese characters expressing condolences were hung about.

Under a tattered canopy No Sin was sitting cross-legged, reading a magazine. Seeing Davies, the boy jumped up and bowed.

"Cozy down here," Davies remarked, noticing that the lad's luggage seemed to consist of a coffee can and a few tiny bundles of clothing rolled up so tightly that they looked like long cigarettes.

A low chant was emanating from the Chinese passengers. "What's the scoop on the praying?"

No Sin put on a morose face. "Oh, nice Chinese lady die last night - they have ceremony for her. Very sad."

"Too bad. You knew her?"

No Sin shook his head.

"Then why do you seem so broken up?"

"She dead. What the matter with you?" He shook his head again.

Even in neutral waters, death seemed inescapable. There was a lot of wailing and flickering candles and smoldering incense. Some people burned hastily made paper money so that the woman's spirit would be able to pay off the lost souls who were sure to accost her on her journey to hell. From hell, she would be judged and allowed to proceed to heaven if her life had been virtuous enough.

Glancing around, Davies saw an assortment of wet clothing that was hanging from ropes strung across the railing to the bulkhead. "What the hell!" he said, pointing to six dress shirts that were flapping in the wind like flags, "those are my shirts! How the devil did you get into my room?'

No Sin looked slightly ashamed of himself. "I think you not want to know." He set his mouth in a determined frown. "It very hard to find iron on this ship, sorry. Your shirts ready in a little whiles, okay? You see, that old fat lady, Mrs. 'Kisser?'" The boy looked upward as if trying to get a glimpse of a passing thought before it slipped away. "Why her amah called 'colored?' She only seem brown to me. Or is she other colors under her clothes?"

"What does this have to do with my shirts?"

No Sin sighed with great disappointment, as if he was being forced to explain something to a small child. "'Colored' amah has steam iron I need to finish your clothes."

"I see. Listen, after last night, have you seen anything or anyone who made you suspicious?"

"Everyone look suspicious to me. You the most."

"Besides me. Listen, Sin, I'll be frank. The person who killed Monica's aunt may be on this ship. If so, they're extremely dangerous."

No Sin shrugged. "You tell me already."

"Very good, but, the fact is, they cut off Madame Lin's bound foot and are keeping it in a fruit jar."

The boy's bored look turned to one of disgust.

"Can you think of any reason why a Chinese would do such a thing? I mean, are there any Chinese legends about cutting off feet? Does such an act have any special meaning?"

No Sin nodded. "Yes."

"Oh? So what does it mean?"

"It mean that the guy who do it is really crazy."

"I see. There's a new passenger staying in cabin six who bears watching. So far, he won't come out of his room; however, with your skills, let's just say that if you learn something let me know."

"You want me to watch cabin?"

"That would be excellent. If anybody comes out tell me immediately."

The boy folded his arms and his eyebrows came together, suggesting a scheme about to be hatched. "So some crazy man try to shoot that little guy, too? I don't think so. I bet your lady friend do it. She very bad, evil woman - this 'Monica.' I bet that phony name."

"You no likee her?" Davies caught himself. "I mean, you don't like her?"

No Sin lowered his head, expressing exaggerated shame and humility. "Please, I just China boy," he said, now a caricature of Asian meekness, "I do not mean to make offense. She half white, so I be half polite - she very nice white girl." A sly smile stole across his face. "But she also half Chinese - so I can be half rude, okay? She very, very wicked China girl."

"Really, Sin, how idiotic can you be? 'I just simple, humble China boy,' dear God, where did you pick up such nonsense? In the future I expect your blunt, indelicate opinion. If you persist in treating me like a superior I shall beat you. Clear?"

No Sin's eyes narrowed. "But how can I treat you like equal? Chinese always be superiors to white man. We just more polite, not bullies."

Davies laughed - again stunned by the lad's cockiness.

Monica suddenly appeared at his side, she had a talent for materializing out of the ether. "I should have known you'd be down here slumming." She sounded like a mother who'd just found her wayward seven-year-old playing with a forbidden friend. Her image was far from maternal, however; she was wearing a white dress with a buttoned-up collar, long sleeves, and tight kid leather gloves. Why was it that the less of herself that she exposed, the more alluring she appeared?

"I thought you were going to stay in your room."

"I probably should have," she answered, softly now, for some reason. "Have you decided to give up grooming altogether? You're starting to look like a bum."

Davies felt a flush of anxiety; these were words a man never liked to hear from a woman. Not because they were critical, but because they implied a desire to control.

No Sin gave her an icy stare. "When you give me your little doll?"

Monica lifted her chin and looked around at the other steerage passengers as if concerned that they might infect her with something.

"I think she want a drink, Mr. Davies." No Sin whispered loudly enough for her to hear.

"Oh, you shut up! Zephyr, he's not to speak to me from now on, is that clear?"

"So it 'Zephyr' now?" No Sin said.

"I will not stand for this!" She strode away.

No Sin folded his arms over his chest and smiled, contentedly.

Davies went after her, wondering why she was behaving in such a beastly manner. After their lovemaking that morning she had been angelic. Had the experience touched something in her that she couldn't handle? "Monica," he said when he reached her side, "what's bothering you?"

"This was all a mistake. Specifically *you* are a mistake. I should never have let you talk me into this ridiculous expedition."

He felt a desire to put his hand comfortingly on her shoulder. Instead, in deference to her hostility, he placed it on the wooden rail. "I know it's tough for you. But consider that any fighting between us only makes you more vulnerable to your growing list of enemies."

"You're my only enemy!"

"So you're no longer worried about your little friend with the cowboy hat?"

"Speak of the devil." He followed her gaze to where the Hatman was standing on the deck above, staring down at them. Realizing he'd been spotted, he immediately scurried off.

"Lord, he gives me the creeps," Monica muttered. "Everybody on this ship is so strange."

"Yeah? Who else?"

"Have you seen that old woman in the wheel chair? The one who has to use a chisel at night to get her make-up off? I'm sorry, actually, she's very nice. I'm just a little cranky because I'm getting the most God-awful headache, no thanks to you. I suppose I slept too much. But what a talker."

"Who?"

"That old lady in the wheelchair - aren't you listening? I nearly had to throw her overboard just now to get away. Why do people have to be so nosy?"

"She's probably lonely," Davies said.

"You know how I hate to talk about myself - so I told her about you - how you want to save humanity and build housing for everyone on earth, a place where all the races can live in love and harmony. She wheeled away fast enough to win the Kentucky Derby. Of course, not before agreeing with me that your character would be improved by a lobotomy."

Her ridiculing of his ideals stung, especially after all they'd been through. "I'm so glad I opened up to you," he said coolly.

Monica took hold of him, digging her fingertips into his arm. "You can open up some more. I've been thinking about it since our little rendezvous last night - what's in this for you? Really and truly. Why do you even want to help me?" The wind blew several locks of hair into her face, and she brushed them away, awaiting his answer.

"Let's just say I love a mystery."

"What a laugh. Damn it, I'm a real person, Zephyr, not your latest damsel in distress." Through the disobedient strands of her hair, her eyes were sharp and accusatory. "I had a beau once who called me his 'little China doll.' Is that all I am to you?"

Still smarting from the way she'd made fun of his ambitions, Davies didn't hesitate to answer. "Yes." He met her expression of hurt with a steady, unblinking gaze. "Come on, it's not as if my affections honestly mean that much to you."

Monica stared at him like she'd been struck by the back of his hand.

"For God's sake, you've been manipulating me ever since we met, Monica - and now you're mad at me for not feeling closer to you - for protecting myself by regarding you as an object? Is your appraisal of me as some kind of jaded playboy any less offensive, or expedient?"

Her full lips pursed as she appeared to think about this. "All right. Maybe you can help me. I guess, things can't get much worse."

"No, they can't. Which brings me to another question. The Kewpie doll from the other night. When No Sin touched it, why did you become so upset?"

"Now we have to go into that?"

He felt remarkably light-headed. He'd been jittery most of the morning, but now all of his energy seemed to sink to the deck and spread out in a silver puddle, leaving him wobbly and boneless, as simultaneously Monica's words faded away like a distant shout from a deep canyon. He was falling into the canyon, and suddenly the floor jumped up and hit him in the face.

* * *

"Zephyr!" Monica cried, after watching him topple over and crash to the deck. She stared down at where he lay sprawled on the wooden planking. Every bit of anger that she felt toward Zephyr Davies instantly mutated into a desperate wish that he be well - she couldn't bear any other outcome.

XXXVIII. JUST PRACTICING

A disembodied voice was talking. "From what I can ascertain, it's an extreme toxicological reaction to a pathogen of some sort. I would not, by any means, rule out exposure to a narcotic. We will probably never know for sure, it might even be food poisoning. But the symptoms are closet to those I've observed in Chinese who've ingested too much opium."

Davies struggled to open his eyes, but only managed to look out through a gritty, hazy slit. Standing over him was a gaunt man with horn-rimmed glasses, a waxed mustache, and hair wet with stickum; a stethoscope dangled from his collar-pinched neck. Beside him, Monica was biting her lower lip, while No Sin stood silently at the foot of the bed. Behind them, the pudgy Japanese captain was pacing the floor and muttering to himself.

"Opium?" Monica repeated skeptically. "What you're really saying is that he was poisoned."

"There are Caucasian addicts, I'm afraid," the gaunt man answered as he placed various gleaming medical tools back in his bag.

The captain shook his head, protesting violently in Japanese, offended by the implication that illegal activities could take place on his ship. Nobody paid any attention to him.

"Is he going to be all right?" Monica asked, folding her arms and looking down at Davies as if he was a sick possum that needed to be put down.

The doctor now removed his stethoscope and placed it carefully in the shiny black bag. "We'll have to watch him for the next twenty-four hours. If he stays well rested, I expect so. There is a chance still of permanent paralysis on the right side. I'll place his arm in a sling, and hopefully his motor skills will make a return in several days."

"Would the Chinese passengers have any kind of antidote?" Monica asked.

"Please," No Sin said, "I ask fellow passengers - some may have Chinese herbs - we make anecdote."

The doctor gave them a look that seemed reserved for ridiculous patients prone to apocalyptic fears.

"I rather think a Chinese antidote, if you should actually find such a thing, would do a great deal more harm than good. Allow me to handle things, would you please?"

Davies groaned as everything went fuzzy and the room began to revolve around him.

"I'd like you to keep an eye on him, Miss Marshall," the doctor said, as if from some distant planet. "I'll return, momentarily, with some medication."

The door closed and Davies felt his right hand enveloped in warmth, was it being stroked and kneaded? He wasn't sure, but could someone now be kissing him? He told himself that he was feeling much better as he lapsed into unconsciousness.

* * *

Despite the doctor's advice that he shouldn't, No Sin had spent an hour searching the ship for an anecdote, getting nowhere until someone told him that he probably wanted an antidote. Soldiering on, he remained out of luck until he found something instead, completely by accident, which was so alarming that he had to alert Mr. Davies as soon as possible. However, as he stood outside his friend's cabin, watching the shadows move inside, it occurred to him that this might not be the most opportune time to relay his discovery. Of course, there was an element of danger in delaying, but if Mr. Davies was in there with *her,* barely conscious, would he be inclined to listen to anything that No Sin had to say, let alone to believe it? There must be some way to get Davies to see the truth about the horrible mongrel woman sitting at his bedside. For the time being, however, the method was elusive.

No Sin crossed to the rail and stared down at dark water, as he listened to the sound of waves splashing against the hull. The sea, black and undulating, certainly didn't care what went on in Zephyr Davies' room. It didn't care what he had found. It didn't care if any of them lived or died.

* * *

The next time he awoke, Davies was aware of Monica slipping a spoon into his mouth. Something warm and salty trickled across his tongue and into his throat. Her silk robe had fallen carelessly off one shoulder, revealing soft, unblemished skin and a delicate arm. Her neck was exquisitely long and slender. Davies could feel the warmth of the soup spreading into his abdomen. He groaned softly and she leaned closer to him, peering into his unfocusing eyes.

"How are you feeling, Wallace?"

"Much better," he murmured hoarsely, and rubbed a dribble of liquid from his mouth. In a hazy glance, he caught sight of something red on his moist fingers. "Am I bleeding?" he asked, more than a little alarmed.

Monica lowered her eyes. "Sorry."

"Sorry for what?"

She was blushing. "Nothing."

"Come on, Monica." He was surprised by his own weakness, which was making it hard to form words. "I'm a sick man. You mustn't keep things from me."

"Look," she answered crisply, "it's just that I kissed you a little. And don't call me stupid, it's hardly news to me." He started to speak and her eyes flashed. "Don't say anything, or it really will be blood - and don't get too full of yourself." She smiled, impishly. "I got bored and decided to practice, you know, so I'll be ready when I meet somebody I really like."

He reached for her; the movement made his forehead feel like it had been cleaved with an ax.

"I'll get the doctor." She placed the soup on the bed stand, tightened her robe, and hurried to the door.

"No!" he said - his voice a fading whisper as she disappeared through the doorway.

* * *

Tuesday, August 28, 1928

Davies slept through the entire night. Monica didn't sleep at all - sitting by his bed until the doctor arrived at about nine the next morning. After determining that Davies was out of danger, he told her that, though he admired the instinctive loyalty of darker races to their betters, she was to be scolded for neither resting nor eating. He ordered her, in no uncertain terms, to go to her room and take a nap.

She was exhausted, yet she had trouble sleeping when she got to her cabin - she was far more worried for Zephyr Davies than she had ever expected to be.

Lying on her bed, Monica clasped her hands together and whispered a little prayer for his recovery. It felt strange to have emotions that were so uncharacteristically unselfish - they were something of a nuisance, yet they made her feel good about herself.

* * *

Later that day, Davies was strong enough, with No Sin's help, to go up on deck. There, he spent the afternoon wrapped in blankets, reclining on a deck chair. Monica and No Sin alternately brought him food while he watched the horizon lift and fall, an action, which didn't make him feel much better. Clusters of clouds would occasionally turn the sea the color of slate. The increasingly awkward movements of the ship, accompanied by jarring crashes and the groans of flexing metal, were a constant reminder of how fragile and unnatural was their journey across the Pacific. At least, China, with its terrors and injustice and whimsy, had seemed the full embodiment of all that was natural and human. China was base and real, but this whole trip to hunt down a killer in the name of vengeance, in theory a very human pursuit, seemed unnatural. The progress of a mechanical vessel on a sea, which was doing its best to shake it off, like a horse shaking off a rider, so underscored the perversity of his task.

Whenever possible, No Sin strategically planted himself so that he blocked the sun from falling on Davies' face. Although he was weary of all this attention, he didn't dare ask No Sin to leave him alone. After attempting to kill the Hatman, it seemed certain that Trees now wanted Davies out of the way - he would surely strike again. But who was Trees - the man in cabin six, whose description by the purser suggested a walking corpse, or someone who'd learned to temper his appearance, and whose monstrous qualities were purely internal? Davies' life depended on finding the answer.

Could someone else have poisoned him, Monica perhaps? On the other hand, it was just as likely that the Hatman had done the dirty deed. It was even possible that Davies had eaten the wrong thing from the wrong vendor back in Foochow, and had no one to blame but himself.

Constantly by his side, No Sin seemed to be increasingly troubled by something. Perhaps he was concerned that Davies might die at any moment. However, when Davies asked what the matter was, the boy tightened his lips and looked away.

The day passed in a chopped-up haze. Davies had soup in his cabin, then returned to the deck for another nap. As he drifted towards sleep, his best time for revelations, he had a minor windfall - for no good reason it came back to him, the irritating, vague thing that had bothered him at his meeting with Elder Brother a full week earlier. It had to do with Elder Brother's exact choice of words, no wonder it had eluded him. Elder Brother had accused the Judge, Chang Wo-tin, of not being a "true patriot," while Hong Fat had been scornfully regarded as "not a patriot."

In Hong Fat's case the adjective "true" was missing. Maybe it was the interpreter's choice of words, but Davies didn't think so - the characterless little man was too meticulous - especially when it came to his English. "Not a true patriot" was someone who misrepresented or exaggerated their patriotism, so Chang Wo-tin's ultimate crime was hypocrisy. But Hong Fat was "not a patriot," and with the additional insult that he was a "traitor," Davies could only assume that this accusation should be taken literally. But how could Hong Fat betray his country, when China, lacking a central government, wasn't a country - at least, not one yet? Chiang Kai-shek was working hard to make China a real nation, and Elder Brother was lending support, hoping, no doubt, to be the power behind the throne. Had Hong Fat somehow stood in the way? Was the forbidden opium shipment only half of the reason why he'd been driven to suicide? And what of 'the clouded twilight,' how did it figure in China's emergence as a nation, if it figured at all? Pondering this question, he lapsed into an unhappy slumber.

When No Sin finally roused him, long shadows mingling with brilliant orange and yellow fingers of light were creeping across the deck. Through the rail, Davies could see that the sun was just setting, framed by glorious, fanciful tropical clouds. With the boy's help, he rose and stumbled toward his cabin, reminding himself of Lo-Chien, as he too was moving only a little faster than the fading fingers of sunlight.

They docked at Tamsui on the island of Formosa at about five-thirty in the afternoon. Davies stood at the rail and watched the Chinese family from steerage load the body of their relative, wrapped securely in white cloth, onto a cart, which took it away. It seemed appropriate that his last glimpse of China would reflect death. Hopefully, it was the last dead body he'd see in a long time. For five years he'd lived in a romantic, sad, charming, and cruel land - he was glad to leave it behind.

Davies returned to his cabin, and No Sin put him to bed. After twenty minutes of fidgeting, Davies finally found a comfortable position on the lumpy mattress and was rewarded with the sound of a note being shoved under his door - at least, he thought so - or had he dreamed the sliding noise? He was so groggy that he couldn't be sure, though the sound of receding footsteps outside on the wooden deck seemed quite real. After ten minutes of sleepy indecision, he rose and crossed to his cabin door. There *was* a note there. He reached down with his good hand and fumbled it into his palm. Rising again, he felt so unsteady that he had to grab onto the ledge of a built-in dresser. Balancing against the dresser, he used both of his trembling hands to unfold the paper, which read, "I'm happy to talk to you now. Please come to cabin six."

IXXXX. THE MAN IN CABIN SIX

Davies wasted no time, but the ordeal of slipping on his greatcoat and his shoes, with one arm in a sling, took nearly ten minutes. When he finally succeeded, he made sure that his Colt was loaded before he stepped out into the night.

No Sin was found in steerage. The boy looked tired, caretaking had taken its toll. "Yes, Mr. Davies?"

"Follow me, will you? I'm going to meet someone, and I'd like you to wait outside, just in case they turn out to be a less than gracious host. Don't worry, you won't have to do anything - unless you hear me screaming." He wasn't entirely exaggerating. He didn't know who was waiting for him in cabin six - if it was Trees, a creature who seemed to have taken perverse delight in slaughtering Madame Lin and Leibowitz, a trap was a certainty. Especially as Davies was in such a weakened condition.

Minutes later, Davies and No Sin were standing outside the mysterious cabin. Davies knocked.

"Who is it?" a heavily accented voice asked from inside; the speaker might be Chinese.

"Davies," he called out.

There was some shuffling, and then the door was unlatched, swinging open with an appropriate creak. The room beyond was dark in shadow, only a faint light coming from behind the closed curtains over the portholes. A figure was standing in a corner, barely discernible, the collar of his heavy coat turned up. Davies had no doubts about what the glimmer of blue steel in the man's hand represented. "Please come in, Mr. Davies," the man said in a coarse whisper.

"I don't mean to be rude," Davies replied, remaining in the doorway, "but could I trouble you to put your gun away?"

"Would you come into the light first?"

"You sound like a missionary. Look, I've got a gun, too - and I've also got a terrific headache; and if I have to shoot you I don't think I could bear the noise. So why don't we both disarm?"

The man sighed and placed his gun on a small table beside his chair. "I didn't mean to be so inhospitable. I'm mistrustful of others on this ship."

Davies entered and shut the door behind him. "You're not the only one."

"I couldn't see you very well, but then your humor gave you away."

"My Achilles' heel. You must know how sorry I am about your wife. Can I sit? As I said, I'm not exactly feeling top drawer."

"Please."

"So, Mr. Lin. What did you want to discuss?"

The slightly-built man sat nervously at a desk chair, while Davies tried to make himself comfortable on the edge of the cabin's single bed. Davies had met Mr. Lin socially several times before, and recognized him almost immediately. His appearance was highly distinctive, even in shadow. A small Chinese, he had a sinister look to him, which had grown more pronounced over the past several years. His face was like a ferret's. He wore a pencil thin black mustache, which was surely dyed because it contrasted so dramatically with the shock of white hair that was cropped close to his scalp. Normally he was immaculately groomed. Tonight, however, he was wearing no shoes, and he hadn't shaved - nor had he combed his hair. He looked pathetic, which was his intention. He was wearing a suit of dark blue burlap, a traditional mourner's outfit, deliberately ill-fitting and shabby to demonstrate how impoverished the lives of the family had become once the deceased had left their realm. "Hasn't Madame Lin been buried?" Davies asked cautiously.

"We buried her two hours before I flew down here to board this ship."

"But your clothes, if you don't mind my mentioning them."

Mr. Lin shrugged wearily. "The ceremony should have lasted no less than five days - but I had to come here; responding, I fear, to a telegram sent by Mr. Arnold, which informed me that he had tracked you down - so I settled for the minimum of three days. I feel so ashamed, the least I can do is stay in these clothes, even though my dear one is now in the ground." His manner was precise and extremely serious. It was strange to think of Madame Lin as having been the easy going, fun loving half of their pairing.

"Let me say that I'm sorry that you are feeling poorly. I don't want to tire you, Mr. Davies, so I'll be blunt - is it your conclusion that Mr. Arnold was responsible for Madame Lin's death?"

"I doubt it," Davies answered, rubbing his aching forehead. "I assume it's yours."

"Yes. At first I thought he could help me. When I offered a reward he came to see me and was very convincing, saying that my niece was the killer, and he knew where to find her. Like a fool, I advanced him some money."

"So what made you question him?"

"Well, he had sent me a note. Here, I'll show it to you. 'I have information,' that sort of thing." Mr. Lin rose, and as he handed over a slip of paper, Davies noticed that the small man's hands were shaking even more than his own. "But when I settled into this cabin, and was going through some of my dear wife's things, I found this."

He gave Davies a second note, the one demanding that Monica meet with her "best friend" at the Willow Pattern Tea House. The two slips of paper were unmistakably in the same handwriting.

Mr. Lin returned to his chair, sitting with a minimum of superfluous motion. "My wife had mentioned a belligerent man who'd threatened her - this is when he came to our door in Shanghai searching for Monica. I, myself, never saw the person. However, when I discovered this note I became suspicious. It occurred to me that this Huey Arnold might have killed my wife. The more I thought about it, the more sure I became. What do you think? Would you disagree with me?"

"I certainly can't disagree with your logic. However, you say you *flew* to Amoy?"

"I did hire a junk, but I didn't sail on it, needing, of course, to attend to Madame Lin's burial. You see, Mr. Arnold told me that you were sheltering Monica. Your servants directed us to the train station, telling us you'd left for Peiping. I was taking Mr. Arnold to the train when we saw the police interrogating your driver in that car of yours. Since the car was down by the Bund, it was Mr. Arnold who suggested that you may have hired a junk. I talked to some men, sailors, and one in particular who had wished to be part of your crew but wasn't strong enough to be allowed to go. He knew your junk and your destination. How ironic that I didn't become suspicious until I'd chosen to look through my dear wife's things, just for sentimental reasons. Once I knew, my anger may have gotten the better of my reason."

"So you rather impulsively came out and tried to shoot him?"

"Yes. Should I be sorry that I missed?"

"Perhaps you should - if for no other reason than that his men attacked our junk, making him responsible for a number of needless deaths. So what is it you want now? My blessing?"

Mr. Lin seemed to deflate. "So now I learn I must also be blamed for needless deaths. I am so bitterly sorry."

"If you want my truthful opinion," Davies said, "I don't think Mr. Arnold killed your wife. He was my prime suspect for awhile. But after I searched his cabin, and spoke to him, well, I just don't think he did it. Let me ask you, have you seen a very pale man in a heavy overcoat?"

"Only myself."

Davies chuckled. "I'm afraid you won't do. And you know about 'the clouded twilight,' of course?"

"Yes, my wife tried not to tell me - but she could never keep secrets."

"I see. Who do I think did it? Not your niece, let's make that clear."

"Who then?" Mr. Lin asked.

"Frankly, I don't know. And, believe me, I want to find them as much as you do."

"What should I do?"

Davies shrugged, sparking a dull pain in his shoulders. "That's up to you. I'll not spoil your game - just keep me informed and visa versa. Oh, you didn't find a baggage tag amongst your wife's things?"

"A baggage tag? No, I believe not. Is it important?"

"Nah."

For the balance of their talk, Mr. Lin sat with both hands dangling impassively from the arms of his chair. He didn't move or gesture, didn't even seem to breathe - but his voice was steadily becoming more weary with sadness. "By the way, I would rather you did not tell Miss Marshall of my presence on this ship."

Davies nodded. "I'm sure she'd prefer it that way - she thinks you have a remarkable temper."

Davies could hear the man deeply inhale. "She's right."

"I have a question or two for you, Mr. Lin. How much is 'the clouded twilight' worth?"

Mr. Lin raised his right hand about two inches, then let it drop - this was by far the most dramatic gesture he'd attempted. "Well, to me it's priceless - it's a matter of familial pride. On the open market, I suppose it's not worth much. One probably couldn't get more than several hundred pounds."

"Did you ever offer to buy it from Monica's mother?"

"Certainly not. I think I offered to pay expenses if she ever returned it to the family, but that's all. However, I see what you mean. Monica actually did try to sell 'the clouded twilight' to my wife, and requested an absurd sum. We thought it very strange."

"How absurd?"

"Fifty-thousand dollars."

"Fifty,...? That is strange." Davies made a sore, half-hearted attempt to cross his legs, then gave up as he mulled over the implications of Mr. Lin's last statement. Either Monica was a brazen but inept con artist, trying to sell 'the clouded twilight' for a huge amount to someone who already thought he owned it - or she had been deliberately misled by someone.

"It was something that made us think that Monica might not be quite right in the head," Mr Lin said reflectively. "It was the last straw, after the telegrams from her mother's friend."

"Telegrams? Plural?"

"Oh yes, they greatly distressed Madame Lin. He warned us that Monica might try to sell us the artifact, and we should play along. He said that she had stolen it; she'd stolen a lot of things from her mother, actually. She had been institutionalized several years ago, did you know that? She had seemed better for a period, but now this friend felt that she was slipping back into madness, and he advised us to have her committed. He was even able to recommend a doctor that he knew in Shanghai."

"Who exactly are we talking about?"

"I believe the man's name is Willows. Monica's mother has worked for him for a number of years now. He became sort of an informal guardian to Monica, I'm told."

"Willows seems awfully involved for just an employer," Davies said, thinking that the whole affair was starting to smell like a scheme to frame Monica.

"Yes, I know." Mr. Lin placed his hands gently in his lap. "Madame Lin hinted that Willows had an eye for Monica's mother; I gather that their relationship became something more than exclusively professional."

"Does he have a romantic interest in Monica, as well?"

"Well, he did seem very fond of the girl, but I honestly think he is far fonder of her mother. I can't tell you why. Such a difficult woman. Frankly, my wife's sister could drive anyone crazy."

"What does Willows do?"

"I don't know. I believe he's very prominent in the United States - quite wealthy."

"What does he look like?" Davies asked.

"He's a small man with an excessively loud voice, rather like one of your politicians. He's around forty I'm told, but appears younger, and has attempted to age himself with a mustache that is not entirely convincing. I must add that his letter made my late wife uneasy. I think it was the cause of her consulting you, she didn't quite trust this fellow Willows. She was rather worried for Monica."

"Let me clarify something, as Monica wasn't speaking, how did she let you know how much money she wanted for the staff?"

Mr. Lin raised his right arm and stroked his mustache, his movements were becoming downright reckless. "Now let me see. We received a telegram from Monica several weeks before she arrived, and that's when she mentioned a price of fifty-thousand dollars."

"But couldn't someone else have sent the telegram, pretending to be Monica?"

Mr. Lin's eyes moved sideways as he thought. "Yes, I suppose so."

"Would Willows want 'the clouded twilight' for any reason?"

Mr. Lin thought about this too. "I have no idea. His telegrams implied an obsession with Monica. It's conceivable he was trying to disguise an obsession for 'the clouded twilight' - though I can't imagine why he'd want it. He must have known it wasn't worth much; and he's the sort of man who loves to tell people how much he paid for something - the more, the better."

Davies was suddenly very tired - he felt that his heart was barely beating as it was; now he suspected that it had stopped altogether. He took a much needed deep breath, then another. He had a hundred more questions, but this was already more than he could handle. With difficulty, he rose and backed toward the door. "I'm sorry, but I'm about ready to collapse. We'll talk again."

Mr. Lin also rose. "So you don't think we've found my wife's killer?"

"No. But, believe me, we will. Sorry, but I just don't have the energy to talk anymore. You've been a real help. So tell me, what'll you do now?"

The small, once dapper man fingered his ragged lapel. "I can't bear a return to Shanghai; though how can I leave Madame Lin?" He stared at the floor for a long moment. "What do you think? Am I a hedonist to just keep sailing? I have family in San Francisco, perhaps I should visit them."

"Madame Lin would want you to be happy."

'I imagine so. Madame Lin cared about you a great deal. You knew that?'

Davies nodded. "And I had great affection for her."

"I recall that she once said of me, 'my husband is far from ideal, I think that's why I love him so.' No one will ever say that about me again." He looked away to conceal the emotion that had begun to infect his voice. "I don't know why I'm telling you all this. It is funny, isn't it?" Mr. Lin added wistfully, as he turned back to Davies. "The only thing I have now to keep me company is this quest. Perhaps you should tell Miss Marshall that I'm on board. I don't really want to talk to her, but I don't think I can stay in this room much longer - all by myself. You have no idea how difficult it is."

"Okay. I'll handle it for you. Maybe I'll see you tomorrow, out on deck."

Mr. Lin made a slow nod. "We shall see."

"I hope so. It's good for you to take walks. Play games, maybe even whittle. Read books, that sort of thing."

"Oh no, I couldn't read. Madame Lin read to me every night - it was a ritual. We'd sit in bed, sometimes I read, other times she read to me." Again, his voice faded, and he stared at nothing in particular.

"You say you may end up in San Francisco?"

"Yes," Mr. Lin replied weakly, "I have cousins there."

"If you have any trouble with immigration, call me up. I'd give you my card, but I don't have it on me. I can slip it under your door tomorrow. And you can do the same, slip the address where you'll be staying under my door. Unless, of course, you change your mind and decide you'd like company."

Mr. Lin nodded politely, and Davies stumbled out into the hall and closed the door behind him. He stood in the small recess wondering if No Sin had heard any of their conversation. Probably he had, because the boy was trying to look as innocent as possible.

Back in his cabin, and before slipping into another restless sleep, Davies thought of Madame Lin. He imagined how horrible her last moments must have been. The shock and the pain of having been shot, yet remaining alive for perhaps five or ten minutes, all the time looking down and seeing her own blood drenching her beautiful clothes, as she felt cruel, sharp, exhausting pain. Finally mustering enough strength and hope to rise and walk to the telephone, only to stumble, and then - God knows what she felt. After having that thing thrust into the brain, did she have any of her wits left as she went smashing through the window?

The Chinese believe that the soul stays in the body for some time after death. If they're right, she might have experienced the indignity of having hundreds of strangers staring up at her. She might even have been aware of her own autopsy.

When her Chinese dressers had finally arrived to take her away from the police, they would have attempted to close her eyes, straighten her legs, and force her hands to her chest, calling her "auntie" soothingly as they beat her stiff limbs into submission. He could imagine how stubborn she would have been, finally drifting away to go in search of the eighteen levels of hell. Or would she have stayed on earth as a ghost? Even now, was she watching him, waiting with her usual impatience to see him bring her killer to justice? Should he take her husband off the list of suspects? His grief had seemed painfully real, but could it have been a ploy?

He rolled over and thought that he had made so many assumptions about Madame Lin, yet he'd completely underestimated what a remarkable woman she had been. Perhaps because of her fierce and eccentric ways she had been one of his favorite people on the face of the earth. He could certainly understand why Mr. Lin was so devoted to her, and so lost without her. How wonderful their good times must have been. How awful it must have been when they ended.

He remembered the hot evening before he'd first met Monica in his garden. He'd telegraphed his mother in the States to report her old friend's dilemma. "A damsel in distress is she?" his mother had written back in reply. "Give her my best. Though, why she wants to be rescued by you, Zephyr, is difficult to fathom. However, I would consider it a favor if you would do what little you can."

If there was one thing he was finally learning from Madame Lin, it was the value of human life. He'd been as guilty as the Chinese, who too often seemed to view their fellow countrymen as so much night soil, disposable fertilizer on which to build a civilization. Was he any less guilty, dispatching those around him with a glib insult or a trite summary of their character? Perhaps he'd been mistaken to think that he was on a mission of vengeance, because, thankfully, the very act of tracking down Madame Lin's murderer was, in itself, a statement to the gods above that a single human being was a thing of importance. Madame Lin's life had not been a meaningless, abstract thing, for her husband's grief was so heartbreakingly real - as was Davies' grief, for that matter.

He reached out from his bed, opened a nearby dresser drawer, and removed the hard tamarind candy he had stolen from Monica's purse. Rolling the candy around in his palm he thought that, whether or not he found Madame Lin's murderer, there was one thing he could promise - one way he could honor her memory. He would no longer assume that people different from him were simple or predictable or less intelligent. He would struggle with himself, just as Madame Lin had, to always seek the truth - to see people for what they were, and not to settle for whatever image was convenient for him. He was an awful jerk, and he was sure to fail. By God, though, he was going to try.

XXXX. LITTLE BUTTERFLY

Wednesday, August 29, 1928

Davies spent another day on deck recuperating. The rise and fall of the ocean was not exactly soothing, but he enjoyed the feel of sunlight on his face and the smell of salt water. Once or twice he was entertained by the sight of a nearby school of frolicking porpoises, and he was thrilled when a terrific rumble heralded the sudden appearance of a Japanese destroyer, flags snapping in the wind, that passed by them as an express train would sweep by a railway pushcart.

His brain was functioning well enough to torment him with endless worries and doubts. To start with, he couldn't help but test the first spoonful of each day's soup with the tip of his tongue, being on the alert for strange tastes or odors.

Then there was Madame Lin. Replaying the images of her death, he still couldn't understand why his dear, cantankerous friend had been killed. She hadn't screamed or aroused the suspicions of desk clerks when she'd phoned down to them, so it would seem that Trees had her under his control. Yet, if Trees was the monster that Monica had described, why hadn't his grotesque appearance alarmed Madame Lin? Also, it was strange that he would chat calmly with her for half an hour, then shoot her.

Was Davies wasting time to try and find a logical motive for an irrational killer? After all, how often did the police render themselves unable to solve a case because they insisted on a logical accounting of the facts, forgetting that murderers, like most human beings, even sane ones, weren't especially logical?

He was also concerned about Monica. The vigil she'd held at his bedside made him think that she might have developed genuine feelings for him. He thought he was ready for love, but faced with the reality of it, he realized he wasn't. Monica was an enjoyable companion, but so young and troubled that it was absurd to become further involved with her. The physical attraction would be hard to resist - he'd have to train himself to be unmoved by the look of amused scorn on her face whenever their lovemaking commenced, or by the softness of her skin, and the liquid smoothness of her lips. Watching the curves of her body move and forcing himself not to touch would be an additional burden, but it was unrealistic to think he could entertain a close relationship with someone of her station and race. Of course, there was a certain appeal in parading her around as a means of shocking all the stuffed shirts and hypocrites peopling his domain - nonetheless, the time had come to leave adolescent fantasies behind. Somewhere beneath his lust he cared about Monica, and he'd continue to help as best he could, but it wasn't right to lead her on. Now that he'd spirited her away from the Shanghai police, his obligation to her was ended. Besides, the possibility remained that she actually was Madame Lin's killer. Whether she was a murderess, or an unlucky innocent, the responsible thing was to let Monica down gently. He needed to be on the lookout for an appropriate time to tell her that the most they could expect to be was friends - he hoped she wouldn't be too hurt.

Another source of anxiety was No Sin, who had been behaving strangely since the meeting the previous night with Mr. Lin. The boy seemed to be holding back a secret, one that he was desperate to tell, yet was frightened to even mention. Several times he'd said, "Mr. Davies," then fallen silent.

Finally, late in the day, as No Sin was delivering perhaps a hundredth cup of tea, he followed through. "Mr. Davies," he said, squatting beside the deck chair, "I find something very important. Something you must see." The boy's voice was charged with repressed excitement.

"What sort of thing?" Davies asked, both curious and irritated. "I don't think I have the strength."

"You come with me! Okay? Okay? I help you!"

"All right," Davies said, wondering what he was getting himself into. He pulled himself up, leaned heavily on No Sin, and readjusted the sling wrapped round his semi-paralyzed right arm. The two of them hobbled forward, the pitching of the ship doing little to make their trek easier.

No Sin led him inside, then along the dirty passageway to Monica's door. "You have key?" he asked.

"Yes. But where's Monica?"

"She go for walk with Laota. She okay. I very bad boy, I know. I should not spy. I know. But I see her through window last night. Very bad."

"Okay," Davies said, and he unlocked the door and opened it.

They entered Monica's cabin. On tiptoes, No Sin moved across to the dresser and pointed to a heavy table lamp. "Under the lamp. That where I see her put it."

"Put what, Sin? Don't be so damned mysterious."

"Just look. I no touch."

Davies crossed the room and lifted the lamp, which, in his weakened condition, seemed to weigh as much as an obese child. Underneath the thing were several small paper packets. Davies set the lamp aside and tore one of the packets open - it contained dried roots and herbs.

Gravely, No Sin shook his head. "I try to tell you she no good. Now you believe me?"

Davies rewrapped the package and gazed at the boy, hoping he could spot the coldness in his eyes. "Stop it. Monica didn't poison me."

"But you see for yourself! She did it!"

Davies eased himself down onto the bed. "No she didn't, Sin. You did."

No Sin's face went pale. "Why you think,..? Why would I,...? You crazy. I sorry, but you crazy."

"If you really suspected Monica of poisoning me, why did you let her feed me soup all night? Weren't you afraid she'd finish me off?"

No Sin shook his head violently. "Not true, no, no, not true, Mr. Davies. No. No. No." The boy's denials were taking on a nearly musical beat.

"I actually didn't suspect you until now. But this is all too pat."

"No, you wrong." No Sin squeezed his eyes shut and began to tremble, tears trickling down his cheeks. "You wrong."

"I assume you didn't mean to kill me, just scare me, right? All to turn me against Monica."

"But you don't see! I never want to hurt you! But I so scare for you! I only put in tiny, tiny bit, so you get little tummy ache. I just trying to protect you!"

"You have a funny way of doing it."

The boy sank to his knees and began to sob. "She bad!" he wailed in a shredded voice. "I know she is! I try to warn you, but you don't believe me. What else can I do?"

Davies looked down at No Sin and couldn't help but shake his head. The incredible part of it was that the youth probably believed what he was saying. "I suppose I should feel grateful for this display of affection. Jesus Christ, what were you thinking, Sin? You could have killed me! Did that occur to you at all?"

"You hate me now!" No Sin howled, his body starting to convulse. "I know I'm bad. You save my life, and I am worthless. You should kill me! I'm sorry! I'm sorry! I only poison you because I care about you!" He covered his head with his hands and fell into a sobbing fit.

Davies made his own contribution to the hysteria level by threatening to have No Sin arrested, then chastising him for his selfish idiocy, using the most colorful terms he could think of. When most of the bile was purged from his spleen, he said, "All right, Sin, that's enough - I've already seen 'Madama Butterfly.'"

With great effort, Davies rose from the end of Monica's bed. He looked down at the boy and kicked him several times. "Stop it, now. I guess you didn't know you had given me too much, I'm sure you didn't mean to kill me."

"No, no."

"You Chinese are notoriously bad poisoners." He dropped a handkerchief beside the lad's trembling hand. "Clean yourself up. We'll pretend this never happened. But make damn sure you don't do it again!"

"I do not deserve forgiving." No Sin's sobs were finally beginning to subside.

"No, probably you don't. And if my arm doesn't get any better you might as well jump overboard. Come on, get up. I'm tired and I can't get back by my myself."

No Sin rose, using the handkerchief to wipe tears from his cheeks. With a maternal frown of concern, he put the damp cloth back into one of Davies' pockets. "You look bad, Mr. Davies. You must rest; you have too much excitement. I help you go to bed."

They hobbled back to Davies' cabin, stopping several times as No Sin broke down and resumed sobbing; it must have looked rather strange - each time Davies leaned against the rail and waited patiently for his helper to regain his composure.

XXXXI. GETTING COZY

Thursday, August 30, 1928

Davies rose the next day at a little after one in the afternoon, having finally experienced a wonderfully deep sleep. He enjoyed a pleasant luncheon with Monica until he made the mistake of bringing up an indelicate subject - he should have known better. "I was going to ask you something. What was it?" He examined his buttered roll, as if it held the secret to what he was trying to remember. "Oh, yeah. You know a fellow named Willows?"

"Why?"

"Who is he, exactly?"

"A friend of my mother's. She works for him."

"How do you get along with him?"

"He's okay."

He took a bite from his roll; not surprisingly, it was stale. "Well, this Willows sent a letter to Madame Lin warning her that you were a little nuts, and that you'd prove it by trying to sell her 'the clouded twilight' for far too much money."

She stopped eating and stared at him accusingly. "Who told you that?"

"Your uncle, Mr. Lin. He's on our ship."

"You're lying."

"Why would I lie about something like that?"

"Maybe you're jealous," she snapped. "You're trying to turn me against him."

"Against who?"

"Against anyone who isn't you!" She tightened her jaw and glared at the ocean, churning outside the dining room window. "It's pathetic. Truly pathetic. I pity you."

"That may be, but,..."

"God dammit! Dammit! Don't talk about this anymore!"

"Yes, but,...."

"Didn't you hear me? Shut the hell up!"

As he stumbled into his dark little room twenty minutes later, Davies thought that he was starting to regret boarding this ship. He was even developing second thoughts about saving No Sin, aiding Monica Marshall, and closing up shop in Shanghai. Since leaving he'd amassed about four hours of real sleep, despite numerous attempts. As much as he wanted to solve the murder of Madame Lin, a part of him wished to get the whole thing over with so that he could spend about a week happily snoring in bed - without headaches, body aches, and immobile limbs.

He sank onto his mattress and an irony struck him, completely unrelated. He could think of a few wealthy friends who lived like coolies. They spent their days in exercise, removed their clothes and labored under the sun, consuming minuscule amounts of food, usually vegetables. But they did it to appease a narcissistic theory of well-being, in order to have perpetual youth and vigor and to appease their strange philosophy of "moral nutrition." Most of his other friends shunned them, as dark skin and a thin body were the tell-tale signs of poverty - but his health-fixated friends didn't care. The world was a peculiar place.

Based on Monica's reaction, the mysterious Mr. Willows was now a major player in the unfolding drama. Was it possible that his warnings to Madame Lin about Monica's sanity were sincere and completely on the mark? And what of the weird little man in the cowboy hat – did he know that Monica had killed her aunt? Had he come aboard ship to blackmail her – or was he propelled by a different motive? Obviously, the fellow was in love with her. And wasn't it awfully convenient that the little gnome had stolen the staff from Monica right before it would have been confiscated by Elder Brother's agents, who surely manned the docks of Shanghai? Maybe the theft was a ruse to get the artifact past customs and Monica and the man with the big hat were still working together - a reasonable theory, worth contemplating; and one more reason why it was downright irresponsible to take the little, amber-skinned girl seriously. What a shame.

He did his best to relax during the remainder of the afternoon, but he continued to be haunted by how ferocious Monica could be when her mood changed. He'd better be very careful when he actually did break up with her; perhaps he should even be armed.

* * *

Davies' revelations about Horace Willows were so shocking that Monica felt like jumping overboard and swimming to America so that she could strangle her mother's "dear friend" with her own, water-shriveled hands. Dear God, what kind of twisted fun house was she living in?

Sitting in the lumpy armchair that helped to make her tiny cabin an obstacle course, she thought of how absurdly she'd behaved in front of Zephyr Davies. Why the hell couldn't she control her temper? Davies was the first decent thing that had happened to her since little Jimmy Paulson shared his lunch of buttered bread with her back in the first grade. Sure, having a rich boyfriend was a hell of a kick, but the greatest kick came from the way that Davies treated her fairly and with decency. He was fun, he was smart, she loved his wicked, dry humor, and his cautious warmth. He gave her hope. He saw something in her that might actually exist, a Monica that even she could grow to love.

Lord, what a joke - what a stupid, worthless pipe dream. The only man who'd ever treated her well must now think she was certifiable. Perfect. She'd just proven to him that she was only worthy of being tossed in the garbage. She buried her head in her hands and sobbed.

* * *

Near dusk, Davies had a martini out on deck and watched the sun set over the materializing city of Yokohama. They docked at about eight p.m., almost a full day late.

Yokohama had been devastated by a terrible earthquake in nineteen twenty-tree, which had spawned a horrific firestorm accompanied by the loss of over a hundred thousand lives. The fire, amplified by the winds from a typhoon, had been so ferocious that a cyclone of flame had descended, as if from the heavens, and sucked innocents into the sky, where they were incinerated. Despite these horrors, the city had been rebuilt in an exceptionally brief period of time. The city fathers had made a good try of it; there were now some wide boulevards, new parks, and plenty of trees. But the waterfront was comprised of tightly packed, modern, and remarkably characterless buildings, which were already beginning to look old and dingy.

The stopover was marred by several unfortunate incidents. The crew had become surly - after running over the little sampan in the harbor, followed by Davies' poisoning, and the murder attempt made against the Hatman, they now regarded their ship as being jinxed. They stared hatefully at the passengers, and did a sloppy job of docking. Their poor performance confirmed the theory that the ship was unlucky when the gangway was misaligned, taking out a section of the ship's rail and crushing a mate's hand in the process.

After a long wait, Japanese customs officials came aboard the battered freighter to check everyone's papers By this time, it was nearly two in the morning. Making matters worse, No Sin had no passport, and an over-zealous customs official refused to take a bribe. With as much calm as he could muster, Davies tried to reason with the stocky government man. "He's lost his passport, I'm afraid. Don't worry, his papers are in order and we intend to straighten out the matter when we dock stateside."

"You may go ahead, sir," the stocky official replied in a machine-like monotone, "but your friend will have to wait here until he can provide the proper documents."

Davies was not interested in playing the role of messenger boy. "That could take weeks."

"Then he will have to return to China."

Davies glanced at No Sin and wondered why he didn't just hand the boy over to the Japanese and say, "good riddance." How charitable was he supposed to be?

The youth's anxious look strongly suggested that Davies' mind was being read.

Yet, No Sin didn't seem an irredeemably bad sort, and a tragic upbringing had contributed to his mercurial behavior. Did China really need another hatchet man, an heir to Elder Brother - at the very least, another beggar? Was Davies again breaking his promise to Madame Lin - and to himself - to overcome his prejudices - moreover, to contribute something to the world, and cease being a wealthy parasite? If he couldn't master the dilemma of a No Sin, how could he ever deal with the inevitable difficulties that would sprout from future, more grandiose acts of charity?

"Forget about it," Davies said firmly, "he's traveling as my man-servant. I'll be responsible, and that will have to do." He hoped that he wouldn't regret this moment of compassion.

"I'm sorry, sir."

"I'm not interested in your sympathy. I'll be more than happy to give you a deposit of security, which is yours to keep if we don't return." Davies reached for his pocket book.

Incredibly, the official grabbed his arm. "I'm sorry, sir."

"You must be the sorriest man who ever lived! You're useless, let me see your supervisor."

On cue, a tall, distinguished Japanese stepped forward. "What's the trouble here?" he asked with unnerving politeness.

The appearance of the supervisor suggested only that he wished to be cut in, and that his underling didn't dare to act independently. After five minutes of genteel bickering the matter was resolved. No Sin's illegal passage didn't come cheap; Davies handed over enough to pay for several high quality neck ties.

As Davies, Monica, and No Sin strolled triumphantly out of the ship's lounge, the lad whispered, "Thank you, Mr. Davies. You don't regret this. I pay you everything, don't worry."

"I never worry, Sin."

Friday, August 31, 1928

They slept in the Dollar Line's warehouse-like waiting room, reclining on hard wooden benches. By eight in the morning Davies reached his threshold of misery, and he walked a number of blocks to a telegraph office where he wired for a thousand dollars to be sent to a bank in Honolulu. He also telegrammed his brother, asking for information about Willows. Finally, he telegrammed Crockwood, updating him, and asking again for news of Singletone's investigation.

Davies made it back to the dock just in time.

Their new ship was handsome and clean, with astoundingly attractive and comfortable cabins - although a janitor's closet would have been a step up from their last accommodations.

Even No Sin got his own third class cabin, and later he told Davies that he'd been so thrilled that he spent the afternoon sitting up in his bunk and grinning at regular intervals.

Davies and Monica had no trouble napping, and they successfully roused themselves for an eight-thirty seating in the dining room - this time the food matched the fine china instead of the now carpeted floor.

Sunday, September 9, 1928

The first days at sea were relaxing - unfortunately, however, the crossing was not lacking in drama.

Davies had regained enough of his strength to feel up to confronting Monica. He wasn't satisfied with her previous responses, and he wanted to know exactly what had happened the night Madame Lin died. He also wanted to know why this Willows fellow was so intent on getting her committed. However, Monica continued to be obstinate and violently uncooperative.

Able to get so little out of Monica, Davies pestered the Hatman with bribes and questions - had he been at the Astor House - had he seen anyone racing through the lobby in a suspicious manner? Huey Arnold, however, was now overplaying the role of a paranoiac, and he literally refused to so much as open his cabin door. What was he so frightened of - Mr. Lin - or someone else?

Frustrated, Davies retreated to the purser's office and sent off a telegram to Amos Mason, an old friend, who was with the Continental Detective Agency in San Francisco. He asked Amos to find out whatever he could about Huey Arnold, particularly if he had a prison record. Maybe Amos could come up with some ammunition that could be used to convince the Hatman to be a little more forthcoming with information.

Monday, September 10, 1928

Two days before they were due in Honolulu, Monica knocked on Davies' cabin door. It was three in the afternoon, and although the temperature was moderate Davies noted small beads of sweat on her otherwise pristine brow. "I want you to see something!" she said, entering quickly.

"What's the matter?"

She took his hand and led him outside, then back into her cabin. She guided him through the heart of the cozy room, slowing as they approached the bathroom. "In there," she said, pointing.

Sensing her anxiety, Davies left Monica behind and entered the small bathroom. All of her cosmetics had been smashed and pieces of broken glass and ceramic were strewn over the sink top. Beside the sink, and intermingled with white globs of cold cream and moisturizer, was an arrangement of vividly red rose petals - they spelled out the word: "whore."

Davies stood stupidly in the doorway, basking in the sensation of violation that radiated from the message in flower petals. To have a stranger force their way into a private space was bad enough, to have them impose their emotional sickness and hatred into a personal environment was the worst kind of assault. He felt cold in his stomach. He felt cursed. How must Monica feel? He walked back to where she was standing and put his arms around her. She was beyond tears.

"It must have happened while I was out walking on deck," Monica said, barely audible.

"Within the past half-hour?" Davies asked.

"I suppose."

Davies pressed his lips together grimly. Fifteen minutes earlier, he'd discovered that his room had been searched - but this wasn't the time to mention it. Saying, "Damn," was all the response he was willing to muster.

"Can I stay with you?" Monica asked in a faltering voice, which made him feel even worse.

"Of course. I'll have Sin collect your things. In fact, go on to my cabin, lock yourself in, and I'll bring your things over myself."

"Zephyr, I'm frightened."

He hugged her, wondering if the benefits of being her protector were starting to be outweighed by the dangers. "Look, I'll talk to the captain. I think I can persuade him to part with several mates to escort us about. If he won't take my money, I'll remind him of all the stories I can tell my society friends when we dock about this ship's security."

Monica squeezed him, fiercely. In return, he kissed her on the forehead. She smelled like fresh linen and drying nail polish.

The captain wasn't on the bridge and Davies was directed to a lower deck, where much of the crew was being distracted by a minor electrical malfunction. The captain, a lean and craggy Belgium, was extremely distressed to learn of the break-ins, and was more than willing to assign bodyguards to Davies and Monica. His willingness was augmented by some information that was passed on to Davies by the first mate: Mrs. Kissler's cabin had also been broken into, and several of her belongings had been stolen, and others destroyed. The mate didn't mind sharing this information because he believed that vigilant passengers were a neglected resource. Having no reluctance to accept Davies' cash, he went on to reveal that someone had attempted to jimmy the lock to Mr. Lin's door as well. These break-ins appeared to be the work of a common thief, unrelated to the sickening incident in Monica's bathroom. Maybe so, but Davies was finding himself less and less inclined to believe in coincidence.

XXXXII. THE BLOODY DRESS

Wednesday, September 12, 1928

It was a relief to see the Hawaiian Islands, moist emerald hills floating in a sea of azure blue. China had been rich browns and yellows, often austere and threatening. These islands were a multi-hued symphony of brilliant, liquid blues, greens and blacks; their spirit was festive and inviting. More than that, with the Hawaiian devotion to the spirit of Aloha, with their reverence for the land, this place seemed an antidote to China - here life was valued.

Just before noon, Niihau and Kauai appeared off the port bow - then Oahu rose directly in front of them. By late afternoon the pink and white stucco buildings of Honolulu were visible, and far to the southeast they could see the brooding peak of Mauna Loa. With ocean all around it, Honolulu was reminiscent of a tiny frontier outpost, a little reminder of civilization in the middle of nowhere.

No Sin was fascinated by the scenery. As the pilot boat arrived to guide them in he asked, "How those mountains get that color?" He pointed to distant slashes of orange and magenta. "Coolies paint them?"

"Probably," Davies answered.

"Don't say that," Monica scolded, "he doesn't know any better."

"I suspect they're flowers, Sin. And certain trees have colored leaves. Jacaranda and such."

No Sin thought a moment. "You making this up, right?"

"He certainly is," Monica said, "Jacaranda's have colored flowers, not leaves. Don't believe a thing he tells you."

No Sin nodded, tentatively, appearing more confused.

Since Davies' "illness," there had been no more attempts on anyone's life. With four burly mates as their constant companions, the last few days aboard ship had been guardedly pleasant.

However, the string of cabin invasions was hardly comforting, and Davies had to go back to entering his quarters gingerly and searching them thoroughly before he could relax. What a miserable ordeal.

The break-ins had perversely cheered Monica because they added substance to her insistence that the incident with the rose petals was not of her own doing. "You see," she'd said, with a sad sense of relief, "I'm not crazy. He's really out there, *whatever* he is."

In truth, Davies had wondered if Monica could have been acting the role of victim to cover her own guilt. Or perhaps, sensing his determination to drop her romantically, she was angling for his sympathy. He was debating whether or not to bring up this uncomfortable theory when he saw No Sin moving toward him in a provocatively indecisive manner. "Something on your mind, Sin?"

"Mr. Davies," the boy whispered, conspiratorially, "can I talk to you for one minute?"

"Okay." They moved away from Monica, who didn't seem to care. "So what's on your mind?"

"I find something. This time it very important."

"You haven't been poking around in my room, have you?"

The boy looked alarmed. "What you mean?"

"I know you're allowed in, and you tidy up nicely, but I can't forget your little packets of herbs. You sure you aren't up to your old tricks? Tell me the truth."

"I not. I swear at gods."

"You better not be lying."

"Please, Mr. Davies, it really, really, really not me."

"I warn you, Sin, if this is another one of your little stunts you'll be on the first boat back to China. Is that understood? Now what did your want to tell me?"

"I guess it nothing, never mind."

"Come on, out with it."

No Sin frowned and shook his head.

The liner let out several loud blasts to signal its arrival. When the relative quiet of churning water returned, Davies said, "We need to discuss another matter of some delicacy."

No Sin gave a quick nod, apparently expecting the subject to have been brought up. "How much money I owe you?"

"Owe me? Well, let's see - counting sea passage at a hundred and twenty, various bribes, and certain documents, which I will try to purchase here in Honolulu - just shy of two thousand American dollars. At a regular salary of thirty dollars a month, very generous I might add, and assuming you only put aside half of that, you should have it all paid back in, umm, sixteen years."

The news didn't seem to bother No Sin. "I guess we know each other for long time."

Now interested, Monica returned to their side.

"Don't worry, Sin, I was pulling your leg. No, the delicate matter I wanted to discuss is whether you're happy with the name I've been calling you."

"Why? Something wrong with it?"

"No. It's just that, well, it was rather imperious of me to make up a new name for you, and take your old one away. I never asked you what you wanted. Are you happy being called 'No Sin?' Or would you rather be referred to by your proper Chinese name, whatever that was. 'Go' something."

"You not like my name?"

"No, I'm perfectly comfortable with it. Either name, actually. I just want to know what you want."

"You mad at me, right? I don't deserve a name after what I did."

"Don't take this the wrong way, I'm just trying to think what's best for you."

"So what best for me - send me back to China? I still owe you two thousand dollar, too? Huh? Why you do this to me? I was so happy. Why you do this?" He started to cry.

Beside him, Monica was attempting to suppress a snicker.

Davies shot Monica a warning glance and put his hand on No Sin's shoulder. "Listen, you don't owe me any money, and I'm not sending you back to China. You've been a big help, well mostly. Look, it's a misunderstanding. I'll keep calling you No Sin, is that all right? We're friends, okay?"

Sniffling, the boy gave a weak shrug. Then, with his head drooping to his chest, he shuffled off to his prized third class cabin.

Shaking her head, Monica slipped her arm through his. "There's such a thing as timing."

"That's right - *now's* not the time for any lectures."

Davies checked them into the Moana Hotel, nestled in a dark palm grove and overlooking Waikiki Beach. He took two suites, one for himself, one for Monica, and arranged for a place in the staff's quarters for No Sin.

The hotel, a handsome, wooden building, was rendered in a simplified Victorian style - a contradiction in terms, to be sure. Nonetheless, the design was successful, creating a structure that was grand yet sensible. Built in 1903, the hotel had absorbed a number of modifications over the years, which made it unexpectedly up-to-date and nicely appointed. Their suite was wonderfully airy with large windows overlooking the sea. Gleaming pecan flooring set off the room, a different kind of wood being the signature of each floor.

After unpacking, Davies went down to the lobby. At the Moana's front desk, he asked the clerk if the hotel was holding a reservation for an individual named "Trees."

"Trees?" The portly clerk repeated the name, rolling his eyes back slightly. He consulted a ledger, wetting his finger as he turned pages. "No, I'm sorry - no one by that name is registered here."

"Are you sure? Can you check again?"

With a faint scowl, the clerk reinspected his ledger. "No - no Mr. Trees." It was easy to imagine that he was keeping himself from saying, "No Mr. Shrub or Bushes either."

This was impossible. Davies felt thoroughly gutted. For the entire journey, he'd fretted that he would come all the way to Honolulu on a wild goose chase - now this fear had come to pass. Where did he ever get the idea that he had any business being a detective?

With little enthusiasm, he pressed the matter and learned that the reservation for Trees, made in Shanghai, had been canceled a week earlier by a telegraph sent from Hong Kong. At Davies' request, the clerk checked with a number of the Moana's competing hotels, but none of them had anyone registered under the name of Trees - the whole affair was a complete rout.

Discouraged, Davies went ahead and booked passage on a steamer bound for San Francisco in four days, as their liner from Yokohama was heading on to Seattle. Next, he checked with the Moana's telegraph office, expecting to have heard back from Crockwood; but no cables from the baggy-eyed reprobate had arrived. This put a smart little twist in Davies' solar-plexus, more out of annoyance than concern, as images of a three-day weekend drunk played in his head.

There was, however, a lengthy radiogram from his brother, which he accepted and stuffed into his coat pocket.

Somewhat piqued, he sent off a telegram to Crockwood's office, and one to Singletone, asking for news of his old friend. It would serve Crockwood right to stumble to his front door in a soiled dressing gown and find the surly Sergeant Smixon waiting there, demanding an account of his recent comings and goings.

Sitting in a wicker chair, with a marvelous view of the sea, Davies dug into the message from his brother. All was well at home - his father's empire was running nicely without his interference. The mines, lumber yards, steel mills, varnish factories and the brokerage house cranking out more money than anyone could ever hope to spend - while not making nearly enough to satisfy his mother.

The telegram also informed him that Willows was one of their competitors in the lumber and mining industries. Ironically, he also manufactured munitions, and had an impressive list of overseas buyers including several governments. He countered these darker pursuits with philanthropy, donating to a fund set up to build San Francisco a proper opera house, and establishing a medical research foundation dedicated to finding a cure for asthma, motivated by the recent death of the young daughter of one of his servants. His balance sheet was impeccable, he was actually worth more than Davies, and lately he'd been collecting office buildings. In fact, a hearing was scheduled in San Francisco at the end of the week to determine if a new one should be allowed to enter his fold. This revelation was annoying, the building was one that Davies rather fancied himself.

Checking his watch, he realized that the local bank was about to close. He abandoned his comfortable chair and walked several blocks to the bank, which, mercifully, was still open. The money that he'd wired for had arrived and was withdrawn without a hitch.

As he strolled back to the hotel, taking a deliberately roundabout route, the sultry trade winds, the quiet streets, and the quaint architecture tempted him to drop his guard and slip into a relaxed, appreciative mood. Many of the houses that he passed were little more than homemade wooden shacks - in another city they'd be dingy slums, here they seemed whimsical and cozy. Everything was so informal, it didn't seem like being in a real city with real problems. The pleasant mood didn't hold, however. He was still haunted by the break-ins that had occurred on the posh liner, which had brought them here. There had been no sign of Trees, and all he had to go on was the word "whore" spelled out in rose petals. Were there two culprits afoot, a common thief working separately from someone with a more sinister agenda? When Davies added in Monica' refusal to discuss Willows, he was left with an abundance of unanswered questions - the most obvious being: was Monica behind it all? Ending his romance with her was making more and more sense.

As much as he hoped he'd left China behind, and that Hawaii signaled a change in his luck, his long walk caused him to become less aware of palm trees and warm ocean breezes, and more conscious of the vengeful ghosts and malevolent spirits that were rumored to haunt this island. The air began to seem sultry rather than comforting, and distant drums, probably from a band warming up in a gambling house, sounded less like modern jazz and instead hinted of bloody pagan rituals, bleached skulls on sticks, evil faces flickering in torchlight. He wondered if he'd wandered into the notorious River District, built along Nu'uanu Stream, a section of Honolulu that had a reputation as fearsome as any on the globe.

Over dinner, Davies continued to be pensive and preoccupied as he shared many of his findings about Trees with Monica, as well as the things he'd learned about Willows and his real estate purchases. Although initially interested in his report, she soon became bored and he could tell that his stock had plummeted. Behind her placid gaze, he sensed that she no longer regarded him as a dashing and resourceful adventurer, but a silly dabbler, in over his head, who'd wasted weeks of her time by plunging off on a wild goose chase. She remained so subdued through the evening that she wasn't even critical of No Sin. Davies wondered if she was going to quit speaking again.

Fortunately, her mood improved after he poured out a couple of drinks from his flask – as it turned out Hawaii was dry. With Samoan bodyguards standing discreetly by, Davies and Monica went on to enjoy an excellent dinner.

When their dining was completed, they stood on the moonlit balcony of Monica's suite listening to the sound of native drums drifting up from the beach. Compensating for a hot, stifling day, the evening was warm and comforting, with the kind of soft breeze coming up from the surf that made one feel that the world was a happy playground with simple, sensible rules. Candles flickered on the small dining table on an upper veranda, beautifully illuminating Monica who was wearing a new frock - a wispy, white thing with bare shoulders and a sash. She had the freshly scrubbed look of a débutante ready for her coming out party. But instead of pasty white skin and freckles, her perfect amber flesh seemed to glow.

"You enjoy dinner?" he asked.

She smiled in her old, sad way. "It was fine."

"Something seems to be bothering you."

She shook her head.

"You sure?"

"Sometimes I just don't have much to say."

"You made that very clear in Shanghai." Getting no response, he cleared his throat. "Monica, I don't know how to put this - I'm concerned that you may be expecting things from me that I can't provide. I *am* something of a playboy, I'm afraid,.."

"I knew this was coming," she said with resignation. "Things always turn out this way for me. So you want to be friends, is that it - no more living in sin?"

"Yes. I think it best."

He waited for her to explode in fury, to begin breaking up the china, to start crying that nobody ever wants her - but she seemed to have no reaction at all. "Can I ask you a favor then, Zephyr? I know this sounds stupid - but would you be willing to kiss me? Just once more - in an unfriendly way." She was gazing up at him as if she were a little girl asking for her very first kiss. Her reaction was peculiar, but far preferable to what he'd been anticipating. Thinking that her request, more than anything, was a reminder that she was all of twenty-one years old, he put his hand on her waist and kissed her gently on the lips. She blinked at him, and seemed to hold her breath for a moment - then she placed her arms around his neck and melted into him, softly devouring his mouth. Eventually, she pulled away and studied him with the careful intensity of a scientist. "Do it again, please," she said, a trickle of sweat evident on her forehead, "but better this time."

Davies kissed her with effortless passion, abandoning himself to the heat, the perfumed scent of her hair, and the remarkable softness of her skin. He remembered her stroking his hand and feeding him soup and things began to happen. What a time to end their affair.

When they finally managed to force a separation, she studied his face closely, the artery on her neck throbbing as fast as his own heart. She smiled, still with sadness. "I've really enjoyed myself. Thanks for being such a gentleman."

Davies watched her float across the terrace and into her bedroom. Again, she puzzled him. Whatever had been troubling her seemed to have faded into passionate warmth. In the past few moments, he'd felt that they'd been unusually close.

The stillness was broken by the ugly crack of a pistol shot echoing harshly against the colorful ceramic tiles outside her bedroom.

Davies bounded across the terrace, entered her bedroom and ran to her closed bathroom door, his heart thumping wildly. The door was locked. "Monica!" he shouted, pounding his fists feverishly on the door. There was no answer. He took a step back, then heaved himself with all his might into the door, causing sharp pain to his shoulder, but shattering the lock.

Monica was lying on the floor, his pistol in her hand, her skin already a shade paler. Just above the center of her chest, blood was oozing onto her elegant white dress. Davies picked her up and carried her to the bed. "Monica," he said for no good reason, as he felt her pulse. With his other hand, he grappled for the phone.

XXXXIII. FLOWERS

The next hour was chaotic. While waiting for the doctor, Davies stopped the bleeding with a towel. Then, with half the hotel staff crowding through the door into the sitting room, the house doctor, in a full dress suit, finally made an appearance.

The wound was not serious the man announced when he'd finished treating her. The bullet had entered at an angle and come out under her shoulder without striking any organs. She had fractured her collar bone and should expect a lot of pain, but recovery seemed assured.

With the aid of a fat bankroll, Davies convinced the doctor that the shooting had been an accident. He'd given Monica the gun in China for protection. An awful, lawless place, China - not like Hawaii. Surely, the Moana wouldn't turn out a recuperating accident victim, that would be a greater scandal - Davies would see to it. The doctor agreed.

"Is she conscious?" he asked the doctor, as he let him out.

"Yes," the physician replied, "but don't disturb her, Mr. Davies. She must have rest and quiet."

"Of course." Davies shook the doctor's hand and locked the door behind him.

A stout Hawaiian nurse, with several small bottles of pills in her fat hands, had been left behind. He chatted with the nurse, who was friendly and cooperative. When he'd finished, he strode across the carpet and entered Monica's bedroom.

Sitting at her bedside, he grasped her hand - it was no longer smooth, but cool and damp. "What a miserable, ugly thing to do," he said, "I hope you're satisfied."

She took a shaky breath. "The only miserable thing is that I missed."

He squeezed her hand, feeling bones that were tiny and delicate. "Don't you know how much you scared me?"

"What do you care?"

"A lot more than you do, I guess. I don't understand. You seemed fairly happy tonight."

She coughed out a laugh. "The price of patriotism. It's all because of the damned 'Pledge of Allegiance.' I thought my heart was up here." Weakly, she touched the heavy mass of bandages around her right shoulder. "The doctor was terribly mad at me. My ignorance of anatomy offended him. He told me how I could get it right next time."

"I've kissed my share of women; I've never had one shoot herself afterwards."

"Don't worry." Her voice was a whisper, "it's all me."

"I still don't understand. Was it because I broke things off with you?"

She closed her eyes. "I'd like to sleep."

After nearly five minutes of indecision caused by an ignorance of post-suicide attempt etiquette, Davies asked, "Would you like some water?"

She nodded - apparently to reassure him that she hadn't stopped talking, she added, "Yeah, please."

He brought her the water. She drank slowly, using her left hand. "Anything else?" he asked.

"Can you get the lights?"

He hesitated, wondering if he dared press for more answers.

She seemed to sense his conflict. "Put your brain to rest, okay? I've really got to sleep."

"Sure. I'll be in the next room, on the sofa." He kissed her softly on the forehead. She smelled like rubbing alcohol. He went to the door, took another look, switched off the light and left the room.

The thing that bothered him the most about Monica's attempted suicide, Davies thought as he tried to sleep, was the way that it permanently tainted her character. Anyone who was capable of such violence to herself was capable of violence to others. Such a person would always put their own needs and desires, no matter how unreasonable, above anyone else's. This reinforced the fact that he'd never felt that comfortable around her. No, that wasn't true, there'd been moments when he'd felt *very* comfortable. Such moments would never occur again; he'd have to be on his guard with her at all times - just as he now had to be on his guard with No Sin. He'd be sure to keep his Colt with him so she couldn't get her hands on it again. It was all so miserable and exhausting. And sad.

Thursday, September 13, 1928

Before she awakened the next morning, Davies had Monica's room filled with tropical flowers. Not ordinary arrangements in vases, but fanciful, tangled carpets of flowers, which covered the furniture and her bed. When placing the order, he'd been tempted to request a giant horseshoe as if she'd won the Kentucky Derby, and realized that he was motivated as much by anger as concern for her. He suddenly thought of the little engraver, who knows what goes on between two people? Perhaps he was wrong to think that the little Chinese had shot his girlfriend for political reasons, maybe she'd had it coming to her. An excess of foliage might give Monica something to think about, hopefully encouraging her to be less attracted to the idea of doing herself in. Sometimes it was nice to have lots and lots of money.

The smell in the room soon became overwhelming, it would be just too bad if she had an allergic reaction to the flowers. In fact, it would serve her right if she did.

When three Filipino bellboys arrived with her meal, he rose from where he'd been sitting in a corner, reading the newspaper, and went over and kissed her on the cheek. "Good morning, Monica. Time to wake up."

"Go away," she mumbled. "Something smells funny." She opened her eyes a crack, then painfully pulled herself up and took in the room. "Oh, God, I died."

"It's amazing what wonders can be worked when persons are sedated," Davies said. "Let's have some breakfast please."

Grinning ferociously, the bellboys came forward and buried Monica under trays of food.

She put a warm hand on his cheek, causing him to rise and make hastily for the door. Unable to think of anything clever, he saluted to her as he left the room.

Downstairs, the colored maid wearing a gold earring was helping Mrs. Kissler across the lobby. Catching sight of him, the old woman bellowed like a Guernsey being improperly milked, "Oh, Mr. Davies!"

Trapped, Davies crossed over to her. Her hair and gown were both tinted red, accompanied by a red feather boa that made it frighteningly dramatic. Apparently, she wasn't a cripple; she only used a wheelchair when she was tired. She grabbed onto his hand with flesh that was soft and damp and determined, causing him to feel that he'd been caught in the grip of a giant clam. "I am Mrs. Rosamund Kissler of Boston. I think it's thrilling the way you're helping Miss Marshall, simply out of the kindness of your heart." The phrasing implied that she wanted reassurance that he wasn't sleeping with a half-breed. She followed up with an expectant smile

He made an incomplete nod, which seemed to satisfy her.

"And isn't it a shame that you fell ill. To think we all ate the same food, nasty stuff it was, too. I count myself lucky for avoiding your fate. How are you?"

"I'm okay."

"That's splendid. And how is the poor thing? I heard there was an accident. I tried to call on her, but her room seems to be guarded, how very odd. Could you say something to get me through?"

"She's all right," Davies replied, eager to escape. "But Miss Marshall needs to rest for several days. Incidentally, did you find any of your things?"

Releasing his hand, the old woman scowled, her face transforming into that of a gargoyle under an ill-fitting wig. "Isn't it awful? It simply ruined my holiday. No, I still have most of what I need, but the idea. Now, how did you know?"

"The captain mentioned it."

"I thought he was keeping it quiet."

"He was. He only told me."

"Really."

"Well, he thought I might help; I worked with the Pinkertons once. Did you lose much?"

"Thank goodness, no. Somebody must have broken into my cabin while I was at tea. They stole jewelry, mostly - and a few dresses, the good Lord knows why. But they didn't get anything really valuable. Still it's all so bothersome. You haven't found any clues for me, have you?"

He shook his head. "I'm afraid not."

"Oh, well. So now I shall have to sail immediately to San Francisco to buy new things." She smiled, flirtatiously. "Did I hear that you live there?"

"Actually I live in Belvedere, it's a little sort of an island - almost."

"I'm going to be staying at that new Mark Hopkins Hotel. It just opened, you know, and they say it's wonderful. Is that true?"

"I really wouldn't know."

"Oh. I just thought you might because Miss Marshall said you were in construction."

"Not exactly."

She appeared confused. "Don't you want to build homes for unfortunates, or some such thing?"

"Eventually."

"That's what she told me, marvelous homes open to all creeds and races. What ambition."

Davies smiled. "I'm glad you approve."

"Now, I didn't say that. I think it's grand to help the poor. But don't you think that different races and cultures are happier keeping to their own?" She turned to her maid. "Isn't that so, Bernice? You're much happier living with your own sort."

Bernice rolled her eyes and muttered, "uhm hum," in a manner that could be taken as neither agreement nor discord, and which implied that living with her own sort was preferable to living with Mrs. Kissler.

"You see," Mrs. Kissler said, triumphantly. "No use stirring up a fuss, especially when you're casting off into uncharted waters." She dug her fat fingers into his arm. "And you must promise to look me up when you get to San Fran. I won't take 'no' for an answer, you dear man. Oh goodness! There's the taxi. I must run." She released him and hurried away with the grace of a freight train rumbling into a sharp turn.

He finally made it all the way to the telegraph office, located just off the lobby. There, he learned that Singletone had snubbed him, but a reply had come from Crockwood's Shanghai office. He accepted it eagerly. The news wasn't good, however. Crockwood had requested a two week leave of absence and then vanished without ever checking back to see if his time off had been granted. Numerous phone calls to his residence had gone unanswered.

When a worried co-worker had finally dropped by in person, he was told by Crockwood's servants that their master had left six days earlier with nothing but an overnight bag. Far more troubling, they'd observed him being escorted to a large sedan in the company of several Oriental gentlemen. Worried and angry, Davies scribbled a telegram to Elder Brother demanding an explanation.

When he returned to Monica's suite, he was startled to see the effete Chinese from their old Japanese freighter sitting at Monica's beside. Spotting Davies, the slender, nattily-dressed man rose and extended his hand.

"This is my friend, Alexander Wu," Monica called out from where she was comfortably encircled by a mountain of pillows. "He's been cheering me up."

Davies nodded and shook Wu's hand; his fingers were impossibly long and thin.

"I'll be off now, Mon Cheri," Wu said, returning to Monica and kissing her hand. He straightened his slender frame, exhibiting impeccable posture, Monica a wave with his fingers, and walked to where Davies stood. "You take good care of her."

Still somewhat confused, Davies nodded.

Wu placed his soft hand on Davies' arm. "A word?"

Together, they walked to the door. "Such a stylish woman," Wu said quietly. "Her kind of taste can't be learned; she's a true gem," "You must treat her extraordinarily well, Mr. Davies. She loves you so very much. She doesn't realize it, of course, so you must be especially patient with her. Au revoir." And he was out the door; a ghost couldn't have vanished more elegantly.

Davies walked slowly back to where Monica sat comfortably in her bed. What kind of detective was he, who hadn't even noticed that Monica had made a best friend, right under his nose? Then again, when he was recuperating from his poisoning it was No Sin, not Monica, who'd spent the greatest amount of time at his side - giving Monica plenty of opportunities to meet with Alexander Wu with Davies being none the wiser. "When did you two become friends?"

"After that ma chiang game on the old ship. I do have a life away from you, you know."

"He's quite devoted to you."

"He's a homosexual."

"Is he?" Davies mused, stating the obvious, and wondering what that had to do with anything.

"But you mustn't tell anybody. Promise?"

"Of course."

"He's been made fun of all his life, something you wouldn't understand." This was said with a bitterness that Davies didn't care for, but realized he deserved. "He saw how people on the ship were treating me because I'm a half-caste. I suppose he regarded me as a kindred spirit. We hit it off immediately."

"Who was treating you badly?"

"The Hatman, for one. I told Alexander about him that first night, before you sat down for dinner."

Davies nodded, remembering the venomous look that Wu had given Huey Arnold after he'd spilled coffee on himself and was lumbering out of the ship's dining room.

"Alexander is so understanding. I can tell him anything."

"Unlike me."

The visit with Wu had exhausted her, so Monica went back to sleep. Davies spent the remainder of the afternoon in the sitting room outside of where she slept. He had regained nearly full use of his arm, and a sling was no longer necessary, which allowed him to imbibe his dearly needed cocktail with traditional effortlessness.

He joined Monica for supper around five, noting that she had been up for an hour without telling him. After her long nap, she'd grown extremely restless, and had somehow succeeded in having most of his flowers removed without his knowledge, presumably through a maid's entrance. "Didn't you like my flowers?"

"The smell got to be a bit much," Monica replied, hesitantly. "And I don't care for lavish arrangements." She nodded towards two vases, each containing a very simple, almost sparse arrangement done in the Japanese style. Out of the hundreds he had given her, roughly thirty flowers had been permitted to remain. Apparently, she treated plants as ruthlessly as people.

"Zephyr?" she said as she perused a magazine.

"Yes, dear."

"What if I was really, truly bad - even worse than you could imagine?"

"Then I couldn't imagine it," he answered, thinking how interesting it was that she could be frank and evasive all at the same time. He went and sat beside her and poured himself a glass of Scotch from his flask.

"Let's say I'd done something I should go to jail for, and you found out. Would you turn me in?"

"Have you done something like that?" He had a vision of her sitting in a holding cell, wearing his mink greatcoat.

"Of course not. But let's just say I had."

"I guess it would depend on the circumstances."

"You mean you wouldn't turn me in if I'd committed a crime and you knew about it?" She looked offended.

"What brought this on all of a sudden?"

"Nothing. Just sitting here all day with nothing to do, I suppose. My mind wanders."

"All right, what crime did you commit?"

"I don't know. Let's say I stole a car - your car."

"Did you damage it?"

"Mangled beyond recognition."

"I'd kill you. Personally. I wonder what's holding up our food?"

"I'm in no hurry - I'm really not all that hungry. Now seriously, as to my question."

"I told you, it'd depend on the circumstances. I might not necessarily turn you in."

She paused to puzzle this through. "Are you saying we should be above the law, Zephyr?"

"Why not?"

"Come on, be serious."

"Aren't you the girl who thinks I'm too serious?"

With her good arm she punched his shoulder.

"Ow. To answer your question – who writes our laws?"

She shrugged.

"Politicians. Need I say more?" "

They both fell silent.

"Can I ask you something, Zephyr?"

"Shoot." He immediately regretted his choice of words.

"Do you think of yourself as a moral man?"

It was a good question, one that he was still grappling with. "I try to be."

"But do you succeed? Especially when it comes to something tough. I mean, anyone can pick up a dime tip that fell on the floor and give it back to a waiter."

"Let's say I'm practicing. That's all I can do. And you?"

"Oh, I don't have to worry. I'm going to hell so I can do anything I please."

"What are you going to hell for?"

She gave him her trademarked sad smile. "Wouldn't you like to know?"

Davies put down his glass, and scooted over to Monica. "Here," he said, "have a vitamin pill." He fumbled with a little bottle, and then handed her a pill. "Let me get you another pillow." He soon found one and propped it behind her.

"Why are you being so nice to me?"

Davies smiled. "Because you're sickly and pathetic."

"I'm not pathetic," she snapped. Her expression softened. "Am I?"

He brushed her soft, black hair.

She sat up straighter and took a dainty sip from her tea. "I suppose you're sick of me now?"

"Have I been acting like I'm sick of you?"

"No. But that's just because you're being nice. When people are nice there's always a catch, like they don't want to hurt you and show they've lost interest."

"You think I've lost interest?"

She shrugged. "It doesn't matter." She went back to her magazine. "I told you, I'm scheming." Another silence followed as she continued with her reading. "I was thinking just now, if I had the power, I'd have you shot. Then I could live with your memory. It would be much easier to live with your memory than to live with you."

He smiled, but he was feeling increasingly worried that he was responsible for what she had done to herself. Should he have been more diplomatic in the way that he'd suggested they become friends? But what was he to do, never bring up any subject that might upset her? His concern was mixed with a sense of feeling trapped - her attempted suicide hardly made her more endearing to him.

Monica seemed to sense his concerns. "I didn't do this because of you, by the way," she said. "I hope that wasn't what you were thinking."

"It crossed my mind."

"Don't worry, you had nothing to do with it."

"Can I ask what it did have to do with, then?"

"No," she answered serenely.

He decided not to press the matter, aware that his relief was giving away to annoyance. It was nice not to feel guilty, but a little insulting to be told that he hadn't meant enough to her to drive her to suicide.

XXXXIV. THE ALLEY

Friday, September 14, 1928

Davies slept poorly. Monica's suicide attempt, distracting as it was, failed to knock his thoughts off track. He was becoming obsessed with the idea that Trees was in Honolulu, monstrous in appearance, yet somehow blending-in amongst the palm trees. He had to admit that his obsession was probably rooted in a desire to reclaim some of his pride. It was a losing proposition, and he felt like an utter failure - his attempts at detecting disastrous. His assurances about Monica had led Madame Lin to be murdered. His hiring of Leibowitz had resulted in an equally fatal outcome. He'd been wrong in his assumption that Trees had fled to Honolulu, wrong to have left Shanghai, wrong to have embarked on an ill-fated journey, which had netted his own poisoning and Monica Marshall's suicide attempt. All these events were bad enough on their own, what was crippling was the feeling that he could no longer trust his own instincts. In fact, he was wondering if he'd *ever* been able to trust them.

Going through the motions of being a competent man on a mission, he checked with the Moana's telegraph office and learned that not only did the Hatman have a criminal record, but he was bound for jail the moment he stepped onto United States soil - no wonder he was hiding out.

Again, there was no telegram from Singleton, or one from Elder Brother; but a package was waiting for him. Davies accepted the package from the clerk and noted that it simply had "Mr. Zephyr Davies" written on it in an elegant hand.

"Who left this for me?" Davies asked.

The clerk went into the manager's office to check. He returned within five minutes. "I'm sorry, sir" he said with a guilty chuckle, "but I don't know who sent it to you. It seems to have just appeared. I'll continue to investigate, however."

"That would be good," Davies said. "Let's see what's inside."

As the clerk looked on, Davies tore off the brown butcher's paper that enclosed the package. A plain cardboard box, very similar to a shoe box, was beneath the paper – unfortunately, a quick search for a note proved fruitless. "Maybe it's full of beach sand," Davies remarked and removed the lid.

"Oh my," the clerk commented, as he stared at the contents.

* * *

No Sin was not very happy with his new duties. He had been asked to join the team of enormous Samoans guarding Monica Marshall. He would have preferred to watch after Zephyr Davies, but his life had become one of sacrifice. Two native giants stood outside Miss Marshall's door, while No Sin was posted on her back balcony - after two hours, he was to change positions with one of the Samoans.

Every so often, No Sin peered between the slats of the wooden shutters and into the foul woman's room. He was uncomfortable watching her this way, but Mr. Davies had instructed him to do so, and it was his duty to obey. At the moment, he could see that Monica was coming out of her bedroom and crossing to the low table in front of the sofa in her sitting room. She seemed suspiciously healthy for someone who had been recently shot, and she was wearing nothing but her sling and a tiny pair of cream colored silk underpants.

She leaned over the low table and picked up a hair brush. Although her back was to him, modesty prevented No Sin from looking directly at her. From the sofa, she walked back into the bedroom, sat down in front of a mirror and brushed at her hair.

No Sin backed to the edge of the balcony and took several long breaths, collecting himself. She was not wide and thick-hipped and built sturdily like women usually were. Her slender figure was surprisingly delicate, especially considering her fierce temper and demanding ways. But she wasn't a stick, she had many soft, full curves and there was something amusingly perverse about her complete attire: stylish, cream colored silk underwear, and a sling around her arm. In fact, her garb was very similar to what was worn by the women in the picture magazines that the Hatman had kept hidden in his stateroom. No Sin had stolen several of the weird man's magazines. - but he had sold them all to the little Japanese captain before they had landed in Yokohama.

He hated Monica Marshall. She was obviously no better than the women in the Hatman's magazines, but he understood why Zephyr Davies always asked him to leave the room when she was there. From the Hatman's magazines, he knew exactly what kind of things women like that did for men.

He returned to the glass doors and peered through the slats. She had a robe on now, and was sitting on the couch staring blankly in his direction. Afraid that she could see him, he turned away. He would certainly be glad when Zephyr Davies returned.

* * *

The sight of the mysterious present, still lying on the Moana's front desk, made Davies feel physically ill - for inside the cardboard box was a beautifully carved wooden coffin.

Davies left his gift with the clerk. As he headed back upstairs, trying vainly to steady his shaking hands, a short, rotund Hawaiian, dressed in a gaudy, purplish suit, approached him. "Mr. Davies?"

"Yes."

"I'm the house detective. Can I have a word?"

Davies anticipated more inquiries about Monica. "Certainly."

"You enjoying it here?" the small man asked as they gravitated toward the outer terrace.

"A lovely spot."

"We think so. Mr. Davies, did you know we're related?"

Where was this was going? Was he about to be hit-up for a donation to the policeman's ball?

"Yes, indeed," the small man continued, "we both have the same Elder Brother."

Davies felt another jolt; again he tried not to let it show. "How nice."

The little man remained cordial. "I'm afraid, though, that our Elder Brother is disappointed in you. You recently delivered an item to him, and it's my job to tell you that the goods are unacceptable. You must return what is missing."

"I have no idea what is missing," Davies replied, trying to reclaim his emotional equilibrium.

"That's not for me to say. When you're ready to turn over what's missing, let me know."

"And if I don't?"

"I'd hate to have to pass that information on. I would."

Davies stared the man in the eyes. He didn't seem a bad sort, taking no obvious pleasure in being cast as a messenger of doom. Nonetheless, Davies was angry. "I have cooperated with Elder Brother fully, and if something is missing, I'll certainly do my best to find it. - that's because I'm a man of my word. But I won't be threatened, do you understand?"

"Of course. However, this matter must be settled within twenty-four hours. Otherwise," the man made a grimace that could be indigestion, but Davies suspected was distaste for what he was charged to say, "one of your friends will be made to pay the penalty."

"What the hell does that mean?" Davies was livid. "Make sure that Elder Brother understands this - a friend of mine from Shanghai is missing - his name is John Crockwood. If any harm comes to him, all bets are off - Elder brother will get nothing more from me. Do I make myself clear?"

The Hawaiian swallowed hard, probably not because he was intimidated by Davies, but rather because he didn't look forward to passing on bad news to Elder Brother. "I got it."

It tore at Davies' guts to think that Elder Brother's opium-stained claws could reach out and grab him thousands of miles from Shanghai. Just as awful was the thought that harm might come to Crockwood. For that matter, what if No Sin was the friend made to "pay the penalty," or Monica?

After bidding farewell to the house detective, Davies' mind stormed with restless activity. What could be missing? "The clouded twilight" was an old piece of wood. Elder Brother's own man, Dr. Sun, had described it as nearly worthless, adorned with paste jewels, and concealing no hidden compartments nor cryptic treasure maps. Afterwards, he'd gone on to certify the artifact as authentic, so what on earth could the problem be? Moreover, why couldn't Elder Brother's man have told him directly what was missing? Why the need for more games?

Monica might very well know what was missing, but Davies wasn't up for a round of fights and evasions. Perhaps Mr. Lin could provide the same information without the accompanying theatrics.

Unfortunately, Mr. Lin was no help. Theatrics were unavoidable it would seem, so Davies made his way to Monica's apartment. He found her sitting by a window, gazing at the sea. "Feeling better?" he asked.

"Marginally. Did you bring me anything?"

"Like what? You mean a present?"

"Candy would be nice. I was hoping that you were clairvoyant." She looked up at him anticipatively, but he was able to offer nothing but a blank expression. "I can see you're not."

He walked closer, folded his arms over his chest, and looked down at her. "I just received word from Elder Brother."

"Here?" She tilted her head, skeptically.

"I'm afraid so. His tentacles are long. He's dissatisfied with 'the clouded twilight.' He says something is missing."

"And I'm supposed to know what you're talking about?"

Grimly, Davies nodded his head.

"That's absurd. Why don't you go get me some candy? I really need some."

"Monica!" Davies yelled - his burst of anger, fueled by fear and a week's worth of suppressed frustration, surprised even him. "This is serious! Elder Brother is not someone you play around with. I've got to know what he wants!"

"Then why the hell don't you ask him?" Her anger was already up to speed and a full match for his.

"Because he's as ridiculous as you are! Now tell me!"

"I don't know!" she screamed at the top of her lungs. "You don't care that I'm recovering from a serious injury! You don't care that I feel like doing it again! Here I am, trying to get better, and you come in and threaten me? How dare you!"

"You could be in danger! Don't you understand that?"

"Get out!" she shrieked. "Get out of my room! Get out!"

The two Samoan guards burst into the apartment. Davies marched out of her quarters, shaking his head and leaving the giants to deal with her. One came after him, but Davies waved him off. "Stay here," he said, curtly.

The guard remained in the doorway, looking bewildered and slightly dejected.

Davies hurried down the stairs, walked angrily across the lobby, and went outside into the hot Hawaiian sun. He needed to clear his head, he needed to calm down, he needed to forget - not that it was remotely possible. He knew Monica felt like crap and his timing was dreadful - but it wasn't his timing, was it, rather Elder Brother's. How difficult could it be for her to answer one simple question like a reasonable human being?

In no time, he found himself in a shabby section of the commercial district, wondering how he'd gotten there. This part of Honolulu appeared dingy instead of quaint, and he remembered that the city was notorious for gambling, slavery, and vice. The architecture here was of the "Cabinet Of Dr. Caligari" school of design, lacking sidewalks, plumb buildings, or coherence. Violent laughter could be heard coming from the open shutters of ramshackle buildings, accompanied by a tinny, Victrola recording of "Limehouse Blues," which implied that the entire neighborhood was indulging in self parody. Notions of humor were quickly vanquished by other sights and sounds: a disembodied, ritualized chant in Japanese a block away, and the more immediate whine and clatter of traditional Chinese music, the shrieking of a child through the open window of a basement apartment, and glimpses of stark, white painted Kabuki faces through dark, broken shutters, apparently rehearsing in the back room of a decaying theater – this neighborhood seemed more oriental than had many in China, it was utterly foreign and unsettling.

Appropriately, fifty feet behind him, a big, stupid-looking man, wearing a lot of white in the eighty degree temperature, was doing a bad job of trailing him. Great, that was all he needed, after everything else. It was a good guess that the behemoth was from out of town; he was so obviously following what a tourist would assume to be the Hawaiian dress code. When Davies stopped to gaze at store windows, the big lummox also stopped, looking at nothing more than a blank wall.

After getting directions from an impatient, Caucasian cop wearing an ill fitting uniform, and insisting he didn't have time to search for 'possibly suspicious characters,' Davies walked eight blocks, eventually passing through a battered set of doors and climbing a narrow, wooden staircase. At the top of the stairs a frosted glass door said Honolulu News Dispatch. He opened the door and moved into a clatter of cackling typewriters, hoping that the newspaper's morgue might have some information about Crockwood's disappearance in Shanghai.

"May I help you?" a Caucasian girl asked. She was sitting at the first desk, pasting up proof sheets. She looked like the sort who'd come out to the tropics to escape a wealthy family and learn what life was all about - a female version of himself.

"No, thanks," Davies said as he walked across the room. He had already spotted the editor's office and wanted to make his own introductions.

Forty minutes later he said his good-byes and left empty-handed. The editor had been helpful to a fault. Neither he nor his best reporters, however, were able to uncover any mention of John Crockwood in any of the past week's news dispatches from the orient. They assured Davies that they would contact him immediately if anything came in. They were very appreciative of his tips.

By the time he passed the receptionist's desk, the weird, sweet smell of printer's ink was making him feel queasy. The reaction must have been triggered by something in his body that hadn't fully recovered from No Sin's act of jealousy. He made for the landing, desperate for untainted air.

When he reached the bottom of the stairs he searched for his tail. The man was directly across the street, reading a newspaper and leaning casually against a brick wall beside an alleyway. Davies walked over and stood close. "You've been following me around all morning," he said cheerfully. "If you've a couple of minutes, I'll give you some tips on how to be more inconspicuous."

A pair of muscular arms lurched out from the alley behind Davies and encircled his neck. In an instant, he was off his feet and being dragged into gaping darkness.

Davies jammed an elbow into whomever was holding him from behind - he heard a sharp exhale, but the man with the newspaper was in front of him now, sailing a jagged fist into his face. Another blow from behind smashed into his kidneys - that hurt. Then his jaw was whipped to the side by a sledge hammer blow.

He knew he was in bad shape but he had two things going for him; strong, heavy bones, and a ferocious temper. He was a well-skilled fighter, who lost all reason and fear if he got mad, and now he was mad.   He hurtled himself at one of the large shapes, knocking the man off balance and causing the two of them to topple into a pile of garbage cans.   With primal viciousness, he used his already scraped fists to pound on the closest man's pockmarked face.   The fellow was able to strike back several times, and his partner was now beating on Davies from behind, but none of it mattered.   For a moment, all three wrestled and rolled around on the filthy ground, then Davies forced himself free and unsteadily lurched to his feet.   Without hesitation, he kicked his two attackers.   Before they could grab his legs, Davies found an old piece of pipe and really let them have it.   The two attackers shielded themselves and scurried away as fast as they could.

Davies stood, panting, in the alleyway, telling himself that he had to get back to the street where others could see him, in case the thugs came back.   He took a jerky step and decided it would be wise to rest a moment.   He sat down on a concrete step, inhaled deeply, and slipped into a black void of unconsciousness.

It was dark when he opened his eyes again.   At some point, he had tumbled from his little step. With stabs of pain coming from every muscle, he forced himself to his hands and knees and ran a shaking hand over his face - then he fell over backwards.   He tried again, rolling over to a wall and propping himself up.   His left jaw was a swollen mass of pulp with no feeling on the surface - but his teeth were all accounted for and both eyes managed to focus, barely.   Wobbling, he pulled himself to his feet and took a deep, painful breath.   His body parts all seemed to be present, and walking was possible if he kept a cautious hand close to the brick wall.   Moving his jaw caused excruciating pain, and he wondered how bad it looked.

The street was deserted as he stumbled out of the alley and leaned against a street lamp for support.   In the newspaper office, a single light bulb was burning in a window on the second floor.   If he could get back up the stairs, he could phone for a taxi.

XXXXV. SOB STORY

"What in a world happen to you, Mr. Davies?" No Sin asked.

Davies was lying on his bed, his eyes closed, an ice-pack across his forehead. "I fell down."

Having inspected himself in the mirror, Davies was amazed that he didn't look worse, not that he looked good. His arm was back in a sling and about five miles of tape encircled his chest. Nothing serious the doctor had said - a mild concussion, two or three cracked ribs, and a badly bruised shoulder. It had been the same doctor, wearing the same dinner jacket as the night before. When he'd left, he'd expressed the hope that Davies and Miss Marshall were leaving Hawaii soon. He was puzzled by the exact nature of their relationship.

Davies reached for his warm Scotch and took a needed slug, wiping a trail of caustic dribble from his chin - then he closed his eyes again. At the moment, he was far from pleased with No Sin; had Davies not been feeling the lingering ill-effects of his recent poisoning, he might have spotted the second man in the alley. But giving No Sin the tongue-lashing that he deserved would only make the boy feel guilty, leading very likely to resentment, and then who knows what? The past couldn't be fixed, but Davies was a little worried about the present and the future.

Who had sent the thugs? Elder Brother? Unlikely, such a crude attack was not his style. Davies was equally sure that Monica wasn't to blame, so much so that he didn't even intend to quiz her. He had kept her purse, doling out five dollars at a time as she needed it - how could she have paid such hoodlums - how would she have recruited them from her sick bed? Who did that leave then? The mythical, probably nonexistent Trees - or had someone else entered the fray?

A sharp knock rattled the door. "Come in!" Davies yelled in a faltering voice. "Ow!" he added, rubbing his jaw.

Monica entered wearing a golden silk robe and doe skin slippers; her arm was also still in a sling. "Oh, dear God!" she exclaimed, hurrying to his side. "What happened?"

"I fell out of bed. Sin, leave us alone, will you?"

The boy glowered at Monica and marched to the door, slamming it hard behind him.

"Really, Wallace, what did happen?" Monica asked, unfazed by No Sin's performance. "Imitation is the sincerest form of flattery, but this is a bit much."

"Why don't we swap? I'll tell you what happened to me today, and you can tell me why,..."

"Can I get you something?" she said pleasantly, evading the impending question about her suicide attempt.

The physical pain and the frustration hit him all at once. "For crying out loud, this is impossible! You've got me bumping around in the dark - this is what all your secrets and lies lead to - don't you understand that? You have no right to do this to me! You have no right to do this to anybody!" He was overreacting, but, damn it, he felt like hell.

"No one's forcing you to help me!" Her full lips curled as her eyes became swollen slashes. "You don't like my secrets," she hissed, "then why don't you give me one good reason why I should tell you the truth, you God damn son of a bitch!" He was about as mad as he could get, but the ferocity of her anger was far beyond anything he was capable of. "How the hell do I know what you're really after!" she shrieked. "Well?"

"Monica, I've been more than fair."

"Oh, I agree, and just think about it - you've bought me a steamship ticket and new dresses - and spent all this time with me. If you were really a detective you'd be charging me - so why aren't you? Because you like me - is that what I'm supposed to believe? I've never known a single man who wasn't after something - who wasn't a lying son of a bitch, not one! What makes you any different? Go straight to hell!" She turned and marched to the door, which was a relief, she'd frightened him just now.

As she reached for the doorknob, however, she hesitated. Seeming to reconsider, she turned and returned to his side. "Do you need some more ice in that pack? It looks kind of squishy."

Her change of mood was startling. "It's fine. Look, I don't want to fight, either." Then he added cautiously, "But you know that something serious has come up."

"Okay," She said amiably, and sat in a chair within striking distance of his bed. The chair squeaked as she settled in, the sound making her seem oddly vulnerable.

Why was she acting as if their recent shouting match had never happened? All the same, her strange civility was welcome, and it seemed wise to follow her lead. "Earlier today I told you that something is missing from 'the clouded twilight,' and Elder Brother is very upset. Please, if you know what's missing, you must tell me."

"Evidence," she said with a startling lack of hesitation.

"I see." He elected not to make an issue of her coy response; he was exhausted and didn't wish to risk provoking her. "And that's why so many people are after the thing - they want the evidence? What, exactly, is the nature of this evidence?"

She withdrew a cigarette from a pocket in her robe. "I thought it would be obvious to someone like you. It's so simple it's almost funny."

"Give me a clue."

She lit the cigarette. "It involves something very small and revealing in a backwards kind of a way. Come on, you ought to be able to guess." She exhaled a cloud of blue smoke.

"I thought you didn't smoke."

"I do now. Everyone I know smokes; I've given up trying to swim upstream."

He shifted the ice pack on his head - somewhere inside his skull little men with jackhammers were trying to bore their way out. "I don't have the energy to guess."

"I know you can do it, Wallace - even with half your brain. Small and revealing."

"I don't know - your scanties."

"Wallace!"

"This is stupid. 'Small and revealing.' A photograph."

"Very good. But in a backwards kind of way."

"Backwards? The back of the photograph? No, that's too clumsy. Oh, I know - the negative."

Monica smiled. "See how well you do with only half a brain." She ran her fingers lazily along the edge of her sling. He doubted that she was trying to entice him, but the way that she was caressing her sling was strangely seductive. He felt self-conscious watching her as he moved the ice pack from his forehead to his jaw, which made talking a challenge. "All right," she said, "I'll tell you what I can. I have a boyfriend in the States, does that make you happy?"

"What the hell does he have to do with anything?"

"I'm getting there - he's on death row."

"I have no idea how this fits in. All right, death row implies a pretty sensational crime."

"I suppose. Except that he didn't do it."

Her evasions were wearing on him. "If your boyfriend didn't do it, who did?"

"I don't know."

"God damn it, Monica! How much sheer crap are you going to throw at me?"

"Zephyr, I made a promise to my boyfriend. There are secrets I simply can't reveal."

"Then leave right now because I certainly can't help you." With a faded voice that completely lacked conviction he added, "Go on, get out of here."

She remained in her chair. "All right," she said, her voice softening to match his, "my boyfriend is in jail because he shot a waitress back in the States. But, like I said, he didn't do it."

"So who did?"

"Someone else."

He attempted a scolding look.

"I'm not being cute, I don't know the killer's name. Just listen a minute, okay? I was dating a Chinese man and his family owned a restaurant. The restaurant was losing money, and so my boyfriend went to a Tong and took out a loan. Well, it was a stupid thing to do and he couldn't pay it back and the Tong threatened to take the restaurant away. In fact, they'd get the whole building.

"Anyway, late one night, after the restaurant closed, my beau had a meeting with some of the people from the Tong to try and play for more time. The Tong men got mad, and to prove they meant business they killed one of the waitresses right on the spot.

The police showed up and my boyfriend got blamed, and he was thrown in jail.

"So I went to my mother. I begged her to loan me money so I could pay off the Tong. She never liked my boyfriend, but she agreed to help. She didn't have enough money, but said that if I sold that dopey 'clouded twilight' to Madame Lin, I could get enough. She'd make all the arrangements."

"And then she tricked you by making you think 'the clouded twilight' was worth a fortune when it wasn't."

"What do you mean?"

"You are aware, aren't you, that all the jewels were removed from 'the clouded twilight' years ago? It's only worth about a thousand bucks. Maybe less."

She became very quiet. "How do you know this?"

"I had the piece appraised in Shanghai. Besides, Mr. Lin confirmed its value."

"Jesus,' she hissed. "Mother. I should have guessed." She let out a small, bitter laugh. "Well, there you go. She wanted to teach me a lesson, since she didn't want me seeing Jager in the first place."

"Jager?" Davies asked. "Not exactly a Chinese name."

"It's complicated. He was adopted by a white family and took their name. You know how tough the whole immigration thing is."

He decided to continue playing along - he'd already been attacked once today, he didn't savor a repeat performance. "I still don't understand about the evidence."

"When my boyfriend told me he was meeting with the Tong I got worried - so I hid in the kitchen and took pictures, hoping that maybe some of the Tong men would be wanted for something. If I gave the pictures to the police, they could step in and arrest them. I found out I was pretty naive. I had a friend on the police force who told me that they might be able to arrest one or two guys, but they were just 'hatchet men.' The only way to call off the loan was to get something on the head man."

"Still, why didn't you give the evidence to the police?"

She sighed. "Because he'll still owe all that money to the Tong. If I get him out of jail before paying them, they'll surely kill him." She leaned forward in her chair. "I never showed the negatives to my friend at the police, I just described them. Maybe I did get a picture of someone important and didn't realize it."

Davies declined to pass on the ominous implications of this conclusion. The real killer, seen in Monica's photographs, was not a mere hatchet man, but one of Elder Brother's more important associates. Clearly, the head of the Chinese underworld wanted the negatives to insure that his agent stayed out of prison and Monica's boyfriend stayed in. If Davies helped Monica save her boyfriend he'd betray Elder Brother, placing himself in mortal danger - Monica, as well - and perhaps Crockwood, who was very likely Elder Brother's hostage back in Shanghai. If Davies refused to help Monica her disappointment was beside the point, an innocent man would be executed. It was a hell of a dilemma. "Why didn't you tell me this earlier?"

"I was afraid you wouldn't help me if you knew it was to save 'the other man.'"

"You're pretty stuck on him, then?" He couldn't help himself.

"I was."

"What does that mean?"

"Figure it out, you're the detective."

He elected to ignore the flattering and entangling implications of this last statement. "So what happened to the negatives?"

"That's what I'd like to know. I hid them in one of the baggage tags attached to the paper I wrapped the staff in. The tag was kind of thick, I split it in two with a razor and put the negatives inside, then glued it together again. When the staff was stolen the tag and the negatives went with it. Listen, I may as well tell you one more thing."

He raised his head slightly. Now that she was feigning honesty, it seemed best to stick to gestures - he didn't want to risk saying something that would cause her to change her mind.

"No, I'm sorry, Zephyr. That will have to wait until tomorrow, too." She rose from her chair. "Don't bother to tell me what you think."

"Right now I don't know what to think. The more I talk to you, the more my brain turns to soup." In truth, he welcomed her evasion, it was preferable to having her garrote him with her sling. "Look, I'd like to know something else. We might as well get it out of the way."

"What?" She radiated mistrust.

"The other night,..."

"No, please!"

"At least, tell me honestly if I was in any way responsible?"

"Of course not. You're one of the few nice things that's happened to me in some time." She sighed. "You might as well know, I didn't really try to kill myself. I thought about it, I admit that. I took your gun and pointed it at my chest to see if I could go through with it, and I knew instantly that I couldn't. I was putting the gun back when the damned thing went off. The trigger is so damn,..."

"Sensitive, yes I know. I should have it fixed. But why didn't you tell me it was an accident?"

She sighed again. "I was being dramatic, it was stupid."

At least she was honest. "Let me ask this, then. What you did to yourself, I mean, your running a little test on yourself, did it have anything to do with your brother?"

"What do you know about my brother?" There was great subdued pain on her face - it was the look he'd noticed when he'd first met her in his garden in Shanghai - it was remarkable how quickly it could sweep over her and through her.

"Madame Lin told me about an incident,..."

She sighed deeply. "What did she tell you?"

He tried to be gentle. "She thought there was a possibility that you had killed him."

These words were met by one of her long silences. "Auntie was right," she finally said. "I did."

"Can I ask what happened?"

She came to his side and sank back into the chair. "I pushed him, he fell in the water."

"Madame Lin mentioned something about a stick."

Her eyes met his. They glistened with moisture, yet they remained flat and emotionless; and though she was looking at him, she was seeing something far away and private. "Let me be clear - I loved my little brother more than anything. I guess I didn't know it at the time. When I was eleven, he was just this annoyance; this little something that everyone thought was so cute. But after he died, and I got a little older, I realized he was all that I had. He was the only person who had ever loved me, as corny as that sounds." A muted, biting laugh escaped from her throat. "And I found a way to kill him."

She had to stop and compose herself. He'd seen impressive performances before, but this didn't strike him as an act. "I was always doing awful things to him; I was such a bully. I just pushed him down. I pushed him too hard and he fell in the water. Of course, he couldn't swim, he was so scared." With a jagged wail, she burst into tears, shaking violently, her words spitting out in halting bursts. "I tried to grab him, but he was too far out. I jumped in but I couldn't swim either. Smart of me to figure that out once I was in the water." She swatted a tear away. "I managed to get back on shore and I found this long stick and I told him to grab it. He just couldn't - he was too tired." The tears overwhelmed her, she put her head down on the table and sobbed.

He reached out and put his hand gently on her shoulder. After a half minute of crying, she became calmer. "What you don't understand," she said, now lacking inflection and devoid of emotion, "is, that for me, it's never a question of should I or shouldn't I? It's only of when and how."

He felt awful. Her natural will to survive had apparently kept her from intentionally shooting herself a day earlier, but he realized now that this instinct was only a sometime thing. In his most soothing voice he said, "Monica, I suppose this is presumptuous, but if you ever did do something like that to yourself, you'd leave me feeling a lot like you feel now."

"I guess you're pretty stupid then." The intensity of her self-hatred cut into him like a razor slash.

The familiar dead look in her eyes had reclaimed her. "Every breath is so much effort. Every day the same - like having to eat and eat until you're so stuffed you ache, and you can't breathe, but there's never any taste or flavor. I can't do any more of this." She paused, her face etched with terrible sadness. "Do you know what it's like living with this thing? This outside, it's smooth, it's pleasing, it's clean. But inside it's filth, rotten. I hate it." Her voice lowered to a whisper. "The worst part is forgetting and getting on and thinking everything's fine, maybe even dreaming and planning for the future. And then one night, for no reason, you wake up and remember, 'oh that's right.' Then your stomach gets sick, and stays sick for days - and you know that you're something foul, the stain will never go away." She rose slowly. "I'm going to bed."

"I want you to stay here tonight." He tossed the ice pack aside and rose, trying his best to wrap his arms around her.

She stood staring at the floor, her arms dangling impassively at her side.

"Come on, let's go to bed."

She shook her head. "I'd rather be by myself."

"Monica, is there a reason why you chose the other night?"

She actually laughed. "You still hope I did that because of you? Wallace, you've been sweet, and you're not dreadful to look at - well, not usually. But, honestly, if I said that I was in love with you, would you think that I had any idea what I was talking about?"

She had a point. "Okay. Then did something happen?"

She shrugged.

"Monica, please. Can't you tell me what happened?"

She gazed at him, again scrutinizing him. Her probing look faded into one of tranquil sadness. "I'll be fine," she said. "Why don't you just forget about me? I'm not worth it."

He hugged her as fiercely as he could and kissed her. It must have looked odd, both of them trying to embrace, each with one arm in a sling. Still, she allowed the advance, kissing him back mechanically. "Don't worry," she said, pulling away, "I'm not going to kill myself tonight. I couldn't have them finding me with my hair in such a mess."

"Stay here."

She tapped her sling. "I fear we'll both wake up with our arms missing. I'm not used to anybody caring, that's all. Maybe you actually do. We'll see." She gave him another apathetic kiss. Then she left the room.

Against his better judgment, Davies was touched by Monica's story. The damnable fact was that his attraction to her was growing again; particularly as her personality showed more hints of being reasonable, supportive, and sympathetic. Remarkably so, considering all that she'd been through. Perhaps he should give her a second chance.

He heard footsteps in the hall; an instant later his door flew open. "You go to bed now," No Sin commanded as he strode into the room.

"Yes, mother." Davies picked up the ice pack and reapplied it to his jaw. Sin," he said, feeling like an utter criminal, "you'd better go look after her. Right now. Make sure she takes a light sleeping potion; I can't do a damn thing with this arm. Can you handle that?"

No Sin gave him a smug look. "I poison you, remember?"

"Yeah, well you better not poison her. I'll send you back to China in a pine box. Or an urn. Or rolled up like your clothes. Why don't you make her some tea?" Davies added. "And put a nice, damp rag on her forehead. And make sure she goes right to sleep."

No Sin mumbled something and slammed the door.

"Women." Davies muttered as he flopped onto his bed and laid his head back onto the pillow.

The prospect of a full night's sleep was glorious, though unlikely considering his throbbing head, shoulder and ribs. Even if he wasn't in pain, the dilemma of choosing between loyalty to Elder Brother, and a moral obligation to free Monica's innocent boyfriend from jail was sure to keep him up all night. Complicating the whole business was the fact that Monica was not a reliable source of information by any stretch of the imagination. Her little tale may very well be pure fiction. God, what a mess. Too bad the thugs who'd beaten him earlier in the day hadn't left him comatose.

The logical mind was a bully that liked to run the show and didn't tolerate competition. His had already set its sights on the emotional euphoria that he'd felt earlier with Monica - it reminded him that there had been other girls, other lost days that somehow became lost months, mixed in with occasional drugs, too much liquor, and the hovering threat of degradation and ruin. His mind whispered that he was a fool to even consider a happy outcome with a troubled Eurasian over ten years his junior. He reached up and scratched the back of his head. The possibility of being ruined by Monica was something that he would have once looked forward to - now he realized it would involve far more effort than he felt able to muster - in time, he would surely lose interest. True, she was funny and bright, and capable of fierce affection, yet it was easy to argue that he was attracted to nothing more than a figment of his own imagination. At the very least, there was no denying that she was pretty and good for a fling, but it was desperately naïve to hope for more. It was the classic dilemma for him, his heart said to give her another chance, allow her the benefit of the doubt, but his brain said that she couldn't be trusted – which would win?

XXXXVI. BETRAYAL

Saturday, September 15, 1928

With the help of medicinals, Davies slept until noon. No Sin delivered his breakfast, then helped him to dress. One side of Davies' face looked like a battered eggplant. "Did you make tea for Miss Marshall last night?"

No Sin shook his head. "She don't like me, you know."

Standing before the mirror, Davies worked at straightening his necktie, and chose not to press for gruesome details. "Sin, I have some business in town, so I'll be gone most of the afternoon. I want you to look after Miss Marshall."

"You actually do something? Or you just sight-seeing?"

"Patience, Sin. It is said to be a great Chinese virtue."

"Then trail is not so hot, huh?"

"Where do you learn these terms? Actually, Sin, the business concerns you." This was true, partially. Davies had an appointment with an immigration lawyer that afternoon. Of more immediate concern, however, was another meeting with Mr. Lin. Somehow during the night, Davies had come to a clear decision. Despite his current pains and traumas, he enjoyed being alive, so much so that he couldn't bear the idea of denying the pleasures of existence to another human being, even one like Crockwood whose humanness was somewhat in question. Therefore, Davies would do whatever he could to return the negatives to Elder Brother. Finding the negatives would also enable him to confirm that what Monica had told him was true. If so, a photographic copy made on the sly might allow a means of freeing Monica's boyfriend at some future point. The problem, of course, was that the negatives were, in all probability, lying in a Shanghai gutter. Still, there was a remote chance that they were here in Honolulu. Madame Lin may have been killed by someone who believed that she had the negatives, and who had succeeded in pilfering them. Perhaps Mr. Lin could shed some light on his wife's last hours, and who might have expressed interest in a lowly baggage tag.

Davies took a final look in the mirror, tested his walking stick, and went out the door.

Monica was waiting for him in the hall - the night's rest had done her no good; she looked even more defeated than the last time he'd seen her. "I was just coming to get you," she said lifelessly.

"You feeling any better?" He gave her a quick kiss on the forehead.

Behind him he thought he heard No Sin making a tiny hissing sound.

"Just so you know, I'll be gone most of the afternoon."

"But aren't we sailing tonight?" she asked.

"We'll have to delay our sailing, I'm afraid. No Sin's immigration papers are taking longer than I thought."

"Delay? But, Zephyr, I have to get to San Francisco."

"Why? What's the hurry?"

"Are you daft? I can't stand it here after all that's happened."

"I'm sorry, I'm as eager to leave as you. But we'd have to send Sin back to China."

"What's wrong with that? He's thoroughly useless!"

"Come on," he said, stroking her hair, and hoping that No Sin wasn't about to attack from behind.

"I'm sorry, Zephyr, but I really don't want to stay here. It reminds me of things I'd rather forget. You know I don't mean to hurt No Sin, but isn't there some solution? Please."

He hugged her tiny body. "Let me see what I can do. Listen, why don't you take breakfast out on the veranda? Look at the sea."

"I'm not hungry."

"Alright. But can you spare me for a couple of hours? I'll try my very best to wrap everything up this afternoon so we can sail."

"Oh God, yes. Thank you." She hugged him. "You're my hero, darling."

Davies kissed her, and left her under the protection of the biggest Samoan. He took the second largest Samoan with him so he wouldn't risk ending up crumpled in another alley. He ordered No Sin to stay behind as extra protection for Monica, telling the boy to watch after her like a mother bear. He'd promised to help her sail, but, the fact was, even if No Sin's papers were not an issue, Davies intended to stay in Honolulu and try to find the negatives. Sorry, but he wasn't about to let Monica slip away to San Francisco, despite her anxieties.

* * *

No Sin would rather be watching over Davies than the man's silly girlfriend. He had experienced deep pangs of guilt over the beating Davies had suffered. He knew it was his fault, and, worse, this was the second employer who had suffered great bodily harm while in his care. He worried that he was some sort of jinx. Such unpleasant things were never going to happen again he resolved.

A drowsy hour passed, and No Sin noticed that Monica's Samoan guard was signaling to him. He walked to where the guard stood, arriving just as Monica Marshall came out of her room. "Sin," she said as if she owned the world, "Mr. Davies just called. Good news! He wants you to meet him - I think to sign some papers. It looks like everything's set for your immigration. Now, here's the address, and two dollars, which should pay for your cab." She gave him an address and some dollar bills. No Sin put everything in his pocket. "Oh, don't you have a key to Mr. Davies' room?"

No Sin nodded, hesitantly.

"Give it to me please."

"Why?" No Sin asked.

"He needs me to start with his packing while you're gone - we've a boat to catch, remember?"

Everything was happening too fast and it made No Sin uncomfortable.

"Sin, the key please," Monica said impatiently. "I don't have all afternoon. Just show that address to the cabbie, he'll know where to take you. Well, come on! Mr. Davies is waiting!"

No Sin fished into his pocket and gave Miss Marshall the key to Mr. Davies' room.

"Good-luck," she said brightly, and kissed his forehead. "I'm so excited!"

Bewildered, he walked slowly down the stairs to the lobby.

No Sin had gone all the way through the lobby and out into the street, before he turned around. He didn't trust Monica Marshall. How did he know that Mr. Davies had really called? He went back into the lobby and cautiously climbed the stairs. He could see that the Samoan guard was now standing outside Davies' room.

"I forget something," No Sin said when he reached the guard. The Samoan nodded and No Sin twisted the door handle, it was unlocked. He entered, quietly shutting the door behind him.

He could only hear what was going on. Strange noises were coming from the bedroom just off of the sitting room; drawers were scraping open and there was a lot of thumping and rattling. No Sin crept to a half-opened door leading to the bedroom, and peered inside.

All the lower drawers of the bureau had been pulled out and were lying on the floor. Anything that Monica thought was valuable had been tossed into a suitcase sprawled open on the bed. She was wearing a wide brim hat, secured by a glittering hat pin and a veil, which completely hid her face. She looked very wealthy and very Caucasian - and also very suspicious; especially as she was using a metal shoe horn to pry open one of the smaller upper drawers. The lock snapped and the drawer popped open. Monica set the shoehorn aside and lifted out a thick wad of American money. She shoved it into her purse, turned back to the bed, and closed the suitcase.

No Sin stepped into the bedroom. "Going away, Miss Monica?"

XXXXVII. MONEY ON THE FLOOR

As if No Sin was not even there, Monica went ahead and locked the suitcase. Then she picked up the telephone receiver and slipped it beneath her veil. "Yes, send up the manager to room four-nineteen." Her voice was calm and her words made the veil rise and fall slightly. "Please hurry, it's an emergency. Thank you." She replaced the receiver as the faint image of an evil smile formed beneath her veil. No Sin returned her hateful gaze in full.

She opened her purse and removed the cash that she'd stolen - what was she up to? Carefully, she counted out sixty-seven dollars from the thick roll of bills; so much money in one place was impressive to look at. She walked over to No Sin and stuffed the money into his breast pocket.

"What you doing?" he demanded. "You think I want his money?" He took the cash and threw it, contemptuously, on the floor. "I tell everything about you, don't worry! You don't stop me!"

Monica shrugged, then leaned over to pick up the bills. "No!" No Sin yelled, "That not yours!" Before she could reach the money, he swept it up and stuffed it back into his pocket. As he did so, No Sin heard a knock, and then the door opened behind him. Monica put the rest of the stolen money back into the purse, folding her arms over her chest.

A little fat person came in; he appeared to be part Chinese and part Samoan, like one of the guards. He was wearing a brown suit with purple pinstripes that made No Sin's eyes want to cross. "What's the trouble here?" he asked. "Who called the house detective?"

"I did," Monica said, speaking through her veil so that the detective wouldn't see that she was almost as Chinese as he was.

A tall white man in a dark suit and wearing a bow tie entered from the hall. He looked like he never laughed. "Is there a problem here?"

"I am Miss Monica Marshall," Monica said, pronouncing the word "Marshall" very precisely. "I'm staying next door, and saw this Chinese boy entering this room. I was suspicious and I called you."

"She big liar!" No Sin exclaimed.

"Be quiet! Remember your place!" The tall man turned to Monica and eyed her suspiciously. "What are you doing with that suitcase, Miss?"

No Sin smiled inside; now she would get what was coming to her.

"It has some of my new dresses in it," Monica answered with an infuriating lack of concern, "I'm on my way downstairs to have them hemmed."

The house detective grabbed No Sin's arm and drew him aside. "Where do you live?" he asked in Chinese. No Sin answered him in Chinese, then told him a few things that he should know.

"Oh! Do you two know each other?" Monica asked, pretending like she was surprised.

The Chinese house detective wisely ignored her and spoke to the tall, Caucasian manager. "This boy says that he is Mr. Davies' servant. I would suggest that he has every right to be here."

"And she is thief!" No Sin shouted. "She take things from Mr. Davies and put them in that suitcase!"

"You said this was your suitcase, Miss? With your dresses? Would you mind opening it for us?" The manager looked at Monica, and there was not a hint of sympathy in his expression. No Sin felt smug content.

She still didn't seem frightened. "Are you actually accusing me? I was on my way downstairs when I saw him sneaking out, and I could see the mess in here through the open door. I was merely trying to be a good citizen! Is that a crime?"

"Well, Miss, we can verify that if you'll just open the case for us."

"I certainly will not. I will not be insulted that way! Mr. Davies and I are very close - you must have seen the lovely flowers he sent to my room. He told me yesterday that some of his things were missing, and he suspected this servant of his. He asked me to keep an eye on his room; and it's lucky I did because this boy took money out of that bureau and stuffed it in his pocket just now."

"She lying! Why do you lie like this? You evil Miss Monica!"

"Be quiet!" the manager ordered.

No Sin turned to the house detective and gave a loud explanation in Chinese. The detective nodded, appreciatively; again he turned to the white-face Manager. "I think his story is worth considering. For one thing, he tells me that,.."

"Is it all right if I smoke?" Monica interrupted, looking directly at the little half-Chinese detective. "Obviously you're calling the shots here. I wouldn't want to offend the Hawaiian gods."

The tall, white man's face flushed. No Sin was displeased with this reaction, but he couldn't imagine that such a somber looking white man would ever be intimidated by a half-Oriental turtle like Monica - even if she was hiding behind a veil.

"Thank you," she said, lighting her cigarette, although no one had given her the permission she had asked for. "Incidentally, I called you," she added, refusing to shut up. "If I was a thief do you think I'd phone you to report my own crime?"

With a heavy frown, the tall Caucasian said, "Woo, see if the boy has any money on him."

Pretending that he hadn't heard, The Oriental detective asked No Sin more questions in Chinese.

"Well-trained, isn't he?" Monica said.

No Sin wished the detective would give him permission to hit her in the face.

"Woo! Do what I say!" the manager shouted, his cheeks turning scarlet. "Don't stand there talking about old times, see if he has money on him!"

"But she give this money to me!" No Sin cried, pulling the sixty-seven dollars from his pocket.

"I certainly did not," Monica snapped.

"She lying!" No Sin protested, realizing that he'd been tricked. Now the Chinese detective was taking out a set of handcuffs. "Oh please, don't take me to jail again."

The fat detective was stronger than he looked and he clamped the handcuffs onto No Sin's wrists. He dragged No Sin toward the door. "Please! Just listen to me!" No Sin shouted.

The white Manager nodded to Monica. "I'm sorry for any inconvenience to you, ma'am."

"So am I!" Monica replied sharply. She almost bumped into them as she went out the door and headed for the stairs.

Western justice was worse than Chinese justice. No Sin explained everything to the Chinese house detective, but the man had stopped being understanding, and didn't care that Monica Marshall had most of Zephyr Davies' money in her purse, and was making off with his valuables in her suitcase. Chinese boys had no business questioning white people, the detective explained, while they waited for the police to arrive, in the alley behind the hotel. No Sin was sure to be convicted of something, there was no point in fighting it. The practical thing was to plead guilty and accept the punishment. Assuming he was not deported to China, the worst sentence he would receive would be five or six years in prison. The prisons weren't so bad. No Sin would get a straw mattress to sleep on, and probably better food than he had been eating outside the prison. No Sin should be thankful - many poor Chinese and Japanese committed crimes for the sole purpose of getting into prison.

When the police came and took him to the station, No Sin admitted his guilt.

He was locked in a cell with eight other men, most of whom were drunk and had urinated on the floor, making it extremely slick and giving it a smell like the Shanghai zoo. He finally found a nearly dry place in the corner, where he sat down and thought about how much he hated Monica Marshall.

He wondered how a great detective like Zephyr Davies could be so stupid as to let a witch like Monica lead him around by the nose and steal everything he had? Maybe Zephyr Davies was not such a great detective, after all. Maybe Zephyr Davies was not trying to find his friend's killer, but was only interested in going to bed with Monica Marshall and committing the grotesque acts depicted in the Hatman's magazines. Maybe Zephyr Davies was indeed a thief, and he had intended to steal the staff himself. Maybe Zephyr Davies was simply stupid.

As if to confirm this, No Sin thought back to something that had happened in the park by Soochow Creek. As they were searching for a suitable junk to take them down river, the millionaire had been intercepted by a haggard beggar woman with a baby in her arms. No Sin had seen her jab the infant with a pin, waking it, squawking, from its quiet sleep. The mother had held up the miserable, wailing child for Davies' inspection and the great white face had actually been taken-in by the beggar's cheap trick, sympathetically tossing her a few coppers. How could No Sin have been so blind? At that moment, he should have seen what an arrogant, stupid fraud Zephyr Davies truly was.

No Sin finally gave up trying to understand Mr. Davies' behavior. Instead, for some strange reason, he thought about Monica Marshall running around her hotel suite with nothing on but a sling and creamy silk panties.

It had only been a lark, he hadn't been given a new life after all. He was destined to grow old in prison, and his escape from Shanghai had been a minor, celestial mistake. Or perhaps, he'd merely been sent to the wrong prison, and this was the one he was supposed to rot in. He buried his head in his hands. One thing was certain, Davies would not be coming to his aid - not this time, not after all the bad things No Sin had done. The police would tell Davies that No Sin, not Monica, had been caught stealing his money, and, after being poisoned, Davies would believe them.

No matter what happened now, he would never allow himself to be tricked like this again. From this moment on, he would be the trickster, even if all his tricks had to be played in jail. How could he have not seen it coming? It made him very angry with himself.

He was pondering his own stupidity, which made him thankfully oblivious to his surroundings, when a foul smelling man nudged him and pointed to a burly policeman with a clipboard who was standing outside the cell. The policeman gestured for No Sin to come over to him. When he did, the cell door opened and he was led to the front offices of the police station. Zephyr Davies was standing by the high desk looking beautiful in his light blue suit - he was a vision from heaven.

"This the guy?" another policeman, seated behind a desk, asked.

Davies smiled at No Sin, which made him feel so good. "Yes, sergeant, this is the guy."

"He confessed, you know. He took everything you got, buddy. Money, suitcase and all."

"But I prefer not to press charges."

The policeman's eyebrows lifted. "So that's the way it is." He gave them both a look of disgust.

"His confession is meaningless. He had my permission to be in my room."

"What about the sixty bucks we found on him? He earned it, right?"

Davies nodded. "Ten dollars of it. The rest he was to give to a tailor who was due to arrive with some suits, well, right about now, actually. Sergeant, when I got there I looked around, and I can assure you nothing was taken. So there is no crime, is there? You can verify it with your lieutenant there." Davies pointed to an older man wearing a rumpled suit who stood nearby. "We've already gone over this matter in some detail."

The sergeant glanced at the lieutenant who looked up from some paperwork and nodded.

"Get your skinny hineys out of here," the sergeant growled, "you both make me sick."

* * *

Davies waited until they reached their taxi before he spoke. "This is getting monotonous," he said as they got into the car. He slammed the door behind them; and, with the sound of grinding gears, the taxi drove away.

No Sin tried his best to bow, even though he was sitting - then he took Davies' hand and squeezed it warmly. "Thank you, Mr. Davies, thank you - again you save my life."

"Cut it out!" Davies jerked his hand away. "Anyway, they wouldn't slice your head off in there."

"I'm sorry, but you wrong, Mr. Davies," No Sin said, his scolding reminding Davies of one of his old, annoying teachers from prep school, "she stole many things from you, even all your money."

"I know. But if I'd told them that they wouldn't have released you, even with my dropping charges. Besides, she didn't take all of my money." Davies lifted a bundle of bills from his pocket.

No Sin looked at him, astonished. "Where you get that?"

"I'm not totally stupid, Sin. In fact, I wish I'd stop being right about things."

"But how you know?"

He put the money back into his coat. "I phoned her this afternoon around one-thirty, and told her that I couldn't make things work. I said I was sorry, but we'd have to stay in Hawaii for another few days. She took it rather too well, which made me suspicious."

"One-thirty? That when she say you call. But she say you want me to come meet you."

"She had to get rid of you. She was hell-bent to board that ship, and you might have told on her."

"Huh!" No Sin grunted, "So now you know she evil. See, I tell you."

Davies nodded; he felt like a Halloween pumpkin whose goopy insides had been scooped out.

When they got back to the Moana, Davies went to the desk and learned the name of the ship that Monica had sailed on. In fact, it seemed that half the hotel had checked out and sailed to San Francisco. Monica had left first, followed by the effete Chinese from their old freighter, and finally Mr. Lin. Since Davies had talked to Mr. Lin at length earlier in the day, and learned nothing of value, the small, dapper man's departure was not a great loss. As for the saggy businessman and the "retired prison matrons," they had sailed for Seattle the day before.

"Look, I'm going to take a nap," Davies said. "How about I meet you in the lobby in about two hours? Then we'll get a bite to eat."

No Sin's eyes opened wide. "You going to eat with me?"

"Sure," Davies replied. "So dress properly."

Davies went up to his room. As he undressed, he thought again of Monica and her monster. Was it a vengeful demon of her own creation, sent to punish her for the death of her brother? As angry as he was, he already missed her. How pathetic.

He picked up one of her left-over magazines from off the floor and tossed it onto his bed as he went into the bathroom to brush his teeth and shower; tomorrow he'd clean up what remained of the mess Monica had made of his room. At least, room service had tidied up as best they could and pulled back the covers on his bed and fluffed up the pillows, making it highly inviting.

He hated the way he felt, and bathing couldn't wash away the guilt. Monica's departure, and her willingness to send No Sin to jail, had dashed Davies' tenuous belief in her innocence. As soon as he got to San Francisco he'd make every effort to track her down. He'd talk directly to her mysterious boyfriend, if he actually existed. His world would never be right until he could prove to himself that he was not to blame for Madame Lin's death.

When he returned from the bathroom, Davies saw the magazine leaning against the pillow where he'd tossed it. Actually, it seemed to be suspended in the center of the pillow. Odd, it was too heavy to be the pawn of static electricity. He crossed to his bed and picked up the magazine - the pillow came with it. Separating the two was difficult, and then he saw why the magazine had been so securely attached - the shiny black tip of a woman's hat pin was pointing straight out from the pillow, awaiting whatever object it could impale. He found two more hat pins placed carefully in the pillow, all angled out so that it would be easy for them to plunge deep into a cheek, or an ear, or perhaps go straight through an eye. The pillow on the other side of the bed also contained three hat pins. The last of these had a ragged scrap of paper impaled on it. Written on it in Monica's precise handwriting were the words: "Thanks for nothing, Wallace."

Davies sat on his bed and rubbed his forehead. Was Monica that deranged and cruel? Is this what he got for helping someone in need?

He phoned down to the desk to ask if he could be moved to another room; it wasn't much fun playing detective anymore.

XXXXVIII. WITH BITTERS

Davies felt like he'd botched everything. If only he could find some overlooked clue that would finally shed light on the identity of Madame Lin's killer. Unfortunately, it seemed unlikely that the guilty party could be anyone but Monica. How utterly moronic he'd been.

His frustration was underscored by the weather, which had become sultry and foreboding. A strong wind was coming off of the ocean and the dark clouds skirting the horizon rose to astounding heights as they gave off occasional flashes of lightning.

Spurned on by this dramatic performance, Davies decided to ruminate on Monica's final betrayal with something tropical and alcoholic. Unfortunately, he'd recently learned that the scourge of prohibition had struck the Hawaiian Islands so it would be necessary to adjourn to a decent speakeasy. As was generally the case, his bellman had already provided him with a recommendation: a cozy spot a block away, favored by the hotel's guests.

The primary reason why he'd invited No Sin to drinks and dinner was because the occasion represented a last fling - he'd decided to dump the boy in Hawaii. After pulling some strings, he'd already managed to secure a job for the lad on a pineapple ranch – bottom line, Davies was sick of helping people, especially difficult, ungrateful, betraying people. True, the boy had been on his best behavior in Hawaii, despite a certain amount of sarcasm and carping, but it wasn't entirely clear what had happened between him and Monica, and who was actually to blame. All he knew was that Monica's sudden departure had drained him of the will to keep giving people the benefit of the doubt.

On his walk downstairs, he thought that it would take another several days to properly and legally dispose of No Sin, which was frustrating because Davies was now fired up to go after Monica on a mission of revenge.

When he and No Sin actually sat on their barstools in the speakeasy and faced their Filipino bartender, Davies realized that it was futile to conceal his disappointment with something sweet and cloying – he preferred a libation that was harsh and unforgiving - better to look darkness square in the eyes. "Martini, up."

The Filipino got right to work .

"And throw in a dash of bitters," Davies added, aware of the appropriateness of such a request.

"Must be the fashion now," the Filipino said. He made "fashion" sound wet and sumptuous.

Davies shrugged. Then he thought about what the bartender had just said. "What do you mean about 'the fashion?'"

"Second guy today to ask for bitters."

Small, disturbing visions that had been floating around in Davies' head for the past few days started to reorder themselves and take on a new pattern. "The first guy, the one who ordered bitters earlier, what did he look like?"

The Filipino grinned, his impeccable teeth were glorious against his brown skin. "Kind of old English guy. Very funny, make me laugh. You know him?"

Davies felt a sickening rush of excitement. "Did he have bags under his eyes, and did he often stroke his necktie in a strange way?"

"Oh, so you friends?"

It was like being told that a close relative had died. There would be no martini tonight. Davies leaped off his bar stool and hurried back to the hotel.

The Hawaiian house detective was by the desk. Davies took him aside. "I need your help."

"I was looking for you. I don't like telling you this, but our Elder Brother,..."

"Don't worry too much. I think we're both about to make our Elder Brother very happy."

With the house detective's assistance, they determined that the man matching Crockwood's description was staying on the fourth floor. As they were about to go up to his room together, however, the manager appeared. "I need to consult with you, Woo."

The small detective remained cheerful. "I must accompany this gentleman to the fourth floor."

The manager looked concerned. "Is there something I should know about?"

"No, sir, I'll be back down in five minutes."

The Hawaiian detective kept his word. He led Davies and No Sin upstairs and to a room on the top floor. The promise of a storm had been kept, and the sound of hard rain battering the roof of the hotel could be heard as they approached their destination. The air remained sultry, and many of the hotel's windows were still open, their drapes blowing inwardly.

"Who's there?" a familiar voice called out when they reached the room they sought. Davies felt like he'd been sucker punched.

The house detective called back, making an excuse about a stolen cigarette case - was the gentleman inside missing one?

Crockwood opened the door. Seeing Davies caused a blur of emotions to pass over his face reminiscent of a ten year old teacher's pet being caught cheating. "Uh," was all that he could get out.

Davies was rendered equally inarticulate.

"I, uh, this must look odd," Crockwood stammered, his words augmented, almost comically, by a flash of lightning.

"Yes, John, it does," Davies said as he forced his way into the room, followed by No Sin. "I would like to know why you've come all the way to Honolulu, and didn't even bother to say 'hello.'"

Crockwood was unusually pasty-skinned and slack-faced, as if he was slightly hung over, but liquor consumption probably wasn't to blame. "I've an an explanation if you'd care to listen."

"I most certainly would."

"I have to get back downstairs," the house detective said. True to his word, he turned and headed in the direction of the stairs.

Crockwood made a sloppy gesture, which Davies guessed was calculated to demonstrate how calm he was. "Can I offer you anything?"

"Just your explanation," Davies said as he moved toward the center of the room. No Sin closed the door and positioned himself in front of it as if to suggest that escape was futile.

"Oh, right you are," Crockwood said with a cheerfulness that came across as forced. "Well, you know how I was uncomfortable dealing with our Elder Brother, and my anxieties were justified. He, uh, he approached me and all but ordered me to come after you. He didn't trust you, you see, that's why I couldn't be my usual sociable self." As punctuation, Crockwood placed his hand on his tie, then moved it away, undeniably remembering how the action elicited ridicule from Davies.

"You're a liar, John."

Crockwood's face flushed. "That's hardly,.."

"Your servants reported seeing you escorted to a car by several Orientals."

"Yes, that's exactly what I mean. Elder Brother's thugs showed up on my doorstep, and,.."

"No, John. Your servants would never tattle on Elder Brother unless ordered to. Why would Elder Brother want me to know that he'd secreted you away?"

"A warning, obviously. Toe the line or you'll be next."

"Exactly. That would put me on my guard, wouldn't it?"

"I suppose it would."

"So why would he send you to spy on me after I'd been put on my guard? Not a good strategy."

Crockwood opened his mouth, seemingly in hope that a serendipitous explanation would magically follow.

"The fact is, John, Elder Brother's men never came for you. Your Oriental friends were Japanese, weren't they? The Japanese cruiser that anchored in Pearl Harbor the day before yesterday is a great deal faster than most passenger vessels. Traveling on it would allow you to leave Shanghai after me, and yet beat me to Honolulu." As if to add dramatic effect, a deep rumble of thunder shook the room. "To say that I'm disappointed would be a gross understatement."

Crockwood looked like he'd just discovered a crowd of amused strangers watching him undress. "Disappointed?" he stammered. "Good God, man, you seem to think you found me out. I'd think your head would burst with pride." Despite his cavalier manner, sweat was slickening the old Englishman's forehead. Davies felt bad for his friend, but worse for what Crockwood had become in his eyes.

"We were friends, John."

"Ah, well, it is the twentieth century, isn't it? Friendships have grown disposable - rather like the safety razor blade." This was no friendly barb, and Davies felt its sting. How could he have gone for years missing the *true* hostility lurking beneath his friend's acerbic facade? His "old chum" must have always hated him.

"I fear, John, that you're going to be disappointed because I *don't* have what you're after: the negatives. And I have no idea who does."

Crockwood's puffy eyes opened marginally, registering something approaching alarm. "You'll forgive me if I maintain a healthy skepticism."

"Alas, John, you killed Madame Lin in vain. It was you, wasn't it?"

"Why of course, Zephyr, if you say so."

That Crockwood would parry such a serious accusation with sarcasm was insulting, and an affront to Madame Lin's memory - reducing her death to something amusing and trivial. Again, Davies felt gut punched. Of all the people that he knew, this was the one he'd counted on to never betray him. They had a bond of shared eccentricity that seemed unbreakable; they'd been united by a mutual cynicism that came as close to truth as Davies could ever hope for. "When we took 'the clouded twilight' to Dr. Sun together," Davies said, his pulse racing as ironically his speech grew slow and deliberate, "you must have seen there were no negatives accompanying it. I confided in you that I'd given a baggage tag to Madame Lin so she could check up on her niece. Other than me, you're the *only* one who knew that Madame Lin had that tag - not Monica, not Madame Lin's husband, whom I recently spoke to, not Elder Brother, not Dr. Sun, only *you*."

"Yes, well, that's all very circumstantial, isn't it? But then, leave it to you to,.."

"John!" Davies yelled with an anger that took them both by surprise, "I've no patience!"

"That's quite obvious," Crockwood replied, his previous nervousness giving way to an air of infuriating coolness, "but, then are you willing to listen? Or is that too much to ask?"

"I'll try."

"Dammit, Zephyr, you give me no time to think or explain - it's not fair. I'm sorry, she was uncooperative. Your friend. I didn't mean to harm her. You know me, I'm a man of peace. But these things happen. She didn't have that little tag. She claimed she'd brought it with her, then misplaced it, which was patently absurd.

When I called her on it, she started to make a stink. What could I do? I couldn't have her tattling back to you." In prep school, years ago, Davies had won the lead in a school play. He could hardly speak when he had to go out on stage for the first time, but somehow he'd managed to blurt out his first line, and from that point on performing became easier and easier until he was barely aware that he was performing at all. This seemed to be the case with Crockwood, initially flustered and sweating, he was now relaxed and seemingly in control. "Let's be frank, Zephyr, if you hadn't lied to me, if you'd only confided in me, told me that you had it all along, she'd still be alive, wouldn't she?"

"You're blaming me for her death?"

"Think about it, Zephyr, have I done anything differently from you? You've sold arms to warlords, do you think they intended to use them to shoot cans? The fact is, your munitions were used to kill people. You could sleep at night because you assumed that the people who died were the *right* people. We both know that the Chinese have made a mess of their own affairs, and if the Japanese take over they will run things in a far superior manner. In the long run, lives will be saved. If an innocent like your Madame Lin is killed in the process, it's sad, but a price worth paying when peace and order is the ultimate payoff. Can you really blame me for doing my little bit to help create a better China?"

"Utter rubbish."

"That's merely your view. Where is the tag now?" Crockwood said with impatience. "You must have it."

Davies waved his hand, dismissively. "I haven't the slightest idea - maybe lying in a Shanghai gutter. You see, Madame Lin never knew that the tag contained valuable negatives. She could easily have misplaced it, *just as she told you.*"

Crockwood's doughy face remained flaccid, but a subtle change in his expression made Davies think of a man who'd bet his life savings on red, and black had come up. Slowly, he raised his hand and rubbed the back of his head. "You're enjoying this, aren't you?"

In point of fact, Davies wasn't enjoying it at all.

"You've always liked to make me feel small - to ridicule anything that brings me pleasure. I know you, Davies, better than you think."

You don't know me at all, Davies thought - after all these years you're even blinder than I was. "You killed Leibowitz as well, didn't you?"

"Who?"

"The poor wretch I hired to look after Monica. He must have seen you leaving the scene of the crime. I suppose you also had no choice."

"Again, if you say so." Behind Crockwood, tall drapes billowed inward as a hot, sticky wind filled the room, and a great crescendo of rain pounded down feverishly on the roof.

"And those thugs who beat me the other day, I assume you hired them."

"My apologies, but I needed a free hand to search your rooms. Don't look so offended, you're a hearty fellow."

Davies shook his head, emphasizing the disgust that he felt. Everyone had a bombastic friend who was tolerated because they were presumed to be all talk. It had never occurred to Davies that Crockwood would act on his outrageous beliefs, leaving Davies battered, and with a little less luck, crippled. As was the case with so many gangsters and captains of industry that Davies had encountered over the years, Crockwood's acts of violence were the monstrous manifestations of glib thinking. "What I didn't understand, at least until now, was your severing of Madame Lin's foot."

Crockwood's face contorted with revulsion; he appeared sincerely shocked by this accusation - but Davies assumed that this was merely part of his performance.

"Dear God, man, what are you talking about?"

"That's how the police found her."

"I don't believe you."

"Sorry."

"You're grossly overreaching. Why would I commit such a ghastly act? I'm not a beast."

"Perhaps to impress your Japanese associates - they're big on symbolic gestures. I wouldn't be surprised if the severing of an enemy's foot in the Japanese culture renders the dead to a peasant status, or some such nonsense. Perfect for literally cutting the mighty down to size."

"Pish posh," Crockwood slurred. "I have to conclude that you're making this up."

"To what purpose?"

"Slander. I don't know. I must say, these strange accusations are making me feel light-headed." As if to prove this, he mopped his shining forehead with a handkerchief; but the gesture seemed false to Davies.

"Do you also deny secretly checking into the Astor House under the name of 'Trees,' and then checking out, leaving clues behind to deliberately lure me away from Shanghai?"

"I certainly do deny it. And why should I lure you away from Shanghai?"

"A simple precaution - misdirection, throw me off the scent. You assumed Madame Lin had what you wanted, no need to keep me around. However, when you discovered that she *didn't* have the negatives, oh my - you had to drop everything and come after me." Davies smiled, mockingly, slipping into a role that was making him feel increasingly sickened. "Never assume, John. My mother taught me that."

"Rather careless of me," Crockwood murmured. "I have to commend you as a creative thinker. - even if what you accuse me of is wrong."

"Oh, I don't think it is. And to prove it, I can give you the name of the Japanese warship that brought you to Honolulu so quickly. I imagine you're in it for the money."

A guilty grin slipped onto Crockwood's face. "I'm not a materialistic man - unlike you."

"What I don't understand is why it took Elder Brother so long to realize that he *didn't* have the negatives."

"Oh, well, that is one thing I can take credit for. I was provided with some dummy negatives, a crime scene the Japanese fudged. After you'd left, I visited Dr. Sun on my own, and left the counterfeit negatives where he'd stumble on to them. I expected they'd hold off Elder Brother for far longer than a few days, however." Crockwood was drifting from cool skepticism back into amiability, but with none of the premeditated nonchalance that he'd adopted earlier; rather it was if his body was being taken over by a power stronger and more resourceful than himself. The change put Davies on his guard, yet he felt as if they were having one of their traditional mix-ups over a round of cocktails. Not quite, because this was a far different Crockwood, a man who'd always been there, but he'd neglected to see. It was this new Crockwood who took a small revolver from his coat pocket and pointed it directly at Davies. The action was elegant, impressively performed with a magician's ease. "This is all so unnecessary, you must see that. We've had out differences, Davies, but at heart we're friends."

"Madame Lin was a friend," Davies said coolly.

"I concede that, and I feel terrible about what I had to do. But our friendship must count for something. I've stood by you when others wouldn't, and I'm rather amusing to boot – that's worth something."

All valid points Davies had to admit. They had enjoyed a number of good times, and hard ones too. Truly, loyalty do a friend counted for a great deal in his book. He'd looked the other way when it came to Monica's indiscretions, and No Sin's as well – not to mention Elder Brother's. But was he willing to forgive cold blooded murder? "I don't know, John."

"Oh, do grow up. We're talking about my life here, Zephyr - in contrast to your Madame Lin, a fine person in her way, I grant you. But you can't honestly tell me that a Chinese life is worth as much as a White life. You've seen how those people live."

"Sin, go downstairs and fetch the house detective."

The boy put his hand on the latch to the door.

"I wouldn't advise that," Crockwood said sharply.

"It's all right, Sin. He's a terrible shot." Davies felt heat on his cheeks, his body telling him that he shouldn't have said something so provocative.

"A terrible shot? Why don't we see? One thing that I learned in Shanghai is that life is cheap."

"Really? I learned the exact opposite." Davies felt the peculiar calm that so often accompanied his moments of danger. "Life is of considerable value."

"*Mine* is," Crockwood said, like a teacher correcting a student, "not that you ever noticed. I'm not a little man, a trivial man, as you seem to think. I must thank you, however; before our little tete a tete with Elder Brother I never had the courage to volunteer for work in the field. Now I find I'm very good at it." Crockwood reached for a pillow, allowing a nervous smile to break through.

"This worked well before." Crockwood fired through the pillow; the exiting bullet making little sound.

The youth gave a small yelp, slid down the wall, and sprawled out on his side like something spilled.

Crockwood glanced at Davies, eager to gauge his one-time friend's reaction.

Davies was too stunned to have much of a reaction.

"Oh dear," Crockwood said, his voice surprisingly shaky. "My poor aim seems to have robbed me of a critical bargaining chip. Sorry, Zephyr, I know you love the slopes, but I did warn him - and you only urged him on. It is ironic, though, that you saved that lad from execution only a week ago. I suppose an early death was his fate."

Davies stared dumbly at No Sin's crumpled form. As he took in the thin, motionless arms, the twisted jacket, something began to build inside him - at the same time it was outside, bearing down on his shoulders like a wooden beam filled with nails.

"Buck up now, what's one Chinaman more or less? I've had to give up Asian concubines, and it's nothing to blubber over like some neurotic schoolgirl. Remember your roots - be white." Crockwood pointed the gun at Davies and pressed on the trigger.

As the first bullet struck, the indescribable emotions that Davies felt simultaneously dissolved and exploded. With the clarity of fury driving him, Davies sprang at his one-time friend, seeing white feathers spraying out from the pillow. He felt, once or twice, as if he'd been struck by a child's hard, clenched fist. He didn't know for sure, and he didn't care. Then he had his hands around Crockwood's throat and the gun had fallen, clattering, to the teak floor. He forced Crockwood outside, through billowing curtains onto the veranda. Warm, hard rain struck him in the face.

Crockwood was wheezing and trying to get out the words, "Damn it!" and, "Zephyr!"

All Davies wanted was to push his betraying friend as far away as possible, force him over the horizon, make him disappear.

With a choked yell, Crockwood's feet were suddenly high in the air, as if he'd become a drunken can can dancer - one of his shoes striking Davies in the face. Then he was gone.

Davies heard yelling. Four stories below, Crockwood lay on his back, splayed haphazardly on the gray, glistening pavement many feet below.

Breathing raggedly, Davies turned and went inside to see if anything could be done for No Sin. He felt desperate, miserable. Alive, the boy was troublesome, often a nuisance. Dead, he was a marvelous character that only came around once or twice in a lifetime. The world would be barren without him.

As he made his way through the shattered door Davies found himself face to face with the young Chinese. "What the,.." he cried, startled. "Aren't you shot?"

The lad smiled with shy embarrassment. "I fake. I pretend again. I get good now."

"You did a damned fine job."

"Thank you."

IL. A FINAL GIFT

Davies learned that he'd been shot three times. It wasn't so bad because one bullet had passed clean through him, grazing his side and lodging itself comfortably in an overstuffed chair. The other two bullets were found residing, respectively, in his torso and his upper thigh. Neither wound was serious; however, it wasn't much fun to have the bullets extracted. Crockwood had remained loyal to his silly twenty-two, which was why he had so much trouble killing people. It was no wonder that he'd been forced to finish Madame Lin off with a cigarette holder.

Fortunately, No Sin had literally dodged the bullet: he'd not been hit at all; his dying "beautifully," (an encore performance,) had fooled Crockwood most effectively.

Crockwood hadn't been an especially close friend, but his betrayal really hurt. Not as sharp a sting as the betrayal inflicted by Monica, a closer friend, even though Davies hadn't known her for nearly as long. Perversely, the only person he could think of who hadn't betrayed him was Elder Brother - how was that for irony?

What an unimaginable fortnight it had been - incredible events plowing into each other, one after the other, so many as to defy belief. Yet how could he be surprised - hadn't he come from China, Shanghai in particular? Shanghai in the year of nineteen hundred and twenty-eight was a place where anything could and did happen. That was the brilliance of China, with all the madness and turmoil, somehow life went on, growing more outrageous and exuberant as it did.

If only he'd ignored Madame Lin's initial phone call back in Shanghai and stayed in his tub. If he'd never taken the case, Monica Marshall would not have come into his life, which meant that he'd have been denied some amusing and stimulating exchanges, as well as a number of delightful sexual encounters. He would also have been spared her tantrums, her manipulations, and the final insult of her storming away and leaving hat pins in his pillows as a going-away present. Additionally, he would not now be experiencing the hollow and completely irrational sadness that came from missing her.

What he still didn't understand was the note. Why leave it? It was a confession, after all, to attempted assault, at the very least – maybe even to murder. And if the hatpins had found their mark, how could Davies ever be expected to read it – wouldn't he be blind or dead or left in a lobotomized stupor? Stranger was the fact that Monica had punctuated her bitter sarcasm with "Wallace," the term of endearment, which meant that she still liked him. The handwriting was definitely Monica's, he had no trouble recognizing it – yet there was no sign of stress in the good little schoolgirl penmanship, no indication that she had been coerced to write it. The weirdness of the note was going to haunt him until he was face to face with Monica, analyzing her explanation. He'd have to steel himself to the possibility that she'd reveal herself, at that moment, to be even crazier and nastier then he'd so far imagined.

So here he was, back where he started. Monica hadn't killed her aunt, but she'd played him for a fool all the same. With his help, she'd escaped the Shanghai police and was on her way to rendezvous with her incarcerated boyfriend. Now that Davies had served his purpose he was no longer needed. It was an equally reasonable assumption that she had concocted the story of seeing a monster in Trees' room, of finding slivers of glass in her cold cream, and had, herself, smashed cosmetics and scattered rose petals as a way of proving her innocence and victim-hood, while actually only providing verification of her madness.

So many betrayals. It seemed inconceivable that he'd ever be able to trust anyone again.

And what of Trees? Trees might have been Crockwood in disguise, more likely he was an innocent hotel guest who'd been horrified by Madame Lin's killing, had attempted to help, then fled realizing that bloody towels found in his rooms might be incriminating.

As for Madame Lin's foot, it was probably tucked away in some Japanese General's tansu, a gift presented by Crockwood to prove his worthiness. Of all the ghastly acts of violence that Crockwood had committed, that was the hardest to imagine him doing; it seemed beyond his repertoire of cruelty. Still, there didn't seem to be another possible explanation. And yet, could there be another explanation? Had the case really been resolved and the guilty party brought to justice? Maybe his skepticism was being driven by an insane, adolescent desire to reunite with Monica and learn that she truly was a maligned innocent - but rattling around in the draftiest, most inaccessible chambers of his brain was a lost argument, whispering to him that not all the clues had been collected, that not all the dark deeds had been exposed.

At least, Elder Brother had offered a brief reprieve after hearing of Crockwood's death. He believed Davies' exhortations that the negatives were not in his possession, but would be tracked down, one way or another.

Monica's abrupt and not particularly pleasant departure helped to erase any conflicts of interest that Davies felt about agreeing to return to Elder Brother's fold. Moronically, her absence still smarted. He'd begun this journey missing someone he'd never met, it had ended with him missing someone he should *never* have met. What a big, wide, wonderful world.

Freed from the doctor, Davies strolled down to the beach as the sun was setting. No Sin came with him. As they walked, Davies wondered if No Sin would turn into a poster-boy for good deeds rewarded - or would he also continue on as a betrayer? Time would tell.

The house detective met them right before concrete gave way to sand – he was there to take No Sin away to the pineapple ranch. With No Sin anxiously looking on, Davies told the tubby Hawaiian that there'd been a change of plans and the deal was off. Curiously, the detective looked slightly relieved.

Fanciful clouds played along the horizon, suggesting the kind of fabulous, far away places that only existed in storybooks. The clouds glowed bright red and orange and purple. Light from the departing sun glinted on the waves. The beauty was painful - the sort that made one want to cry.

No Sin stood beside him. "Beautiful," he said.

Davies nodded.

"I bring you something." No Sin held out a small cardboard box, attractively wrapped. "You need this, I think."

Taking the box, Davies had a momentary vision of a woman's bound foot resting daintily inside, or perhaps another small wooden coffin.

"I wrap it myself," No Sin said with pride.

The job was masterfully executed. Davies struggled with the elaborate bow, finally undoing it. Not without anxiety he removed the lid from the box, finding inside two dozen pieces of hard, tamarind candy. "I know that your favorite, because you always have piece with you. I never thank you for so many wonderful things you do for me. This not much, I know. But it a start, I think."

Davies smiled at No Sin. "You couldn't have come up with anything better." He selected a piece of candy, then as an afterthought he offered it to No Sin, who shook his head "no."

"Don't worry, I put much less poison in this time." No Sin smiled.

"I expected nothing less."

"No, it okay. You can trust me."

"I trust you completely, Sin." Davies popped the candy into his mouth, and turned back to watch the setting sun. No Sin was right, it was beautiful.

THE END

AFTERWORD

Japanese freighters did occasionally steam with impunity over Chinese sailors in sampans, and Elder Brother, the head of the Chinese underworld, actually did send miniature coffins to people who displeased him. Indeed, he was suspected of dispatching dignitaries with smallpox germs placed on their table napkins.

On the flip side, there were vendors all up and down the Chinese coast who sold remarkable foodstuffs, and the intentionally unfair Chinese justice system maintained remarkable order considering how close China was to a descent into chaos back in the twenties.

ACKNOWLEDGMENTS

My thanks goes to Ann Hogle for her insightful feedback, to Carla Meilstrup, Kit Colman, and Megan Aguilar for reading and reacting to this book in its many incarnations. Additional thanks to Cesar Ayala for his overall support, and to Camela Raymond, Patricia Fogarty, and Elizabeth George for being willing to slog through an early draft.

Mitchell Dwyer and Robert C. Ortwin provided some wonderful anecdotes about their times spent in Shanghai during the 1920's and the 1930's, and Alan Buckhantz gave me important feedback and critical resources.

Ronin Colman was very helpful with his knowledge of guns and eugenics.

As usual, I am extremely grateful to fellow writers Patricia Smiley, Barbara Fryer, Elaine Medosch, Reg Park, Peggy Hesketh, Steve Long, and Tim Polmanteer.

ABOUT THE AUTHOR

T.M. Raymond lives in Los Angeles and has worked in the movie industry for many years.

A PREVIEW OF "MADNESS," THE NEXT BOOK IN THE NO SIN MYSTERY SERIES.

MADNESS

I. HEADING HOME

Thursday, September 27, 1928 – S.S. Malolo - two days east of Honolulu

"**W**hat the hell?" Zephyr Davies stopped short, aborting his evening stroll along the swaying walkways of the S.S. Malolo. After a tumultuous few weeks fleeing the Orient, he was in desperate need of tranquility. Mercifully, the sultry evening was conspiring with a calm sea to soothe his spirit and portray nature as his benevolent companion – now the spell was shattered. On a lower deck he caught sight of his Chinese friend, No Sin, being taunted by three sailors. For a moment Davies thought that the lad's bullying brothers had somehow sneaked aboard the ship, but the burly white men who had surrounded the slender youth were hardly relatives.

"May I ask what's going on here?" Davies called out as he descended the metal stairway that led to where the men were gathered like jays, massing to peck a weaker bird to death.

"We have it handled, if you don't mind," the tallest and most aggressive of the sailors said with a measured politeness that was reserved for white passengers. Turning back to No Sin he barked, "What cabin are you staying in?"

"I, uh.,,"

"Just thought you'd hitch a ride? So sorry, no cabin, no ride'ee." He winked at his mates, who smiled back.

"He's staying in cabin thirty-four on C deck," Davies said.

"Thank you for the information, sir, but I don't think this concerns you." The officer's back remained turned toward Davies.

"Actually, it does," Davies said pointing to a half dozen dress shirts that were hanging from a length of twine and billowing in the wind. "Those are my shirts." Apparently No Sin had committed the unspeakable act of stringing up a clothesline in order to dry Davies' laundry.

"Are they now?" The man finally turned toward Davies and he forced a smile that had probably taken weeks of training to perfect. His uniform identified him as the associate chief steward and he had the kind of face that begged to be smacked: smug, with a tiny nose and a slackening overly-square jaw that implied good genes gone bad from centuries of cousins marrying cousins who'd all come over on the Mayflower. "I know we all like to find a bargain, but have you considered that there are certain protocols to be followed on a first-class ship? Didn't your people ever explain that to you?"

Evidently this associate chief steward assumed that Davies had hired No Sin to wash his clothes out of a gauche desire to save a few pennies over what the Malolo's laundry charged.

"Come on," Davies said, "this ship goes overboard, pun intended, to create an atmosphere of fun. You have people lying about half naked on the deck in bathing suits, you organize turtle races and ladies' nail driving contests - in that context is it so awful that he's hung some laundry out to dry?"

Instead of replying, the associate chief steward resumed his harassment of No Sin. "Are you hard of hearing, boy, or just stupid? Let me see your room key! Chop! Chop!"

No Sin hesitated, looking to Davies for guidance.

It was outrageous that this twit felt he had license to insult No Sin because of his race. Despite his youth, No Sin had an intelligence, strength, and depth of experience that few people could match. "I can assure you that he has all his proper documentation, and his room is paid for," Davies said, struggling to stay calm.

With his back still turned to Davies, the officer raised his hand in a cautionary gesture. "Sir, please allow us to do our jobs." Consistent with the man's curt, manufactured personality, there were no rings on his slender fingers to imply a hint of humanness, however Davies was surprised to catch sight of a Cuban link bracelet adorned with tiny, green Hawaiian stones hidden within the dark cave of the fellow's sleeve.

Meanwhile, No Sin began to remove a shirt from the improvised clothesline, probably believing that this would diffuse the situation.

"Leave that!" the associate chief steward barked. "I asked you a question!"

No Sin took hold of a second shirt.

The associate chief steward lurched at the offending rope, trying vainly to rip it down with one, masterful stroke.

No Sin stepped in to help, doing his best to untie the knot. As he struggled with the obstinate tangle of rope, he accidentally jabbed the associate chief steward in the stomach with his elbow. The blow was light and glancing, but the associate chief steward reacted as if he'd been swatted by a grizzly bear.

"Did you see that," the young officer cried, spinning toward his mates, "he struck me! I want this boy held for criminal assault!"

Raw panic swept across No Sin's face. He didn't stand "a Chinaman's chance," of making it to America if was held for even a minor offense. In no time, he could be back on the streets of Shanghai, begging for food. The young officer was a twit, but in all counties twits wearing the right uniform wielded real power.

"Look, why don't we all just calm down," Davies said.

"No, you look! He attacked me! That's a very serious offense!" The associate chief steward turned back to his mates. "Didn't I tell you to take this filthy Chinaman below!" To emphasize his authority, he succeeded in tearing the remaining shirts off the line - holding them possessively in his arms.

The mates went to No Sin, each taking hold of an arm.

"This is very easily resolved," Davies said.

"Sir, as an officer of this ship, I have the authority to restrain any passenger who questions my authority and compromises the safety of this vessel."

"I was just saying,..."

"We're done here, right?" This time the artificial smile signified finality as he turned away from Davies. "Right."

The officer's dismissal was stunning. Davies felt like he was back in prep school where privilege created an especially odious brand of bully. The concept of fair play would be as foreign to this man as the surface of the moon. It was time to play a hunch, and he'd better be right as No Sin's entire future was at stake. "How's your father?"

Slowly, the associate chief steward turned back to face Davies. "I beg your pardon."

"Associate chief stewards are usually working class and have to make their way up through the ranks, but here you are, young, brash,..." Davies paused for emphasis. "How did you make it so young? You aren't wearing a class ring, which implies a less than stellar scholastic experience, resulting, perhaps, in bitter memories. The only possible explanation," Davies continued pleasantly, "is that daddy got you this job. Unless I miss my guess he's a director of the line."

The associate chief steward cocked his head in a reflective manner, studying the gray sea as if he'd suddenly discovered beauty in nature.

Behind the associate chief steward, the mates tightened their grip on No Sin, but did little else; they seemed quite interested in hearing Davies' appraisal of their superior officer.

"You would also like to be a director, wouldn't you?" Davies said softly, "at least a vice president. So why aren't you? Is it because your father has no confidence in you?"

The young officer's face remained rigid, but his cheeks had turned scarlet and his lips were tight. "You must really enjoy hearing yourself talk."

"To make matters worse, I can't imagine that dad is pleased with your Hawaiian girlfriend." Davies was now wearing a practiced expression of concerned empathy. "Or is it a secret?"

"What gave you that idea?" the young man said, his voice an octave higher and his face turning several contrasting colors.

"The charm worn around your wrist. It's a Cuban link adorned with peridots - a green, volcanic gem known as 'the poor man's emerald.' You don't fancy jewelry; your fingers are bare, so obviously it's a gift from someone special. Someone Hawaiian. Your sweetheart I presume."

Both mates glanced at their superior officer as if seeing him in a new light.

"I have more important things to do. You deal with this." The associate chief steward threw the shirts at his mates, turned sharply on his heels, and stalked away.

Embarrassed, the mates released No Sin, then did a clumsy job of folding the shirts and handing them back to Davies. "Sorry 'bout that, sir," the shorter of the two said. "He's a bit in over his head." The two sailors gave Davies a little salute and climbed the stairs to a higher deck.

No Sin let out an audible exhale of relief. "Let me thank you, Mr. Sir." he said, clasping his hands together and executing an exaggerated bow. No Sin's playful sarcasm was a welcome signal that things were creeping back to normal; he had an arsenal of methods designed to keep Davies from slipping into the role of a smug, celestial white face looking after his little yellow brother, and such reminders were extremely helpful.

Davies held up the damp shirts that were clutched in his arms. "They have a perfectly good laundry service on this ship, you know."

"Laundry man too fat."

"Mr. Wissman?"

"How can he be as good as me? I do not understand why those guys get so mad. I do it before, you know that, and it okay."

"That was on a tramp steamer in Chinese waters. You were in steerage."

"Ahh, so peaceful. So lovely to sleep on deck and look at stars."

"Okay, but now you know that the Malolo isn't like that. They don't have steerage on this ship, in fact they don't even have second class."

With a loud sigh, No Sin took the bundle of damp shirts out of Davies' arms. The boy appeared strange holding the laundry, his sleek, elegant looks rendered him unconvincing as a domestic, and belied his impoverished background. Thinking about this renewed Davies' fury at the associate chief steward's ignorance and bigotry. "I bring these to you later," No Sin said, "maybe. I have little problem with Mrs. Kisser's colored amah, so we see."

"Again?" Mrs. Kissler was a fussy matron who dressed lavishly, if badly, usually in a chiffon gown, which was color-coordinated to match her wig. No Sin helped her with odds and ends now and then.

"Yes. I need to borrow iron. But amah won't let me borrow iron until after I help her repack Mrs. 'Kisser's' dresses."

Davies stared blankly at him, awaiting an explanation.

"Mrs. 'Kisser,' she buy too many dresses in Honolulu, no room left in steamer trunk. Now you understand?" He rolled his eyes and muttered, "Sometime I think I too nice to you."

"Alright," Davies said, amused that No Sin never lacked for a cutting remark, a remarkable feat considering the young man's tenuous grasp of the English language.

"And sometime you too nice to me."

"I'll try to correct the matter."

"Don't joke. People think you strange; it serious problem. Sometime you act like you own world; other time you act like world own you, it very confusing. Worst thing of all, you dress too much like money. Rich people supposed to be old and ugly, and boss everyone. Then you come along, very handsome, very polite, you supposed to be thirty-five or something but you looking very young, always patient, always watching. What going on? You gigolo? Maybe some kind of crook casing joint? Even sissy? That what people think because pieces don't add up." The unsolicited criticism came as no surprise to Davies; he knew from experience that many people grew to resent those who shackled them with bonds of gratitude. No Sin felt that his imminent immigration to America made him the luckiest person in the world, but also the most indebted. "One thing I do not understand," No Sin said, causing Davies to wonder what the boy had planned for an encore, "why Mrs. 'Kisser' buy more dresses? I mean, everything she wear so ugly. And she ugly too. What difference does it make what she wear?"

"I imagine it makes a difference to her. And it's Mrs. Kissler, not 'Kisser' as you insist on calling her. I should add, Sin, that you'll be old yourself someday, so try to be nice."

"Why? You not nice to that guy, *for once*." No Sin drew out the last two words so there'd be no mistaking his scorn for Davies' regular, excruciatingly reasonable modus operandi. "I love it so much, so perfect. How you know what to say to get him to leave?"

"Logic. And a touch of luck."

"But how you know you right?"

"I don't. I take bits of information and form a logical conclusion. Then I run it by my instincts. If my conclusion *feels* right I take a deep breath and plunge ahead; nine times out of ten I get away with it."

"You can't imagine how scare I am. I hope some big fish jump up and eat that guy." No Sin glanced down at the laundry in his arms and smoothed a barely wrinkled collar. "So how long before we be in America? It that way, right?" He pointed with his chin toward the ship's bow.

Davies turned to look. "I must say, your aim is quite accurate."

"Of course. I not stupid."

"In all fairness, sometimes you play dumb."

"And sometimes I *am* dumb, that what you think?"

"Occasionally naïve, simply because you are nineteen years old. Also because you are more intelligent than most people. How should I put this? Bright people are often labeled as naive because they can imagine things and see fantastic possibilities that are beyond the abilities of those with duller, more closed minds."

No Sin squinted at Davies. "Okay, that pretty good answer. I forgive you this time."

Leaving No Sin to deal with the laundry, Davies took another aimless turn around the deck. Tonight the sea resembled an undulating landscape of small, gray hills; dull, smooth waves conspiring to create a vista that seemed solid and geographic. He made a search for the horizon, but the slate-colored sky was such a perfect match for the ocean that the space where the two met was an illusive smudge, slipping by too briefly to be clearly made out. It was an appropriate metaphor for his life.

An entire evening loomed ahead, offering him nothing but a return to worrying. The impending reality of returning home and adopting a mundane, normal life, getting up in the morning and trudging off to an office for ten hours a day, was weighing on him. Living a life of adventure, running guns, and moonlighting as a detective had been alternately exciting and terrifying; it made sense to give it up. Yet had he chosen the best alternative? Becoming a respectable businessman simply didn't suit him. His very identity was at stake.

He headed toward the front of the ship, enjoying the twilight, which was gloomy and warm. He hoped to catch sight of performing sea life, frolicking dolphins, that might be silhouetted by glowing wakes of green phosphorous. He preferred natural entertainment to a movie, and he wondered how many passengers would be tempted to sit huddled on an upper deck, pointed toward an outdoor screen, as Hollywood's latest streamed from the projection booth built into the Malolo's rear smokestack. Sleek and modern, the Malolo was the pride of the Matson Line. It felt almost sinful to be enjoying its comforts after weeks spent on leaky junks and battered tramp steamers.

Passing the English flavored, dark paneled smoking room Zephyr Davies overheard a loud table of drunken card players. Through a window he could see several sturdy men in evening clothes, who seemed to be all noses and earlobes, sitting at the bar and telling stories of their travels. When younger, Davies would have prided himself on having endured greater miseries than these seasoned old men, now he was in awe of them for having maintained a spirit that he had lost. Unlike them, adventure was something he no longer believed in - instead, sadly, he believed in cruelty, injustice, physical injury, stupidity, sudden, meaningless death, and irony. When he'd left for the Orient at the brash age of twenty-seven he'd told himself that there could be nothing worse than a safe, predictable life filled with dull routine, generating mental stagnation. Now he was wondering if there could be anything better.

His anger reignited as he entered his cabin. It was outrageous that No Sin had been treated so badly, simply because of his race. He'd probably brood about it all night and there seemed little point in doing much of anything except try to sleep, which was becoming the high point of his day. He'd hoped that, with this journey, the traumas and tragedies of the past five years would fade into oblivion. However, the run-in with the associate chief steward, the fragility of No Sin's prospects, the tumultuous sea suggested to him that China was following him home. Dammit all, it was disgraceful for a person with his advantages to indulge in even a moment's self-pity. Resolving to embrace a more positive attitude he flopped onto bed and quickly dozed off.

Right before midnight, when he'd finally descended into a full, welcome sleep, there was a loud, banging on his door. It would be just his luck if some crewman was outside waiting to tell him that the ship was sinking. He lumbered out of bed and put on his greatcoat, all that he could find in a hurry. Still groggy, and unintentionally dressed as an exhibitionist, he swung the door open; the slack faced associate chief steward, the one he'd sparred with earlier, was standing in the doorway. Oh, God, now what? Had they rounded up No Sin and thrown him in irons after all?

"Would you be so good as to come with me?" the officer said with a formality that caused Davies' anxiety level to shoot up a notch. "The Captain would like a word with you."

II: THE SEALED ROOM

Leaving his cabin, Davies anticipated a late night scolding by the crew, maybe even a hazing led by the Captain, surrounded by all the sailors wearing robes made of seaweed, and accessorized with hats rendered from giant clams. Therefore, he was surprised to be told simply that his assistance was needed.

The night was thick with mist, making the ship's wooden planking treacherous. Pearls of moisture glinted on the top of the associate chief steward's cap, and the shoulders of his uniform, as he led the way. "You did such a good job of putting me in my place earlier," he said, brusquely, "that I thought you might be able to help with a situation that's come up. Also, I'm told that you know the gentleman in question."

Not quite an apology, but close. Davies appreciated the man's change of attitude, though he didn't sound any more pleasant than he had that afternoon, and a certain level of tension remained. Davies wasn't ready to become bosom buddies with this fellow, and would be glad to get on to whatever matter was at hand. "Who exactly is the 'gentleman in question?'"

"His name is Huey Arnold. I believe you sailed with him from China."

Huey Arnold was a slovenly, portly fellow, slight of stature, who went by the nickname of "the Hatman" for the forged passports, or covers, that he provided for a fee. Davies and Huey Arnold were not on the best of terms, and the odd, little man had become strikingly paranoid since a haphazard attempt had been made on his life a week earlier on another ship. He was now such a committed recluse that he wouldn't come out of his room even to eat.

They went down a deck, and through a heavy door into the welcome warmth of the ship. Arriving at the narrow corridor outside the Hatman's cabin, Davies saw that No Sin was already present, crammed in amongst a crowd of curious and groggy passengers. In the confusion, Davies heard a bald man ask No Sin to fetch him clean towels. The passenger didn't realize how lucky he was that his request was merely ignored.

The ship's stately, bewhiskered Scottish Captain, a studious, thoughtful appearing purser, and several mates were pounding on the cabin door and demanding entrance. "Ye must open the door! We cann'o help you unless you let us in!" The Captain called out in his lilting, Scottish brogue.

"Oh, God! Oh, God!" the Hatman wailed from inside his locked cabin.

"Mr. Arnold," the Captain yelled back, "please open the door!"

"I can't open the door!"

"Of course, ye kin," the Captain hollered.

This appeal was answered by a piercing scream, which caused many of the bystanders to gasp.

"Mr. Arnold?"

Not so much as a moan came from beyond the Hatman's door.

The bald passenger scratched the back of his gleaming skull. "What's happened to him?"

"Something's wrong with the poor guy," an elderly man said, as if he was the only one aware of the obvious.

The Captain fumbled a passkey from his tunic and unlocked the door. He twisted the handle and pushed the door inward, but it refused to budge.

Elbowing his way through the small crowd, Davies tried pushing on the door himself; something was jamming it.

Mrs. Kissler and her colored maid joined the onlookers. Tonight her red wig and alabaster make-up had apparently been slapped on in a hurry, making her appear that much more like a demonic circus clown. "What the hell is going on?" she demanded, angry that her sleep had been interrupted.

"I don't know what all the fuss's about," a sharp-faced woman muttered. "The guy's drunk."

Another woman, wearing a tweed coat and with traces of cold cream on her face, found this statement so absurd that she snorted out a contemptuous laugh and shook her head.

"Well, he is," the sharp-faced woman said defensively.

Davies wasn't surprised that the Hatman's last, truly horrific scream had rattled some of the passengers into various spasms of denial. It had certainly rattled him.

While Mrs. Kissler advised, ordered and complained it took nearly five minutes of pounding and straining to break the door down. They timed their efforts to match the rolling of the ship. Each time the corridor wall moved downward, capturing their weight, four broad shoulders heaved against the obstinate door. It finally yielded, accompanied by the snapping and crunching sound of splintering wood. As the door swung into the room, hot, musty air billowed out.

The lights in the cabin wouldn't work, and the purser came back with a torch and shone it into the blackness. The darting cone of light revealed a room that was a mess - clothes strewn about, the Malabo's trademark table lamp with a single flower painted on its green shade lying broken beside a slender mattress that had been cast to the floor, dangling like a dog's tongue from the built-in bed. There was no sign of Huey Arnold.

Davies was the first to enter, calling out a cautious, "Huey?" The warm air inside added to Davies' apprehension, particularly as it was not unreasonable to assume that the Hatman had committed suicide, considering his bizarre behavior. However, no body lay on the floor, which didn't mean that one wasn't sprawled in the tiny shower in the equally tiny bathroom. A passing thought chilled him, was the Hatman's paranoia justified and some hulking, murderous thug was lurking in the gloom of the cabin?

"Where is he?" the Captain demanded as he peered into the darkness. "We'ar we not just talkin' to him?" He seemed teed off, but Davies had seen fear take many strange forms.

"He must be in here somewhere," Davies said. "Maybe in the loo." He took a determined breath and moved deeper into the cabin, whose current darkness muted the fact that it was freshly painted and cheerfully decorated. Were the lights not working to facilitate an ambush?

Hesitantly, the Captain followed after him.

They pushed open the door to the bathroom and shined the torch on the shining walls; no one was there.

Together they continued their search. Each time Davies opened a drawer, or lifted up something that had fallen on the floor, he was afraid of what he might find. However, no bodies were under a lumpy pile of bed sheets and blankets, no hacked-up body parts had been placed in the cupboards built into the base of the bed.

"This is impossible," the Captain muttered, his voice losing much of its previous steadiness. He was a stately man, the sort who seemed to have nerves that were never rattled, therefore the anxiety in his voice was unsettling. "We all he'ard him. And the door was locked from the inside. Boarded up fer that matter. Where is he?"

Davies said nothing. The experience of being inside the dark, hot room where a man had inexplicably vanished was simultaneously unreal and overly real, causing his emotions to operate on a primal level, and making him feel mildly nauseated.

"Conn'l 'ave the torch?" The Captain asked in loud, steady voice intended to mask his unease.

Davies handed the torch to the Captain, who used it to carefully examine the portholes; they were securely locked from the inside with latches that proved themselves to be difficult to operate.

Davies reclaimed the torch from the Captain and reinspected the inside of the door. Not only had the stubborn inner safety latch been activated, but also boards, secured by nails pounded deep into the center of the door, were firmly in place. When shut, five bed slats had stretched from the center of the door to where more nails had been driven deep into the wooden outer molding surrounding the door. This was why the door had been so hard to force open. The boarded-over door indicated that the Hatman had been trying very hard to keep something from getting in. Then it seemed he had lost his battle, and simply vaporized into thin air.

"Who's that?" Davies called out, aware that another figure had joined his party.

"It me," No Sin said, coming closer to where Davies could see him. "This place so scary. Why it so hot?"

Abandoning a peek under the mattress, which lay on the floor, Davies went to check the vent above the bed. "Heat's on full blast for some reason." He found the rheostat and turned the cock, shutting the heat off. "Even aboard ship, someone must have heard him pounding all those nails." Davies glanced out at the crowd of curious passengers. "Did any of you hear strange noises in this room?"

The passengers looked at each other and shook their heads.

"Nothing?" Davies persisted. "What time did you all go to dinner?"

"I dined at seven," Mrs. Kissler said in an overtly helpful tone.

"I went about seven-fifteen," the balding man added hesitantly.

"Was anybody here between seven-fifteen and, say, eight?"

The passengers looked at each other a second time; nobody responded.

"What time did you get back?" Davies asked Mrs. Kissler.

"About eight-twenty I expect. I left the dining room ahead of the others."

"So this could have happened while everyone was eating, that's why nobody heard anything. Sin," Davies said, "you stayed in the hall after we broke the door down. Could someone have slipped out with all the confusion?"

"How could anyone get by?" No Sin asked. "We could hardly move it was so crowded."

This observation was so self-evident that Davies wondered why he had even bothered to pose the question. "Can we be sure that his screams were actually coming from his cabin?" Davies asked the Captain.

"Ye were here, weren't you? Ye hear'd him." The Captain looked at Davies as if challenging him to disprove his words.

"Yes, I suppose you're right," Davies conceded. "Sin, would you go into the cabin beside this one, shut the door, and shout back at us?"

No Sin shrugged, went into an adjacent cabin and shouted, "Hello, I dying! Help me, please! Oh no!"

Davies knew that No Sin was not trying to be funny, nonetheless his performance elicited nervous titters from the onlookers. More to the point, his shouts sounded like they were coming from the cabin next door, not the Hatman's cabin.

"All right, Sin, that's enough."

"I've seen many a stray'ange thing over the years." The Captain wiped his brow with a handkerchief. "Boot this beats all."

"Mr. Davies! Come look at this!" No Sin called from inside the Hatman's cabin. It was surprising that he could move about so quickly and stealthily.

Davies abandoned the hall and crossed to the center of the room where No Sin was looking at a spot, illuminated by the purser's torch, which had previously been covered by the mattress that No Sin had moved back on to the bed frame. The feeble beam of the torch illuminated a long, streaked trail of something wine colored and glistening on the floor.

"Wha' did ye find?" the Captain asked as he poked his head into the cabin.

Beneath where the mattress had lain, long, dark fingers of purple exploded from the filmy pool of liquid. Davies crouched and put his finger into the sticky stuff. The sharp metallic odor of iodine gave it away. "Blood," he said to the Captain. "Let me see that torch for a moment."

The purser handed it to him. "Close the door, would you?"

The purser did so. Alone in the cabin, and suppressing a creeping sense of panic, Davies used the torch's soft, yellow shaft of light to follow a trail of plum-colored drops that led from the clotting pool back toward the hall. "Jesus," he hissed as he saw something that he hadn't noticed before: down low, crimson handprints were smeared on the inside face of the shut door. Above them, written in blood was, "IM DEAD."

CPSIA information can be obtained
at www.ICGtesting.com
Printed in the USA
LVOW11s0234200517
535226LV00001B/211/P